TWO WOMEN

Other books by Alberto Moravia

THE WOMAN OF ROME

CONJUGAL LOVE

TWO ADOLESCENTS
(*Agostino* and *Disobedience*)

THE CONFORMIST

THE TIME OF INDIFFERENCE

THE FANCY DRESS PARTY

BITTER HONEYMOON

A GHOST AT NOON

ROMAN TALES

ALBERTO MORAVIA

TWO WOMEN

TRANSLATED FROM THE ITALIAN BY

ANGUS DAVIDSON

NEW YORK FARRAR, STRAUS AND CUDAHY

Library of Congress catalog card number 58-7439

Second Printing, 1958

Published in Italy as *La Ciociara*

Manufactured in the United States of America

TWO WOMEN

Chapter 1

Ah, those good days when I was a young bride and left my native village and came to Rome! You know the song:

Quando la ciociara si marita
A chi tocca lo spago e a chi la ciocia.

But I gave my husband everything, strings and sandal and all,[1] because he was my husband and also because he was taking me to Rome, and I was pleased to be going there and did not know that it was in Rome that misfortune was awaiting me. I had a round face, big, staring black eyes, and black hair that grew almost down to my eyes and was coiled into two thick, thick tresses like ropes. My mouth was red as coral and when I laughed I showed two rows of close-set, regular white teeth. I was strong in those days and was capable of carrying as much as fifty pounds balanced on the pad on my head. My father and mother were peasants, to be sure, but they had given me a trousseau just like a young lady, thirty of everything: thirty sheets, thirty pillow

[1] "When a girl from Ciociaria is married, some get the strings and some the sandal." The Ciociaria is a country district to the southeast of Rome, of which Frosinone is the center. The name is derived from the *ciocia*, the shoe worn by the local peasants, which resembles the Roman sandal, being formed of a piece of leather cut to the shape of the foot and fastened by strings round the ankle and the calf of the leg.

cases, thirty handkerchiefs, thirty chemises, thirty pairs of drawers. It was all of fine quality, in heavy hand spun and hand woven linen made by my mother herself on her own loom, and some of the sheets even had parts embroidered with all sorts of beautiful needlework. I had some coral jewelry, too, of the dark red coral, the most valuable kind—a coral necklace, coral and gold earrings, a gold ring set with coral, and even a brooch, a beautiful gold and coral brooch. Besides the coral, I had some plain gold jewelry that had belonged to my family, and I had a medallion to be worn around the neck, with a very beautiful cameo in which was depicted a shepherd boy with his sheep.

My husband owned a small grocer's shop in the Trastevere district, in the Vicolo del Cinque, and he fitted up a little flat right above the shop, so that if I leaned out of the bedroom window I could actually touch with my fingers the maroon-colored sign on which was written *Pane e Pasta.* The flat had two windows looking on to the courtyard and two on to the street; there were four rooms in all, very small and low, but I furnished them nicely; some of the furniture we bought at the market in the Campo di Fiori and some came from our families. The bedroom was entirely new, with a double bedstead of iron painted to look like wood and the head and foot ornamented with bouquets and garlands; and in the sitting room I placed a fine sofa with curly ornamental carving on it and a flower-patterned cover, two small armchairs with the same covers and the same carving; a round dining table, and a sideboard to keep the plates and dishes in, these being all of fine china, with a gold border and a decoration of fruit and flowers in the middle.

When my husband went down to the shop I would do the cleaning. I scoured and swept and polished and dusted, I cleaned every corner and every single object; after the cleaning the house would shine like a mirror and a quiet, soft light would come in at the windows, in which we had little white curtains, and I would look around the rooms and when I saw them so tidy and clean and shining, with everything in its right place, an indescribable kind of joy would rise up in my heart. What a lovely thing it is to have your own house, with nobody coming into it and nobody knowing it, and you could spend a whole lifetime cleaning it and putting it in order! When I had finished my cleaning, I would dress and carefully do my hair; then I would take my bag and go off to the market to do the shopping. The market was close by, only a few steps from the house, and I used to walk around among the stalls for more than an hour, not so much in order to buy things, for we had the greater part of the stuff in our own shop, as to have a good look. I would walk around the stalls looking at everything—fruit, vegetables, meat, fish, eggs; I understood these things, and I enjoyed calculating prices and profits, estimating quality, finding out the tricks and dishonesties of the sellers. I enjoyed bargaining, too, and judging the weight of things by lifting them in my hand, then putting them down and leaving them, and then going back and bargaining again and in the end not taking anything at all. Some of these dealers used to make a play for me, too, giving me to understand that they would give me stuff for nothing if I would listen to them; but I answered in such a way that they would quickly understand that the person with whom they had to do was not a woman of *that* sort. I have always been proud and it doesn't take much to make my blood boil, and then I see red, and it's just as well women don't carry knives in their pockets as men do, otherwise I'd be quite capable of killing someone. There was one dealer who annoyed me even more than the rest and who went on and on making suggestions to me and trying to insist on giving me things; so one day I ran around behind him with a hat pin and it was lucky the police intervened or else I should have planted it in his back.

Well, I used to come home quite pleased with myself, and after I had put on the water to boil for the stock pot, with some flavorings and a few bones and pieces of meat, I would go straight down to the shop. There, too, I was happy. We sold all kinds of things—*pasta,* bread, rice, dried vegetables, wine, oil, tinned foods—and I stood behind the counter like a queen, my arms bare to the elbow and my medallion with the cameo in it pinned to my breast: I would fetch things and weigh them, make out the bill as quick as anything with a pencil and a piece of yellow paper, do up the parcel and hand it to the customer. My husband, on the other hand, was slower. Talking of my husband, I forgot to say that he was already almost an old man when I married him and there were some people who said I had married him for money; and certainly I was never in love with him; but I swear by God I'm telling the truth when I say that I was always faithful to him, though he, on the contrary, was by no means so to me. He was a man who had his own ideas, and the chief of these ideas was that he was attractive to women, which was not really the case at all. He was fat, but not with a healthy kind of plumpness, and he had black bloodshot eyes and a face which was all yellow and looked as if it was stained with tobacco crumbs. He was bilious and secretive and rude, and woe betide anyone who contradicted him. He continually absented himself from the shop and I knew he was going off to meet some woman or other, but I would be ready to swear that women never paid any attention to him except when he gave them money. With money, as everyone knows, you can get anything you want; you can even get a young bride to lift up her skirts. I knew at once when his love affairs were going well, because then he was almost cheerful and you might even say kind. But when he didn't have a woman he became silent and gloomy and answered me rudely and sometimes even hit me. But I said to him once: "You can go with your sluts as much as you like, but don't you touch me or I'll leave you and go back home." As far as I was concerned, I didn't want any lovers, although plenty of them, as I have already said, came after me; I put all my passion into my home, into the shop, and, after I had my baby, into my little daughter. Love didn't mean anything at all to me; in fact—and this may perhaps have been because I had never known any man but my ugly old husband—the idea of it almost disgusted me. All I wanted was to be left alone and not to be in need of anything. In any case, a woman ought to be faithful to her husband whatever happens, even if her husband, as in this case, is not faithful to her.

My husband, as the years went by, could no longer find women who would take any notice of him, even for money, and had become quite intolerable. For some time I had not been to bed with him, and then, perhaps because he now had no girl friends, he took a fancy to me all over again and wanted to force me to start making love with him again, not in the ordinary straightforward way, like husband and wife, but in the way tarts do with their lovers; he would take hold of me by the hair and try to make me do things I never liked and had never wanted to do, even when I first came to Rome as a young bride and was so happy that I very nearly deceived myself into thinking I had fallen in love with him. I told him I did not wish to make love with him ever again, either as a wife or as a tart. He started hitting me, even going so far as to make my nose bleed; then, seeing that I was quite determined, he gave up annoying me in that way but took to hating me and persecuting me in every possible manner. I bore it patiently, but in real truth I hated him too and couldn't bear the sight of him. I told the priest in the confessional that we were heading for disaster; and the priest, like a typical priest, advised me to have patience and to dedicate my sufferings to the Madonna.

At that time I had taken on a girl to help me with the housework, a young girl called Bice, who was only fifteen and whose parents had asked me to look after her, since she was almost a child. My husband started making advances to her, and when he saw that I was busy with customers he would leave the shop, rush upstairs fours steps at a time, go into the kitchen and fall upon her like a wolf. I took a firm stand and told him to leave Bice alone; then, when he persisted in tormenting her, I told her she must go. After this, he took to hating me more violently than ever, and it was then that he started calling me a booby: "Has that booby come back?" "Where's that booby?" What with one thing and another, it was a heavy cross to bear, and when he fell seriously ill I am bound to confess I was almost relieved. I looked after him lovingly, however, just as a wife ought to look after her husband when he is ill; and, as everyone knows, I neglected the shop and stayed beside him all the time and hardly even allowed myself any sleep. In the end he died; and then again I felt almost happy. I had the shop, I had the flat, and I had my daughter who was an angel, and really there was nothing more I asked from life.

Those were the happiest years of my whole life: 1940, 1941, 1942 and 1943. It is true that the war was going on, but of war I knew nothing; since I had just this one daughter, it meant nothing to me. Let them slaughter each other as much as they pleased, with airplanes, with tanks, with bombs; my shop and my flat were all I needed in order to be happy, which indeed I was. In any case I knew little about the war because, although I can do accounts and even go so far as to put my signature on a picture post card, to tell the truth I am not much good at reading and I only used to read the papers for the crime reports, or rather I made Rosetta read them to me. Germans, English, Americans, Russians—they were all the same to me. When soldiers came into the shop and said we shall win there, we shall go here, we shall become such and such, we shall do this and that, I used to answer: for me, everything's all right as long as the shop goes well. And the shop *was* going well, although there was that tiresome business of ration cards, and Rosetta and I were running about all day with scissors in our hands just as though we had been dressmakers instead of shopkeepers. The shop was going well because I was clever and always managed to gain a little on the weight, and also because, with the rationing, we both of us did a little black market business. Rosetta and I used to shut up the shop every now and then and go off to my own village, or to some other country place that was nearer. We would start off with two big, empty fiber suitcases; and would bring them back filled with all sorts of things—flour, hams, eggs, potatoes. I had come to an understanding with the Food Control policemen, for they were hungry too, and thus it was that I sold more under the counter than I sold openly. One day, however, one of the police took it into his head to try and blackmail me. He came and said that, if I didn't go to bed with him, he would report me. "All right," I said, perfectly calmly, "all right . . . come up to my flat later on." He went very red, just as though he had received a blow, and went away without saying anything. At the time arranged he came up. I led him into the kitchen, opened a drawer, took out a knife and, pointing it suddenly at his neck, said: "Go and report me if you like, but I'll cut your throat first." He was frightened and said hurriedly that I was crazy and that what he had said was simply a joke. And he added: "Aren't you made like other women? Don't you like men?"

I answered him: "These are things that you must go and ask other women. I am a widow, I have my shop, and I don't think about anything except my shop. Love doesn't exist for me; remember that, and act accordingly." He didn't believe me at first, and for some time went on paying court to me—in a respectful way, however. But what I had said really was the truth. After Rosetta's birth I had taken no further interest in love; perhaps I hadn't even before. I am made like that; I have never been able to bear anyone putting his hands on me; and if my parents had not, at the right moment, arranged a marriage for me, I believe I should still today be exactly as my mother bore me.

But appearances, in my case, are deceptive, for I am attractive to men and, although I am rather on the short side and have grown rather square as I have got older, my face is smooth and without a wrinkle, my eyes are black and my teeth white. At that period—which, as I have said, was the happiest of my life—there was no counting the number of men who asked me to marry them. But I knew that what they were after was the shop and the flat, even the ones who declared that they loved me seriously. Possibly even they themselves didn't know that the shop and the flat were more important to them than I was, and they deceived themselves about their own feelings; but I judged the matter from my own self and I thought: "I would give any man in the world for my shop and my flat . . . and why ever should they be different from me? We're all made in the same mould." If they had at least been—I don't say rich, but comfortably off, but they weren't. They were more or less desperate types who, as you could see a mile off, were badly in need of a settled way of life. There was one man from Naples, a policeman, who acted the lovesick swain more than any of them and tried to get me by flattery, smothering me with compliments and even going so far as to call me, in the Neapolitan manner, "Donna Cesira," and so I said to him, frankly: "Come now, if I hadn't the shop and the flat, would you come and say these things to me?" He, at any rate, was sincere. He answered, laughing: "But you *have* the flat and the shop." However it was quite true that he was sincere, because by that time I had taken away all possible hope from him.

All this time the war was going on, but I paid no attention to it and when, after the light music on the radio, they read the communiqué, I used to say to Rosetta: "Turn it off, turn that radio off. Let the bastards cut each other's throats as much as they like but I don't want to hear about it. What does their war matter to *us?* They started it among themselves without asking the opinion of the poor people who have to go and get mixed up in it, and so we, who *are* the poor people, are justified in taking no notice of it." And yet I must admit that, from another point of view, the war was doing me good: I was selling more and more in the black market at fancy prices, and less and less in the shop at the prices fixed by the government. When the air raids began at Naples and other towns, people came and said to me: "Let's get away or we'll all be killed;" and I used to answer: "No, they won't come to Rome, because the Pope's here . . . besides, if I leave, who's going to look after the shop?"

My parents, too, wrote and invited me to stay with them at our village, but I refused. Rosetta and I were going more and more often into the country with our suitcases and bringing back everything we could find to Rome: the country districts were full of stuff, but the peasants didn't want to sell to the government because the government paid very little, so they waited for us of the black market who paid them the proper market prices. We loaded ourselves up with heaps of things besides what we put into our suitcases; I remember once coming back to Rome with several pounds of sausages tied round my waist, under my skirt, so that I looked as if I was going to have a baby. And Rosetta used to put eggs inside her bodice, and then, when she took them out later, they were all warm, as if the hen had just that moment laid them. These journeys, however, were long and dangerous; and once, in the neighborhood of Frosinone, an airplane machine-gunned the train, and the train stopped in open country and I told Rosetta to get out and hide in the ditch; but I myself didn't get out because our suitcases were crammed with stuff and I saw some faces round me in the compartment that were not very reassuring and it doesn't take long to steal a suitcase. So I lay down on the floor, between the seats, with the seat cushions over my body and head, and Rosetta got out with the others and hid in the ditch. The plane, after the first burst of machine-gunning, circled round in the sky and then returned to the attack, flying low over the train, with a terrible roar of engines and a fierce crackle of machine guns, like a hailstorm. It passed over and went off into the distance and then there was silence, and finally everyone came back into the compartment and the train started again. They even showed me some of the bullets, which were as long as your finger; and some of them said it was the Americans and some that it was the Germans. But I said to Rosetta: "You've got to put together your trousseau and your dowry. Soldiers come back from the wars, don't they? They come back, even though, in the war, they are shot at all the time and other soldiers try every possible means of killing them. Well, we shall come back too from these trips of ours into the country." Rosetta said nothing, or rather she said she would go wherever *I* went. She was a sweet character, quite different from me, and God knows, if ever there was an angel on this earth, it was she.

I always used to say to Rosetta: "Pray God the war may go on another couple of years, then you'll not only put together a nice trousseau and dowry but you'll become rich." But she did not answer, or she would just give a sigh, and in the end I came to know that she had, in fact, a sweetheart in the war and was fearing all the time that he would get killed. They used to write to each other—at present he was in Yugoslavia—and I found out about him and discovered that he was an honest young man from Pontecorvo, and that his parents owned a little bit of land, and he was studying to be an accountant and had broken off his studies because of the war but expected to take them up again when it ended. So I said to Rosetta: "The first thing is for him to come back from the war. I'll see to everything else." Rosetta, in her happiness, threw her arms round my neck. And I was at that time able to say truly: "I'll see to everything": I had the flat, I had the shop, I had money put aside; and wars, as we all know, have to come to an end some day and then everything falls into place again. Rosetta also made me read her fiancé's last letter, and I remember one sentence particularly: "We're leading a really hard life here. These Slavs don't want to give in to us and we're always in a state of alarm." I didn't know anything about Yugoslavia, however I said to Rosetta: "What on earth are we doing in that country? Couldn't we stay in our own homes? Those people don't want to give in to us and they're perfectly right, I tell you, they're perfectly right."

In 1943 I did a good piece of business. There were a number of hams, about ten of them, which had to be brought from Sermoneta to Rome. I found means of making an arrangement with a truck driver who was bringing cement to Rome, and he put the hams underneath the sacks of cement and thus the hams arrived safe and sound and I made a lot of money out of them because everyone wanted them. It may perhaps have been this business of the hams that prevented me from realizing what was going on. On my return from Sermoneta I was told that Mussolini had run away and that the war was really and truly on the point of coming to an end. My answer to this was: "As far as I'm concerned, whether it's Mussolini or Badoglio or someone else, it makes little difference, as long as business goes on." In any case Mussolini had never meant anything to me; I always disliked him, with those goggle eyes and that arrogant mouth that could never keep quiet, and I always felt that things began to go wrong for him from the day he took up with that Petacci woman, because, as everyone knows, love makes elderly men lose their heads and Mussolini was already a grandfather by the time he met that young woman. The only good thing about that night of July 25th was that an Army Service Corps storehouse in the Via Garibaldi was turned upside down and I went there with everyone else and brought home a whole Parmesan cheese balanced on my head. There was every sort of good thing there, and everything was carried away. One of my neighbors brought back, on a handcart, the terra cotta stove which had been in the manager's office.

During that summer I did plenty of good business; people were afraid and were piling up stuff in their homes and never seemed to have enough. There was more stuff in cellars and larders than in the shops. I remember taking a ham to a lady in the neighborhood of the Via Veneto. She lived in a beautiful house, and a manservant in livery opened the door to me. I had the ham in my usual fiber suitcase, and the lady, who was beautifully dressed and perfumed and covered with jewels till she looked like the Madonna, came to meet me in the anteroom, and behind her was her husband, a funny little fat man. The lady almost kissed me, and said: "My dear, come this way, make yourself at home. Come, come now." I followed her down a passage and the lady opened the storage room door and there I saw all the good things God ever made. There were more things there than in a delicatessen shop. It was a biggish room without any windows, and there were rows of shelves all round it, and on the shelves you could see, in one place, a lot of big tins, the kind that weigh about two pounds, of sardines in oil, and in another place a lot more tinned foods, of the finest kind, American or English, and also packets and packets of macaroni, and sacks of flour and of beans and pots of jam and at least ten hams and *salame* sausages. I said to the lady: "Why, ma'am, you've got enough here to last you for ten years!" "You never know," she replied. I put the ham beside the others and the husband paid me on the spot, and as he was taking the money from his wallet his hands were trembling with joy and he kept repeating: "As soon as you get something good, remember us. . . . We're ready to pay twenty or even thirty percent more than other people."

Everybody, in fact, wanted things to eat and paid any price for them without a murmur, and so it was that I failed to make any provision for myself, for I had grown accustomed to considering money as the most precious thing in the world, whereas, on the other hand, you can't *eat* money, and when the real shortage came I had absolutely nothing. The shelves in the shop were empty; there was nothing left but a few bundles of macaroni and a few tins of poor quality sardines. Of course I had money, and I no longer kept it in the bank but at home, because it was said that the government intended to close the banks and seize the poor people's savings; but now nobody wanted money, and, furthermore, it was a painful thing for me, after making my money by selling in the black market, to spend it in the black market again when prices were rising to the stars. In the meantime the Germans and the Fascists had come back, and one morning, as I was passing through the Piazza Colonna, I saw the black standard of the Fascists hanging from the balcony of Mussolini's palace, and the whole square was filled with men in black shirts armed to the teeth, and all the people who had made an uproar on the night of July 25th were now running away, keeping close along the walls, like so many mice when a cat appears. "Let's hope," I said to Rosetta, "that they'll win the war quickly now and that we'll get something to eat again."

It was now September and one morning I was told that there was to be a distribution of eggs in the vicinity of the Via della Vite. I went along, and indeed there were two lorries full of eggs. But they weren't distributing anything, and there was a German with a tommy gun across his shoulders superintending the unloading of the eggs. The people had gathered into groups and were watching the eggs being unloaded without saying a word but with their eyes starting out of their heads like starving people, as indeed they were. You could see the German was frightened that they would attack him, because he kept turning round, his hand on his tommy gun, jumping from side to side like a frog on the edge of a swamp. He was young, fat and white, and all reddened with sunburn, with marks of scorching on his thighs and arms as though he had spent a day at the seaside. The crowd, seeing that the eggs were not being distributed, began murmuring, gently at first and then louder and louder, and the German raised his gun and pointed it at them, saying: "Go away, go away!" Then I lost my head, partly because I had had nothing to eat that morning and was hungry, and I shouted at him: "You give us those eggs, and then we'll go." He repeated: "Go away, go away!" and pointed the gun right at me, and then I made a movement, bringing my hand up to my mouth as much as to say that I was hungry. But he gave no sign of having understood and all at once thrust the point of his gun against my stomach, pushing it right into me, so that he hurt me, and this made me furious, and I shouted: "It was too bad you ever threw Mussolini out; we were much better off with him. Since you people have been here, there's nothing to eat." I don't know why, but at these words the crowd started laughing and several of them shouted "Booby!" at me, just as my husband used to do, and one of them said: "Don't you read the papers at Sgurgola?" I answered snappishly: "I come from Vallecorsa, not from Sgurgola, and anyhow I don't know you and I'm not speaking to you." But the others still went on laughing, and the German was almost laughing too. In the meantime men were taking down the eggs in their open boxes, all white and lovely they looked, and carrying them into a warehouse. Then I shouted out: "Hey, you, we want those eggs—d'you understand? We want those eggs." A policeman came out from the crowd and warned me: "Come on, you'd better be moving on. Have you had anything to eat?" I replied; "*I* haven't." Then he gave me a slap and pushed me back among the crowd. I could have killed him, I swear, and I struggled and told him exactly what I thought of him; but everyone round me was pushing me to get me to go away and in the end I was forced to go, and I lost my handkerchief in the confusion, into the bargain.

I went home and I said to Rosetta: "If we don't get away from this place soon, we shall end by starving to death." Then she burst into tears and said: "Mum, I'm so frightened." I was upset because up till then Rosetta had never said a word; she had never complained, in fact more than once she had given me courage because of the calm way in which she had behaved. "You silly," I said to her, "why are you frightened?" "People say," she answered, "that they'll come with their airplanes and kill us all. They say that first they'll destroy all the railways and the trains and then, when Rome is thoroughly isolated and there's nothing left to eat and no one can get away into the country, they'll come and bomb us and kill us all. Oh I'm so frightened, Mum . . . and Gino hasn't written to me for a month and I don't know what's happened to him." I tried to comfort her by telling her the usual things that even I now knew were not true—that in Rome there was the Pope, that the Germans would soon win the war, that there was nothing to be frightened of. But she was sobbing violently and in the end I had to take her in my arms and rock her up and down as I used to do when she was two years old. All the time I was stroking her and she was still sobbing and saying over and over again; "Oh Mum, I'm so frightened," I was thinking that really she was not in the least like me, for I had no fear of anything or anybody. Moreover, she did not at all resemble me physically: she had a face rather like a little sheep, with big eyes that had in them a soft, almost melting expression, a delicate nose drooping slightly downward over her mouth, and a beautiful, full-lipped mouth that jutted out a little over a curved back chin. Her hair, too, reminded one of lamb's wool, very thick and curly; and her skin was white and delicate with a mole here and there; whereas I have black hair and a dark, sunburned-looking complexion. At last, in order to soothe her, I said: "Everyone says the landing of the

English is only a question of days and then they'll come here and there won't be any more food shortage. But d'you know what we'll do in the meantime? We'll go to your grandparents in the country, and we'll wait there for the end of the war. They have plenty of things to eat, they have beans, they have eggs, they have pigs. Anyhow, you can always find something in the country." "What about the flat?" she asked. "My dear child," I replied, "I've thought about that too. We'll let the flat to Giovanni—or rather we'll let it to him *nominally* . . . and when we come back, he'll hand it over to us exactly as it is. But I'll shut the shop altogether; there's nothing in it anyhow and there won't be anything to sell for some time."

I must tell you that this Giovanni was a coal and wood merchant who had been a friend of my husband. He was a great big tall man, bald and red-faced, with bristling mustaches and a mild look in his eyes. When my husband was still alive, he used to keep him company at the inn in the evenings, together with the other shopkeepers of the neighborhood. He wore ample, loose clothes and always had a dead, cold half-cigar gripped between his teeth, under his mustache, and I have never seen him without a notebook and pencil in his hand; he was forever doing accounts and taking notes and jotting down observations. His manners were like the expression in his eyes, gentle, affectionate, familiar, and whenever he saw me, at the time when Rosetta was a small child, he would always ask me: "How's the little one? What's the little one doing?" There is one thing I want to relate, and yet I am not entirely sure about it, because with some things that happen you are not certain afterward whether they happened at all, especially if the person who did these things never mentions them again and behaves as though they hadn't really ever happened. Giovanni, then, while my husband was still alive, came up to the flat one day while I was cooking, making some excuse or other, and sat down in the kitchen while I was at the stove and began talking about one thing and another, finally bringing the conversation around to my husband. I thought they were friends; imagine my surprise, therefore, when, all of a sudden, I heard him say: "Tell me now, Cesira, how can you put up with that old carcass?" That was the word he used, "carcass"; and I could hardly believe my ears and I turned to look at him: and there he sat, gentle and calm, with his dead cigar in the corner of his mouth. Then he went on: "He can hardly stand on his feet, even now, and one of these days he'll die. Besides, he goes with the girls so much that one of these days you'll find you've caught some nasty disease." "Well," I said, "I suppose *I* know what happens with my own husband. When he comes home at night, he gets into bed and I turn the other way and that's that." And then he said, or anyhow I *think* he said: "But you're still young; you don't want to live like a nun, do you? You're young and you need a man who's fond of you." "What's that got to do with you?" I asked him. "I don't need any men, and even if I did, how do you come into it?" At this point he got up—or so I seem to remember—came over to me and took my chin in his hand, saying: "With you women everything has always to be made as clear as crystal. It's myself I'm talking about. Haven't you ever given a thought to *me?*" So many years have gone by since that day that my memory is a bit confused as to what happened after that. I am almost sure, however, that he suggested that I should go to bed with him; and I am also almost sure that, when I answered: "Aren't you ashamed of yourself? Vincenzo is your friend," he replied: "What d'you mean, friend? I'm not a friend of anybody." And then—I could swear to it—he told me that if I would take him into the bedroom and do what he wanted, he would give me some money. And he opened his wallet and began to put down, on the kitchen table, a whole lot of notes, one after the other, looking straight at me and repeating: "Shall I put some more? Or is that enough?" And finally, it seems to me, without getting angry I told him to go away. And he picked up the notes and went. All this certainly happened, because I couldn't have invented it; and yet next day he never mentioned it, nor the following days either, nor ever again. And his behavior was again exactly as before, simple, affectionate, gentle, so that I began to wonder whether I had dreamed it all—that he had called my husband an old carcass and had suggested that I should go to bed with him and had put down money on the kitchen table. This feeling that the thing had never happened grew stronger with the years, and sometimes I thought I had really been dreaming. But all the time, for some reason or other, I knew that Giovanni was the only man who was truly fond of me, for my own sake and not for my belongings; and that, in a difficulty, he was the only one to whom I could turn.

I went therefore to see Giovanni, and found him in his pitch-dark basement, which was full of piles of faggots and sacks of coal, the only merchandise to be found in Rome that summer. I told him what I wanted and he listened to me in silence, blinking his eyes at his half-smoked cigar. Finally he said: "All right then. I'll keep an eye on the shop and the flat for you all the time you're away. They'll both of them be a worry, especially in times like these, and really I don't know why I do it. For the sake of my old friend Vincenzo, I suppose." I was upset at these words because I seemed again to hear his voice saying: "How can you put up with that old carcass?"; and, once more, I could scarcely believe my ears. All of a sudden I burst out with: "I hope you'll be doing it for my sake too"; and I don't know why I said it, perhaps because I was convinced that he was truly fond of me and it would have given me pleasure at that difficult moment to hear him say he was doing it for me. He looked at me for a moment, then took the cigar out of his mouth and put it down on the edge of the table. Then he went over toward the door of the basement room, up the short flight of steps, closed the door and barred and bolted it, so that all at once we were left in complete darkness. I understood now, and I held my breath and my heart was beating violently, and I cannot say that the thing was displeasing to me: I felt deeply excited, disturbed. I suppose this was due to the circumstances, with all Rome upside down and the shortage of food and the general fear and my despair at leaving the shop and the flat and the feeling of not having a man in my life, like all other women, a man who, in a situation like this, would help me and give me courage. However that may be, for the first time in my life I felt my whole body slacken and become limp and yielding, as he came toward me in the darkness; when he came close to me, still in the dark, and took me in his arms, my immediate impulse was to cling to him and to place my own panting mouth upon his. And so he pushed me back on to some sacks of soft charcoal, and I gave myself to him and felt, as I did so, that it was the first time I had truly given myself to a man; and in spite of the fact that the sacks were rough and he was heavy, I had a feeling of lightness and relief; and after it was finished and he had left me, I still lay for quite a long time on the sacks, feeling surprised and happy, and it almost seemed to me that I had gone back to that youthful period of my life when I had come to Rome with my husband and had dreamed of experiencing a feeling like this and yet had never done so and had been left with a sense of repugnance both for men and for love. . . . After some time his voice came out of the darkness asking if I felt ready to talk about our business, and I raised myself up and said yes, and then he lit a little bright yellow lamp and I saw him sitting at the table as before, as though nothing had happened, with his cigar sticking out from under his mustache and his mild eyes half closed.

I went over to him and said: "Swear you won't ever tell anybody what happened today—swear it." And he smiled and answered: "I don't know anything—what are you talking about? I don't understand . . . you came about the business of your shop and your flat, didn't you?" Again I had that feeling I have already spoken about, of having dreamed everything; and if my clothes had not been mussed and I hadn't had dirty marks here and there from having turned this way and that on top of the charcoal sacks, I might really have persuaded myself that nothing had happened. "Yes, of course," I stammered, disconcerted, "you're quite right. I've come about the house and the shop." Then he took a sheet of paper, wrote on it a declaration in which I said that I gave him a lease of the shop and the flat for the duration of one year, and made me sign it. He put the paper in a drawer, then went and opened the door, saying: "That's understood, then . . . I'll come and take over the place today, and tomorrow I'll come along and fetch you both and see you off at the station." He was standing at the door and I passed in front of him to go out, and then, as I went past him, he gave me a slap on the bottom with his open hand, smiling, as much as to say: "It's understood about that other business too." I thought to myself that I no longer had any right to protest, that I was no longer an honest woman, and I even went so far as to think that this, too, was an effect of the war and the shortage of food—that an honest woman should feel a slap on her bottom and not be able to protest, just because she is, in fact, no longer honest.

I went back home and at once began preparations for leaving. I was sad, indeed my heart bled, at having to leave this home in which I had spent the last twenty years, without ever going away except for my black market trips. It is true that I was convinced the English would be arriving very soon indeed, in a matter of a week or two, and in fact I made my preparations for an absence of not more than a month; but at the same time I had a kind of presentiment not merely that my absence would be longer but also that some sadness or other was awaiting me in the future. I had never taken any interest in politics, and I knew nothing of the Fascists, the English, the Russians or the Americans: nevertheless, from having heard people talking all around me, I had come to see that, as things now were, there was nothing good for poor people like ourselves. It was just as when, in the country, the sky becomes black before a thunderstorm and the leaves on the trees turn all the same way and the sheep huddle against each other and, even though it is summer, a cold wind comes from nowhere and blows close along the ground: I was afraid, but I did not know of what; and my heart sank at the idea of leaving my home and my shop just as though I had known for certain that I would never see them again. However, I said to Rosetta: "Now mind you don't take too many things, because we shall be away for not more than a fortnight and it's still warm." It was about the fifteenth of September and it was very hot, more so than in other years.

So we packed two small fiber suitcases, mostly with light clothes, and put in no more than a couple of sweaters in case it should happen to get cold. In order to comfort myself for leaving home I described to Rosetta the great welcome my parents would give me in our village: "You'll see they'll make us eat until we're fit to burst. We'll get fat and we'll have a good rest. All the things that make life so difficult in Rome don't exist in the country. We shall be comfortable and we'll sleep well and above all we'll have plenty to eat. You'll see: they've got pigs, they've got flour, they've got fruit, they've got wine, we shall live like kings." But this prospect did not cheer Rosetta; she was thinking of her fiancé in Yugoslavia. It was a month since he had sent any news of himself, and I knew that every morning she got up early and went to church to pray for him, to pray that he should not be killed and that he should come home and that they should be able to get married. Then, so as to make her see that I understood her, I said, hugging and kissing her: "My darling child, don't worry, because the Madonna sees and hears you and she won't allow anything bad to happen to you." Meanwhile I went on with my preparations, and, now that the moment of apprehension was over, I could hardly wait to get away. This was partly because, what with air raid warnings, shortage of food, the idea of leaving and a number of other things, life for me had ceased to be what life ought to be; I had even lost the desire to do my housework, I who usually threw myself down on my knees to polish the floors and ran out of breath with polishing them and making them shine like mirrors. It seemed to me, in fact, that life had fallen to pieces, like a box that falls off a cart and breaks open and everything in it is scattered all over the street. And when I thought about that incident with Giovanni and of how he had given me that slap on the bottom, I felt that I too, like life, had fallen to pieces, and that I was now capable of anything, even of stealing, even of killing, because I had lost my self-respect and was no longer the woman I had once been. I comforted myself with thinking of Rosetta, who at least had her mother to protect her. She at least would be what I myself now no longer was. True it is that life is made up of habits, and even honesty is a habit; and once habits change, life becomes a kind of hell and we ourselves so many devils let loose, with no more respect either for ourselves or for anyone else.

Rosetta, moreover, was also worried on account of her cat, a fine tabby which she had come upon in the street when it was a small kitten and had brought up on scraps, and which slept with her at night and followed her about during the day like a puppy. I told her to ask the caretaker's wife in the building next door to look after it, and she said she would. She was now sitting in her room, at the foot of the bed upon which lay her suitcase already closed, holding the cat on her knee and gently stroking it, while the cat, poor creature, ignorant that its mistress was on the point of deserting it, was purring, its big eyes tight closed. I felt sorry for Rosetta because I knew she was suffering, and I said: "My blessed child, once this bad moment is past, everything will be all right, you'll see it will. The war will come to an end, we shall have plenty of everything again, and you'll get married and be with your husband, and then you'll be happy." Just at that moment, as though answering me back, came the sound of the air raid warning, that accursed noise which seemed to me to bring ill luck and made my heart sink every time I heard it. Then a rage came over me and I opened the window facing the courtyard and raised my fist toward the sky and shouted: "May you come to a bad end, *and* the people who sent you too, *and* the ones who asked you to come!" Rosetta, who had not moved, said: "Why d'you get so angry, Mum? You said yourself that everything will come right soon." And then, for love of that sweet angel, I calmed myself, though it needed a great effort, and I answered: "Yes, but in the meantime we've got to leave our home, and goodness knows what more is going to happen."

That day I suffered the pains of hell. I seemed no longer to be myself: now I was thinking of what had happened with Giovanni, and at the thought of having yielded to him, just like a common streetwalker, with all my clothes on, on top of those coal sacks, I could have bitten my fingers with rage; and then again I was looking round the flat which had been my home for twenty years and which I now had to leave, and it gave me a feeling of despair. In the kitchen the fire had gone out, in the bedroom where I slept in the double bed with Rosetta the sheets were thrown back in disorder, and I couldn't bring myself to tidy the bed in which I knew I should soon no longer be sleeping, nor yet to light the fire in the stove which tomorrow would no longer be *my* stove and where *I* should not be cooking. We ate some bread and sardines on the bare table; every now and then I glanced at Rosetta who was looking so sad, and then the mouthful would stick in my throat because the sight of her distressed me and I was frightened on her account and thought how unlucky she was to be born and to live in times like these. About two o'clock we threw ourselves on the bed, on top of the untidy sheets, and slept for a little; or rather Rosetta slept, all huddled up against me, while I myself lay with my eyes open, thinking of Giovanni, of the coal sacks and of the way he had slapped me on the bottom, and of the home and the shop I was going to leave. At last there was a ring at the doorbell, and I released myself gently from the pressure of the sleeping Rosetta and went to the door. It was Giovanni, smiling, cigar in mouth. I didn't even give him time to draw breath. "Now listen," I said to him furiously, "what happened happened and I'm no longer the same woman I was before, I admit that, and you're quite right to treat me like a slut. But you give me another slap like you did this morning, and I swear by God I'll kill you. Then I'd go to prison, but in these times I daresay it's quite comfortable to be in prison and I wouldn't in the least mind going there." He raised his eyebrows very very slightly in surprise, but didn't say anything. Then he walked past me into the hall and murmured almost inaudibly: "Well then, let's get on with the taking over of the flat."

I went back into the bedroom and fetched a sheet of paper on which I had made Rosetta write down all the things I had both in the flat and in the shop. I had made her write down even the smallest objects, not so much because I did not trust Giovanni but because it is best not to trust anybody. And so, before we started on the inventory, I said, very seriously, to Giovanni: "Now mind, all this is hard-earned stuff that my husband and I collected together in twenty years of work. Be sure and let me find it all when I come back, and remember that not one single nail in the place must be missing." He smiled and said: "Don't worry, you shall find all your old nails again."

I started with the bedroom. I had made two lists; he held one and Rosetta held one, and I myself pointed out the things to him. I showed him the bed, big enough for two, made of iron painted to look like wood, and very beautiful with all the veinings and knots in the wood so well done that you could really mistake it for walnut. I lifted the covers and pointed out to him that there were two mattresses, one of horsehair and one of wool. I opened the cupboard and counted out the blankets and sheets and all the rest of the linen. I opened the doors of the bedside tables and showed him the china chamber pots with red and blue flower patterns on them. Then I went through the list of the furniture: one chest-of-drawers with a white marble top, one oval gilt-framed mirror, four chairs, one bed, two bedside tables, one wardrobe with double doors and mirrors inset. I counted over all the knicknacks and ornaments: a bunch of artificial wax flowers that looked perfectly real, under a glass bell, which I had had as a wedding present from my godmother, a china dish for sweets, two statuettes representing a shepherd and shepherdess, a blue velvet pin cushion, a box from Sorrento that played a tune when you opened it and whose lid was inlaid with a picture of Vesuvius, two water bottles with glasses to match, all made of massive engraved glass, a colored china flower vase in the shape of a tulip, with three peacock's feathers, ever so lovely, stuck into it in place of flowers, two pictures printed in colors, one showing the Madonna and Child and the other a sort of theatrical scene with a Moor and a blonde lady, which I had been told was taken from an opera called *Othello*, and indeed the Moor in the picture was Othello himself. From the bedroom I led him into the dining room, which I used also as sitting room and where I kept my sewing machine. Here I made him touch and feel the round table of dark walnut, with its embroidered table center and flower vase to match the one in the bedroom and the four chairs round it upholstered in green velvet, and then I opened the sideboard cupboard and counted out, piece by piece, the whole china dinner service with the flowers and wreaths on it, very beautiful indeed and complete for six people, off which I had eaten perhaps twice in my whole life. At this point I warned him: "Now mind, this dinner service is as dear to me as the light of my eyes. Break it and you'll see. . . ." He answered with a smile: "Don't worry." I went on with my list and showed him all the other things: the two flower pictures, the sewing machine, the radio, the small repp-covered sofa and its pair of armchairs to match, the pink and blue glass bottle for cordials and its six little tumblers, a few more dishes and boxes, a lovely fan, painted in colors with a view of Venice, which I had hung up on the wall. Then we went through into the kitchen and here I counted over, piece by piece, all the crockery and all the pots, some of aluminum and some of copper, and the stainless steel knives and forks, and I pointed out to him that nothing was lacking—neither an oven, nor a potato-masher, nor a little cupboard for brooms, nor a zinc rubbish-bin. In fact I showed him everything, and then we went downstairs and into the shop. The inventory for the shop was shorter, because, apart from the shelves, the counter and a chair or two, there was nothing left; everything had been sold, and the place had been cleaned and swept during these last months of food shortage. Finally we went upstairs again into the flat, and, feeling much discouraged, I said: "What's the use of this inventory? Somehow I feel as if I should never come back here again." Giovanni, who had sat down and was smoking, shook his head and replied: "In a fortnight's time the English will be here;

even the Fascists admit it. You go off for a couple of weeks' holiday in the country, and then come back again and we'll have some fine celebrations in honor of your return. What are you getting into your head?" Giovanni spoke these words, and a great many more, to comfort us, Rosetta and me, and he almost succeeded; so that when he went away we felt much relieved, and this time, even though we were alone in the hall, he did not give me a slap as he had done before, but contented himself with giving me a slight caress on my cheek, such as he used often to give me even when my husband was still alive, and I was grateful to him for this, and it almost, almost seemed to me that really nothing had happened between me and him and that I was still the woman I had always been.

I spent the rest of that day finishing my preparations. First of all I made up a good parcel of things to eat during the journey: a *salame* sausage, one or two tins of sardines, a tin of tunny fish and some bread. For my father and mother I made up a separate parcel: for my father an almost new suit of my husband's, which he had had made shortly before he died and had asked me to put on him after he was dead, but at the last moment this had seemed to me a pity—such a lovely suit of dark blue woolen cloth—and so I had wrapped him up in an old sheet and had saved the suit. My father was almost of the same height as my husband, and with the suit I put also a pair of his shoes, old ones, but still good. For my mother I decided to take a shawl and a skirt. I added to the parcel all I had left in the way of groceries, that is, a few pounds of sugar and coffee and a few tins and a couple more *salame* sausages. I put all these things into a third suitcase, so that we now had three suitcases, as well as a bag into which I put a blanket and a pillow in case we were forced to sleep in the train. Everyone told me that the trains were taking even as much as two days to get to Naples, and we had to go to a point half way between Rome and Naples, and I thought that such precautions could not be overdone.

In the evening we sat down to table, and this time I had done some cooking to keep us from being too depressed, but we had scarcely started eating when the air raid warning sounded, and I saw that Rosetta had turned pale with fear and had started to tremble. I realized that, after holding out for a long time, she was now unable to do so any longer and that her nerves were all upset, so I resigned myself to leaving the supper on the table and going down to the cellar—a precaution which in point of fact served no purpose at all, because if a bomb had fallen that old house of ours would have crumbled into dust and we should have been buried underneath it. So we went down into the shelter, and there were all the other tenants living in the house, and we spent three quarters of an hour sitting on benches in the dark. They were all talking about the arrival of the English as being a question of only a few more days: they had landed at Salerno which was near Naples and to get from Naples to Rome they would take possibly a week, if they went slowly, for the Germans and the Fascists were now running like hares and would not stop till they reached the Alps. But some of them said that the Germans would give battle at Rome, because Mussolini attached great importance to Rome and did not in the least mind reducing it to ruins to keep the English from entering it. I listened to these things and thought we were doing right to leave; Rosetta was clinging to me, and I realized she would not calm down until we were right away from Rome. Then somebody said: "You know what people are saying? That they'll drop parachutists and the parachutists will come into the houses and do all sorts of things." "What d'you mean by that?" "Well, first they'll help themselves to what they want and then it'll be the women." "I'd like to see the man," I said, "who'd dare to put a hand on *me*." From the darkness came the voice of a man called Proietti, a baker, a man of unspeakable stupidity, always very solemn in his speech, a person I had never been able to bear; he was saying, with a guffaw: "Nobody said they would lay hands on *you;* you're too old, but on your daughter, they certainly will." "Be careful what you say," I retorted, "I'm thirty-five, because I married at sixteen, and there are plenty of men who would like to marry me now. I haven't married again simply because I don't want to." "Oh yes," he replied, "sour grapes." I was really angry now, and I said: "You'd better think about that slut of a wife of yours. She makes a fool of you already, even when there aren't any parachutists. Just imagine what it'll be when they arrive!" I thought the wife was away in the country; they came from Sutri and I had seen her going away a few days before; but not at all, there she was, by ill luck, in the air raid shelter, and I hadn't seen her because of the darkness. Now, in a flash, I heard her shouting at me: "Slut yourself, you ugly, common slut, you mean, miserable wretch!" And then I was aware that she had seized hold of Rosetta by the hair, thinking it was me, and Rosetta was screaming and the woman was hitting her. So I hurled myself at her in the dark and we rolled together on the floor, punching each other and tearing at each other's hair while everybody was shouting and Rosetta was crying and begging for help and calling to me. In the end they had to separate us—still in darkness, of course—and I believe the peacemakers came in for a slap or two as well, because, all of a sudden, as they were separating us, the all clear went and someone turned on the light and we found ourselves face to face, panting and disheveled as they held us by the arms, and some of the people who were holding us had scratches on their faces and some had their hair disarranged. Rosetta was sobbing in a corner.

That night, after this angry scene, we went to bed very early, without even finishing the supper which had been left on the table and which was still there next morning. In bed, Rosetta cuddled close up to me as she had used to do when she was small. "Are you still frightened?" I asked her. "No, I'm not frightened," she said, "but oh Mum, is it true that parachutists do things like that to women?" "Don't pay any attention to that silly fool," I said. "He doesn't know what he's talking about." "But is it true?" she insisted. "No, it's not true," I replied, "and in any case we're leaving tomorrow and going to the country and nothing will happen there, so don't worry." She was silent for a minute or two, and then she said: "But, for us to be able to come home, which is it who ought to win—the Germans or the English?" I was put out by this question, because, as I have said, I had never read the papers and, into the bargain, had never taken any interest in knowing how the war was going. "I don't know what plans they've got," I said; "all I know is that they're bastards, the whole lot of them, both English and Germans, and that they make these wars without consulting unfortunate people like us. But I tell you this: as far as we're concerned, somebody's *got* to win, and to win seriously, so that the war can come to an end. Whether it's Germans or English doesn't matter, provided one of them is really stronger."

But she still insisted. "Everybody says the Germans are bad, but what have they done, Mum?" "What they've done," I answered, "is that, instead of staying in their own country, they've come here to make a nuisance of themselves to *us*. That's why people hate them so." "But where we're going now," she asked, "is it the Germans who are there or the English?" I really didn't know what to answer, so I said: "There aren't either Germans or English there. There are nothing but fields and cows and peasants, and everything is all right. So now you had better go to sleep." She said nothing more, but she cuddled up against me and in the end she appeared to fall asleep.

What an unpleasant night that was! I woke up at every moment and I don't believe Rosetta closed her eyes all night long either, even though she may have pretended to be asleep in order not to distress me. At times I thought I woke up when in fact I was asleep and dreaming that I woke up, at other times I thought I was asleep when I was in fact awake, and weariness and nervous restlessness gave me an illusion of being asleep. I doubt if Jesus Christ in the Garden, on the night before Judas came to lay hold on Him, suffered as much as I suffered during that night. My heart sank at the thought of leaving the home in which I had lived for so many years, and I wondered whether our train would be machine-gunned during our journey, or whether the train was no longer running, for people said that any day now Rome might be left isolated. I thought about

Rosetta too, and reflected that it had been a real misfortune that my husband should have been the man he was and that he should have died, for indeed two women alone in the world, without a man to guide and protect them, are in a sense like two blind people who walk along without seeing and without understanding where they are.

At one moment—I don't know what time it was—I heard the sound of shooting in the street, but I was accustomed to this by now, for there was shooting every night and it sounded like shooting at a target; but Rosetta started up and asked: "What is it, Mum?" "Nothing," I answered, "nothing. . . . Just those same bastards amusing themselves with firing. Let's hope they all kill each other." Still later a long convoy of trucks went past the house, and the whole place shook and the convoy seemed to go on for ever and when it appeared to have finished yet another truck went rumbling past with such a din you could hardly believe it. I held Rosetta in my arms, with her head against my chest, and all of a sudden—perhaps because I had her head against my breast—I remembered the time when she was a baby and I was feeding her, and my breasts were swollen with milk, as always happens with us Ciociaria women who are known as the best wet-nurses in all Latium, and she was absorbing all that milk and becoming more beautiful every day and was indeed such a perfect flower of beauty that people in the street used to stop and look at her; and all of a sudden I said to myself that it would have been much better if she had never been born if she now had to live in a world like this, surrounded with troubles and dangers and fears. But then I said to myself that those were ideas that come to one in the night and that it was a shame to have such thoughts, and in the darkness I made the sign of the Cross and implored the protection of Jesus and the Madonna. I heard a cock crow in the flat next door, a flat belonging to a family that kept a complete poultry house in the lavatory, and then I knew that it would soon be day and I believe I fell asleep.

I was awakened with a start by the sound of the doorbell

ringing and ringing as though it had been ringing for a long time. I got up in the dark and went into the hall and opened the door, and there was Giovanni, who said, as he came in: "My goodness, how you sleep. I must have been ringing for an hour at least!" I was in my chemise; and even now my bosom is still so firm that it stays in place without the support of any brassière; and at that time it was even more beautiful, with heavy, solid breasts and nipples turning upward as though they insisted on attracting attention to themselves. Well, I noticed at once that he was looking at that part of me and that his eyes were lighting up beneath his eyebrows like two pieces of coal beneath the ashes. I realized that he was on the point of catching hold of my breasts, so I drew back hastily and said: "No, Giovanni, no. For me, you no longer exist, and you must forget what happened. If you were not already married, I would marry you, but you *are* married and there mustn't be anything more between us." He did not say yes or no, but it was obvious that he was making an effort to control himself. Finally he succeeded, and said, in his normal voice: "You're right, but let's hope that nasty old wife of mine will get killed during this war, so that when you come back I shall be a widower and we can get married. Plenty of people are getting killed in air raids, so why shouldn't she?" Once again I was shocked and surprised to hear him say such things, and I could scarcely believe my ears, just as when he had said that my husband was an "old carcass" although up till then he had been his friend and they had been, as you might say, inseparable. I did, as a matter of fact, know Giovanni's wife and had always thought he really loved her or at any rate was quite fond of her, since they had been married for a great many years and had had three children; and yet here he was, speaking of her with hatred and hoping she would be killed, and the way in which he spoke of her implied that he had hated her for goodness knows how long and felt nothing for her now except hatred, if indeed he had ever had any other feeling for her in the past. To tell the truth, I was almost frightened at the thought that a man can be a friend and a husband for so many years and then talk like that, with such a degree of coldness and unkindness—"that old carcass" and "that nasty old woman"—of his friend and his wife. But I said nothing of all this to Giovanni, who meanwhile had gone through into the kitchen, where I could hear him making jokes with Rosetta. "I know what it'll be, you'll both come back fattened up, and that will be the only consequence of the war for you. In the country there's cheese and eggs and lambs; you'll have plenty to eat and you'll be very well off there."

By this time everything was ready and I took the three suitcases and the bag with the parcels in it to the door, and then Giovanni took up two of the suitcases and I took the bag and Rosetta the smallest of the suitcases. They went downstairs, while I stayed behind with the excuse of locking the door. As soon as they were around the corner of the staircase, I went back into the bedroom, where I pulled up one of the floor tiles and took out the money I had hidden there. It was quite a big sum for those times, all in thousand-lira notes, and I had not wanted to take it out in the presence of Rosetta because, with money, you never know, and an innocent person may easily commit an imprudence and say the wrong thing and anyhow in matters of money you can't trust anyone. In the hall I lifted up my skirt and put the money into a cloth pocket which I had sewn on underneath for that purpose. Then I went down and joined Giovanni and Rosetta in the street.

There was a cab waiting at the door, for Giovanni had not wished to use his coal wagon for fear of its being requisitioned. Giovanni helped us in and then got in himself. The cab moved off, and I could not help turning round to look back at the crossroads and at my home and my shop, for I had a presentiment that I should never see them again. It was not yet day, but night was over and the air was grey, and in this grey air I saw my home at one corner of the crossroads, all its windows shut, and on the ground floor below, the shop with its blinds lowered. Opposite it was another house which also formed a corner, and on the first floor of this house there was a framed niche with an image of the Madonna under glass, surrounded with gold swords and with a little lamp perpetually burning. It seemed to me that this little lamp that burned even in time of war, even in time of famine, was rather like my own hope of coming home again, and I felt a little relieved: this hope, I thought, would continue to warm and comfort me when I was far away. In that grey light the whole of the crossroads could be seen, like an empty stage after the actors have left it; and you could see that the houses were the humble homes of poor people, rather crooked, as though they were leaning one against the other, the plaster peeling off here and there, especially at ground floor level, because of the handcarts and vehicles; and right beside my shop was Giovanni's coal shop, and it was all black round the door like the mouth of a furnace, and at that hour of the day you could see the black very clearly and for some reason it seemed to me intensely sad. And I could not help remembering that during the daytime, in the good old days, the crossroads would be full of people, with women sitting on straw-seated chairs outside the doors, cats prowling round on the cobblestones, children skipping and playing leap frog, and young men working in workshops or going into the inn which was always full; and at this thought I had an ache at my heart and I realized that these humble houses and this crossroads were dear to me, no doubt because I had spent most of my life there and had been very young when I saw them for the first time, and now I was a mature woman with a daughter already grown up. I said to Rosetta: "Aren't you looking at our house, aren't you looking at the shop?"—and she answered: "Now, don't worry, Mum, you said yourself that we should be back in a couple of weeks' time." I sighed and said nothing. The cab started down toward the Tiber and I turned my head and ceased to look back at the crossroads.

All the streets were empty, and the grey air at the far end of each of them looked like steam from the washing when the clothes are very dirty. On the ground the early morning dampness made the paving stones shine so that they were like iron.

There were only dogs to be seen: I saw five or six of them, ugly, starved-looking and dirty, sniffing at corners of houses and then pissing against walls from which hung torn colored posters inciting people to war. We crossed the Tiber by the Ponte Garibaldi, went along the Via Arenula, through the Piazza Argentina and into the Piazza Venezia. From the balcony of Mussolini's palace hung the same black banner that I had seen a few days before in the Piazza Colonna, and armed Fascists stood at each side of the door. The square was deserted and appeared even larger than usual. At first I did not see the gold stripe in the black banner and I really thought it was a mourning banner, all the more so as there was no wind and it was hanging straight down, looking just like one of those pieces of black cloth that people hang outside the door when there is a dead person in the building. Then I saw the gold stripe amongst the folds, and realized that it was Mussolini's own banner. "Why, is Mussolini back again?" I asked Giovanni. He was smoking his usual half-cigar, and he answered emphatically: "Yes, he's back again and let's hope he'll stay for good." These words left me open-mouthed with astonishment, because I knew that he disliked Mussolini; but then he was always giving me surprises, and I could never foresee what might pass through his head. Then I felt his elbow nudging me in the ribs and saw that he was winking in the direction of the driver, as much as to say that it was from fear of *him* that he had spoken like that. This seemed to me exaggerated, for the driver was a nice little old man, with white hair like a wig sticking out from under his cap in all directions, and I felt he might have easily been my grandfather and that he would certainly not act the spy; however I said nothing.

We turned up the Via Nazionale, and the air was becoming less grey and there was a pink shaft of sunshine on the top of the Torre di Nerone. But when we reached the station and went in, it was just as though it had still been the middle of the night, with the lamps all lit and the place otherwise in darkness. The station was full of people, mostly humble folks like ourselves, with their bundles, but there were also a lot of German soldiers laden with arms and haversacks, standing about in groups, close together, in the darkest corners. Giovanni went off to buy the tickets, leaving us with our suitcases right in the middle of the station. All of a sudden there was a great clatter and about ten motorcyclists, all dressed in black like devils out of hell, came rushing in right under the roofed part of the station. After the black flag in the Piazza Venezia, these motorcyclists, all in black too, made me feel impatient and angry, and I thought to myself: "Why *black*, what's all this *black* for? The wretches, the bastards —they've well and truly cast the evil eye on us with their blasted black." The motorcyclists stopped their machines, leaned them up against the entrance columns, and then took up positions beside the doorways, their faces expressionless under their black leather helmets, their hands on the revolvers in their belts. I caught my breath with fear and my heart started beating violently, for I thought these black motorcyclists must have come to the station to block the entrances and arrest everyone on the spot, as indeed they often did, and then they took away all the people in trucks and nothing more was ever heard of them. So I looked about in the hopes of finding a way out by which we could escape. But then I saw that, at the entrance on the side where the trains came in, there was a group of people arriving, while others were repeating: "Make way there, make way!"— and I realized that the motorcyclists were there because of the arrival of some important personage. I did not see him because the crowd prevented it, but after a little I heard once more the clatter of those hateful motorcycles and knew that they had ridden off behind the important person's car.

Giovanni came to fetch us, holding the tickets and telling us that these tickets would take us as far as Fondi: we would be able to reach the village from there, through the mountains. Then we went out to the platform, where the train was. There was sunshine there, falling in long rays on the paving stones and looking like the rays of sunshine you see in hospital wards and prison yards. There was not a soul to be seen, and the long, long train, drawn up along the platform, appeared to be empty. But when we got in and started walking along the corridor, I saw that it was crammed full of German soldiers, all fully armed, with their haversacks over their shoulders, their caps over their eyes, and their rifles between their legs. There must have been I don't know how many of them; we went from compartment to compartment and in each were eight German soldiers with all their equipment on, sitting still and silent and looking as if they had been given the order not to move and not to speak. At last, in a third class coach, we found Italians. They were crammed together in the corridors and in the compartments, like beasts being taken to the slaughter—and therefore, as they are so soon to die, it doesn't matter whether they are comfortable or not; and they too, just like the Germans, were neither speaking nor moving; but you could see that their immobility and silence were due to weariness and despair, whereas, with the Germans, it was obvious that they were holding themselves in readiness to jump out of the train and immediately start fighting. I said to Rosetta: "You see, we shall have to stand the whole way." And in fact, after hunting about, with the sun coming in through the dirty windows of the train and making the carriages red hot already, we put down our suitcases in the corridor, just in front of the lavatory, and squatted down as best we could. Giovanni, who had followed us into the train, then said: "Well, I'll be leaving you now; the train will be starting soon." But another man, dressed all in black, who was also sitting on his suitcase, snapped back at him, in a gloomy sort of way, without raising his eyes: "Quite soon—don't you believe it! We've been waiting three hours already."

Well, Giovanni said good-bye to us, and kissed Rosetta on both cheeks and me on the corner of the mouth; perhaps he really wanted to kiss me right on the mouth but I turned my face away in time. When he had gone, we remained sitting there on our suitcases, I myself perched up high and Rosetta lower down, her head resting against my knees. After we had squatted there, without speaking, for half an hour, Rosetta asked: "When do we start, Mum?" and I answered: "My dear girl, I don't know any more about it than you do." I sat like that, quite still, with Rosetta crouching at my feet, for I don't know how long. The people in the corridor dozed and sighed, the sun became scorching, and not a sound came from the platform outside. The Germans, too, were silent; it was just as though they hadn't been there. Then, all of a sudden, in the compartment nearest to us, they began singing. It cannot be said that they sang badly; they had low, hoarse voices but they sang in tune; yet I had so often heard our own soldiers singing gaily, as they do when they are in the train traveling together, I felt depressed because these Germans were singing something that seemed to me sad. They sang slowly and it really seemed that after all they hadn't such a great wish to go and fight, for their song was truly sad. I said to the man in black who sat beside me: "*They* don't like war, either. After all they're human beings too. Listen how sadly they sing." But he answered sullenly: "You don't know what you're talking about. It's their National Anthem. It's like the *Marcia Reale* with us." And then, after a moment's silence, he added: "It's we Italians who have the real sadness!"

In the end the train moved off, without a whistle or any sound at all, as though it were starting by pure chance. I wanted to put myself and Rosetta, once and for all, in the hands of the Madonna, so that she might protect us from all the dangers we might meet. But I was overcome by such an intense desire to sleep that I hadn't the strength. I merely thought: "Oh, those bastards. . . ." and I didn't know whether I was thinking about the Germans or the English or the Fascists or the Italians. The whole lot of them, I daresay. Then I fell asleep.

Chapter 2

I WOKE UP after an hour or so and the train was standing still, in silence. Inside the coach the heat was now so great that it was almost impossible to breathe; Rosetta had got up and was looking out of the window at something or other. A number of other people were also looking out, standing in a row all down the corridor. I got up with some difficulty, feeling stunned and sweaty, and I too looked out. There was the sunshine, there was the blue sky, there was the green countryside, composed all of hills covered with vineyards; and on one of those hills, right opposite the train, there was a little white house which had been set on fire. Out of its windows came red tongues of fire and clouds of black smoke, and these flames and this smoke were the only moving things, for everything else in the countryside was still and quiet, on that truly perfect day, and there was no one to be seen. Then, inside the coach, everyone suddenly cried: "There he is, there he is!"; and I looked up at the sky and in an angle of the horizon saw a black insect which almost immediately assumed the shape of an airplane and disappeared. And then, all of a sudden, I heard it above my head, flying over the train with a terrible din, and inside the din you could hear a hammering noise like a sewing-machine. The din lasted for a moment and then died down and immediately afterwards there was a terrible explosion quite close to us, and everyone in the coach threw themselves down on the floor except me; I wasn't in time and didn't even think of it. Thus I was able to see the burning house vanish in a great grey cloud which at once started spreading out over the hillside and coming down in great puffs towards the train; now there was silence again and people were getting up from the floor almost unable to believe that they were still alive; and then they all turned and began looking out of the windows again. The air was now filled with a fine dust which made you cough; then the cloud slowly dispersed and we were all able to see that the little white house was no longer there. The train, after a few minutes, started off again.

That was the most notable thing that happened during our journey. There were several stops, always in open country, sometimes for half an hour or an hour, so that the train took almost six hours to accomplish a journey which in normal times would have taken about two hours. Rosetta, who had been so frightened during air raids in Rome, now, after the little white house had blown up and the train had started again, said to me: "It doesn't frighten me so much in the country as it did in Rome. Here there's sunshine and open air. In Rome I was terrified of the house coming down on my head. Here, if I was killed, I should at least be able to see the sunshine." Then one of the men who was traveling with us in the corridor said: "I saw people who were killed in the sunshine, in Naples. There were two rows of them on the pavements, after an air raid. They looked like piles of dirty clothes. *They* were able to take a good look at the sunshine before they died." And someone else commented: "What is it they say at Naples, in that song? *O sole mio?*"—and he smiled ironically as he said it. But no one really wanted to talk, still less to make jokes; and so we kept silence for the rest of the journey.

We were to get out at Fondi and, after we had passed Terracina, I told Rosetta to get ready. My parents lived up in the mountains, in a little village in the direction of Vallecorsa where they had a small house and a bit of land, and from Fondi this was a journey of one hour by car, by the main road. But as it turned out, when we arrived opposite Monte San Biagio—which is a village perched high up on a hill, looking out over the Fondi valley—I saw that everyone was getting out of the train. The Germans had already got out at Terracina; and there was no one left in the train but Italians. They all got out and we two remained in our empty compartment, and all at once I felt better because we were alone and it was a lovely day and we should soon be arriving at Fondi and would go on from there to my parents'. The train was standing still, but I was not surprised, it had stopped so many times; and so I said to Rosetta: "You'll see how you'll come to life again in the country; you'll eat and sleep and everything will be all right." I went on talking about what we would do in the country, and still the train did not move. It must have been about one or two o'clock and it was very hot, and I said: "Let's have something to eat"; and I took down the small suitcase in which I had packed the provisions, opened it, and proceeded to make a couple of sandwiches with the bread and *salame*. I had also a small bottle of wine, and I gave a glass of it to Rosetta and drank one myself. We were eating and the heat was intense and there was a great silence, and through the windows all you could see was the plane trees round the open space in front of the station, white with dust, parched, with the crickets chirping amongst the foliage as though we had still been in mid-August. This was the country, the real country, where I was born and where I had lived till I was sixteen, my own native country, with its smell of dust lying hot in the sun, of dried dung and scorched grass. "Ah, I feel fine," I couldn't help exclaiming, putting my feet up on the seat opposite; "just listen to the silence! How pleased I am not to be in Rome!" At that moment the door of the compartment was thrown open and a man put his head in.

It was a railwayman, thin and dark, with his cap on one side, his jacket unbuttoned, his chin unshaved. He put his head in and said: "*Buon appetito!*"—but in a serious, almost an angry, way. Thinking that he was hungry, as so many people were in those days, I pointed towards the piece of yellow paper upon which the slices of *salame* were lying, and said: "Won't you take some?" But he retorted, getting more and more angry: "Take some—get along with you! You've got to get out." "We're going to Fondi," I said, and showed him the tickets. He scarcely glanced at them and replied: "Can't you see everyone's got out here? The train finishes here." "Doesn't it go to Fondi?" "What d'you mean, Fondi? The line's cut." After a moment he went on, a little more kindly: "You can get to Fondi on foot from here in half an hour. But you'll have to get out because the train goes back again to Rome soon." And he went out, banging the door.

We sat just as we were, staring each other in the face, our half-eaten sandwiches in our hands. Then I said to Rosetta: "It's a bad beginning." Rosetta, as if she had guessed my thoughts, answered: "No, no, Mum, we'll get out and find a cab or a car or something." I was no longer listening to her. I took down the suitcases, opened the door and got out of the train.

There was no one on the station platform. We went through the waiting-room: no one there; and out on to the open space outside: no one there either. From thence there was a straight road in front of us, a real country road, white, covered with fine dust, blinding in the sunlight between hedges veiled in dust and a few dusty trees. In one corner of the open space there was a small drinking-fountain; heat and anxiety had dried up my mouth, and I went across to have a drink, but it was dry. Rosetta had stayed with the suitcases and was looking at me with a frightened face. "Oh Mum," she said, "what shall we do?"

I knew that this road went straight to Fondi. "Well, child, what *is* there we can do?" I said. "We must start walking."

"And how about the suitcases?"

"We'll carry them."

She said nothing but gazed in consternation at the suitcases; she did not see how we could possibly carry them. I opened one of them, took out two table napkins and made a couple of head pads, one for each of us. While I was making the pads,

I said: "Now Mum will show you how we manage." Rosetta, relieved, smiled.

I placed the pad on my head, well pressed down, and told Rosetta to do the same. Then I took off my shoes and stockings and made Rosetta do so too. On the pad of my own head I arranged the biggest of the suitcases, the medium-sized one, and the parcel of provisions, in order of size; and on Rosetta's, the smallest of the suitcases. I explained to her that she must walk with her head and neck erect, holding the suitcase steady with her hand at one corner. When I saw she had understood and was already walking away with the case on her head I said to myself: "She was born in Rome but, after all, she's a *Ciociara* girl too: blood will always tell." And so, with the suitcases on our heads, bare-footed, walking at the edge of the road where a little grass grew, we started off toward Fondi.

We walked for some distance. The road was deserted and even in the fields there was not a living soul to be seen. To a town person who did not understand such things, it might have looked like a normal countryside; but I who had been a peasant before I had been a city dweller could see that it was a countryside abandoned. You could see signs of this everywhere: the clusters of grapes in the vineyards ought to have been harvested, instead they were still hanging among leaves that were yellowed, over-golden, some even brown and withered, the grapes half eaten by wasps and lizards. The maize, in some places, was lying flat and in disorder and full of weeds, and the ears were ripe, almost red. All around the fig trees there lay quantities of figs which had fallen from the branches through being too soft, and were now broken and burst open and pecked by birds. There was not a peasant to be seen and I supposed they must all have run away. And yet it was a beautiful day, warm and serene, a real country day. That is what war is like, I said to myself: everything looks normal and yet, underneath, war penetrates like a boring worm in wood and people get frightened and run away, while the countryside, for its part, continues with complete indifference to throw off fruit and corn and grass and trees as though nothing were happening.

We arrived at the gates of Fondi with our legs white with dust up to the knee, our throats parched, both of us exhausted and speechless. "Now," I said to Rosetta, "we'll go to an inn and have something to eat and drink and have a rest. And then we'll see if we can find a car or a cart to take us to your grandparents'." An inn, indeed, a car, a cart! Far from it! As we walked into Fondi we very soon realized that the town was deserted and abandoned. Not so much as a dog to be seen; and all the shops had their blinds lowered, with bits of white paper stuck on to them here and there explaining that the owners had been evacuated; all the doors to houses and courtyards were bolted and barred, the windows were shuttered, even the cat holes were stopped up. It was like walking through a town in which all the inhabitants had died of the plague. And to think that generally at Fondi, in this season, the streets are crowded with people, men, women, and children, cats and dogs and donkeys and horses, to say nothing of hens—all going about their business and enjoying the fine weather as they walk about or sit in the cafés and in front of the houses. A few small side streets gave an impression of life because of the brilliant sunlight striking on the paving stones and the fronts of the houses; but when you looked closer you found the same shuttered windows, the same bolted doors. The sunshine flooding the stones became almost frightening, just as the silence and the sound of our own footsteps were also frightening. I stopped from time to time and knocked at a door and called out, but no one answered me. Finally we came to the Cock Inn, with its wooden sign with a painting of a cock, discolored and defaced. The door was shut, an old door painted green with an old-fashioned lock with a big keyhole; and I put my eye to the keyhole and looked in. I could see through the half-darkness of a big room to a window facing on to a garden, beneath a pergola which was full of light and over which hung a green vine with many clusters of black grapes: I could also see a table lit up by the sunshine, but that was all. Here again nobody answered me; no doubt the innkeeper had run away, like everyone else.

So this was the country: worse than Rome. And when I reflected on how I had deceived myself into thinking that I should find in the country everything that was lacking in Rome, I turned to Rosetta and said: "Do you know what *I* say? Let's rest now and then go back to the station and catch the train to Rome again." That is what I should have done. But I saw Rosetta's face take on a frightened expression—she was obviously thinking of the air raids—so I added hastily: "However, before we give up altogether, I want to have a last try. This is Fondi. Let's try the country. It may be that we shall find some peasant or other who will let us sleep in his house for a night or two. After that we'll see."

So we sat on a low wall, without speaking because in that deserted place we found our own voices almost frightening; and then we put back the suitcases on our head pads and left the town on the opposite side to the one by which we had come in. We walked for perhaps half an hour along the main road, in the blazing sun and through the same white, floury dust, and then, as soon as the orange groves began on each side of the road, I took the first path through the orange trees, thinking "it will lead us to some place or other; in the country paths always lead to some place." The orange trees were thick and close, their foliage clean and without dust, and beneath them there was deep shade; this gave us new vigor after the sun-scorched, dusty high road. As we followed this path which turned and twisted through the orange trees Rosetta asked: "When do they pick the oranges, Mum?" I answered without thinking: "They begin picking them in November. And you'll see how sweet they taste." And then I bit my tongue because it was barely the end of September and I had kept saying that we would stay away from Rome not more than ten days, although I knew in my innermost heart that it was not true, and now I had given myself away. But luckily she paid no particular attention to what I said, and we continued on our way along the path.

At last the path came to an end in a clearing, and in the middle was a cottage which once must have been painted pink, but now, with dampness and age, was blackened and peeling. An outside staircase went up to the second floor, where there was a terrace with a wide archway from which hung many strings of sweet peppers and tomatoes and onions. In front of the house, on the threshing-floor, quantities of figs were strewn about, drying in the sun. A peasant's house, obviously, and inhabited. The *contadino* himself, in fact, came out immediately, even before we called, and I realized that he had been hiding somewhere to see who was coming. He was an old man, frighteningly thin, with a small, bony head, a long nose like a beak, deep-sunk eyes and a low, bald forehead like a kite's. "Who are you?" he said, "what do you want?" and in his hand he held a small scythe, as though ready to defend himself. I did not falter, however, particularly because I was with Rosetta, and people have no idea of the strength you can derive from a person weaker than yourself who is in need of your protection. I answered that we didn't want anything, that we came from Lenola —which indeed was more or less true because I was born in a place not so very far from Lenola—that we had walked so far that day that we couldn't go any further, and that if he would give us a room for the night I would pay well, just like at a hotel. He stood quite still, his legs wide apart, in the middle of the threshing-floor, listening to me; and with his ragged trousers, his patched coat and his scythe, he looked exactly like a scarecrow; and I believe all he grasped was that I would pay well, because, as I discovered later, he was half daft and, apart from self-interest, understood nothing at all. But even self-interest must have been, for him, a thing hard to understand, for he took I don't know how long to make out what I was saying and kept on repeating: "We haven't any rooms, and you'll pay, but what will you pay with?" I did not want to pull out the money that I had in the little bag under my skirt; you never know, in wartime anyone may turn thief or murderer, and he already had the face of a thief—or even a murderer, come to that; so I shouted myself hoarse, telling him that he needn't worry, I would pay all right. But still he didn't understand. And already Rosetta was pulling at my sleeve and telling me in a whisper that it would be better to go away again, when luckily the old man's wife appeared, a thin little woman much younger than he, with a breathless, excited look on her face and eyes that sparkled. Unlike her husband, she understood at once and almost threw her arms round our necks, repeating: "But of course, of course you shall have a room, why not? We'll sleep on the terrace or on the hay in the barn and give you our room. We've got food too and you can eat with us, simple food, you know, country fare; you can eat with us." The husband by this time had moved away to one side and was gazing gloomily at us, looking just like a sick turkey cock that rolls its eyes and goes all flabby and won't peck at its food. She took me by the arm and kept on saying: "Come along, come along, I'll show you the room, come along, I'll give you my bed, my husband and I will sleep on the terrace"; and she took us up the outside staircase to the second floor.

And so began our stay in the house of Concetta, for that was the woman's name. The husband, who was called Vincenzo and was about twenty years older than his wife, was the tenant farmer of a certain Festa, a business man, who, like so many others, had fled from the town and was now living in a cottage high up on one of the mountains that encircled the valley. There were also two sons, Rosario and Giuseppe, both of them dark, with massive, brutal faces, small eyes and low foreheads, who never said anything and who were only rarely to be seen: they were hiding because, when the armistice came, they were both in the army and had run away and not presented themselves again, and now they were afraid of being arrested by the Fascist patrols who were going around seizing men to be sent to work in Germany. They were hiding in the orange groves; they turned up at mealtimes, ate their food in haste, almost without speaking, then disappeared again. Although they were quite polite to the two of us I did not like them, and I did not understand why, and often told myself I was being unjust. Then, one fine day, I realized that my instinct had not led me astray and that they were indeed a pair of good-for-nothings, as I had suspected from the beginning. I must tell you that, not far from the house, among the orange-trees, there was a big green-painted shed with a tin roof. In this shed, Concetta told me, they put the oranges as they picked them, and this may well have been true; but at present they were not picking oranges, the oranges were still on the trees, yet in spite of this I noticed that not only Vincenzo and Concetta but the two sons as well were very often occupied at the shed. I am not inquisitive, but finding myself alone with my daughter in the house of people I did not know, and whom —to tell the truth—I did not trust, curiosity was, so to speak, forced upon me. So, one afternoon when the whole family had gone to the shed, I followed them, after a short interval, hiding behind the orange trees. The hut stood in another, smaller clearing, and looked like a mere ruin—discolored, the roof crooked, the planks seeming to hang together by a miracle. In the middle of the clearing stood Vincenzo's cart with a mule harnessed to it, and heaped up on the cart I saw a large and varied collection of things—bed springs, mattresses, chairs, little tables, bundles. The door of the shed—a very large, double door—was wide open, and Concetta's two sons were untying the ropes that held all these things together. Vincenzo, half-vacant as usual, was sitting to one side on a tree stump, smoking his pipe; Concetta was inside the shed and I could not see her, but I heard her voice: "Come on, hurry up, be as quick as you can, it's late already." The two sons, whom I had always seen silent and inert, as though frightened, now appeared transformed: they were nimble, diligent, busy, energetic. I was struck by the thought that one ought always to see people doing the things that interests them, peasants in the fields, workmen in their workshops, shopkeepers in their shops, and indeed—let us be frank about it—thieves with the stuff they have stolen. For these bed springs and mattresses and chairs and tables and bundles were all stolen goods; I at once suspected this but it was confirmed that same evening by Concetta when I plucked up courage and asked her, in an unpremeditated sort of way, who all that furniture and stuff belonged to which they had unloaded and put into the shed that day. The sons, as usual, were not there, they had already gone away; Concetta was disconcerted, I think, just for one moment: but she recovered immediately and said, with her usual enthusiastic, excited gaiety: "Ah, so you saw us . . . but what a pity you didn't come out, you could have helped us! We've nothing to hide, you know, absolutely nothing. That stuff comes from a house in Fondi. The owner, poor man, has run off into the mountains and goodness only knows when he'll come back. Rather than leave all those things in the house to be destroyed in the next air raid, why, we thought it better to take them ourselves. After all, like that they're some use to somebody. There's a war on, you know, and we all have to manage as best we can, and things that are left behind are lost, my dear. Besides, the owner of that house will get repaid by the government for the things he has lost, when the war is over—no doubt about it; and then he'll buy even better stuff than before." To tell the truth, this left me feeling uncomfortable, in fact positively frightened, and I think I must have turned pale because Rosetta looked up at me and said: "Why, what's the matter, Mum?" I was frightened because, being a shopkeeper, I had a very strong sense of property, and I had always been honest and had always considered that mine was mine and yours was yours and there mustn't be any confusion about it, and if there is, everything is turned topsy-turvy. And now, lo and behold, I had fallen among thieves and, what was worse, these thieves had no fear because in that area there were now neither laws nor police, and not only had they no fear but they were very nearly boasting about their thieving. I said nothing, however; but Concetta must have realized that there was some thought in my mind, for she added: "Let it be understood, though, that we take these things because, in a manner of speaking, they don't belong to anybody. We're honest people, Cesira, and I can prove that to you at once: knock on this wall here." She got up and knocked on the kitchen wall, to the left of the stove. I got up and knocked too, and I could hear a kind of resonance as though there were an empty space behind the wall. "What is there behind this wall?" I asked. And Concetta cried enthusiastically: "There's all Festa's belongings, there's a positive treasure, there's the whole of his daughter's trousseau and all the household stuff too—sheets and blankets and linen, silver and china, all sorts of valuable things." I was flabbergasted, because I hadn't expected this. Then Concetta, still with that strange enthusiasm which she put into everything she did or said, explained to me: Vincenzo and Filippo Festa were, as they say, "San Giovanni" to each other, that is, Festa had held Vincenzo's son at his christening and Vincenzo Festa's daughter; thus, bound together by this tie, they were, in a manner of speaking, relations. And Festa, trusting in this "San Giovanni" relationship, had, before he took refuge in the mountains, walled up all his belongings in Vincenzo's kitchen and made him swear to give him back everything, just as it was, at the end of the war, and Vincenzo had sworn to do this. "For us, these things of Festa's are sacred," concluded Concetta emphatically, as though she were speaking of the Most Holy Sacrament; "I would die rather than touch them. They have been there a month, and there they'll stay till the war is over." I still felt a bit doubtful; and I was not convinced even when Vincenzo, who had hitherto kept silent, took his pipe out of his mouth and said in a hollow voice: "That's it, sacred. Whether it's Germans or Italians, they'll have to pass over my dead body before they touch them." At her husband's words, Concetta looked at me with shining, excited eyes, as much as to say: "You see? What d'you say now? Are we honest people or are we not?" But I was as though frozen, and remembering how I had seen the two sons busily unloading the stuff from the cart I thought to myself: "In the long run, once a thief, always a thief."

It was this question of thieving that was the main reason why I began to think of leaving Concetta's house and going elsewhere. I had that money hidden in the little bag under my skirt, and it was quite a lot of money and we were just a couple of lone women without anyone to protect us and there were no laws or police now and it wouldn't be very difficult to get the better of us and run off with everything we had. It's true that I had never shown Concetta my money bag; but from time to time I paid a small sum for food and lodging and I had told them I intended to pay, and they must certainly have known that I had some money somewhere or other. They stole property that had been abandoned; tomorrow they might easily steal my money and murder me into the bargain; there was no knowing. The two sons had the faces of brigands, the husband appeared half-witted, Concetta was always in a state of excitement; you couldn't tell what might happen. And the house, although it was only a short distance from Fondi, was buried in the orange groves, hidden away and lonely, and you could easily slit a person's throat there without anyone noticing. True, it was a good hiding place; but it was one of those hiding places where worse things can happen than in the open, underneath the airplanes. That same evening, in our room after we had gone to bed, I said to Rosetta: "This is a family of crooks. It's possible they may not do us any harm, but it's equally possible that they might kill us both and bury us under the orange trees for manure: it might be one or the other." I spoke in order to give vent to my uneasiness; but I did wrong, for Rosetta, who had never recovered from her terror of the air raids in Rome, immediately started crying, clinging to me and whispering: "Oh Mum, I'm so afraid, can't we go away at once?" So I went on to say that really it was all my imagination; it was all due to the war; that after all Vincenzo and Concetta and their sons were no doubt excellent people. She did not seem fully convinced, and finally she said: "In any case *I* would much rather go away; partly because it's so uncomfortable here." And I promised her that we would leave as soon as we could, because, from that point of view, she was perfectly right: it was extremely uncomfortable.

Uncomfortable it was, and now, looking back, I can say that, in all that time during the war that we spent away from home, I was never so uncomfortable as I was at Concetta's. She had given us her own bedroom, in which she had slept with her husband since the day they were married; but I must say that, though I am a peasant like her, I have never in my life seen such a filthy hole. The room smelt so bad that, although the windows were always wide open, there was no air and one seemed to be suffocating. What was it the room smelt of? Of stuffiness, of old, sour dirt, of caterpillars, of urine. Looking around to trace the cause of the stink, I opened the two bedside tables: they contained two very tall, very narrow chamber pots, without handles, like two tubes, of white china with pink flowers; these chamber pots had never been washed and inside they were of all colors, and it was from them that a great part of the smell came. I put them outside the door and Concetta was so angry that she very nearly hit me, saying that these chamber pots had come to her from her mother and belonged to the family and she could not understand why I did not want them in my room. Then, on the first night we slept in that big double bed, on a mattress all holes and depressions and full of lumps and rustling, prickly stuffing and covered with a cheap material so thin that it seemed on the point of bursting at every movement, I was conscious of a continual itching, and so was Rosetta, who was unable to lie still and kept changing her position and could not get to sleep. In the end I lit a candle and, candlestick in hand, examined the bed: by the light of the small flame I saw, not one or two, but entire groups of bugs fleeing in all directions–dark red and big and swollen with our blood which they had been sucking for hours. The bed was black with bugs, and I am telling the truth when I say I had never seen so many of them all at once. It had happened perhaps a couple of times in Rome that I had discovered one or two; then I had immediately had the mattress re-made and no more had been seen. But here there were thousands of them; it was evident that they were lying concealed not only in the mattress but also in the wooden frame of the bed and, in fact, all over the room. When Rosetta and I got up next morning, we went over and looked at ourselves in the wardrobe looking glass: our whole bodies were covered with red spots, the bugs had bitten us everywhere, and we looked as if we had some disgusting skin disease. I called Concetta, showed her Rosetta who was sitting naked on the bed, crying, and told her it was a disgraceful thing to make us sleep with bugs in the bed; and Concetta, in a state of excitement as usual, replied: "You're right, of course it's disgraceful, it's shocking; yes, I know there are bugs, it's disgusting. But we're poor country people and you're a town lady: it's bugs for us and silken sheets for you." She agreed enthusiastically that I was right, yet in a strange sort of way, as though she were mocking me; and in fact, having admitted I was right, she concluded in an unexpected manner by saying that even bugs were God's little creatures and that, if God made them, it was a sign that they served some purpose. In the end I said that in future we would sleep in the hut where they kept the hay for the mule. The hay was prickly and there was an occasional insect even there, but these were clean insects, of the kind that walk over you and even tickle you a bit but don't suck your blood. However, I came to the conclusion that we couldn't go on like that for very long.

In that house everything was disgusting, not only the sleeping arrangements but the food. Concetta was slovenly, dirty, always in a hurry, always slapdash, and her kitchen was a black corner in which pans and dishes had the dirt of years upon them and there was never any water and nothing was ever washed and the cooking was always done in a headlong, happy-go-lucky style. Always, every day, Concetta cooked the same food, the dish that in Ciociaria is called *minestrina*: a number of thin slices cut from a home-made loaf and placed one on top of another, enough to fill a *spasetta*, which is a shell-shaped earthenware dish; and then, poured over the bread, a small potful of bean soup. This dish is eaten cold, after the bean soup has soaked thoroughly into the whole of the bread, reducing it to a mush. I never thought *minestrina* was good: but in Concetta's house, partly owing to the dirt, which meant that there were always a few flies or caterpillars to be found in it, partly because she was unable to make even this very simple dish properly, it positively turned my stomach. Besides, they ate it in the real peasant way, without bowls, dipping into the dish all together with their spoons, putting their spoons in their mouths and then plunging them into the mush again. And would you believe it? One day I made a remark to her on the subject of the large number of dead flies I found mixed up among the bread and the beans, and she, like the boorish creature she was, answered: "Never mind, eat them up, eat them up! What's a fly, after all? It's meat, isn't it?—just as much as veal." In the end, seeing that Rosetta could no longer bring herself to eat this filth, I took to going with Concetta, every now and then, out of the orange grove on to the main road. This was where the market was now held; it was no longer in the town, where, what with the air raids and the Fascists and their requisitionings, nothing was now safe. On the main road you could find peasant women selling new-laid eggs, fruit, a few bits of meat and even, sometimes, fish. The prices of all these things were crazily high, but if anyone tried to argue and get the price reduced, they would say: "All right then, you can eat the money and I'll eat the eggs." They too, of course, knew that there was a food shortage and that money in a time of food shortage is useless, and they made my blood boil. However, I always bought something or other; and thus I ended up by providing things to eat for Concetta's family as well, to such an extent that my money melted away like water and this in itself became another cause for uneasiness.

We thought of going away, but where to? One day I told Concetta that, since the English had not arrived, we now felt the time had come for us to go on, either by cart or even on foot, to my parents' village and await the end of the war there. She at once approved this idea with enthusiasm. "Why of course you'd be doing the right thing! It's only in your own home you can ever feel really comfortable. And who can ever take the place of a mother? Of course it's the right thing to do; you're not satisfied with anything here, there are bugs and the *mines-*

trina is bad; but in your parents' house the same bugs and the same *minestrina* will seem to you like heaven. Why, of course they will! Rosario will take you in the cart tomorrow, and you'll enjoy the drive." Happy and confident, we awaited the next day, when Rosario was to come back from I don't know where. He came back, but, instead of the cart and the mule, he brought with him a load of bad news: the Germans were requisitioning men, the Fascists were arresting anyone who ventured on to the roads, the English were dropping bombs, the Americans were descending by parachute; and there was hunger everywhere, and a food shortage, and revolution; and soon the English and the Germans would be fighting in the very district where my parents' village lay; and in the meantime—this information came from German headquarters—the village had been evacuated and all its inhabitants had been taken away to a concentration camp near Frosinone. He also said that in any case the roads were not safe because of planes coming down low and machine-gunning people, and they did not stop machine-gunning until they saw that the people were dead; nor were the mountain roads safe because they were full of deserters and brigands who killed you for no good reason at all; and that, in fact, the best thing for us two was to wait for the English here at Fondi—which was a question merely of days, because the Allied army was advancing and would be arriving in not more than a week. Finally he told us a whole lot of things both false and true, but all mixed up in such a way that the true things made the false things appear true as well. It was true that there were bombings and machine-gunnings, but it was not true that a battle was about to take place in the area of my parents' village and that the village had been evacuated. But we were frightened and alone and had no other information than what he gave us; and we did not realize that he was giving us all this bad news in order that they might keep us at their house and continue to make money out of us. Moreover the times were seriously bad and I had a daughter and could not take upon myself the responsibility of starting out even if there were only one chance in a hundred of encountering the dangers he had described. So I decided to put off the journey to my village to some other time and to wait at Fondi for the arrival of the Allies.

It became essential, however, for us to leave Concetta's house as quickly as possible, all the more because, as I have already said, anything might happen in that lonely spot amongst the orange groves; and the more I saw of Concetta's sons, the more they frightened me. I have said they were taciturn; but when they spoke they revealed characters which I did not like at all. They were capable of saying, for instance, in a joking manner: "At one village in Albania they opened fire on us and we had two wounded. What d'you think we did as a reprisal? Since all the men had run away, we seized the women, the best looking ones, and had them all. . . . Some of them did it willingly, dirty sows who were just waiting for an opportunity like that to deceive their bloody husbands, others had to be made to do it by force . . . and some of them were had by so many of our chaps that they couldn't stand up afterward and really looked as if they were dead." I listened to these tales with a stony expression; but Concetta laughed and kept on saying: "Ah well, young men will be young men. We all know young men like the girls. Young men are hot-blooded." But the effect on Rosetta was much worse; I saw her turning pale and almost trembling. So much so that one day I said to him: "Stop it, can't you? My daughter's listening to you, and that's not the way to talk in front of an unmarried girl." I would have preferred them to protest, or even to swear at me; but they said nothing, they merely looked at Rosetta from under their eyelids with coal-like, glittering eyes that were so frightening, while their mother kept on repeating: "Young men, as we all know, hot-blooded young men. But you needn't be afraid for your girl, Cesira. My sons wouldn't touch your girl, not even for a million. You're our guests, and guests are sacred. Your girl is as safe here as if she was in church." As for me, what with the silence of the sons and the excitement of the mother, my fear was redoubled. I had managed to procure a clasp knife from a peasant, and I kept this with my money.

You never know: if they had attempted anything, they would have had to face me first and I felt quite capable of cutting their throats.

What finally convinced us that we must leave was an incident that happened a couple of weeks after our arrival. One morning Rosetta and I were sitting on the threshing floor, busy shelling ears of maize—mainly in order to have something to do—when suddenly two men emerged from the footpath. I realized at once who they were, not only from the guns they carried slung across their shoulders and the black shirts that were visible under their coats, but also from the fact that Rosario, who had been sitting not far from us eating bread and onions, ran off and disappeared among the orange trees the moment he saw them. I said quietly to Rosetta: "They're Fascists, don't you say a word, leave it to me." I knew all about the new Fascists—the ones since the 25th of July—from having seen so much of them in Rome: toughs of the worst kind, vagabonds who found it paid to put on black shirts now that honest people no longer wanted such things; but always big, strong fellows, of whom there are so many in Trastevere and Ponte. These two, on the other hand, as I could see with half an eye, were mere physical trash, a couple of poor fish, unfortunates who were far more afraid of their own guns than the people those guns were intended to frighten. One of them was partly deformed, with a bald head and a face as withered as a dried chestnut, pitifully narrow shoulders, deepset eyes, a turned-up nose and an unshaven chin; the other was almost a dwarf, with a big head like a professor, bespectacled, serious, plump. Concetta, who had at once come downstairs, greeted the first man by a nickname that fitted him perfectly: "Well, Apeface, what are you looking for over here?" Apeface, the thin, bald one, answered in a blustering sort of way, rocking backward and forwards as he spoke and striking his hand against the butt of his rifle: "My good Concetta, now listen, my good Concetta, let us understand each other. You know what we're looking for. You know perfectly well." "Honestly, I don't understand you. D'you want wine? Bread? We haven't much bread, but we can give you a bottle of wine and we can give you a few dried figs too. Just country stuff, you know." "My good Concetta, you're very clever, but this time you've found someone cleverer than you." "Apeface! What are you saying? Me, clever?" "Yes, you're clever, and your husband's clever, and the cleverest of all are your two sons." "My two sons? Who's seen my two sons, I should like to know? It's a long time since *I* saw them. They're in Albania, my two sons. My poor sons, they're in Albania fighting for the King and for Mussolini—may God preserve them both in good health!" "King! What d'you mean, King? We're living in a Republic, Concetta." "Well, long live the Republic, then!" "And your sons aren't in Albania, they're here." "Here? Would to God that was true!" "Yes, they're here, and no longer ago than yesterday they were seen selling stuff in the black market on the Coccuruzzo road." "What ever do you mean, Apeface? My sons *here?* As I said before, would to God it was true! Why, I would be able to kiss them again, and I'd know they were out of danger. As it is, I cry myself silly every night, and I have more sorrows than the Madonna of the Seven Sorrows herself!" "That's enough; tell us where they are and be done with it." "How should *I* know? I can give you some wine, I can give you some dried figs, I can even give you a little maize flour, though I've got very little of it; but how can I possibly give you my sons when they're not here?" "Well, let's have a look at that wine in the meantime."

So they sat themselves down on a couple of chairs on the threshing floor. And Concetta, brimming over with enthusiasm as usual, went and fetched a bottle of wine and two glasses and also brought a little basket of dried figs. Apeface, who had settled himself astride his chair, drank his wine and then said: "Your sons are deserters. You know what it says in the decree about deserters? If we catch them we are to shoot them. That's the law." She appeared delighted. "You're quite right," she said. "Deserters deserve to be shot. Scoundrels, they are . . . they ought all to be shot. But my sons are not deserters, Apeface." "What are they then, if not . . . ?" "They're soldiers. They're fighting for Mussolini—may God preserve him for a hundred years." "Fighting in the black market, eh?" "Will you have some more wine?" Whenever she failed to find any other answer, she offered them some wine; and the two men, who had come mainly for the sake of the wine, accepted and drank.

We two were sitting to one side, on the stairs. Apeface, as he drank, never took his eyes off Rosetta; and he didn't look at her in the way a policeman does, who perhaps wants to find out whether there's anyone present whose papers are not in order; he looked at her legs and her bosom, like a man whose blood has been stirred by the sight of an attractive woman. Finally he asked Concetta: "And who are these two?"

I myself answered for Concetta, hastily, because I didn't want the Fascists to know that we came from Rome. "We're cousins of Concetta's," I said, "we come from Vallecorsa." Concetta confirmed this enthusiastically. "Yes, they're cousins of mine," she said; "Cesira is the daughter of an uncle of mine. They're of my own blood, and they've come to stay with us; blood is thicker than water, we all know."

But Apeface did not appear convinced. It was obvious that he was more intelligent than he looked. "I didn't know," he said, "that you had relations at Vallecorsa. You always told me you came from Minturno. And what's this pretty girl called?"

"She's called Rosetta," I said.

He emptied his glass, then rose and came over to us. "Rosetta, I like you," he said. "It so happens that we need a maid up at headquarters, to do a bit of cooking for us and make our beds. Will you come and join us, Rosetta?" So saying, he put out his hand and took Rosetta by the chin. Quickly I gave his hand a good slap, and said: "Keep your hands to yourself."

He opened his eyes wide and stared at me, feigning astonishment. "Well, well," he said; "what's wrong with *you?*"

"What's wrong with me," I replied, "is that I don't like your touching my daughter."

Arrogantly he took his rifle from his shoulder and pointed

it at me, saying: "Do you know who you're talking to? Put your hands up!"

Then, quite calmly—just as though, instead of a rifle, he had leveled a *polenta* ladle at me—I pushed the barrel aside slightly, and said contemptuously: "Hands up, indeed! D'you think you frighten me with your rifle? What's the use of a rifle to you—shall I tell you? Just to cadge some wine and a few dried figs—that's all the use it is to you. Even a blind man could see that you're just a starving beggar and nothing more."

Strangely enough he calmed down and said laughingly to the other man: "Really she almost deserves to be shot—what d'you think about it?" But the other man shrugged his shoulders and muttered something like: "They're women, don't lose your head." Then Apeface lowered his rifle and said emphatically: "This time you're forgiven, but let me tell you, you came within an inch of death: whoever touches the militia gets lead in his body." *Chi tocca la milizia avrà del piombo;* this was a slogan written up on the walls in Rome and also in Fondi, and that was where this wretched creature had learnt it. After a moment he added: "But it's understood that you send us your daughter to our headquarters at Coccuruzzo, as a maid." "As for my daughter," I answered, "all you can do is dream about her. I'm not sending you anything." Then he turned to Concetta. "Let's make a bargain, Concetta," he said. "We'll stop looking for your sons—who are here, and you know it, and if we *really* looked for them we'd arrest them without the slightest doubt. In exchange, you'll send us your young cousin. That's agreed, eh?" That miserable Concetta, all the more enthusiastic because the suggestions made to her with both criminal and impossible, answered with the greatest emphasis: "But of course, tomorrow morning, as ever is, Rosetta shall be at your headquarters. I'll come with her myself, don't worry; Rosetta shall come and be your cook and your housemaid and anything you wish. Of course, I'll bring her along tomorrow morning." This time, although my blood was boiling, out of prudence I said nothing. Those two wretched men stayed on a little longer; they drank two more glasses of wine and then, one carrying the bottle and the other the basket of dried figs, went away by the same path by which they had come.

The moment they had disappeared, I said at once to Concetta: "Why, you're crazy, not even dead would I send my daughter to be a servant to the Fascists."

I did not say this very forcefully because I was hoping that Concetta had agreed simply as a matter of form, in order not to contradict the two Fascists and to send them away happy. But I was much upset when I saw that she was not in the least indignant. "Well, after all," she said, "they wouldn't *eat* Rosetta. And the Fascists, my dear, have *everything:* they have wine, they have flour, they have meat, they have beans. They eat spaghetti and veal every day at their headquarters. Rosetta would live like a queen there."

"What on earth are you talking about? Are you crazy?"

"I'm not saying anything, all I'm saying is that there's a war on, and the important thing, in wartime, is to keep on the right side of people who are stronger than yourself. At present it's the Fascists who are the strongest and we must keep in with *them.* Tomorrow it may easily be the English, and then we'll be on the side of the English."

"But you don't understand that they want Rosetta for some quite different reason. Didn't you see that wretched man, how he stared at her breasts all the time?"

"Well, well, well! Whether it's one man or whether it's another, that time has to come. Well, well! There's a war on, and we all know that in wartime women mustn't be too particular and can't claim the same respect as in peacetime. Besides, some people's bark is worse than their bite, my dear. I know that Apeface: what *he* wants is to fill his belly." It was, in fact, as clear as daylight that she had taken Apeface's suggestion seriously: you give me Rosetta and I'll leave your sons alone. And I am not saying that from her own point of view she was exactly wrong: if Rosetta had gone as servant girl, or worse, to the Fascists, those two scoundrelly sons of hers could have slept quietly in their own home and no one would have looked for them any more. But it was with my daughter that she intended to pay for this freedom for her sons; and I, a mother too, realized that she, for love of her sons, was perfectly capable of summoning the Fascists next day and handing Rosetta over to them, and that therefore it was no longer a question of making a protest but simply of running away. So I changed my tone all of a sudden and said, calmly: "Well, I'll think it over. It's true that Rosetta, as you say, would live like a queen with the Fascists, but all the same I shouldn't like. . . ."

"Nonsense, my dear. We have to keep in with the strongest side. There's a war on."

"Well, we'll decide tonight."

"Think it over, think it over. There's no hurry. I know these Fascists, I'll tell them Rosetta will go to them in a couple of days' time. They'll wait. But in the meantime you can be sure you wouldn't lack anything. The Fascists have everything; they have oil, they have wine, they have pigs, they have flour . . . All they do is eat and drink. You'll get fat, you'll be comfortable."

"Yes, of course."

"It was Providence, Cesira, that sent those Fascists here, because, to tell you the truth, I was really beginning to feel I couldn't keep you much longer. It's true that you pay, but there *is* a food shortage and in times of shortage provisions count for more than money. Besides, my sons couldn't go on with their present life any longer—always on the move, like gipsies. Now they'll be able to stay quiet, to sleep in peace and to work. Yes, it was really Providence that sent us those Fascists."

She seemed, in fact, to have made up her mind to sacrifice Rosetta. And I had equally made up my mind to leave that same night. We had our usual evening meal, the four of us—we two, Concetta and Vincenzo, for the sons were at Fondi; and the moment we were safe in our hay shed, I said to Rosetta: "Don't imagine I'm in agreement with Concetta. I pretended to be, because with people like that you never know. Now we're going to pack our bags, and at the first light of dawn off we go."

"But where are we going, Mum?" she asked in a tearful voice.

"We're going away from this house of crooks. We're going right away. We're going where we can."

"But *where?*"

I had already thought many times about this flight, and I had my own ideas. I answered: "It's not possible to go to your grandparents' because the village has been evacuated and goodness knows where they've got to. So we'll go first of all to Tommasino's: he's an honest man and we'll ask his advice. He's told me many times that his brother is up in the mountains and living comfortably up there, with all his family. He'll be able to make some suggestion. Don't be afraid, you've an old Mum who loves you, and we've got the money too—always a man's best friend and the only one you can trust. We'll find a place to go to, all right." And so I reassured her; partly, too, because she knew Tommasino, who was the half-brother of Festa, the owner of the property farmed by Vincenzo. This Tommasino was a shopkeeper who, though he was frightened out of his wits, had been unable to make up his mind to join his relations up in the mountains, and this out of love for the black market, in which he had dealings, selling every sort of thing. He was living in a cottage at the edge of the plain, just at the foot of the mountains; and he was making plenty of money, though at the peril of his life, by carrying on his trade in the midst of air raids and machine-gunnings, Fascist bullying and German requisitioning. But as is well known, even cowards become courageous for the sake of money, and Tommasino was one of that kind.

So, by the light of a candle, we put back into our suitcases the small amount of stuff that we had taken out since our arrival; and then, fully dressed as we were, threw ourselves down on the hay and slept for perhaps four hours. Rosetta, indeed, would willingly have slept longer; she was young and a sound sleeper, so sound that the village band might have come and played in her ear and still she would not have woken up. But I, not so young as she, slept lightly, and indeed since the time we had fled from Rome, partly from anxiety and nervousness I had slept very little. And so, when the cocks began to crow—it was still dark, but dawn was near and the cocks knew it—at first very faintly, far away on the plain, then nearer and finally close beside us, in Vincenzo's chicken house, I got up from my bed of hay and started shaking Rosetta. I say "started" because she was most unwilling to wake up and kept repeating in a tearful voice between sleeping and waking: "What is it? What is it?"—as though she had forgotten we were at Fondi, in Concetta's house, and thought we were still in Rome, in our own home, where we never used to get up before seven. At last she was fully awake, though still complaining, and I said to her: "Perhaps you would rather go on sleeping till noon and be woken up by a man in a black shirt?" Before leaving the hut I peeped out of the door and looked towards the threshing floor: I could just make out the figs scattered about on the ground to dry, a chair upon which Concetta had left a basket of maize, the peeling, smoky pink wall of the house. I placed the suitcases on my head pad and on Rosetta's, as we had done on our arrival at Monte San Biagio station, and we left the hut and ran nimbly to the path through the orange trees.

On the main road I turned in the direction of the mountains that rise to the north of the plain of Fondi. Day was just dawning, and I remembered that other dawn when I had fled from Rome, and I thought: "I wonder how many more dawns like these I shall see before I go home again." There was a grey, mysterious look over the whole countryside; the sky was vaguely white with a few yellow stars here and there, as though it were not day which was about to appear but a second night, less black than the former one; and heavy dew lay on the sad, motionless trees and on the broken stones of the roadway, which were cold beneath my bare feet. There was a numbed silence, but this again was not a nocturnal silence; it was full of dry creakings and flutterings and rustlings; slowly the countryside was awakening. I walked in front of Rosetta and looked at the mountains that rose into the sky all round us, bald, barren mountains, with a few brown patches upon them here and there, mountains that appeared deserted. But I belong to the mountains and I knew that, once we were on those mountains, we should find cultivated fields, woods, thickets, huts, cottages, peasants and evacuees. And I reflected that all sorts of things were going to happen on those mountains and I hoped that they would be good things and that I was going to find good people there and not crooks like Concetta and her family. Above all I hoped that we should have to stay there only for a little and that the English would come as soon as possible and that I should be able to go back to Rome, to my flat and my shop. Meanwhile the sun had risen, but only a few moments earlier, behind the rim of the mountains; and the peaks and the sky around them now began to be tinged with pink. There were no stars left in the sky, which had turned pale blue; then the sun shone out, bright as gold, beyond the olive groves, through their grey branches; and its rays fell across the road, and though they were still feeble it seemed to me at once that the ground under my feet was less cold. Cheered by this sunshine, I said to Rosetta: "Who would ever know there was a war? You'd never think, in the country, that there was a war going on." Rosetta hadn't even time to answer me before an airplane appeared with incredible speed from the direction of the sea: first I heard its violent noise, steadly increasing, and then I saw it coming straight at us, nose down, out of the sky. I only just had time to seize Rosetta by the arm and throw myself with her across the ditch into a maize field where we fell flat on our faces amongst the crop; then the plane, flying low above the road and apparently following it, passed by us with a deafening din, furious and evil, so close that it seemed right on top of us. It went on as far as a distant bend in the road, turned, suddenly reared up over a row of poplars and then flew off along the line of the mountains, at half their height, looking like a fly moving from one place to another in the sunshine. I had remained lying on my face, holding Rosetta tightly, but I was looking at the road where lay the small suitcase which Rosetta had dropped when I pulled her away by the arm. At the moment when the plane passed along the road I saw a number of little clouds of dust rising from the surface and moving swiftly in the direction of the mountains, together with the plane. When the noise had completely died away, I left the field and went to look; and I saw that there were several small holes in the suitcase and that there were a few brass shell cases, as long as my little finger, on the road. There was no doubt about it, then: the plane had been aiming at *us*, for there was no one else on the road. "Curse and blast them," I said to myself, and I was filled with an intense hatred for the war: that airman did not know us, he was, I daresay, a nice young man of Rosetta's age and merely because there was a war going on he had tried to kill us, just for an idle whim, so to speak, like a sportsman out walking in the woods with his dog who shoots haphazard into a tree and says to himself: "I'll kill something, even if it's only a sparrow." Indeed we were just a couple of sparrows, we two, shot at in an idle moment by a sportsman who, if the sparrows fall dead, leaves them where they are since they're of no use to him. "Mum," said Rosetta after a little, as we walked along, "you said in the country there wasn't any war, and yet that man tried to kill us." "My dear child," I answered, "I was wrong. The war is everywhere, in the country just as much as in the town."

Chapter 3

AFTER ABOUT half an hour's walking we came to a fork in the road: to the right there was a bridge over a stream and beyond the bridge a white cottage where Tommasino lived. Looking down from the bridge I saw a woman kneeling on the rocks at the edge of the stream, washing clothes in a pool. "Is this where Tommasino lives?" I shouted to her. She finished wringing out a garment she had just washed and then replied: "Yes, he lives here. But he's not here now. He went early this morning to Fondi." "He's coming back?" "Yes, he's coming back." There was nothing to be done but wait, therefore, and this we did, sitting on a stone bench at the end of the bridge. For some time we sat in silence, in the sunshine which was becoming steadily warmer and brighter. Finally Rosetta asked: "D'you think I shall find Pallino safe and sound at Annina's when we get back to Rome?" I was deep in thought, and for a moment I did not understand. Then I remembered that Annina was the caretaker's wife in the building next door to us in Rome, and Pallino Rosetta's tabby cat which she had placed in Annina's care before we left. I reassured her, saying that I was sure we should find Pallino both larger and more beautiful, especially as Annina was the sister of a butcher and they would never lack meat, in spite of the general shortage. My words seemed to comfort her, and she fell silent again, half-closing her eyes in the sunshine. I have mentioned this question put to me by Rosetta at that very critical moment in order to show that, even though she was now over eighteen, she still had the character of a child. And this was to be seen in her preoccupation about the cat, when we still did not know where we were going to sleep that night or whether we should get anything to eat.

At last there appeared, at a corner in the road, the figure of a man walking slowly along eating an orange. I at once recognized Tommasino, who was the living image of a Jew from the ghetto, with his long face, his week-old beard, his hooked nose and prominent eyes, and his shuffling walk with his feet turned outward. He also recognized me, for I was his customer and had bought a great deal from him in those last two weeks; but he was suspicious and did not respond to my greeting as he came forward eating his orange and looking down at the ground. When he came quite near, I said to him at once: "Tommasino, we've left Concetta's. You must help us now because we don't know where to go." He leaned back against the parapet of the bridge with his foot against the low wall, took a bite out of another orange that he had pulled out of his pocket, spat the peel into my face and then said: "You're just talking. In these times, it's everyone for himself and God help us all. How d'you think I can help you?" "D'you know some peasant or other in the mountains," I said, "whom we could stay with until the English arrive?" "I don't know of anyone," he said, "and all the cottages are occupied, from what I hear. But if you go into the mountains you'll find something or other, a hut or a haystack." "No," I said, "I'm not going like that, at random. You have your brother up there in the mountains, and you know the peasants. You must give me some advice." He spat another piece of orange peel into my face, and said: "D'you know what I would do, in your place?" "What?" "I'd go back to Rome. That's what I would do."

I realized that he was turning a deaf ear because he thought we were a pair of paupers, and I knew that he thought of nothing but money and that unless money was introduced into the question he would do nothing for anybody. I had never told him that I was carrying a large sum of money on me, but I now saw that the moment had come to let him know about it. I could trust him because he was of the same breed as myself: like me, he was a shopkeeper, with a grocery shop at Fondi, and he was now dealing in the black market exactly as I had done; and of course there's honor among thieves as they say. And so, without more ado, I said: "I'm not going back to Rome, because there are air raids there and a shortage of food and no more trains anyhow, and my daughter Rosetta, here, is still suffering from the shock of the bombs. I've made up my mind to go into the mountains and find somewhere to stay there. I'll pay. I also want to get together a store of provisions–that is to say, oil, beans, oranges, cheese, flour, a bit of everything, in fact. I'll pay everything in ready cash, because I have the money here, I have almost a hundred thousand lire. You don't wish to help me: all right then, I'll find someone else. You're by no means the only person here at Fondi, there's Esposito, there's Scalise, there are plenty of them. Come along, Rosetta." I had spoken in a determined fashion; then I replaced the suitcase on my head pad and Rosetta did the same and off we went along the road in the direction of Monte San Biagio. When he heard me say that I had a hundred thousand lire, Tommasino opened his eyes very wide and paused for a moment with his teeth pressed against the orange he was in process of peeling. Then, throwing away the orange, he ran after me. Owing to the suitcase which I was holding balanced on my head, I was unable to turn in his direction, but I heard him beseeching me, in a hoarse, breathless voice: "One moment, please wait a moment . . . what the devil . . . what's the matter with you? Please stop and let us talk . . . let's discuss. . . ."

Well, in the end I stopped, and after a certain amount of cavilling I consented to turn back and go into the cottage with him. He led us into a small, white, bare room on the ground floor, in which there was nothing but a bedstead and mattress and some untidy sheets. We sat down, all three of us, on the bed and he said, in an almost kindly tone: "Well, now let's make a list of the provisions you need. I don't make any promises, mind you, because it's a very bad moment and the peasants have grown cunning. In the matter of prices, therefore, you must leave it to me and not argue: we're not in Rome in time of peace, we're at Fondi in time of war. As for finding a cottage in the mountains, I really don't know. There were plenty of them, before the air raids, but since then they've all been let. However, since I'm going up to see my brother this morning, you two had better come up with me and probably some arrangement can be made, especially if you're prepared to pay at once. With regard to the provisions, however, you'll have to give me at least a week. In the meantime, if you find a lodging up there, my brother or one of the other evacuees will be able to lend or sell you something." Having uttered these words in a practical, sensible tone of voice, he took a torn, greasy notebook out of his pocket, selected a blank page, took a copying pencil, wetted the point in his mouth, and then resumed: "Well now, let's see: how much flour d'you want?"

So I dictated the list to him, carefully; so much best-quality flour, so much maize flour, so much oil, so many pounds of beans, so much sheep's-milk cheese, so much lard, so much *salame*, so many oranges, and so on. He wrote everything down and then put the notebook back in his pocket and left the room, returning shortly afterwards with a loaf of bread and half a *salame* sausage. "Here's the first instalment of your provisions," he said. "Have something to eat now and stay and wait for me here. In about an hour's time we'll start up the mountain. Meanwhile you might as well pay me for this loaf and the sausage . . . then we shan't get into a muddle." So I took out a thousand-lire note and gave it to him, and he, having examined it against the light, gave me my change in a whole lot of small notes that were more torn and sordid than any I had ever seen. These are the notes that are to be found in the country, where there is little money and that little is passed round and round, always through the same pockets, and is never renewed because peasants are reluctant to take money to a bank, and keep it hidden in their homes. I gave him back some of these notes because they were really too dirty, and he exchanged them for me, with the remark: "If only I had a cartload of these notes, I would make a bargain at once."

Well, Tommasino left us, informing us that he would be back soon, and we ate the bread and *salame* sitting on the bed without speaking, but feeling quiet and calm now because we knew that soon we should have both house and provisions. I only made one remark—and I don't know why, except that perhaps I was following a train of thought. "You see, Rosetta, what money means?" And she answered: "The Madonna helped us, Mum, I know that, and she will always help us." I didn't dare contradict her, for I knew she was religious, very religious indeed, and always said her prayers in the morning when she got up and in the evening when she went to bed, and it was I myself who had brought her up like that, according to the custom of my own part of the country; but I could not help thinking that, if what she said was true, the Madonna's help was a bit strange: the money had persuaded Tommasino to help us, but that money I had made in the black market thanks to the war and to the food shortages, and had the Madonna perhaps *wanted* the war and the food shortage, and if so why? To punish us for our sins?

After we had eaten the bread and *salame*, we lay down on Tommasino's sordid sheets and slept for about half an hour, for we had risen with the day and now sleep was overcoming us, making us muzzy in the head, as wine does if you drink it on an empty stomach. We were still asleep when Tommasino returned and came over and slapped our faces, saying cheerfully: "Wake up, wake up, we must be off!" He was pleased, and you could see that he was already enjoying the thought of the money he intended to make out of us. We got up and followed him out of the house. On the open space in front of the bridge stood a very small grey donkey, laden, poor little beast, with a quantity of parcels on top of which Tommasino had already tied our suitcases. And so we started off, Tommasino holding the donkey by the bridle, a switch in his hand, he himself all dressed up in his town clothes, with a black hat, a black coat and black striped trousers but no tie, and on his feet army boots of yellow hide all covered with mud; we two walked behind.

At first we walked along the flat ground around the foot of one of the mountains, then, when we reached a mule track that led off from the high road—a track all stones and dust and holes, between two bramble hedges—we began to climb and very soon found ourselves in a steep, narrow valley between two mountains which contracted like a funnel the higher it went and finally, as we could see, became, at the top, merely a pass, up under the sky, between two rocky summits. As soon as I placed my foot on the first stones of the mule track, amongst the dried dung and the dust and the holes, I had a feeling of joy. As a peasant of the mountains, I had climbed up and down many mule tracks of this kind up to my sixteenth year, and when I found this one beneath my feet it seemed to me that at last I had found something familiar again, as though, in the absence of my parents, I had at any rate rediscovered the places where they had brought me up. Until now, I said to myself, we have been in the plain, and the people of the plain are false, dishonest, dirty and treacherous; but now, with this beloved mule track, full of stones and asses' dung, dusty, steep—now I was finding the mountain lands again and my own people. I said nothing of all this to Tommasino because in the first place he would not have understood me and also because he was a real man of the plain himself, with his Jewish-looking face and his mania for making money. But to Rosetta I said in a low voice, as we were passing along in front of a fine hedge with quantities of cyclamen growing at its foot: "Pick some of those cyclamen and make a bunch and put it in your hair, it'll look nice." I had remembered that I myself used to do that when I was a little girl: I used to pick cyclamen (which we in Ciociaria called, I don't know why, *scocciapignatte*, "pot-breakers") and make a bunch of them and put it in my hair, just above the ear, and then it seemed to me that I was twice as beautiful. When we stopped to get our breath Rosetta picked a bunch for herself and one for me and we put them in our hair. I said laughingly to Tommasino, who was looking at us in astonishment: "We're making ourselves look pretty for the new house we're going to move into." But he didn't even smile: he was all the time gazing into the void and making calculations in his mind about the things he intended to buy or sell, about possible profit and loss. Like a true black marketeer, and a plainsman into the bargain.

The mule track first led past a group of houses at the opening of the valley and then turned off to the right, along the mountainside, through the scrub. It zigzagged very slowly upward, keeping apparently almost level, with an occasional short, steep rise. I did not feel I was making any effort because my legs had been used to climbing almost since I was born, and had now immediately fallen into the slow, regular mountain step, so that I did not get out of breath even at the steepest parts of the climb, whereas Rosetta, who was a Roman, and Tommasino who was a plainsman, had to stop every now and then to get their breath again. In the meantime, as the mule track rose, the nature of the valley was revealed—or rather the cleft, for it was too narrow to be called a valley: an immense flight of steps, of which the widest were at the lowest point and the narrowest at the summit. These steps were the cultivated terraces which we in Ciociaria call *macere*, which consist of so many long, narrow strips of fertile soil, each one being supported by a low wall of unmortared stones. All sorts of things grow on these strips—corn, potatoes, maize, vegetables, flax; not to mention fruit trees, which are to be seen sprinkled here and there amongst the other crops. I knew these *macere* well; as a girl I had worked like a beast of burden, carrying baskets of stones on my head for raising the low supporting walls, and at that time I had grown accustomed to going up and down by the steep little paths and short flights of steps that connect one *macera* with another. They require an enormous effort, these terraces, for in order to make them the peasant has to break up the slope of the mountainside, getting rid of the scrub, tearing out the rocks one by one and carrying up by hand not only the stones for the walls, but the soil as well. Once made, however, they assure his living, providing him with everything he needs, to such an extent that he hardly needs to purchase anything.

We followed the mule track for a considerable time as it wandered, clambering for some distance along the mountain on the left side of the valley and then crossing to the other side and starting to climb up the mountain on the right. We could now see the whole of the valley rising up to the sky: at the point where the gigantic staircase of the *macere* ended, the dark band of scrub began; then the scrub thinned out and you could see a number of trees scattered over a bare slope; finally the trees also came to an end and you could see nothing but white broken stones right up to the blue sky. Just below the top of the ridge there was a kind of tuft of projecting greenery, and among this vegetation you could catch a glimpse of some red rocks. Tommasino told us that amongst these rocks was the entrance to a deep cave which, many years ago, had been the hiding-place of the famous shepherd of Fondi who had burned his betrothed alive inside a hut and had then gone away to the other side of the mountain and married someone else and had children and grandchildren, and by the time they at last discovered him, he was a fine-looking old man, father, father-in-law and grandfather, with a white beard, loved and respected by all. Tommasino added that beyond that ridge were the mountains of Ciociaria, among which was the Monte delle Fate, the Fairies' Mountain. I remembered that when I was a child the name of that mountain had always set me dreaming and often I had asked my mother whether there really were fairies on that mountain and she had always answered me that fairies didn't exist and that the mountain was so called for no reason at all. I had never believed her; and even now, when I was grown up and had a grown-up daughter, I was almost tempted to ask Tommasino why the mountain was so called and whether there had really been a time when the fairies lived there.

At a turn in the mule track, we saw a white ox harnessed to a plow in the middle of the staircase of terraces, and a peasant guiding the plow on one of those long, narrow little strips. At once Tommasino put up his hand to his mouth and shouted: "Hi, Paride!" The peasant went on a little farther with his plow, then stopped and came forward, without haste, to meet us.

He was not a tall man but well-proportioned, as they are in Ciociaria, with a round head, a low forehead, a small, hooked nose, a heavy jaw and a mouth like a slit which looked as if it could never smile. Tommasino, with a wave of the hand toward us, said to him: "Paride, these are two ladies from Rome and they're looking for a cottage up in these mountains . . . until the English come, of course—just a matter of a few days." Paride took off his little old black hat and looked at us fixedly, without expression, in the dazed, stolid way peasants look at you when they have been alone for hours on end, face to face with an ox, a plow and a furrow; then, slowly and grudgingly, he said that there were no more cottages, the few there were had already been let, and in fact he didn't see where we could possibly find a lodging. Rosetta immediately looked sad and disappointed; but I remained calm because I had money in my pocket and I knew that in the end everything can be arranged if you have money. And indeed, the moment Tommasino said to him, almost roughly: "Listen, Paride, let's understand each other, the ladies will pay . . . they don't expect anything from anybody . . . they'll pay in ready cash . . ."—Paride scratched his head and then, lowering his eyes, admitted that there was a kind of stable or lean-to at the side of his own house in which they kept the loom for weaving materials to make clothes and where we might be able to accommodate ourselves if it was really only a question of a few days. "Well," said Tommasino to him at once, "there *was* a house, you see. . . . All that's needed is a little thought. All right, Paride, you go back to your work. I'll see about introducing the ladies to your wife." Paride, after a few more words, went back to his plow and we continued on our way up the path.

We had not much farther to go now. In barely a quarter of an hour we came upon three cottages arranged in a semicircle on the flat ground of a *macera.* They were small cottages of no more than two rooms, with their backs against the slope; the peasants build them for themselves, often without the help of a mason. The peasants merely sleep in these little houses; the rest of the time they are at work in the fields. When it rains, or when mealtimes come around, they go to their huts; these are even easier to build than the cottages and can be put up in a single night, with nothing but a dry-stone wall and a straw-thatched roof. There were many of these huts scattered about here and there, around the cottages, forming a kind of tiny village. Smoke was coming from some of them, showing that cooking was being done, while others appeared to be for keeping hay or for shutting in the beasts at night, People were coming and going between the cottages and the huts, on the narrow open space of the *macera.*

When we finally arrived on the level ground in the middle of the houses and huts we saw that these people who were coming and going were in process of laying a big table in the open air, almost at the edge of the terrace, in the shade of a fig tree. They had arranged plates and glasses on a table cloth, and were now busy bringing up big tree-stumps which were to serve as chairs. One of these people, as soon as he saw us, came over at once to Tommasino, calling to him: "You've arrived just in time for dinner."

It was Filippo, Tommasino's brother, and never have I seen two people so different. Just as Tommasino was reserved, silent, secretive and almost gloomy, always busy calculating his profits, biting his nails and gazing down on the ground, so was Filippo expansive and cordial. Like Tommasino, he was a shopkeeper, except that Tommasino had a grocer's shop while he kept a sort of emporium where he sold a bit of everything. He was a small man with a head fixed, almost without any neck, on to very broad shoulders, so that it looked like a cooking pot turned upside down, with the narrowest part at the top and the widest part at the bottom and a nose shaped exactly like the mouth of a pot. His legs were short, the upper part of his body massive, with a prominent chest and a paunch, so that his trousers, supported by a belt, were always below his stomach and seemed to be on the point of coming down at every movement.

Filippo, when he heard that we were refugees and were going to live up there with them and that we had money and were shopkeepers (all these things were told him by Tommasino, in a gloomy, reticent sort of way, as though he were talking to himself) very nearly threw his arms round our necks. "Now come and sit down to dinner with us," he cried. "We've got spaghetti and beans today, and you can eat with us, and until your own provisions arrive you can share ours. And then of course the English will come, and they'll bring everything and there'll be plenty again, and what matters most now is to eat and be cheerful." He rambled on, going this way and that round the table, and introduced his daughter to us, a gentle, rather sad-looking brunette, and his son, a shortish young man with broad, slightly bent shoulders, so that you almost thought he was a hunchback, which he wasn't at all. He was very dark, with the strong glasses of the short-sighted, a doctor, or so his father said: "May I introduce my son Michele . . . he's a doctor"; and then he introduced his wife, a woman with a very white, frightened face, lustreless, black-encircled eyes and an enormous bosom: she suffered from asthma and also, in my opinon, from fear, and looked ill. As I have already said, as soon as he knew that I had a shop in Rome, Filippo became cordial, not to say brotherly, and, after asking me whether I had any money and learning that I had, confided to me that he also had a large sum in his trouser pocket, which would suffice even if—supposing it to be possible—the English delayed their coming for a whole year. He spoke to me in a confidential tone, as between equals, as between one shopkeeper and another, and I felt reassured. I did not yet know, nor did he, that that large sum of money would gradually have less and less value as the war went on, and that, in the end, the amount that would support his family for a year would no longer suffice to keep them going for a month. Filippo said: "We're staying up here until the English come, and we're going to eat and drink and not worry about anything. When the English arrive, they'll bring wine and oil and flour and beans and there'll be plenty of everything and we shopkeepers will start up our businesses again as though nothing had happened." I objected–if only in order to say something–that there was a possibility that the English would not come at all and that the Germans would win the war. "Well, what does that matter to us?" he asked. "Germans or English, it's all the same thing, provided one of them wins decisively. All that matters to us is business." He spoke these words in a loud voice, with great assurance; and then his son, who was standing alone at the edge of the terrace, looking at the panorama of the Fondi valley, twisted round like a viper and said: "It may not matter to *you* . . . but if the Germans win, *I* shall kill myself." He said this with such seriousness and conviction that I was surprised and asked: "But what have the Germans done to you?" He looked at me sideways and then said: "To me personally, nothing. But now tell me: if someone said to you, 'Look, I'm bringing this poisonous snake into your house, please take special care of it,' what would you say?" I was astonished, and answered: "Well, I shouldn't like to have a snake in my house." "Why? The snake wouldn't so far have done you any harm, would it?" "Perhaps not, but everyone knows that sooner or later a poisonous snake will bite." "Well, it's just the same thing; even if they've done me no harm personally, I know that the Germans, or rather the Nazis, will sooner or later start biting, like snakes." At that moment, Filippo, who had been listening to us impatiently, started shouting: "Come along, come along, dinner's ready. Never mind about the Germans or the English. The soup's on the table," and his son, thinking perhaps that I was a peasant woman and that it was not worth his while to waste words upon me, also walked off, toward the table.

And what a sight that table was! I shall remember it as long as I live, partly because of the strangeness of the place and partly because of the abundant spread. A strange setting indeed—a long, narrow table on the long, narrow terrace, below us the gigantic staircase of the *macere* reaching down to the Fondi valley; around us the mountainside; and above us the blue sky illumined by the warm, mild September sunshine. And, on the table itself, abundance: dishes of *salame* and ham, mountain cheeses, loaves of homemade bread, crisp and fresh, mixed pickles, hard-boiled eggs and butter, and soup with *pasta* and beans in it, in great bowls filled to the brim which were carried to the table by the daughter, mother and wife of Filippo, who came one after the other from the hut where they were cooking. There was also wine in flasks, and even a bottle of brandy. No one could have thought that down below there was a shortage of food and that one egg cost eight lire and that in Rome people were dying of hunger. Filippo circled round the table, rubbing his hands, his face shining with satisfaction. He kept on saying: "Let's eat and drink . . . The English will be coming soon and then there'll be plenty of everything again." Where he had got hold of this idea that the English would bring abundance with them, I couldn't say. But up there they all believed it and never stopped saying so to one another. I think this conviction of theirs was derived from the radio, on which—so they told me—there was an Englishman who talked Italian like an Italian and made propaganda by repeating day after day that, once the English arrived, we should all he swimming in plenty.

When the soup had been served we all sat down to table. How many of us were there? There was Filippo, his wife and his two children; there was Paride and his wife Luisa, a small, fair woman with curly hair and blue eyes and a sullen expression, and their little boy Donato; there was Tommasino and *his* wife, a long, thin woman with a mustache and a surly face, and his daughter, who had the same horselike face as her mother but with a gentle expression and kindly black eyes; there were four or five men, badly dressed and unshaven, who, from what I understood, were people from Fondi who had been evacuated to this place and who hovered around Filippo, looking upon him as their acknowledged leader. They had all been invited by Filippo to celebrate his wedding anniversary. But this I only learned later; at the moment I had the impression that Filippo had such quantities of provisions that he could afford to throw them out of the window by entertaining the local people every day.

We ate for three hours at least. We started with the *pasta* and bean soup; the *pasta* was light, made with plenty of egg and golden yellow, and the beans of the best quality, large, white and tender, and they melted in the mouth like butter. The soup was so good that everyone had two, or even three plates of it, full to the brim. Then came the *hors d'oeuvres:* mountain ham, slightly salted but appetizing, homemade *salame*, hard-boiled eggs, pickles. After this the women rushed off to the hut, nearby and came back with dishes full of large, roughly carved hunks of roast meat—the very best veal, tender and white; a calf had been killed just the day before, and Filippo had bought several pounds of it. After the veal there was a hash of lamb, tender and delicate, with an extremely good bitter-sweet white sauce; then we had sheep's-milk cheese, hard as a rock, pungent, made specially to be eaten while drinking wine; and, after the cheese, fruit—oranges, figs, grapes and dried fruit. There were also little sweet cakes—yes indeed there were—baked in the oven with *pasta margherita* and sprinkled with vanilla sugar; and to end up we had, with the brandy, little biscuits out of a big box which Filippo's daughter brought down from their cottage. And how much did we drink? At least a quart each, though there were some who drank more than a quart and some who drank less than a cup full, such as, for instance, Rosetta, who never drank at all. The gaiety of everyone at that table cannot be described: they all ate and drank and talked of nothing but of things to eat and drink, of what they were actually eating and drinking or of what they would have liked to be eating and drinking or of things that they had eaten and drunk in the past. For these people of Fondi, as indeed also in my own village, eating and drinking was as important as, in Rome, having a car and a flat in the Parioli quarter; to them, anyone who eats and drinks little is a hopeless creature, so that anyone who wishes to be considered a gentleman tries to eat and drink as much as he possibly can, knowing that this is the only way to be admired and esteemed. I was sitting next to Filippo's wife, that white, white woman with the enormous bosom, who, as I have already said, looked ill. She, poor thing, was not at all gay, obviously because she was not well; nevertheless she boasted to me of the things that they habitually kept in the house: "Never less than forty new-laid eggs and six hams and as many *salame* sausages and cheeses. . . . Never less than a dozen pillows. . . . We used to eat so much bacon that one day I gave a belch and a piece of bacon I had already swallowed came up again and stuck out of my mouth just as if it had been a second tongue, only this one was white." I repeat these words because she said them like that, simply to impress me. They were, in fact, country people who still did not know that real gentlefolk, the ones in the towns, eat little, very little in fact, especially the women, and put their money into their houses, into jewels and clothes. These people here, on the other hand, went about dressed like ragamuffins, but they were as proud of their eggs and their bacon as the ladies of Rome are of their evening dresses.

Filippo drank more than anybody, partly because—as he suddenly announced to us—it was his wedding anniversary; and partly because it was a failing of his. More than once, on later occasions, I saw him with glazed eyes and a red nose, even at nine in the morning. And so, perhaps because he was drunk, he started to become confidential. "I tell you this," he began suddenly, glass in hand, "it's only for fools that war is a bad thing, not for others. You know what I should like to write up in my shop, above the cash desk? *'cca' nisciuno è fesso'*: 'No fools here'. That's what they say in Naples, but we say it here too, and it's the absolute truth. I'm no fool and I never shall be, for in this world there are only two kinds of people, stupid and clever, and no one, as far as I know, would ever want to belong to the first kind. It all depends on knowing certain things, it all depends on keeping your eyes well open. The fools are the ones who believe what's written in the papers and pay their taxes and go and fight in the war and are even so silly as to get killed. The clever ones—ha! ha!—the clever ones are the opposite, that's all. And these are times when the man who's a fool comes to a bad end and the man who's clever comes safely through, and the man who's a fool can't help being more foolish than usual and the man's who's clever has to be very clever indeed. Well, you know the saying: better a live ass than a dead doctor; and this one too: a bird in the hand is worth two in the bush; and this other one too: only a coward makes promises and keeps them. I'll go further: I'll say that from now on there won't be any place in this world for fools, never again can anyone allow himself the luxury of being a fool, not even for one single day. From now on it's going to be necessary to be clever, to be very clever, very clever indeed, because these are very dangerous times and if you give them an inch they'll take a mile. You know what happened to that poor fool Mussolini who thought he was going to make a nice little war in France; he plunged into it up to his neck with the whole world against him, and now he has nothing left and is compelled to act the fool, he who always wanted to be thought so clever. You mark my words, governments come and go, and they make wars at the expense of poor people's lives and then they make peace and then they do whatever they like, but the only thing that counts, the only thing that never changes, is business. Whether the Germans come, whether the English come, whether the Russians come, the one things that must come first for us shopkeepers, always, is business; and if business is good, everything's all right."

This little speech must have cost him a most extraordinary effort, for by the end of it his forehead and temples were running with sweat, and, after emptying his glass in one draught, he began mopping his brow with his handkerchief. The evacuees who, as I said, constituted his band of followers, immediately showed their warm approval, all the more so as they were sponging on him for the food they were eating and were anxious to ingratiate themselves with him, like the starving parasites and flatterers they were. "Three cheers for Filippo, three cheers for business!" cried one of them. Another remarked, with an ironical smile: "You may well say that business never changes: all sorts of things have happened, but business goes on, and you're doing pretty well, eh, Filippo?" A third, who seemed rather perplexed but also rather knowing, said: "Let either the Germans come, or the English, I quite agree; but don't say, Let the Russians come, please, Filippo." "Why not?" asked Filippo, who had by now drunk so much wine that I am sure he understood very little. "Because the Russians wouldn't let you carry on your business, Filippo—didn't you know that? Shopkeepers are just what the Russians dislike most of all." "Bastards," said Filippo in a quiet, reflective sort of way, pouring himself a drink from the flask and observing the wine lovingly as it rose gradually in the glass. Finally a fourth man cried: "You're a great man, Filippo, and you're quite right; no fools here, that's certain, what you said was absolutely true."

At this point, while everyone was laughing at this perfectly sincere remark, Filippo's son jumped up from the table and said, with a dark look on his face: "No fools here—except me. *I'm* a fool." There was silence, after this outburst, and we all stared at each other in astonishment. The son went on after a moment: "And since fools don't get on very well in the company of clever people, excuse me, but I shall go and take a little walk." Having said this—while some of those present hastened to protest—he pushed back his chair and walked off along the terrace.

Everyone turned to watch him as he went away; but Filippo was too drunk to take it ill. He raised his glass in the direction of his son and said: "Here's to his health. After all, you must have *one* fool in a family; it doesn't do any harm." Everyone started laughing when they saw the father who thought he was so clever drinking the health of the son who proclaimed himself a fool; and they laughed all the more when Filippo, raising his voice, shouted: "You can be the fool if you like, because I'm always there to be the clever one." Someone remarked: "It's quite true: Filippo works and makes money and his son spends all his time reading books and giving himself airs." But after a moment Filippo, who seemed to be secretly proud of this son who was so different from himself and so learned, lifted the tip of his nose from his glass and added: "Understand this, however: my son, really and truly, is an idealist . . . But, in these times, what is an idealist? A fool. Of course it's not his fault, he's forced into it, but all the same, he's a fool."

Late afternoon was upon us, the sun had hidden itself behind the mountains, and finally everybody had risen from the table: the men went off to play cards in Filippo's cottage, the peasants went back to work, and we women began to clear the table. We did the washing in a tub filled with water near the well, and then made a pile of plates which I carried into the room occupied by Filippo and his family in the middle cottage. It was a cottage with two floors; you went up to the top floor by outside steps, straight from the terrace. I was surprised when I went in: Filippo and his friends were sitting on the floor, in the middle of the room, with their hats on and the cards in their hands: they were playing *scopone*. There was no furniture in the room, nothing but mattresses rolled up and leaning against the walls in the corner, and a great number of sacks. I don't know how many of these sacks there were; and I must admit that, as regards provisions at any rate, Filippo had applied his ideas in a practical way and acted as a clever man rather than a fool. There were sacks of flour, all white and dusty, there were sacks of maize flour, these being yellow, there were smaller bags which appeared to contain beans, chick peas, lentils and dwarf peas. There were also large numbers of tins, especially tins of tomato purée. In the window hung a couple of hams, and on top of the sacks were a few large cheeses. I also noticed numbers of pots with paper covers, full of lard, big bottles of oil, a couple of demijohns of wine, and, dangling from the ceiling, strings of homemade sausages. Inside that room, in fact, was the basis for a good meal, for when there is flour and fat and tomato you can always, whatever happens, make a dish of spaghetti. As I said, Filippo and his band were playing *scopone* in the middle of the room; Filippo's wife and daughter were lying together on a mattress, coiled up one against the other, half undressed, stupefied with heat and digestion. When he saw me come in, Filippo said to me, without raising his eyes from the cards: "You see, Cesira, how comfortably we've installed ourselves up here. But you get Paride to show you your room . . . you'll see, you'll be in clover." I said nothing; I put down the plates on the floor and went out to look for Paride so that I could get the question of the house settled.

I found him splitting logs near his hut and at once told him that I was ready: would he show me the room he had promised me? He rested his sandal-shod foot on a stump of wood and held his chopper in his hand as he listened to me from under the brim of his little old black hat. Then he said: "Well, Tommasino talks as if he was the master but the real master here is me. I did tell you before that I could give you a room, but now, after thinking it over, I'm afraid I can't let you have that room after all. Luisa works there all day at the loom . . . and what would you do while she's working? You can't stay out in the fields all the time." I realized that, like a true peasant, he was still suspicious; so I took a five hundred lire note out of my pocket and held it out to him, saying: "Are you afraid we shan't pay? Here's five hundred lire, I'll leave you that as a deposit; then, when we go away, we'll settle the account." He was silent and took the money; but he took it in a particular manner which I want to describe because it has its importance in the understanding of the mentality of these mountain peasants. He took the note, held it in both hands at the level of his stomach and gazed at it for some time with a kind of somber, embarrassed admiration, as though it were some strange object, twisting it this way and that. Afterward, I saw him make this gesture every time any money happened to come into his hands. These people never see any money because everything they need they make at home, including their clothes; and the little money they have they collect together by the sale of the faggots they carry down to the town during the winter; so that money, for them, is a rare and precious thing, it is not so much money as a kind of god. These mountain peasants with whom I spent such a long time are not, in fact, at all religious and are not even superstitious, and for them it is money that is the most important thing, partly because they haven't any and never see any, partly because it is from money—from their point of view, anyhow—that all good things come; at least that is what they think, and I, as a shopkeeper, really couldn't say they are wrong.

And so, after he had had a good look at my bank note, Paride said: "Well, if you don't mind the noise of the loom, you can have the room." I followed him toward his cottage, which was at the lefthand side of the settlement and like all the others had its back against the supporting wall of the terrace. At the side of the cottage, which had two floors, there was a small structure set against the rocky wall of the mountain, with a tiled roof, a small door and a small unglazed window. We went in and I saw that half the room was occupied by a loom for weaving materials for clothes, one of the old-fashioned kind, made entirely of wood. In the other half there was a countrified bed, by which I mean two iron trestles with planks laid over them and, on top, a big sack of some thin material stuffed with dried maize leaves. It was scarcely possible to stand upright in this room under the sloping roof; the back wall was of bare, rough rock, the other walls covered with spiders' webs and patches of damp. When I looked down, I saw that the floor was paved neither with bricks nor stones but was of bare earth, just as in a stable. Paride scratched his head and said: "This is the room. See if you can make yourselves comfortable here." Rosetta, who had followed us, said in a tone of some dismay: "Why Mum, have we got to sleep here?"; but I reproved her by replying: "Half a loaf is better than none," and then I turned to Paride and said to him: "Now, we haven't any sheets; can you give us some?" Then an argument began; he did not want to let us have the sheets, he said, because they were part of his wife's trousseau; but in the end we agreed that I should pay him so much for the hire of them. Blankets, however, he had none; but he promised us his black cloak, it being understood, of course that we should pay for the hire of that too. And so it was with everything else: a large copper pot for us to fetch water for washing, towels, crockery, even a chair, so that at least we could sit down in turns—everything had to be forced out of him by fighting tooth and nail and was only obtained after I had promised to pay a certain sum for the hire of each object. Finally I asked where we could do our cooking and he answered that we could use the hut where they did *their* cooking. "Let's have a look," I said, "so that I can get an idea of it."

I went with him to the hut, which was situated on the terrace immediately below. The lower part of this hut was of unmortared stones, with a thatched roof. I knew these huts quite well; in my own country they keep implements and beasts in them, and huts like this can be built in one day if you work hard. First you make the wall, placing the big, roughly hewn stones and fitting them one into the other, without mortar. Then, at the two ends of the enclosed space, which is oval in shape, two forked branches are placed upright. Horizontally, resting on the forks of these branches, is placed another, long branch. Finally the straw, in bundles tied together with vine-tendrils, is laid on in superimposed layers, on both sides. There are no windows; the door is made with two upright stones as door posts and a horizontal one as architrave, and it is always a small, low door that forces you to bend down in order to enter the hut. Paride's hut was exactly the same as the ones in my own village; near the door a bucket of water with a ladle hung from a nail. Before entering, Paride took the ladle, drank some water, then handed it to me and I drank also. We went into the hut. For a moment I saw nothing because, as I said, there were no windows, and Paride had closed the one and only door behind him. Then he lit an oil lamp and I began to see. The floor appeared to be of beaten earth; in the middle was a dying fire with an iron tripod over it on which was placed a small black kettle. I raised my eyes and saw, high up in the darkness, strings of sausages and black puddings put there to smoke, as well as a large number of frail, black streamers of soot which made me think of decorations for a Christmas tree, but a Christmas tree decked out for mourning. Around the fire were several blocks of wood arranged in a circle, and I was surprised to see, sitting on one of these blocks, an old woman, very old, with a face that looked like the waning moon, all nose and pointed chin, spinning with a distaff, all alone in the dark. It was Paride's mother, and she greeted me with these words: "Come, my dear, sit down here, they tell me you're a lady from Rome . . . Well, this isn't a Roman drawing room, it's only a hut, but you'll have to be content with it now. Come over here and sit down." To tell the truth, I hadn't any desire to sit down on one of those narrow blocks of wood and I almost wanted to ask where the chairs were; but I restrained myself in time. Later I discovered that in the huts there are never any chairs; they keep them in their cottages, regarding them as a luxury to be used only on feast days and solemn occasions such as weddings, funerals and the like, and in order not to spoil them they hang them upside down, like hams, from the ceiling. One day when I went into Paride's cottage I knocked my forehead against a chair, and I thought to myself that this was a truly rustic spot that I had chanced upon.

Well, I was used to the light in the hut now and I could see that it was a place fit only for beasts—cold and dark, with a muddy floor, and the stones of the low walls and the inside straw of the roof blackened and encrusted with soot. The air was smoky from the dying embers, perhaps because the wood was green; and this smoke hung stagnant inside the hut, issuing very slowly through the roof, so that in a short time Rosetta and I began coughing and our eyes began watering. An ugly mongrel dog and an old mangy cat were squatting down almost hidden among the wide folds of the old woman's skirt, and they—impossible as it seems—were also weeping, poor things, just as if they had been Christian beings, owing to this acrid, pungent smoke; but they wept without moving, their eyes wide open, showing that they were quite accustomed to it. I have never been fond of dirt, and indeed my house in Rome, though modest, was as bright as a mirror. When I saw this hut my heart sank at the thought that henceforth Rosetta and I would have to cook, eat, and also live in it, like a couple of goats or sheep. I said, as though I were thinking aloud: "Luckily it's only a matter of a few days, until the English arrive." "Why?" asked Paride; "don't you like the hut?" "In *my* village," I said, "we use the huts to keep the beasts in." Paride was a curious type, as I discovered afterwards, insensitive and with no pride, so to speak. He answered, with a faint, strange smile: "Well, *here* human beings live in them." The old woman remarked, in her shrill, cricket-like voice: "You don't like the hut, eh? Anyhow it's better than living in the middle of a field. I'm sure those poor soldiers in Russia, the husbands of the women up here, would willingly agree to come back and live all their lives in a hut like this. But instead of that, they'll never come back and they'll all be killed, and they won't even get a Christian burial, because in Russia nowadays they know neither Christ nor the Madonna." I was surprised at these gloomy conjectures; and Paride, with another faint smile, said: "My mother looks at everything in a black sort of way because she's old and she sits alone all day and then she's deaf into the bargain." Then he raised his voice and said: "Who says they won't come back? Of course they'll come back, it's only a question of days now." But the old woman muttered: "Not only will they not come back, but we up here will all be killed too, by the airplanes." Paride smiled again, as though this were something comical; but I, alarmed by such pessimism, said hurriedly: "Well, we'll see you later . . . good-bye." She replied: "We'll see each other, never fear, especially as you won't be going back to Rome as soon as all that; very likely you won't ever go back there." Paride laughed at this, but I thought to myself there was little to laugh at, and I couldn't help making mental conjurations against the evil eye.

I spent that afternoon cleaning the little room where our bed was, not knowing we should have to live there for a long time. I swept the floor, scratching the filth of years from the bare earth; I handed over I don't know how many spades and hoes which were piled up in the corners to Paride; I dusted the spiders' webs off the walls. Then I put up the bed in a corner against the rock wall, fixed the planks firmly on the trestles, gave the sack of maize leaves a good shake-up and wrapped the sheets round it—the sheets were very fine, of heavy hand-woven linen, clean and fresh—and spread Paride's black cloak over it as a blanket. Paride's wife, Luisa, the little fair woman with the sullen face, blue eyes and curly hair, had in the meantime settled herself at the other end of the room in front of the loom and was working it up and down with strong, muscular arms, without a pause, and with a clatter that was unbelievable, so much so that I said: "My goodness, will you always be in here, making that noise?" Laughing, she answered: "Oh, I don't know how long I'll be here. I've got to weave cloth to make trousers for Paride and the boys." "How nice for us," I said. "We'll be deafened." "*I* haven't gone deaf," she replied. "You'll see, you'll get accustomed to it." She remained there for about two hours, working the loom all the time, up and down, with the sharp, resounding noise of wood slamming against wood; and after we had tidied up the room, we sat down, Rosetta on the chair which I had hired from Paride and I on the bed. There we remained, staring at Luisa as she went on weaving, open-mouthed, doing nothing, like a pair of idiots. Luisa did not talk much but she answered our questions willingly. In this way we came to know that, of all the men who had lived in the neighborhood before the war, Paride was the only one who had not gone away, owing to his having two of the fingers of his right hand missing. All the others were in the army, and almost all in Russia. "Except for me," said Luisa with an ambiguous smile, in a tone almost of complacency, "all the other women up here—it's just as if they were widows already." I was surprised, and thinking that Luisa must be as pessimistic as her mother-in-law, I said: "But why should the whole lot of them die? I think they'll come back, myself." But Luisa smiled and shook her head. "You don't understand what I mean," she said. "I find it difficult to believe they'll come back, not because they'll be killed but because the Russian women like our men. A foreigner's always attractive, you know. It's quite possible that when the war's over those women will force them to stay, and then no one's likely to see them again." In fact, she thought of war as an affair of males and females, and you could see she was very pleased to have been able to keep her own male, thanks to those two missing fingers, while the others were going to lose theirs to the Russian women. We talked also about the Festa family and she told me that Filippo had managed to avoid having his son sent to the front by means of recommendations and favors; whereas the peasants who had neither money nor influence had to go to the war and very likely got killed. I recalled, then, what Filippo had said about the world, how, according to him, it was divided into fools and clever people; and I realized that in this case too he had conducted himself like a clever man.

Evening came in God's good time, and Luisa stopped making that terrible din with the loom and went off to prepare supper. We two were so tired that for a whole hour we remained exactly as we were, without moving or speaking, I sitting on the bed and Rosetta on the chair at the head of the bed. The oil lamp cast a feeble glimmer, and, in that light, the room really seemed like a small cave: I looked at Rosetta, Rosetta looked at me, and each time our glances expressed something different, and we did not speak because we understood each other perfectly, and we knew that words would be superfluous and would add nothing to what our eyes were saying. Rosetta's were saying: "What are we to do, Mum, I'm frightened, what ever sort of a place have we come to?" and so on, and mine answered: "My darling daughter, don't worry, you've got your Mum beside you, you mustn't be afraid," and other things of the same kind. And so, dumbly, we exchanged a great number of reflections, and in the end, as a kind of conclusion to this despairing conversation, Rosetta drew up her chair to the bed and put her head in my lap and her arms around my knees, and I, still in silence, started very slowly stroking her hair. We stayed like that for perhaps half an hour; then the door was unlatched, someone pushed it open, and a small child's head appeared around the door post. It was Paride's son, Donato. "Daddy says would you like to come and have supper with us?" We were not very hungry as we had eaten so much at Filippo's table at midday; however, I accepted the invitation, for I felt tired and discouraged and I did not like the idea of finishing the evening supperless, alone with Rosetta, in that dreary little room.

We followed Donato, who scampered in front of us in the dark like a cat. We found Paride surrounded by four women—his mother, his wife, his sister and his sister-in-law. These last two each had three children. Paride's sister, Giacinta, was, like him, very dark, with an intense, wild look in her eyes and a broad, heavy face: she looked like someone possessed and never spoke except to scold her three children in a harsh manner. They clung to her clothes like puppies to a bitch and never stopped whimpering; sometimes she did not even speak to them but merely hit them, silently and hard, on the head, with her closed fist. Paride's sister-in-law was called Anita and was the wife of a brother of Paride who, in peace time, lived in the neighbourhood of Cisterna; she was a dark, pale, thin woman with an aquiline nose, quiet eyes, and a calm, thoughtful expression. In contrast with Giacinta, who was almost frightening, Anita gave the impression of tranquillity and sweetness. She also had her children round her, but instead of clinging to her clothes they were sitting politely on the benches, waiting silently and patiently to be given something to eat. As we came in, Paride said to us with his usual strange smile, half embarrassed and half sullen: "We thought that, as you were alone, you would like to join us." After a moment he added: "Until your own provisions come, you can have your meals here with us; we'll settle the account later." He made it clear, in fact, that the food was not given for nothing; but I was grateful to him, all the same, because I knew they were poor and there was the food shortage and it was a considerable thing that they should agree to give us food in exchange for money, for in times of shortage anybody who has a few provisions keeps them for himself and does not share them with others even for money.

Paride lit an acetylene lamp and a fine white light illuminated the whole party of us as we sat on benches and stumps of wood round the tripod, upon which a small pot was boiling. We were all women and children except Paride, the solitary man; and Anita, the sister-in-law, made a joke about this—a joke not unmixed with melancholy because, like most of the men, her husband was away in Russia. "You must be pleased, Paride," she said, "to have so many women all to yourself; it ought to make you happy." "A happiness that won't last long," replied Paride with a half-smile; but his pessimistic old mother immediately snapped at him: "Long? Why, *we* shall be finished before the war is." Luisa, in the meantime, had placed an earthenware soup-tureen on top of a small, shaky table; then she seized a loaf of bread, and, holding it tightly against her chest, quickly cut it into thin slices with a very sharp knife, allowing the slices to drop into the tureen until it was full of bread to the brim. Then she took the little pot off the fire and poured its contents on to the slices of bread as they lay on top of each other: it was, in fact, the usual *minestrina* which we had already eaten at Concetta's house—the mush of bread and bean soup.

While we were waiting for the bread to get thoroughly soaked, Luisa placed a big basin on the floor in the middle of the hut and poured water into it from a pitcher which was warming in the ashes beside the tripod. They all then started removing their sandals, in a leisurely manner and with a certain solemnity, as though they were doing something very serious which was repeated every evening and always in the same way. At first I did not understand, but then, when I saw Paride take the lead in thrusting his bare foot, all black with earth between the toes and round the heel, into the water in the basin, I saw what was happening: we in the city wash our hands before eating; but they, poor things, having walked about all day in the mud of the fields, wash their feet. The whole family, however, washed in the same basin and without changing the water, and you can imagine what the water was like after all those feet had been through it, including the children's. We two did not wash; and one of the children innocently asked: "Why aren't you two washing?" To which the old mother, who hadn't washed either, answered in a somber tone: "They're two ladies from Rome. They don't till the soil as we do."

By this time the *minestrina* was ready; Luisa removed the basin full of dirty water and placed the table with the tureen on it in the middle. We all began eating at the same time, each one helping himself straight from the tureen with his own spoon. I do not think Rosetta and I ate more than two or three spoonfuls each; but the others plunged in with such vehemence—especially the children—that in a short time the tureen was empty and I could see, from their disappointed and still eager faces, that several of them still remained hungry. Paride distributed small handfuls of dried figs, one handful for each person, then he took a flask of wine from a hole in the wall of the hut and poured out a glass. Everyone, including the children, drank from the same glass, and each time Paride wiped the rim of the glass with his sleeve, poured out more wine, scrupulously, and handed the glass to the next person, naming in a low voice the person to whom he was handing it; it was like being in church. The wine was harsh, almost like vinegar—mountain wine; still, it was made of grapes. When the meal was over the women took up their spindles and distaffs again and Paride, by the light of the acetylene lamp, began correcting his son Donato's arithmetic exercise. Paride was illiterate but he had some knowledge of keeping accounts and wanted his son to learn too. It was quite clear, however, that the boy, a child with a big head and a simple, expressionless face, was extremely dull, for, after trying again and again to make him understand some problem or other, Paride would fly into a rage and give him a violent blow on the head, saying: "You blockhead!" The blow resounded as though the child's head were made of wood; but he did not even seem to notice it and started quietly playing on the floor with the cat. I asked Paride afterward why he was so keen for his son—who, like him, could neither read nor write—to learn arithmetic; and I realized that, to him, numbers, not letters, were of importance, because with the former you could at least count your money, whereas the latter, according to him, served no purpose at all.

I wished to describe this first evening of ours with the Morrone family (that was their surname) before anything else, because, having once described the first, I have described all those which came afterward, for they were all just the same; and also because, during that same day, I had a midday meal with the evacuees and an evening meal with the peasants and so was in a position to note the differences. Now, I am telling the truth: the evacuees were richer, at least some of them were; their food was better; they knew how to read and write; they did not wear sandals and their women were dressed like women in a town; and yet, from that very first day, and increasingly as time went on, I preferred the peasants to the evacuees. This preference was perhaps derived from my having been a peasant myself before I was a shopkeeper; but it was due, in my opinion, more particularly to the strange feeling I had toward the evacuees, especially when I compared them with the peasants, a feeling that they were people whose education had served merely to make them worse. It is the same thing that happens with some good-for-nothing little boys; as soon as they go to school and learn to write, the first thing they do is to cover the walls with rude words. What I mean is that it is not enough to educate people; you have also got to teach them how to make use of their education.

Finally everyone was half asleep and some of the children had dozed off altogether, so Paride announced that it was time to go to bed. We left the hut and said good night to one another, and then Rosetta and I were left alone at the edge of the terrace, both of us gazing intently into the darkness toward the point where we knew Fondi to be. There was not a single light to be seen, all was dark and quiet, the only living things were the stars which shone brilliantly and seemed to be winking in the black sky as though they were so many golden eyes looking at us and knowing all about us while we knew nothing about them. Rosetta said to me in a low voice: "Mother, what a lovely night," and I asked her if she was content that we had come up to that place and she answered that she was always content when she was with me. We stood there for a few moments longer looking at the night, and then she pulled me by the sleeve and whispered that she wanted to pray in order to thank the Madonna who had brought us all the way up there, safe and sound. She said this in a low voice, as though she feared to be overheard, and I was rather surprised and asked: "Here?!" She nodded and then let herself fall gently on her knees in the grass at the edge of the terrace, pulling me down with her. This move of hers by no means displeased me; Rosetta had interpreted my own feeling, amid the silence and quiet of that night, after so many anxieties and so many fatigues: a feeling as it were of gratitude toward somebody or something that had helped and protected us. I joined hands with her and, moving my lips briskly, I recited the prayer that is usually said before going to bed. It was some little time since I had prayed; I had not done so since the day when I had given myself to Giovanni, and I knew I should not pray any more after that day because I considered myself in a state of sin, and yet, on the other hand–I don't know why–I couldn't bring myself to recognize it. And so, to begin with, I asked Jesus for forgiveness for what I had done with Giovanni and once more promised myself that I would never do it again. Then, influenced, by the immensely vast, black night which embraced so many lives and so many things and in which there was nothing to be seen, I prayed for all living beings, for myself and for Rosetta and also for the Festa family and for Paride's family and then for the people who were scattered all over the mountains, for the English who would be coming to set us free and for us Italians who were suffering and also for the Germans and the Fascists who were making us suffer but who after all were human beings too. As my prayer gradually extended itself more and more widely I felt deeply moved and my eyes were full of tears, and although I thought that this might be partly the effect of weariness I said to myself that this feeling was a good one and that it was a good thing I experienced it. Rosetta, too, was praying with bowed head, but then suddenly she seized me by the arm, exclaiming: "Look, look!" I looked and saw, far away in the darkness, a luminous streak rising into the air; when it reached a great height it transformed itself into a green flower that fell back, very slowly, lighting up for a moment the mountains around the valley, the woods, and even—it seemed to me—the houses of Fondi. Later I came to know that these green lights, beautiful as they were, were star-shells and that their purpose was to light up the darkness so that points might be chosen as targets for gun fire and bombing from the air. But at the moment it seemed to me a good omen, a signal by which the Madonna allowed me to understand that she had heard my prayer and was disposed to grant it.

My intention in telling about this prayer was chiefly to give an idea of Rosetta's character, which I have not so far described. Since, later on, this character changed to its exact opposite, I wish to say now what Rosetta was like at that time, at the moment when we reached that mountain village—or at any rate how she appeared to me and how she had always appeared to me up to that time. Mothers, as everyone knows, do not always know their children; but anyhow this was the idea I had formed of Rosetta, and even now—when, as I have said, she has changed from white to black—I think that this idea, taken all in all, was not far wrong. Well, I had brought up Rosetta with great care, just like a daughter of gentlefolk, shielding her from all the ugly things that there are in the world. I am not what is called a very religious woman, although I am a practicing Catholic: with me, religion goes up and down, and there are times—that night, for instance, on the terrace—when it seems to me that I really believe in it, and other times—as for example during the days when we were on the point of fleeing from Rome—when I don't believe in it at all. In any case religion does not make me lose sight of reality, which remains always what it is; and however much the priests struggle to explain and justify it, reality often contradicts their assertions point by point. But with Rosetta things were different. I do not know whether it was due to my having entrusted her to the nuns, as a half-boarder, until she was twelve, or whether she was led to it by her own character, but Rosetta was deeply religious, all of a piece, without hesitations or doubts; so sure, so convinced that you might almost say she never spoke, or perhaps even thought, about it. For her, religion was as the air we breathe, which goes in and out of our lungs and we attach no importance to it and do not even notice it. It is difficult for me now, after so many things have changed, to explain what Rosetta was like at the time of our flight from Rome. All I will say is that at times I thought she was perfect. She was one of those people whom you cannot find any flaws in even if you are unkind. Rosetta was good, frank, sincere, disinterested. I have ups and downs of humor, I may fly into a rage, or scream, or even hit somebody, because I lose my head. But Rosetta never answered me angrily, never nursed any resentment, never showed herself anything but a model daughter. Her perfection, however, did not consist merely in having no defects; it consisted also in the fact that she always did and said the right thing, the one thing in a thousand that *ought* to be done and said.

Very often I felt almost frightened and said to myself: I have a saint for a daughter. And really there was good reason to think she might be a saint, because to behave so well and in so perfect a manner, having no experience of life and being in truth only a child, is indeed saintly. She had done nothing in life except live with me and, when her education with the nuns was finished, help me with the household jobs and sometimes also in the shop; and yet she behaved as if she had done everything and known everything. Now, however, I think that the perfection which appeared to me almost unbelievable came, in truth, from inexperience and from the education the nuns had given her. Religion and lack of experience, fused together, gave shape to the perfection which I thought as firm as a tower but which was, instead, as fragile as a house of cards. I did not in fact realize that true sanctity lies in knowledge and experience, even if it is only of one particular kind, and cannot result from lack of experience and ignorance, as was the case with Rosetta. But how was I to blame? I had brought her up with love; and like all mothers in this world had taken care that she should know nothing of the ugly things of life because I considered that, once she had left home and got married, she would come to know about these things only too soon. On the other hand I had not reckoned with war, which forces us to know things even when we do not want to, and compels us to have experience of them before the proper time, in a cruel, unnatural manner. Well, that was how it was: Rosetta's perfection was of the kind that was suitable to peacetime, with the shop going well, and me thinking about putting money together for her dowry, and an honest young man who would love her and marry her and give her children, so that she, after being a model baby and a model girl, could also be a model wife. Her perfection was not of the kind that is suitable to wartime, which demands qualities of a different kind—what, I do not know, but certainly not the qualities that Rosetta had.

We got to our feet and went off in the darkness along the terrace toward our room. We passed underneath Paride's window, and I could hear that Paride and his family had not yet gone to sleep but were moving about and talking in subdued voices, just like hens in a hen house that set up a fuss before they go off to sleep. Then we came to our own little room against the side of the house and the wall of the terrace, with its door made of planks, its sloping, tiled roof and unglazed window. I pushed open the door and we found ourselves in darkness. But I had matches with me; and the first thing I did was to light a small piece of candle; then, out of a band of linen torn off a handkerchief, I manufactured a wick which I put into the oil lamp. In this bright but melancholy light we both sat down on the bed, and I said to Rosetta: "We'll take off only our skirts and bodices. We've nothing but the sheets and this cloak of Paride's, and if we undress altogether I'm sure we shall be cold later on." So we did this, and got into bed, one after the other, in our petticoats. The sheets were of cool, heavy, hand-woven linen; but that was the only normal thing about this bed that was not really a bed at all. At the slightest movement I became aware of all the maize leaves rustling and dividing into two separate heaps, so that my back, through the thin material of the sack, touched the hard planks underneath. I had never slept in a bed like that, even as a child, in my own village: we had ordinary beds, with springs and mattresses. At one moment, indeed, as I turned over, it was not merely the leaves but the planks also which opened beneath me, and I felt myself falling down through the gap until my behind actually touched the floor. I pulled myself up in the darkness, replaced the planks and the sack and then got into bed again, clasping my arms closely round Rosetta whose back was turned to me and who was curled up in a ball against the wall.

But, even so, it was a very restless night. And I don't know what time—after midnight, I daresay—I heard a little chirping noise, a very, very thin sound even fainter than the chirping of birds. It came from under the bed, and so, after a short time, I wakened Rosetta and asked her if she could hear it too, and she replied that she could. Then I lit the lamp and looked under the bed. The chirping, I at once realized, came from a box which appeared to contain nothing except bunches of camomile and mint. But on looking more closely we discovered a round nest made of straw and down containing eight or ten new-born mice, no bigger than my little finger, pink and naked and almost transparent. Rosetta said at once that we must not touch them; it was our first night up there and to kill them would bring us bad luck. So we got back into bed again and settled ourselves to sleep as best we could. But, not more than a hour later, suddenly, in the darkness, I felt something soft and heavy walking over my face and chest. I uttered a cry of fright, Rosetta awoke again, we lit the lamp and, lo and behold, after the mice, the cat. It was in fact a pretty little black kitten with green eyes, thin but young and glossy, and it was sitting at the bottom of the bed gazing fixedly at us, all ready to jump back out of the window by which it had come in. Rosetta, however, called it in her own special way, for she had a passion for cats and knew how to treat them, and immediately the cat advanced confidently, and in a very short time it was under the sheets with us, purring happily. This kitten slept with us the whole time we stayed there, and it was called Gigi. It had its own habits, coming in every night after midnight and creeping under the sheets between the two of us, and there it would stay till dawn. It was good-tempered and fond of Rosetta, but if either of us dared to make a movement while it was sleeping there was trouble, you could immediately hear Gigi growling in the darkness as much as to say: "My goodness, can't we be allowed to get a little sleep?"

That same night I woke up several times more, and each time I had difficulty in recognizing the place where I was. During one of these wakeful moments I heard an airplane flying low, very slowly, with a regular, solemn, pleasant sound, as if its engine were grinding water instead of air, and it seemed to me that this sound was speaking to me and telling me things that reassured me. It was explained to me afterward that these planes were called Storks and that they went out patroling and for that reason flew slowly; and in the end I became accustomed to them, to such a degree that sometimes I stayed awake on purpose to hear them, and if I failed to hear them I was almost disappointed. They were English planes, these Storks, and I knew that in the end the English were bound to come and give us back our freedom and allow us to go home.

Chapter 4

AND SO BEGAN our life at Sant'Eufemia, for that was the name of the place. It began as though it were to last, provisionally, for only a couple of weeks; actually it was to be prolonged for nine months. In the mornings we used to sleep as late as we could, seeing that there was nothing at all to do; and, I must tell you, we were so exhausted by the privations and anxieties of Rome, that during the first week we slept sometimes for as much as twelve or fourteen hours at a stretch. We went early to bed, and would wake up during the night and then go off to sleep again, and wake up again at dawn and then sleep would again take possession of us, and day would come and all we had to do was turn toward the rock wall of the terrace, with our backs to the light coming in at the window, in order to plunge back into sleep and go on sleeping until late in the morning. I have never slept so much in my life, and it was a good sleep, solid and full, with the sound flavor of home-made bread, a sleep without dreams and without anxieties, a sleep so truly refreshing that with every day that passed we recovered the strength that we had lost in Rome and during our stay at Concetta's. This sleep, so deep and so sound, truly did us good, and indeed, by the end of a week, we were both of us transformed, our eyes fresh and bright, without any rings round them, our cheeks taut and full, our faces smooth and firm, our heads clear. I felt, in that sleep, that the soil upon which I was born and which I had abandoned for so long had taken me back into its bosom and was communicating its strength to me—just as happens with plants that have been uprooted and then replanted: they recover their strength quickly and start putting forth leaves and flowers again. Yes, indeed, we are plants, not human beings, or rather we are more plants than human beings, and it is from the soil upon which we are born that all our strength comes and if we leave it we are no longer either plants or human beings but mere frail wisps, to be tossed hither and thither by life, according to the wind of circumstances.

We slept so much and so readily that the hardships of life appeared slight to us and we faced them with cheerfulness and scarcely noticed them; rather like a well-fed, well-rested mule that pulls a cart up a hill all in one go and, having reached the top, still has the strength to start off at a good, regular pace, just as if nothing had happened. And yet, as I have already said, life up there was hard. The morning began with washing. In the first place it was necessary, as we got out of bed, to take care not to dirty our feet, and for this purpose I arranged some flat stones on the floor in such a way that we should avoid getting muddy on rainy days when the floor was a pool of water. Then we had to draw water from the well, which was just in front of our hut. As long as autumn lasted, there was no difficulty about this; but with the winter—the place being at a height of more than three thousand feet—the water at the bottom of the well froze and every morning when I threw down the bucket my hands were numbed with cold and the water I drew up was so icy that it took one's breath away. I feel the cold very much, and I limited myself, generally, to washing my hands and face; but Rosetta, who preferred cold to dirt, undressed completely and, standing in the middle of the room, upset the entire bucket of icy water over her head. So robust and healthy was my Rosetta that the water slithered over her body as though she had oil on her skin, and then there was nothing left of it but a few drops on her breasts, her shoulders, her belly and her bottom. After our toilet we went out and started on jobs connected with our cooking. With the cooking, too, things went fairly well as long as the autumn and the fine weather lasted; the real difficulties began with the winter. We had to go out in the rain into the scrub and cut a good quantity of fuel from reed beds and bushes with pruning knives. Then we went into the hut and the maddening task of lighting the fire would begin. The green wet wood refused to burn, the reeds made a dense black smoke; we had to get down on the floor with our cheeks against the muddy ground and blow until the fire caught. In the end we were covered with mud, our eyes were filled with burning tears, and we were exhausted and exasperated; and all this to cook a little potful of beans and fry an egg.

We formed the habit of arranging our meals as the peasants do —a first, very slight meal about eleven in the morning, and a second meal, our proper dinner, about seven in the evening. In the morning we had *polenta* seasoned with sausage gravy, or, perhaps an onion and a piece of bread, or just a handful of carob beans; in the evening we had the *minestrina* I have already described and a few pieces of meat, almost always goat's meat, she-goat, kid, or he-goat. After we had finished our morning meal there was nothing to do but wait for our evening meal. If it was fine weather we would go for a walk: we would follow the line of the mountain, keeping all the time on the same *macera* or terrace, until finally we reached the scrub, where we would choose a pleasant, shady spot under a tree and lie down on the grass, with the great panoramic view in front of us, remaining there all the afternoon. But when the bad weather came—which, that winter, lasted for months—we stayed in our room, I sitting on the bed and Rosetta on the chair, without doing anything, while Luisa did her weaving at the loom with the deafening din I have already spoken of. As long as I live, I shall remember those hours that I spent in that room during the bad weather. The rain never ceased to fall, thickly and steadily, and I listened to it murmuring on the roof tiles and gurgling down the pipe from the gutter before falling into the well; inside the room, in order to save oil, we sat in semi-darkness, our only light coming in, rain-veiled, at the little window—or rather the cat hole, so small it was, and we sat silent because we no longer had the heart to speak of the usual subjects—which were only two, anyhow: the shortage of food and the arrival of the English. And so the hours passed, till one was reduced to a state of exhaustion; and I had lost all sense of time and no longer even knew what month it was or what day of the week, and it seemed to me I had become half-witted, since I had ceased to use my head, and sometimes I felt I was almost going mad, and if it had not been for Rosetta, to whom as her mother I had to set an example, I do not know what I should have done: I might have rushed outside screaming, or I might have started hitting Luisa, who seemed to be making that din with her loom on purpose to deafen us and who always had a particular kind of sly smile on her face, as much as to say: "This is the life we peasants usually lead. . . . Now you have to do the same, you ladies from Rome. . . . What do you think of it? Do you like it?"

Another thing that almost drove me mad during that time was the restricted space in which we lived, especially when compared with the vastness of the Fondi panorama. From Sant' Eufemia we could see the whole of the Fondi valley, with its dark orange groves and white houses here and there, and also, to the right, in the direction of Sperlonga, the narrow band of the sea; and we knew that in that sea lay the island of Ponza—which in fact could be seen in very clear weather—and we knew, too, that at Ponza were the English or, in other words, freedom. But notwithstanding this vast expanse of landscape, we continued to live and move and wait on our long, narrow terrace, so confined that if you took four steps forward you ran the risk of falling down on to another terrace of equal dimensions. We sat up there like so many birds perching on a branch during a flood and awaiting a favorable moment to take flight toward some drier place. But that moment never came.

After that first invitation, the Festa family invited us a few more times but more and more coldly, and then they no longer invited us at all because, as Filippo said, he had a family, and as it was a question of things to eat, it was his family that he had to think of first. Luckily, Tommasino appeared from the valley a few days after our arrival, pulling at the bridle of his little donkey, which was laden like a true beast of burden with parcels and suitcases. In these were our provisions, which he had raked up from all over the Fondi valley in accordance with the list we had made together. No one who has not found himself in similar circumstances, with money that from a practical point of view has lost all its value, a stranger amongst strangers, on the top of a mountain, and has never experienced what it really means to be without anything to eat in time of war, will be able to understand the joy with which we welcomed Tommasino. There are things which it is difficult to explain. Usually people live in towns, where the shops are full, and make no provision for the future since they know that the shops are there, well furnished with everything. People get the illusion that this matter of full shops is almost a fact of nature, like the progress of the seasons and rain and sunshine and night and day. This is nonsense: there can be a lack of foodstuffs all of a sudden, and then all the millions in the world are not enough to buy a crust of bread, and without bread you die.

Tommasino arrived panting and out of breath, hauling at the bridle of the donkey, which could scarcely go any further. "Here," said Tommasino, "here you have enough to eat for at least six months"; and then he handed over the things to me, checking each item on a piece of yellow paper upon which I had written the order. I remember the list, and I give it here so as to show what people's lives were like in the autumn of 1943. *Our* life–Rosetta's and mine–was dependent upon one fifty-kilo sack of white flour, for making bread and *pasta*, one other, smaller sack of yellow maize flour for making *polenta*, one small sack containing about twenty kilos of beans of the worst quality (the ones with eyes), a few kilos of chick peas, dwarf peas and lentils, fifty kilos of oranges, a pot of lard weighing two kilos and a couple of kilos of sausages. Besides these, Tommasino had also brought up a small sack of dried figs, walnuts and almonds, and a good quantity of carob beans which are usually given to horses but which now were too good even for us. We put all this stuff into our room, for the most part under the bed, and then I settled the account with Tommasino and discovered that in one single week prices had already risen by almost thirty per-cent. Someone may imagine that it was Tommasino who had caused them to rise, since he would have done almost anything to make money; but I myself am a shopkeeper and when he told me that prices had risen I believed him at once, because I knew from experience that it could not but be true and that if things went on as they were now going—that is, with the English held up at the Garigliano and the Germans carrying off everything and terrifying people and preventing them from working—prices would go up still further and even, I daresay, reach the stars. I therefore believed Tommasino and paid him without hesitation, more especially because I felt that a man like him, greedy enough to face the dangers of war simply in order to make money, was a treasure in times like these and must be carefully cherished. I paid him, and what is more, I let him see the big bunch of thousand-lire notes that I kept in the bag under my skirt; and when he saw the money he fastened his eyes upon it as a kite does upon a hen. He said that we were made to understand one another and that he would find things for me whenever I wished —always, however, at the current price, not a penny less and not a penny more.

I noticed once again the degree of consideration which money, or in this case provisions, can produce. Recently the Festas, observing that our provisions failed to arrive, and that we turned to Paride for help, and that he, albeit very unwillingly, allowed us—for payment, of course—to eat with his family, had avoided our company and, when mealtimes came, slunk away in an almost shamefaced manner to eat on the quiet. But as soon as Tommasino arrived with his donkey their attitude changed completely. Smiles, greetings, caresses, conversations, and even—now that we had no more need of it—invitations to dinner. They actually came to gaze at our provisions, and on this occasion Filippo, genuinely pleased because he liked me—not quite enough, perhaps, for him to give me anything to eat but enough to be glad that I had something—said to me: "You and I, Cesira, are the only people up here who can face the future calmly, because we're the only ones who have the money." His son Michele looked even blacker than usual, and said with clenched teeth: "Are you quite sure of that?" His father burst out laughing and clapped him on the shoulder. "Sure?" he cried, "it's the only thing I *am* sure about. Don't you know that money is a man's best friend, the most faithful and most constant friend he can have?" I stood listening to them and said nothing. I thought to myself that it wasn't really quite true: that very day the trusted "friend" had played the joke on me of lessening his purchasing value by thirty per cent. And today when a hundred lire are barely enough to buy a little bread, whereas before the war you could live for half a month on that sum, I can say truthfully that in time of war there is no friend that can be trusted, neither man nor money nor anything else. War throws everything into disorder and destroys, together with things that can be seen, a great many other things that cannot be seen but that nevertheless exist.

Our normal life at Sant'Eufemia began with the day when the provisions arrived. We slept, we dressed, we collected sticks and wood for the fire, we lit the fire in the hut, then we walked about a little, chatting about this and that to the other evacuees, we ate, we walked about again, we cooked and ate for the second time, and finally, in order to spare the oil for the lamp, we went to bed with the hens. The weather was fine and mild and calm, windless and cloudless, a truly magnificent autumn, with the woods on the mountains around us sprinkled with red and yellow, and everyone was saying that this was ideal weather for the Allies to make a rapid, overwhelming advance and get at least as far as Rome, and no one could persuade himself that they would not do so but would linger in the vicinity of Naples or a little farther north. People talked perpetually about the Allies and when they were coming and why they didn't come and how on earth this and why ever that. It was the evacuees particularly who talked of all this because they wanted to go back to Fondi as soon as possible and take up their ordinary lives again; the peasants talked about it less, partly because the war meant good business for them, since they had let their cottages and made many other small but profitable deals with the evacuees; and partly because they were leading the same life as they had led in peacetime and little or nothing would change, for them, with the arrival of the Allies.

What a lot of talk I had about the Allies, up and down the terraces, in the open air, looking out over the wide view to Fondi and the blue sea so far away; or in the evenings in Paride's hut, almost in darkness in front of the half-dead fire with the smoke making our eyes water; or again at night in bed, holding Rosetta in my arms before we fell asleep! I talked about them so much that gradually these Allies had become like village saints who bestow favors and bring rain and fine weather, and at one moment a man prays to them and next moment he insults them and always he expects something from them. Everyone was expecting extraordinary things from these Allies, exactly as from the saints; and everyone was sure that with their arrival life would not merely return to normal but to something much better than normal. You ought to have heard Filippo, especially. I believe he pictured the army of the Allies as an endless column of trucks filled with all God's good things, with soldiers perched on the top for the express purpose of distributing all these things, gratis, to us Italians. And this was a man of middle age, a shopkeeper, and one who claimed to be included in the category of clever men; whereas according to his ideas the Allies would have to be such utter fools that they would confer benefits upon us Italians who had made war upon them and killed their sons and made them spend their money!

Of trustworthy news about the coming of these blessed Allies we had extremely little, in other words, none at all. Sometimes Tommasino would appear at Sant'Eufemia, but since he was not interested in anything but the black market and money-making, it was difficult to get anything out of him but inconclusive remarks; sometimes some peasant would come up, and being a peasant, would say things that did not make sense. There were also some young men from Pontecorvo who used to turn up occasionally with knapsacks on their backs, selling salt or leaf tobacco, the two things which were scarcest. The tobacco was damp and bitter, and the evacuees used to chop it up and make cigarettes of it with pieces of newspaper; the salt was extremely bad quality, the kind that is given to cattle. These young men also brought news, but mostly it was news of a fantastic sort which you believed at first but which on closer examination you found to resemble the salt they sold, which weighed twice as much because of the water it contained. In the same way their news was so mixed up with fancy that it appeared to have the weight of truth; but then, under the hot sun of examination, the fancy evaporated and you realized there was mighty little truth in it. They told us a story of how there was a great battle going on, one of them saying it was to the north of Naples, in the direction of Caserta, another that it was near Cassino, yet another that it was very close indeed, at Itri. Lies, from beginning to end. In truth all these young men cared about was selling their salt and tobacco; as for news, they tried to say the things that would give pleasure to those who questioned them.

One morning we heard explosions of some kind in the direction of the coast, more or less where Sperlonga lies. These explosions were heard distinctly, and later a woman who came up bringing oranges told us that the Germans were blowing up the dikes of the marshes and canals in the reclaimed land in order to hold up the English advance. Soon everything that was above water would be submerged and a large number of people who had worked all their lives to cultivate a small field would be ruined, because water, as everyone knows, devastates cultivated land and it takes years to get rid of it and to make the soil workable again. These explosions followed one another like fireworks at a village *festa*, and they had a curious effect because there was something festive about them and yet I knew that they meant misery and despair for the people who lived on the reclaimed land. It was a magnificent day, calm and serene, the sky cloudless, the whole green and prosperous plain of Fondi stretching away to the hazy line of the sea, so lovely to look at, so blue and so smiling. And once more, as I listened to these bangs and looked at this landscape, I thought to myself that men go one way and nature the other, and when nature lets loose a storm, with thunder and lightning and rain, men are very often happy inside their houses; whereas, when nature smiles and seems ready to promise eternal happiness, what happens is that men despair and long to die.

Several days went past like this and all the time the war news was vague. People who came up to Sant'Eufemia from the valley told us that a big English army had started along the road to Rome. But this big army must have been advancing at the pace of a tortoise, for even if they were proceeding on foot and stopping from time to time to get their breath, the English ought to have arrived by now, but there was nothing to be seen of them. I myself, feeling I could not go on talking about the English and when they would arrive and the abundance they would bring with them, tried to occupy myself in some way, for instance by knitting. I had bought some wool from Paride and was knitting a sweater, for by this time I suspected that we should have to stay up there for an indefinite time, and the cold weather would come and we two should have nothing to put on. The wool was greasy and dingy and smelt like a stable; it came from the few sheep that Paride possessed, and every year they clipped it and then spun it with spindle and distaff, in the old-fashioned way, and made stockings and sweaters. Everything up there was conducted in that sort of manner, as in the good old times. Paride's family had everything they needed not only for food but also for clothes, such as flax, wool and leather—and just as well for them, since, as I have said, they had no money at all, or scarcely any, and if they had not made provision of this kind, they would have had to go about naked. Therefore they grew flax and kept sheep for wool, and when they killed a cow they used the leather for sandals and waistcoats. As for the wool and the flax, after they had spun them in the way I have described, they wove them into cloth on the loom in our room—sometimes Luisa, sometimes Paride's sister or sister-in-law; but not one of the three was any good at the work, and in spite of all their toil with spindle and distaff and loom, they did not manage well. They dyed their cloth an uneven blue with certain bad dyes of their own and cut it to make trousers and coats (and I have never seen stuff so badly cut; it looked as if it had been done with a hatchet); and it didn't last a week before it went through at the knees or elbows. Then the women had to sew patches over the holes, so that barely a fortnight after their new clothes had been put on for the first time the family were going about patched up and in rags. Everything they needed they made themselves, but they made everything badly and clumsily. Michele, Filippo's son, to whom I mentioned my observations, answered me seriously, with a shake of the head: "Who makes things by hand nowadays, when there are machines? Only miserable wretches like these, only the peasants of a miserable, backward country like Italy." You must not think from these words that Michele despised the peasants; on the contrary. It was just that he always expressed himself in this way, crudely, abruptly and very harshly, but at the same time—and it was this that impressed me most—in a quiet voice without any violence in his tone, as though he were saying things that were obvious and indisputable but which had long ceased to make him angry and which he now merely uttered, just as anyone else might remark that the sun was shining in the sky, or that rain was falling.

He was a curious type, Michele; and since we afterward became friends and I was to become as fond of him as if he had been my own son, I want to describe him, if only in order to have him, for one last time, before my eyes. He was rather short, but broad-shouldered and even slightly hunchbacked, with a big head and a very high forehead. He wore glasses and walked very upright, in a proud, dignified sort of way, with the air of a person who does not allow himself to be put upon or oppressed by anyone. He was extremely studious, and as I learned from his father was either going to take his degree, or *had* taken his degree—I don't remember which—that same year. He was about twenty-five, although what with his glasses and his very serious appearance he looked at least thirty. But it was above all his character which was unusual, quite different from the characters of the other evacuees and also from those of the people I had known hitherto. As I said before, he expressed himself with absolute assurance, like one who is convinced of being the only person who knows and speaks the truth. It was this conviction that gave rise to the curious fact I have already mentioned: even when he said harsh and violent things, he never became in the least heated, in fact he said them in a calm and reasonable tone, in a tone almost casual, and without emphasis, as though it were a question of some stale subject about which everybody had now been agreed for a long time. This, on the contrary, was quite untrue, at least as regards myself. To hear him talk of Fascism and the Fascists, for instance, always gave me a feeling of astonishment. For twenty years—that is, ever since I had started to think for myself—I had never heard anything but good spoken of the government; and although now and then I had found fault with one thing or another, particularly as regards my shop, I thought that, when all was said and done, if the newspapers always approved of the government they must have good reasons for doing so, and it was not for us poor ignorant creatures to criticize things we neither knew about nor understood. But here was Michele denying everything; where the papers had always said one thing, he said the opposite; there was nothing that had been good during those twenty years, and everything that had been done in Italy during those years had been wrong. According to Michele, Mussolini and his ministers and all the bigwigs and all the people who counted for anything were just a lot of gangsters—that was what he said: gangsters. These assertions, made with such complete assurance, such indifference, such calm, left me open-mouthed. I had always heard that Mussolini was at least, *at least*, a genius; that his ministers, to put it mildly, were great men; that the party secretaries, as shown by their willingness to remain modest, were intelligent, honest persons; and that all the other, smaller officials, unassuming as they always were, were people whom you could trust blindly. And now here was Michele upsetting the apple cart, and calling the whole lot of them gangsters. I wondered how he had come to think in this way; for it did not seem that he had begun to have such opinions, like so many people in Italy, the moment the war had started to go badly; on the contrary, he seemed to have been born with these opinions, holding them in a perfectly natural way, just as other children normally give names of their own to plants and animals and people. To put it simply, he had a long-standing, unshakable, hardened mistrust in everybody and everything. And this appeared to me even more surprising in that he was only twenty-five and had never known anything except Fascism, and had been brought up and educated by Fascists, and so, if education counts for anything, ought to have been a Fascist too, or at the least one of those people—of whom there were so many at that time—who did indeed criticize Fascism, but only half-heartedly and without assurance. But no. Michele, for all his Fascist education, was violently antagonistic to Fascism. And I could not help thinking that there must have been something wrong about that education, otherwise Michele would not have expressed himself in that way.

It may perhaps be thought that Michele had had exceptional experiences, to make him speak like that: we all know that, if someone has an unpleasant experience—and this may happen even with the best governments—he is afterward led to generalize, to see everything as black and ugly and misguided. But this was not so, as I came to know Michele I was more and more convinced that he had had very little experience and that what he had had was insignificant, common to all young men of his position and age. He had grown up at Fondi with his family; and at Fondi he had first gone to school and, like all the other boys of his age, had been first a "*balilla*" and then an "*avanguardista*".

Then he had gone to Rome University and had studied and lived in Rome for some years, living in the house of an uncle who was a magistrate. That was all. He had never been abroad; in Italy, besides Fondi and Rome, he scarcely knew even the chief towns. In short, nothing extraordinary had ever happened to him; or, if it had happened, it had been always a case of things happening in his head, not in his life. In the matter of women, for instance, he had never, in my opinion, had any experience of love —which in so many cases, in the absence of other experience, opens a young man's eyes to what life is. He himself told us many times that he had never been in love, that he had never been engaged, that he had never paid court to any woman. At the most, as far as I could understand, he had made advances to one or two tarts, like all young men of his kind who have neither money nor acquaintances. And so I came to the conclusion that these deeply rooted convictions had been formed in him almost without his noticing it. For twenty years the Fascists had used their energy to proclaim that Mussolini was a genius and all his ministers great men; and Michele, as soon as he had begun to think for himself, had—as naturally as a tree sends out its branches in the direction of the sun—thought the exact opposite of what the Fascists proclaimed. These are mysterious things, I know, and I am a poor ignorant woman and cannot pretend to understand and explain them, but I have often observed that children do the exact opposite of what their parents tell them to do or of what they do themselves, not so much because they really understand that their parents are doing wrong but for the sole and excellent reason that they are children and their parents are parents and they want to have a life of their own, just as their parents have had *their* life. That's how I think it was with Michele. He had been brought up by the Fascists so that he should become a Fascist; but for the sole reason that he was alive and wanted to have a life of his own, he had become an anti-Fascist.

Michele took to spending almost the whole day with us. I do not know what attracted him, for we were just a couple of simple women, not so very different, fundamentally, from his mother and sister; moreover he did not even feel any particular attraction toward Rosetta. Probably he preferred us to his family and to the other evacuees because we came from Rome and did not talk in dialect and did not, like the others, discuss Fondi matters, which bored him stiff. He used to come in the morning, soon after we had got up, and did not leave us except at meal-times, so that he was with us practically the entire day. I seem to see him still as he used to appear in the doorway of our little room where we would be sitting doing nothing, I on the bed and Rosetta on the chair. He would announce in a cheerful voice: "Well, what do you say to going for a nice walk?" We would accept, though in any case these nice walks of his were always the same: either you started out along the terrace, following around the mountainside and then, by walking on the same tier, you could end up in another neighbouring valley, exactly similar to the Sant'Eufemia valley; or you could go up as far as the pass, among rocky slopes and forests of oak; or you could go down toward the valley. We almost always chose the level path, and following the terrace, went as far as a spur of the mountain on the left which stuck out vertically above the valley. There was a great carob tree there and the scrub was all green and full of sunshine, and on the ground soft moss to serve as a cushion. There we would sit down, almost on the topmost point of the spur, not far from a blue-grey rock from which you could survey the whole panorama of Fondi down below, and there we would stay for hours. What did we do? Well, now I come to think about it, I couldn't say. Rosetta sometimes wandered about in the scrub with Michele, and they picked cyclamen, which at that season grew thick and beautiful and tall, their bright pink petals rising amongst the dark leaves wherever there was a particular kind of moss. She would pick a big bunch and bring it to me, and later I would put it in a glass on the table in our room. Or sometimes we just sat there and did nothing: we looked at the sky, at the sea, at the valley and the mountains.

We were a couple of ignorant women and he was a man who

had read many books and who knew many things. Yet I myself had an experience of life which he had not; and I think now that, with all the books he had read and the things he knew, he was at heart a simple creature who knew nothing of life and formed mistaken ideas about many matters. I remember, for instance, some remarks that he made to me on one of those first days. "Cesira," he said, "it's true that you're a shopkeeper and that you think about nothing except your shop, but you haven't been spoiled by being a shopkeeper; luckily for you, you've remained exactly as you were when you were a child." "And what's that?" I asked. "A peasant," he replied. "That's certainly no compliment," I said. "Peasants don't know about anything except the land, they are ignorant and they live like beasts." He started laughing, and answered: "Some time ago it wouldn't have been a compliment, but today it is. Today it's the people who read and write and live in towns and are gentlefolk who are the really ignorant, the really uncultivated, the really uncivilized ones. With them there's nothing to be done, but with you peasants one can begin from the very beginning." I did not quite understand what he meant: "What d'you mean, beginning from the very beginning?" "Well," he said, "making new men of them." "It's quite clear," I exclaimed, "that you don't know anything about peasants, my dear boy. With peasants, there's nothing to be done. Why, what d'you think peasants are? They're the oldest people in the world. New men, indeed! They were peasants before anyone else existed, long before there were people in towns. They are peasants and they will always be peasants." He shook his head as if he were sorry for me and said nothing. I had the impression that he saw the peasants as they were *not* and as they never would be; rather as he himself wished to see them, for reasons of his own.

It was only of peasants and working men that he spoke well; but in my opinion he knew nothing about either of them. One day I said to him: "Michele, you talk about workmen but you don't know them." "And you," he asked, "do *you* know them?" "Of course I know them," I replied, "plenty of them come into my shop . . . they live all about." "What sort of workmen?" "Well, small artisans, plumbers, masons, electricians, carpenters, all of them people who have to work hard for a living—all sorts of people." "And what are these workmen like, in your opinion?" he asked with a kind of teasing look, as though he were preparing to hear a lot of nonsense. "My dear Michele," I answered, "I don't know what they're like. For me these differences don't exist. They are men just like other men. There are good ones and bad ones. Some are lazy and some work hard. Some are fond of their wives and others run after tarts. Some drink and others gamble. In fact there's a bit of everything, as there is everywhere, just as there is among the gentry and the peasants and the office workers and all the rest of them." "Perhaps you're right," he said. "You see them as men like all other men and you're right to see them like that. If everybody saw them as you do, that is, as men like other men, and treated them accordingly, certain things would not happen and perhaps we shouldn't be up here at Sant'Eufemia." "How do other people see them?" I asked. "They see them," he replied, "not as men like other men but simply as working men." "And you, how do *you* see them?" "As working men, too." "Well then," I said, "it's partly *your* fault that we're up here. Of course I'm just repeating what you said yourself, although I don't understand you: you said that you also considered them as working men and not as men like other men." "Yes, indeed," he said, "I *do* consider them as working men . . . but you must understand why. . . . Some people find it convenient to consider them as working men in order to exploit them better; *I* find it convenient to do so in order to defend them." "You're a revolutionary, then, are you?" I asked suddenly. He was disconcerted, and demanded: "What's that got to do with it?" "I've heard about it," I said, "from a police superintendent who used to come to my shop. All these revolutionaries, he said, were acting as agitators among the working men." "All right," he said after a moment, "let's suppose I *am* a revolutionary." "But," I insisted, "*you* haven't ever acted as an agitator among the working men, have you?" He shrugged his shoulders and admitted, in the end, unwillingly, that he had not done so. So I said: "You see, you *don't* know the working men, do you?" This time he made no answer.

However, in spite of his difficult conversation Rosetta and I always preferred his company to that of the other men who were living up there. He was, in short, more civilized, and besides, he was the only one who did not think about self-interest and money, and this made him less tiresome than the others, for self-interest and money are certainly important but hearing them spoken about all the time gives you, in the long run, a feeling of oppression. Filippo and the other evacuees talked about nothing but money-making—that is, about things to be bought or sold and about price and profit, and about how things were before the war and how they would be after it was over. When they were not talking about money-making, they were playing cards. Assembled in Filippo's little room, sitting cross-legged on the floor with their backs against flour or bean sacks, their hats on their heads and cigars in their mouths, in a foul atmosphere of stink and smoke, they would spend hours and hours slamming their cards down on the table with yells and oaths that sounded as if they were murdering one another. There were always at least four others looking on, as in village inns. I, who have never been able to endure card games, was quite unable to understand how they could spend entire days gambling, with cards so nasty and greasy and worn that you couldn't see the figures on them. But it was even worse when, instead of playing cards or talking about money-making, Filippo and his companions discoursed about nothing in particular—that is, made conversation. I am an ignorant woman and I don't understand about anything except shopkeeping and the land, but I felt that these bearded, grown-up men, whenever they went outside the field of their own interests, talked great nonsense. I felt this all the more because I had Michele as a standard of comparison; he was not an ignorant man, and I used to feel that the things he said, though often I did not understand them, were nevertheless just. These other men talked like idiots, or like beasts—if indeed beasts could talk: and when they were not talking pure nonsense, they were saying things that were offensive in their crudity and coarseness. I remember a man called Antonio who was a baker, a tiny, very dark man with one sightless eye which looked smaller than the other and had a little eyelid that flickered all the time as though it had a mote in it. One day four or five of the evacuees, including Antonio, were sitting on the stones of the terrace, talking about the war and about what was going on and the sort of things that happen in wars; Rosetta and I were nearby, listening. This Antonio had been in the war in Libya when he was twenty, and he liked talking about it because that war had been an important thing to him and it was there, incidentally, that he had lost the sight of his eye. Well, at one moment we heard him say: "They had killed three of our men—but 'killed' is hardly strong enough. They had put out their eyes, cut out their tongues, torn off their nails, so we decided on reprisals. Early in the morning we went into one of the villages and burned down all the huts and killed everyone, men, women and children . . . as for the little girls, the bastards, we shoved our bayonets into them, you know where, and then chucked them onto the pile with the others. That was how we taught them to carry out atrocities." Someone, at this point, coughed slightly because we two were within hearing, and Antonio had perhaps not noticed it, because we were standing behind a tree. I heard Antonio excuse himself, saying: "Oh well, things like that, and others too, happen in wartime," and then I ran off after Rosetta who had hurried away. She was walking with her head down and finally she stopped and I saw that her eyes were full of tears and that her face was very pale. I asked her what was the matter; and she said: "Did you hear what Antonio said?" I could find nothing better to say than to repeat Antonio's last remark: "In wartime things like that do happen, my dear child, and others too." She was silent for a moment and then said, as if speaking to herself: "I should always rather be among the ones who get killed than among the ones who do the killing." After that we kept more and more away from the group of evacuees, for Rosetta wished at all costs to avoid finding herself near Antonio and having to speak to him.

With Michele, however, Rosetta was in agreement, up to a point; but on the subject of religion there was no question of agreement. Michele had two pet aversions: the Fascists, as I have already said, and—not far behind them—the priests; and it was difficult to understand whether he hated the former or the latter more; and he himself used often to say, jokingly, that Fascists and priests were the same thing, the only difference being that the Fascists had cut short their soutanes and turned them into black shirts, while the priests wore them complete, down to their feet. I was quite unmoved by his furious attacks on religion, or rather, on the priests: I have always thought that in these matters each person must decide according to his own feelings; I am religious, yes, but not to the point of wishing to impose my religion upon others. Besides, I was aware that Michele, for all his harshness, was fundamentally without malice; sometimes it almost seemed to me that he spoke ill of the priests not so much because he hated them *as priests*, but because it displeased him that they were not truly priests and did not always behave like priests. In fact, it is even possible that he himself was religious, but with a kind of disillusioned religiousness, and often it is just the people like Michele, people who *might* have been more religious than others, who, owing to their disillusionment, attack the priests with the greatest violence and harshness. Rosetta, on the other hand, was quite a different type. She believed in religion and would have liked everyone else to believe in it too; and she could not endure to hear it spoken ill of, even—as was the case with Michele—in good faith and without any real malice. No sooner had he made his first furious attack on the priests than she warned him, clearly and plainly: "If you want to go on seeing us, you must give up that sort of talk." I was expecting that he would persist in his remarks, or fly into a rage, as he sometimes did when he was contradicted. Instead of this, much to my surprise, he did not protest, he did not say anything; all he did was to observe, after a moment or two: "Some years ago, I was like you. In fact I thought seriously of becoming a priest . . . but then I gave up the idea." I was astonished at this unexpected piece of news: never would I have thought that he could have entertained such an ambition. "Did you seriously want to become a priest?" I asked him. "Certainly I did," he said; "you can ask my father, if you don't believe it." "But why did you give up the idea?" "Well, I was only a boy then, and I realized that I hadn't a vocation. Or rather," he added with a smile, "I realized that I *had* a vocation and that, for that very reason, I oughtn't to become a priest." This time Rosetta said nothing; and that was the end of the conversation.

In the meantime things were changing, slowly, and not for the better. After so many contradictory rumors, a precise piece of news arrived: a German division was encamped in the plain of Fondi; and the front had been brought to a halt at the Garigliano river. This meant that the English had ceased to advance and that the Germans were preparing to spend the winter with us. People coming up from the valley told us that the Germans were everywhere, concealed, for the most part among the orange groves, with their tanks and their tents all speckled with green, blue and yellow patches—camouflaged, as they called it. But it was still a question of rumors; no one had ever *seen* the Germans, I mean no one up at Sant'Eufemia, for no German had come up there. Then something happened that put us into contact with the Germans and made us understand what sort of people they were. From that moment, things changed; and it was then, in a sense, that the war arrived up there for the first time, never to leave the place again.

Well then, among the evacuees who played cards with Filippo there was a tailor called Severino, the youngest of all, a small, thin man with a yellow face and a little black mustache and an eye that seemed perpetually to be winking in an understanding way. This was a result of his occupation, because as he sewed, huddled up on a chair in his shop, he always kept one eye half closed. Severino had fled from Fondi like all the others, at the time of the first air raids, and was staying in a cottage not far from ours, together with his little girl and a wife who was as small and modest as he was himself. He was more worried than any of the other people up there because, since the beginning of the war, he had invested all his money in a quantity of English and Italian cloth, which he had hidden in a safe place—but not, it appeared, so truly safe as to save him from a state of permanent anxiety about his little patrimony. Severino, however, passed from anxiety to hopefulness whenever, instead of thinking about the present, with the Germans and the Fascists and the war and the air raids, he turned his mind toward the future. To anyone who was willing to hear it, Severino would expound a plan which he said would make him rich as soon as the war was over. His plan was to exploit to the full the period—perhaps of six months, perhaps of a year—that would come between the end of the war and the return to normality. During those six or twelve months there would be a shortage of everything, owing to the lack of transport and of trade and commerce, and Italy would be occupied by the military and shopkeeping would be difficult or impossible. During that period Severino would put his cloth on a truck and would rush to Rome, and there, with prices soaring to heaven because of the shortage, would become rich by selling retail, piece by piece, the materials he had bought wholesale. It was a reasonable plan, as could be seen later, and it proved that Severino—alone, perhaps, of the people who happened to be staying up there—really understood the way prices worked. It was, I repeat, a reasonable plan; but unfortunately reasonable plans are always the ones that don't succeed, especially in wartime.

One morning a boy who had been Severino's assistant arrived from the plain, all out of breath. Even before he reached the terrace he shouted from down below to the tailor, who was nervously awaiting him at the edge of the low mall: "Severino, all your cloth has been stolen. . . . They found the hiding-place and stole all your materials." I was quite close to Severino and at these words I saw him stagger as though someone had hit him over the head with a stick. In the meantime the boy had come up onto the terrace; and Severino, agitated and breathless, seized hold of him by the front of his shirt and with eyes starting out of his head stammered: "It can't be. What are you talking about? The cloth? My materials? Stolen? It can't be. Who stole them?" "I don't know," replied the boy. All the evacuees had run up, and they gathered round him as Severino waved his arms, rolled his eyes and struck his hand against his forehead and pulled at his hair. Filippo tried to calm him down, saying: "Don't distress yourself. It may only be a rumor." "Rumor, indeed!" answered the boy. "I saw it myself, with my own eyes—the wall pulled down and the hiding place empty." Severino waved his hand in the air in a gesture of despair, as though he wished to express his anger with Heaven; then he rushed off down the path and disappeared. We were all deeply impressed by this occurrence: it meant that the war was going on and in fact getting worse, that there was no conscience left and if people were committing robberies now, they would no doubt soon be committing murders too. Somebody said to Filippo, who was criticizing what had happened more energetically than anyone and blaming Severino for not having taken adequate precautions; "You be careful, Filippo, you who have put your belongings behind the wall in your tenant's house, be careful the same thing doesn't happen to you." Remembering the way in which Concetta and Vincenzo had talked, I said to myself that the man was quite right: that was another wall which might at any moment be knocked down. But Filippo, full of assurance, shook his head confidently: "My tenant and I are 'San Giovanni' to each other," he said. "I held his son at his christening and he held my daughter at hers. Don't you know that *San Giovanni non Vuole inganni?*—that we can trust each other absolutely?" I thought then that it's all very well being clever, as Filippo imagined he was, but there's always some point or other in a man's life where he's a fool; for it seemed to me that to believe in "San Giovanni" in the case of Concetta and Vincenzo was an utter folly; charming, but a folly nevertheless. I said nothing, not wanting to make him suspicious. All the more so since someone else had already brought up the subject and it had served no purpose at all.

That same evening Severino came up again from the valley, covered in dust, defeated and sad. He had been into the town and had found the wall broken down and the hiding place empty. They had taken everything and he was ruined; he said it might have been either Germans or Italians but he believed it had been Italians; in fact—from what he had been able to gather by questioning the few people who had remained in the town—it had probably been the Fascists. After he had said these things he fell silent, sitting hunched up on a chair in front of the door of Filippo's house, more yellow and more black than usual, hugging the back of the chair and looking with his one eye down toward Fondi where his cloth had been stolen, while his other eye seemed to be winking in an understanding way; and perhaps this was the saddest thing of all because people generally wink when they feel cheerful whereas he was very near killing himself out of despair. From time to time he shook his head and repeated in a low voice: "My cloth. . . . I've nothing left. . . . They've taken away everything," and then he would pass his hand over his brow, as though he were unable to persuade himself that it was true. Finally he said: "I've become old in a single day," and went off to his own cottage, refusing an invitation to stay to supper with Filippo, who was trying to soothe and comfort.

Next day it was evident that he was still thinking about his cloth and wondering how he could recover it. He was sure it had been stolen by local people; he was almost sure that it was the Fascists, or rather those who were now called Fascists and who had been known in the valley as vagabonds and desperadoes. These vagabonds, immediately on the return of Fascism, had enrolled themselves in the militia with the sole purpose of sponging on the local inhabitants for food and other good things of life, and the population was left completely at their mercy. Severino was determined to discover his missing cloth, and went down to the valley every day or so, returning in the evening tired, dusty and empty handed but more determined than ever. This determination changed his entire manner, he was silent all the time, with glittering eyes and an air of concentration, and a nerve that never ceased twitching under the tight-drawn skin of his jaw. If anyone asked him what he did at Fondi, he would answer: "I go hunting"—by which he meant that he went hunting for his cloth and for the people who had stolen it. Gradually, from Severino's conversations with Filippo, I came to understand that these Fascists who, according to him, had stolen his cloth, had barricaded themselves in a farm house in the neighborhood known as Uomo Morto. There were a dozen of them, and they had carried to this house quantities of provisions which they extorted from the peasants, and there they ate and drank and enjoyed themselves, waited on hand and foot by some strumpets who had previously been servants or work-girls. At night these Fascists would leave the farmhouse and go into the town, and visit, one by one, the deserted houses of evacuees, stealing anything that was left in such houses and knocking on each wall and floor with their rifles to see if there were any hiding-places These Fascists were armed with tommy guns, bombs and daggers, and they felt quite safe because in the whole valley there were no *carabinieri* left—they had all run away or been arrested by the Germans some time ago—nor any police or civil authorities. There was, it is true, one municipal inspector left. But he was a poor man, burdened with the responsibility of a large family, and he went around ragged and hungry from one farm to another, imploring the help of the peasants, who would give him a piece of bread or an egg. There was no law left, and the German military police, who were distinguished from the other soldiers by a kind of band which they wore across their chests, were the only people to maintain the law; but it was *their* law, not our own Italian law, and—for us at any rate—it was law only in a manner of speaking, for it appeared to have been made with the express purpose of permitting them to comb out men for forced labor, to steal property and to commit all kinds of arrogant actions. To give you an idea of the sort of thing that used to happen at that period, let me tell you about a peasant from a place not so very far from Sant'Eufemia who one morning stabbed his nephew, a boy of eighteen, and then let him die from loss of blood in the vineyard. This happened at ten in the morning. At five o'clock on the same day, the murderer went to a black market butcher's shop to buy a pound of meat. The crime was already known; everyone knew about it, in fact, but no one dared say anything to him: it was his affair, and besides, everyone was a little frightened. However one woman remarked: "How do you have the face to do it? You've killed your nephew and now you come here calmly to buy meat." And he answered: "That concerns whom it may. No one's going to arrest me because there's no law nowadays and everyone does as he likes." And he was right, for they did not arrest him and he buried his nephew under a fig-tree and continued to go about unmolested.

Severino, then, decided to take the law into his own hands, seeing that public justice no longer existed. I do not know what arrangements he made during those expeditions to Fondi; but suddenly, one morning, a young peasant arrived, his tongue hanging out of his mouth from having run so hard uphill, and cried out that Severino was coming up with some Germans and that the Germans were going to get back his cloth for him. All the evacuees came out of their cottages, and Rosetta and I too, and there must have been about twenty of us on the terrace watching the path along which Severino would appear with the Germans. Everyone was saying how clever and sensible Severino had been, and that after all it was true that the Germans now held the authority, and they were not vagabonds and crooks like the Fascists, and that not only would they get back his cloth for him but would punish the Fascists as well. Filippo was the one who strove hardest in favor of the Germans. "They're serious people," he said, "and they do everything seriously, whether it's war or peace or business. Severino has done right to appeal to them. The Germans are not like us Italians, lawless and undisciplined . . . They cultivate discipline, and in time of war stealing is an act contrary to discipline. Severino went straight to the kernel of the question. Who holds the authority in Italy today? The Germans. So it's to the Germans one must appeal." Filippo thought all this aloud, strutting up and down and smoothing his mustaches. It was quite obvious that he was thinking about his own belongings concealed in the house of his tenant; and that he was pleased at the prospect of Severino getting his cloth back and of the thieves being punished because he also had property concealed and he also was afraid of being robbed.

All this time we were watching the path, and at last Severino came into sight, but instead of the armed patrol of Germans there was only one single German to be seen, and he a mere ordinary soldier, not one of the military police. When they reached the level of the terrace, Severino, proud and pleased, introduced him to us by the name of Hans, which in German, I believe, means Giovanni; and they all gathered round him with hands outstretched, but Hans did not shake hands with anybody; he merely gave a military salute, clicking his heels, with his hand to his cap, as though to put a distance between himself and the evacuees. This Hans was a small, slight, fairish man with wide hips like a woman and a white, rather puffy face. He had two or three large scars across his cheek, and when somebody asked him where he had got them he answered curtly: "Stalingrad." Owing to these wounds, his soft, sort of squashy face looked like a peach or an apple that has fallen off the tree onto the ground. It lies there all bruised and cut, and then when you split it open you see that it is half-decayed inside. His eyes were blue but not beautiful; their color was washy, inexpressive, too pale, as though they were made of glass. In the meantime Severino, very proud of himself, was explaining that he had struck up a friendship with this man Hans because it so happened that Hans in peacetime was also a tailor. And so, both of them being tailors, they had understood one another, and he had told Hans the story of the robbery and Hans had promised to get back the cloth for him. To sum it all up, he was not one of the police, he was not a number of Germans but one single German; and, furthermore, it was not an official, but a private, matter, a thing between friends who were of the same trade, being both of them tailors. The German, however, was in uniform, with a tommy gun slung across his shoulders, and his behavior was that of a German soldier; and they all vied with one another to flatter him. One of them asked him how long the war would go on, another asked him about Russia, someone else wanted to know whether the English would start a battle, someone else asked whether it would not more probably be the Germans who did so. The more questions people asked him, the more swollen with importance did Hans become, like a flabby balloon when someone blows it up. He said the war would last only a short time now because the Germans had secret weapons; he said that the Russians fought well but the Germans fought betters; he said that the Germans would battle the English and throw them back into the sea. In short, he commanded respect; and in the end Filippo decided to invite him, and Severino too, to lunch in his cottage.

I myself was also present at this lunch. I had already had something to eat, but I was curious to see this German, the first to turn up at Sant'Eufemia. They had already reached the fruit when I went in; and the whole of Filippo's family was assembled —with the exception, however, of Michele, who hated the Germans and who, shortly before, while Hans was talking importantly of the great victory which the Germans were soon going to win over the English, had glared at him in a dark and threatening manner, as though he would have liked to jump on him and pummel him with his fists. Now, thanks partly to the wine he had drunk, the German had become confidential. He kept slapping Severino on the shoulder and repeating that they were both tailors and that they were friends for life and that he would get back Severino's cloth for him. Then he took out his wallet, and from it a photograph in which there was to be seen a woman twice as tall and twice as big as himself, with a good-natured face, and said that she was his wife. Then they started talking about the war again, and Hans began again: "We make an offensive and throw the English into the sea." Filippo, whose aim was to flatter him and keep him in a good temper, agreed enthusiastically: "Why of course, certainly. We'll throw them into the sea, the whole lot of them. Murderers." But the German retorted: "No, murderers no, brave men, soldiers." "Yes," said Filippo hurriedly, "they're brave soldiers, of course; we know they're brave soldiers." But the German answered: "You admire English soldiers . . . You are traitors." "Who's admiring them?" asked Filippo, frightened, "didn't I say they were murderers?" But the German was not content. "Murderers no, brave soldiers," he said; "but traitors like you, who admire the English—*kaputt*," and he made the gesture of cutting a throat. He wanted it both ways, in fact, and nothing would please him and we all became frightened because he seemed to have turned nasty. Then he said to Serverino: "Why not at the front—you? We Germans, we fight, and you Italians, you stay here. You—at the front." Severino, too, was now frightened, and replied: "I was rejected . . . a weak chest." And he touched his chest, and it was true, he had been very ill and it was even said that he had only one lung. The German, however, thoroughly nasty by now, took him by the arm and said: "You come with me then, quickly now, to the front." And he actually made as if to rise and drag him off. Severino had turned white and was making an unsuccessful effort to smile, and everyone was in dismay and I myself so frightened that my heart was jumping in my chest. The German was pulling Severino by the arm and he was trying to resist, clinging to Filippo, who was also terrified. Then the German burst out laughing and said: "Friends . . . friends. . . . You tailor, me tailor. . . . You have your cloth back and get rich. I go to the front and fight and die." And, still laughing, he started slapping him on the shoulder again. The whole scene had a strange effect upon me, it was like finding yourself face to face with a wild beast which at one moment purrs and the next moment shows its teeth, and you don't know what its intentions are or how to take it. It seemed to me that Severino was deluding himself, like people who say: "This animal knows me . . . It will never bite *me*." And it will be seen that I was not wrong.

After this scene, the German became kindly disposed and drank a great deal more wine and slapped Severino on the shoulder. Severino's fear gradually evaporated and at a moment when the German's attention was distracted he said to Filippo: "I shall get my cloth back *this very day* . . . you'll see. A short time afterward, the German rose from the table and buckled on his belt (he had taken it off when he sat down), pointing out to us, in a joking way, that owing to the large amount he had eaten he had had to buckle it one hole less tightly than before. Then he said to Severino: "We go down, you come back here with your cloth." Severino got up, the German gave a military salute, clicking his heels, and then strutted off with Severino along the path that led across the *macere* down to the valley. Filippo, who had come out with the others to watch them as they went, expressed the feelings of everyone when he finally said: "Severino trusts that German . . . I wouldn't be quite so trustful myself, if I were him."

We kept a lookout for Severino all that afternoon and part of the night and still he did not come. Next day we went to the cottage in which Severino lived with his family and found his wife weeping in the dark, with the little girl on her knee. With her was an old peasant woman who was spinning wool with distaff and spindle and repeating from time to time, as she pulled the thread: "Don't cry, child . . . Severino will be back soon and everything will be all right." But the wife shook her head and replied: "I know he won't come back . . . I knew it within an hour of his going away." We tried to comfort her but she went on weeping and saying it was all her fault because Severino had done all this for her sake and the little girl's, so that they might be rich and comfortable, and she ought to have stopped him and prevented him from buying that unlucky cloth. There was nothing, alas, to be said, for Severino did not come back; and this was a hard fact, and all the kind words in the world are worth nothing in face of a hard fact. We stayed with her all day, saying first one thing and then another, making every possible kind of suggestion to explain Severino's disappearance; but she kept on weeping and repeating that he would never come back. Next day, the second day after Severino's disappearance, we went again to the cottage but found neither her nor the child: at dawn she had taken the child on her shoulder and gone down to the valley to see what had happened.

For some days we heard nothing more either of Severino or of his wife. In the end, Filippo—who, in his own way, was fond of Severino—determined to find out what had happened and sent someone to fetch Nicola, an old peasant who had given up working in the fields and usually spent the day with the children. He said he wanted him to go and get news of Severino, and he also told him he must go to the place known as Uomo Morto, where those Fascists who had stolen the cloth had barricaded themselves in a farmhouse. At first the old man refused to go, but Filippo promised him three hundred lire, and the old man, who would have gone into a blazing furnace for money, went off to get his donkey ready. He said that he would spend the night with some relations and return the next day, and he put a loaf and some cheese in his knapsack. We waved to him as he went off, sitting erect in the saddle, his little old black hat on his head, his pipe in his mouth and his legs hanging down stiffly on each side, in their sandals and white cloth wrappings. Filippo advised him to get into touch with a man known as Il Tonto, the Dolt, he was the least bad of the whole lot of Fascists. The old man said he would do so, and rode away.

The day passed and half the following day, and then toward twilight the donkey appeared from the terrace below, led by the old man and with Il Tonto in the saddle. They came up and Il Tonto dismounted: he was a man with a dark, thin, unshaven face, melacholy, deep-set eyes, and a long nose that drooped almost into his mouth. Everyone gathered round him, and Il Tonto looked embarrassed and was silent. Old Nicola took the ass by the bridle and said: "The German took the cloth himself and sent off Severino to work on the fortifications at the front—that's what happened." After flinging these words at us he went off to feed his donkey.

We were all terrified. Il Tonto was standing to one side, ill at ease, and Filippo said to him angrily: "And you—what have you come up here for?" Il Tonto stepped forward and said, in a very humble manner: "Filippo, you mustn't think hardly of me. I came here just in order to please you. I wanted to describe how it all happened, so that you shouldn't think it was we who did it." Everyone looked at him with dislike, yet everyone wanted to know what had happened, and in the end Filippo—though much against his will—invited him to come and drink some wine in his cottage. Il Tonto accepted, with all the rest of us following behind in a kind of procession. Inside the room Il Tonto sat down on a sack of beans and Filippo handed him the wine, standing in front of him, while all the rest of us assembled near the door, also standing. Il Tonto drank some wine calmly and then said: "It's no use denying it, we *did* take the cloth. In these times, Filippo, each man for himself and God help us all. Severino thought he had hidden it well, but several of us knew where it was and we thought: if it's not us it'll be the Germans, they won't take long to spy out the place, so we might as well take the stuff. Besides, what's a man to do, Filippo?"—and he clasped his hands together and looked at us—"We have families too, and in these times every man has to think first of all of his family and of other things afterward. I'm not saying we did right, I'm saying we acted out of necessity. You, Filippo, you're a shopkeeper, Severino's a tailor, and we—we get along somehow. . . . But Severino did wrong to go to the Germans, who had nothing to do with it. Why, hell take it, Filippo, if Severino hadn't turned nasty we might have been able to come to some agreement; we might even have sold the cloth and shared the profit—or anyhow we could have made him a present. After all, as neighbors we should have got together somehow. But instead of that, Severino turned nasty, and what happened, happened. That blasted German came along, the Severino said all sorts of things and then the German pointed his tommy gun at us and said he had to search the place. We couldn't do anything because in a way we depend on the Germans. The German found the cloth and loaded it on a truck and off he went with Severino, who shouted to us as he drove away: 'There's justice in this world, after all.' Fine justice indeed. You know what that German did? A few miles further on they met another truck full of Italians who had been rounded up to be sent to work on the fortifications at the front. So he stopped his truck and forced Severino to get into the other truck. And so Severino, instead of getting back his cloth, has been sent to the front; and the German, who is a tailor too, will send the cloth, a small amount at a time, to Germany, where he will make use of it to open a tailor's shop in defiance of Severino and all of us. Now, Filippo, what I say is, why bring in the Germans? When two people quarrel it's the looker-on who gets the best of it: that's what has happened, and I swear I'm telling you the truth."

After this speech Filippo and all of us remained silent; partly because Il Tonto had mentioned this matter of rounding up men. We had heard of this, but never so clearly and so quietly, as though it were a normal thing. Finally Filippo plucked up courage and asked what these round-ups were. Il Tonto replied indifferently: "The Germans go round with lorries and carry off all the able-bodied men and send them to the front either at Cassino or Gaeta to strengthen the defenses." "And how do they treat them?" Il Tonto shrugged his shoulders. "Well, plenty of work, army huts, and not much to eat. It's well known how the Germans treat people who aren't Germans." We were all silent but Filippo persisted: "They take the men who stay down in the plain; but the evacuees, the ones who are up in the mountains, they don't take them, do they?" Il Tonto again shrugged his shoulders. "Don't trust the Germans. It's like eating an artichoke: they eat the leaves one by one. First it's the people who live down in the plain, soon it'll be the ones in the mountains." By this time everyone had forgotten Severino; they were all frightened and each man was thinking of himself. Filippo asked: "But how d'you know about this?" "I know about this," answered Il Tonto, "because I have to do with the Germans all day long. Mind what I say, either get into the militia like us or else hide yourself well—really well, I mean. Otherwise the Germans will catch you one after another." Then he added a few explanations. The Germans were combing out the whole plain, carrying off all able-bodied men. In the second stage they would start on the mountains, and would operate in this way: very early in the morning, while it was still dark, a company of soldiers would climb to the highest ridge of a mountain and then, toward noon, they would start coming down again, spreading out across the whole width of the slope, in such a way that all those who happened to be half way down, like us, would be caught like so many fishes in a net. "They think of everything," remarked someone at this point, in a voice full of fear. Il Tonto had now recovered himself and had returned to his usual impudent manner. He tried to ingratiate himself with Filippo, whom he knew to have more money than the others. "How about you and me coming to an agreement?" he suggested; "I could put in a word for your son with the German captain. I know him well." Filippo, now that he was really frightened, might have agreed to discuss the matter with Il Tonto, but quite unexpectedly Michele stepped forward and said in a harsh voice to Il Tonto: "What are you waiting for? Why don't you go?" Everyone fell silent in astonishment, especially as Il Tonto was armed with hand grenades and a rifle and Michele had no arms at all. But Il Tonto, for some reason, was subdued by Michele's tone. Hesitatingly, he said: "Oh well, if that's how it is, you can manage for yourselves. . . I'm off." Then he got up and went out of the cottage. Everyone followed him; and Michele shouted to him from the top of the terrace, before he disappeared: "And instead of going around offering your services, look after your own affairs. One of these days the Germans will take your rifle away from you and send you to work like Severino." Il Tonto turned round and made a sign at him with his fingers held up like a pair of horns, to avert ill luck. We never saw him again.

After Il Tonto had gone we went with Michele to our hut. Rosetta and I spoke of how sorry we were for poor Severino, who had lost his cloth and then his freedom as well. Michele, gloomy and silent, with head bowed, shrugged his shoulders and said: "It's all right for him." "How can you say such a thing?" I protested. "That poor man is ruined, and now he may even lose his life too." For a moment Michele said nothing, then he cried: "Until they've lost everything, they won't understand anything. They've got to lose everything and suffer and weep tears of blood. Only then will they grow up." "But Severino didn't do it for his own interest at all. He did it for the sake of his family," I objected. He started laughing disagreeably. "His family!" he exclaimed. "His family! The grand justification for every kind of meanness in this country! Well, so much the worse for his family!"

Michele—since I am on the subject—was really an odd character. Two days after the final disappearance of Severino I was talking to him about one thing and another and the remark was made that, now winter had come and it became dark so early, it was difficult to know what to do. Michele said that if we wished he would read a book to us. Pleased with the idea, we accepted, although we were not in the habit of reading books, as I think I have already explained; but in a situation like that even books might provide some distraction. Thinking that he intended to read us a novel, I remember saying: "What will it be? A love story?" He answered with a smile: "That's right, you've hit the nail on the head; that's just what it is, a love story." It was decided that Michele should read to us after supper—that is, at the time in the evening when one did not know what to do. I recall the scene extremely well, perhaps because Michele on that occasion revealed another aspect of his character. I can see the two of us and Paride's family sitting on the tree stumps and benches round the dying fire, with a little oil lamp hanging up behind Michele so that he could see to read. The hut was dark and gloomy indeed; from the ceiling of dry branches hung black trails of soot that quivered lightly at every breath, and at the farthest end of the hut, almost swallowed up in the shadows, sat Paride's mother, looking like the witch of Benevento, so old and wrinkled was she, ceaselessly spinning wool with her distaff and spindle. Rosetta and I were pleased to have the reading; not so much so Paride and his family, for after working all day long they could hardly keep awake in the evening and usually went to bed at once. The children were already asleep, crouching down half on top of their mothers.

Michele took a little book from his pocket and said: "Cesira wanted a love story and that's just exactly what I'm going to read." One of the women, more out of politeness than because she was genuinely interested, asked if it was a thing that had really happened or if it had been invented; and he replied that possibly it had been invented; but it was just as though it had really happened. He opened the little book, adjusted his spectacles on his nose, and announced that he was going to read some episodes in the life of Jesus, from the Gospel. We were all a little disappointed for we had expected a real romance, besides, everything to do with religion always seems rather boring, perhaps because we carry out our religious activities more from duty than pleasure. Paride, interpreting the general feeling, remarked that we all knew the life of Jesus and therefore the reading would not reveal anything new to us. Rosetta said nothing, but later when we were back in our own room she remarked simply: "If he does not believe in Jesus, why doesn't he leave him alone?" She spoke as if shocked but not hostile, for she liked Michele although she did not understand him.

Michele's only reply to Paride's words was to say, with a smile: "Are you quite sure?"; then he announced that he would read the episode of Lazarus, adding: "Do you remember it?" Now we had all heard of this Lazarus; but, at Michele's question, we realized that we did not really know who he was nor what he had done. Rosetta knew, but again she kept silent. "You see," said Michele, in a characteristic tone of quiet triumph, "you said you knew the life of Jesus and then you don't even know who Lazarus was. And yet this episode is shown, like so many others, in the paintings of the Passion that you see in churches. You can even see it in the church at Fondi." Paride, thinking perhaps that these words contained a reproof for himself, remarked:

"You know that to go to church down in the valley means losing a whole day?. . . We have to work and we can't afford to lose a whole day even to go to church." Michele said nothing and began to read.

As I am sure that the episode of Lazarus is well known to all those who are likely to read these reminiscences, I will not copy it down here, especially as Michele read it out without adding anything to it; as for those who do not know it, they can go and read it in the Gospel. I will merely observe that the further Michele progressed in his reading, the more the faces of the peasants around him expressed indifference and disappointment. They had expected a nice love story; instead of which Michele was reading them the story of a miracle which—at least, as far as I could gather—they did not believe, any more than Michele himself believed in it. But there was a difference. They were bored—so much so that two of the women started chattering together again and quietly laughing, and the third one did nothing but yawn, and Paride himself, who seemed the most attentive of all, displayed an expression of obtuseness and insensibility. The difference was that Michele appeared to be truly moved by this miracle in which he did not believe. In fact, when he came to the sentence: "And Jesus said, I am the resurrection and the life," he broke off for a moment and could not go on because he was crying. I realized he was crying because of what he was reading and that it was all related in some way to our present situation, but one of the bored women inquired anxiously: "Is the smoke troubling you, Michele? There's always too much smoke in here. . . . But of course this is only a hut." This woman was anxious to make excuses to Michele for the smoke, but he abruptly wiped away his tears and jumped up and cried: "Smoke indeed! Hut! That has nothing to do with it! I won't read to you any more because you people don't understand. . . and it's no use trying to make people understand who will never be able to understand. But remember this, now: each one of you is Lazarus. . . and in reading the story of Lazarus I was speaking of *you*, of all of you. . . of you, Paride, of you, Luisa, of you,

Cesira, of you, Rosetta, and of myself too, and of my father and of that scoundrel Il Tonto and of Severino with his cloth and of the evacuees up here and of the Germans and the Fascists down in the valley, of everybody, in fact. You are all dead, we are all dead and we think we're alive. As long as we think we're alive because we have our possessions, our fears, our trifling affairs, our families, our children, we shall be dead. Only on the day when we realize that we're dead, utterly dead, putrefied, decomposed, that we stink of corruption from a mile away, only then shall we begin to be just barely alive. . . Goodnight." He jumped up, upsetting and putting out the oil lamp and left the hut, banging the door behind him. We were left in darkness, stupefied. Finally Paride, after rummaging about, succeeded in finding the lamp and re-lighting it. But no one had any desire to discuss Michele's outburst; Paride merely said, with the embarrassed, sullen air of the peasant who thinks he is being clever: "Well, well, Michele's tongue runs on very fast. He's the son of gentlefolks, he's not a peasant." I believe the women thought likewise: all this sort of thing was the concern of gentlefolks who don't dig or earn their living by the sweat of their brow. So we bid each other goodnight and went off to bed. Michele, next day, pretended not to remember the scene, nor did he ever suggest reading aloud to us again.

That occasion confirmed the opinion I had formed when Michele had told us that as a boy he had seriously thought of becoming a priest. It seemed to me that for all his anti-religious speeches, Michele was much more like a priest than an ordinary man such as Filippo or one of the other evacuees. That outburst to which he had given vent when he realized that the peasants did not understand him, were not listening to him, and were also bored, might easily have been uttered with only a few changes by some country priest during his Sunday sermon, on noticing, as he waved his arms about in the pulpit, that his parishioners below him had ceased to pay him any attention. It was the outburst, in short, of a priest who considers everyone else as a sinner to be instructed and led back to the straight path, not that of a man who holds himself to be like other men.

To finish my account of Michele's character, I wish to tell of one other incident. As I have mentioned, he never talked of women or of love and appeared never to have had any experience in that field. Not so much for lack of opportunity but because in this respect he was different from other young men of his age—as will be seen from what I am about to relate. The incident was as follows. Rosetta had a habit of taking off all her clothes and washing herself naked every morning as soon as she got out of bed. I would go outside the hut, throw the bucket down to the bottom of the well, draw it up full of water and then hand it to her; and she would pour half of it over her head, then soap her body all over, and then pour the other half over herself. She was extremely clean, was Rosetta; and the first thing she wanted me to buy from the peasants, when we reached Sant'Eufemia was some of their homemade soap; and she went on washing herself in this manner even in the middle of winter, when we were having real mountain cold up there and the water in the well was frozen in the morning and the bucket bounced off the ice before breaking it and the rope cut my hands, and the few times I tried to follow Rosetta's example and pour a bucket of water over my head it took my breath away and left me open-mouthed and almost fainting. Well, one morning Rosetta had been washing as usual and was standing beside the bed, her feet on a small plank of wood so as not to get dirty on the muddy floor, rubbing herself hard with a towel. Rosetta's body was far more robust than you would ever have expected from looking at her gentle, delicate face, with its big eyes, its rather long nose and full mouth jutting out a little over the curved-back chin which made her look slightly like a little sheep. Her bosom was not really big, but as well-developed as that of a fully grown woman who has already been a mother; it was white and prominent, as though full of milk, with dark nipples that turned upwards as if seeking the mouth of a baby she had brought into the world. Her belly, on the other hand, was that of a virgin girl, smooth, flat, almost hollow, so that the hair between her strong, rounded thighs stuck out, curly and thick, looking like a little pin cushion. From behind, too, she was really beautiful; she looked just like a statue, one of those white marble ones that you see in the public gardens in Rome: her shoulders full and rounded, her back long, and in the lower part of her back a deep curved hollow, such as you see in a young mare, throwing into full relief her round, white, muscular buttocks, so lovely, so clean that you wanted to devour them with kisses just as when she was two years old. Indeed I always thought that any man who *was* a man, on seeing my Rosetta standing naked, rubbing the hollow of her back with a cloth and at each stroke making her splendid firm, high breasts tremble slightly—such a man, I say, ought at least to be disturbed at the sight and to go red or pale, according to his temperament. And this because, even if a man's mind is set on other things, the moment a woman shows herself naked his thoughts all fly away like so many sparrows out of a tree if you fire off a gun; and nothing is left but the troubled excitement of the male, face to face with the female. Now one morning, when Rosetta was standing naked, drying herself in a corner of the room, Michele came to see us unexpectedly and pushed the door half open, without knocking. I was sitting near the threhold and could easily have told him of his mistake and said: "No, don't come in, Rosetta's washing." But I must confess that I was not exactly displeased at his coming in so unexpectedly, because a mother always takes pride in her daughter, and at that moment my vanity as a mother was stronger than my surprise or even my disapproval. "He'll see her undressed," I said to myself: "no harm in that, especially as he didn't do it on purpose. He'll see how beautiful my Rosetta is." With these thoughts in my head, I kept silent; and he pushed the door wide open and found himself right in front of Rosetta, who now sought—quite in vain—to cover herself with the towel. He paused for a moment in uncertainty, almost annoyed at seeing Rosetta naked; then he turned to me and said hurriedly that I must excuse him, perhaps he had come too early. In any case, he wanted to tell us the important news that he had just that moment heard from a young man from Pontecorvo who went round the mountain districts selling tobacco: the Russians had launched a big offensive against the Germans and the latter were retiring all along the front. Then he added that he wanted to speak to us and would see us later, and went away. That same day I contrived to talk to him alone, and said to him with a smile: "Well, Michele, it's really true then, you're not made like other young men of your age?" His face clouded and he asked: "Why is that?" "You had a pretty girl like Rosetta," I said, "naked, right under your eyes, and all you thought about was the Russians and the Germans and the war, and indeed, you never even saw her, so to speak." He was embarrassed and in fact almost angry, and said: "What nonsense you talk! I'm surprised that you, her mother, should speak in that way." "Even a black beetle," I said to him, "is beautiful in its mother's eyes—didn't you know that, Michele? Anyhow, what's the trouble? *I* didn't tell you to come this morning and burst in without knocking. But, once you had come in, possibly I might have been angry if you had looked too intently at Rosetta—though in real truth, just because I am her mother, it wouldn't have displeased me at all. But there was nothing like that: you never even saw her." He smiled in a forced kind of way, and then said: "For me those things don't exist." And that was the first and last time I ever spoke to him about such things.

Chapter 5

SOON AFTER the visit of Il Tonto it began to rain. For the whole of October the weather had been brilliant, the sky serene, the air fresh, clear and windless. With such weather, during those endless days that we spent up there, we had at least had the amusement of going for walks or simply sitting in the open looking at the wide view toward Fondi. But one morning the weather changed quickly. As we got up we were aware that it was warmer, and then, when we looked in the direction of the coast, we saw that the sky was overcast and that great masses of dark, swollen clouds hung suspended over the grey sea as over a boiling pot. By the end of the morning these clouds had invaded the whole sky, impelled by a lazy, moist wind which was also coming from the sea. The evacuees, who understood these matters because they had been born in the district, told us that these clouds meant rain and that the rain would go on until the *scirocco*, blowing in from the sea, was replaced by the *tramontana*, coming from the mountains. And indeed it was so: towards midday the first drops began falling and we retreated into our hut to wait till it stopped. But it did not stop: it rained all that day and all night and then next day the seacoast looked more dingy than ever and the entire sky was a tangle of dark clouds and the mountains were hooded with clouds and up from the valley, with the gusts of the moist wind, came other clouds swollen with rain. After a brief pause it started raining again and from then onward, for more than a month it rained all the time, day and night.

For people who live in towns, rain does not matter. If you go out, you walk on a pavement or an asphalt road, under an umbrella; if you stay at home, you move about on wooden or marble floors. But up at Sant'Eufemia, on the *macera,* among the huts, the rain was truly a punishment from Heaven. We stayed all day in the hut, in that dark room with its sloping roof, the door open because there were no windows, and we watched the rain falling and forming, as it fell, a sort of wet, steamy curtain in front of the door. I would be sitting on the bed and Rosetta on the chair that I had managed to get from Paride by paying him for the hire of it. We watched the rain like a pair of idiots, and if we spoke at all it was of the rain and the discomforts it brought with it. Going out was not to be thought of: we left the hut only when absolutely necessary; to gather wood or in order to satisfy the needs of nature. And at this point—although the subject is not a very pleasant one—I must state that anyone who has not led that sort of life and who lives in a town where each house has its own lavatory and even, perhaps, its bathroom, cannot possibly know what it is to live in a place where no kind of latrine exists. We had to go out along the terrace and there, lifting up our skirts, squat down behind a hedge, just like animals. Toilet paper there was none, naturally, nor even newspapers or such like; and so we used the leaves of a fig tree that stood just outside, near the hut, and cleaned ourselves with them. With the coming of the rain all this became much more difficult and disagreeable: to go out through fields, plunging up to the ankles in mud, and then, in the pouring rain, to pull up one's skirt and feel the rain beating cold and repellent on one's bare bottom, and then to rub oneself with a wet, clammy fig leaf—these are things that I would not wish for anyone, even my worst enemy. The rain brought discomfort not only out of doors but indoors as well: the mud was such that in the mornings, when we got out of bed, we had to hop here and there, like frogs, on large stones placed especially for the purpose.

The rain penetrated everywhere with a wetness not to be described; and whatever we did, even if we made the smallest movement, we at once discovered that we were splashed with mud, that we had mud on our skirts or our legs or somewhere. Mud on the ground and rain in the sky. Paride and his family were accustomed to it, and comforted themselves by saying that this rain was a normal thing and was needed and that it came back each year and there was nothing to be done but wait for it to stop. But for us two it was a positive torment, worse than anything we had hitherto experienced.

The worst effect of this rain, as we finally came to know, was that, the English had come to a halt at the Garigliano, and there was no further word of their advancing. And naturally, as soon as the English gave up the idea of advancing, the Germans decided not to retire any further and to entrench themselves where they were. I understand nothing about wars and battles; I only know that, on one of those rainy mornings a peasant arrived, bringing with him a large sheet of printed paper: it was an order which the Germans had put up in all inhabited localities. Michele read it and explained to us what it contained: German headquarters had decided to evacuate the entire area between the sea and the mountains, including the locality in which we were living and which was in fact mentioned in the order. The day on which the evacuation of each locality was to take place was given. People were not to take any suitcases or bags with them, merely a small quantity of food. They had, in short, to abandon houses, huts, livestock, agricultural implements, furniture and all other possessions, take up their children in their arms and go, by almost impassable muletracks, away over the mountains, in the rain, back and back toward Rome. And naturally the Germans, the miserable bastards, threatened the usual penalties for those who did not obey: arrest, confiscation, deportation, shooting. Our district was detailed for complete evacuation within two days. In four days the whole area had to be left empty so that the Germans and the English could have more room to kill each other at their leisure.

Filippo and the other evacuees and the peasants too had become accustomed by this time to considering the Germans as the sole remaining authority in Italy; and so their first reaction was not so much to rebel as to give themselves over to despair: the German authorities demanded something impossible, yet, nevertheless, they were the authorities and there was no other authority apart from them: therefore one must obey, or . . . or . . . they themselves did not know what could be done. The evacuees, who had already left their houses at Fondi and knew what it meant to be fugitives, despaired at the prospect of fleeing yet again over mountain mule tracks, at that icy time of year, in rain that never ceased to fall from morning till night, with mud that made it impossible to walk even to the far end of the terrace, let alone to Rome, with no fixed direction, no guide, no exact place to go to. The women wept, the men cursed and swore or sat silent and dejected. As for the peasants such as Paride and the other families, all of them people who had toiled their whole lives, creating the terraces with their own hands, cultivating them, building cottages and huts—they were in a state beyond despair: they were stupefied; they scarcely believed it. Some kept repeating: "Wherever shall we go?"; some wanted the decree read over to them again, word by word; some of them, after it had been read to them, said: "It's impossible, it can't be so." They did not understand that for the Germans the impossible did not exist, especially in the case of things which were to be done at other people's expense. Paride's sister-in-law, Anita, whose husband was in Russia and who had three little children, expressed the general feeling when she suddenly declared, without vehemence: "Rather than leave here, I shall first kill my children and then myself." And I realized that she said this because she was aware that to take to the mule tracks in the mountains, in the middle of winter, with three small children, meant condemning them to death, and so she might just as well kill them at once: she would merely be anticipating.

The only one who did not lose his head on this occasion was Michele; and this, I believe, was due to the fact that he had never recognized the authority of the Germans, considering them, as he often said, to be robbers, gangsters and crooks who were, for the moment, in the stronger position because they had the weapons and made use of them. After he had read the proclamation from German headquarters, he merely gave a sarcastic laugh and said: "Anyone who said that the Germans and the English are all the same, and that one's as good as the other, let him step forward now." No one breathed a word; least of all Filippo, his father, at whom these words were aimed. We were all assembled in the hut, round the fire, in the evening, and Paride said: "You may laugh, but for us this means death. We have our homes here, our livestock, our belongings, everything we possess; if we go away, what will happen to all these things?" Michele, as I think I have already made clear, was a curious type, good-hearted but at the same time hard, generous, if you like, but cruel as well. He started laughing again and said: "Oh well, you'll lose everything and I daresay you'll die into the bargain. What is there strange about that? What about the Poles, the French, the Czechs and everybody who's come under the German occupation—haven't they lost everything, including their lives? Now it's the turn of us Italians. As long as it happened to other people, no one found fault with it. But now it's our turn; first one and then the other." Everyone was thrown into consternation by these words, most of all Filippo, who was trembling so violently that he was more or less incapable of thinking or speaking coherently. "You're always making jokes," he said, "but this isn't a time for joking." "But," said Michele, "why should it matter to you? Haven't you always said that, as far as you're concerned, the Germans and the English are just the same thing?" "Anyhow," asked Filippo, "what are we to do?" And I saw that all his wisdom, based on the doctrine of "No fools here," was worth absolutely nothing, not only for us but for himself too. Michele shrugged his shoulders. "Aren't the Germans the masters?" he said. "Go to the Germans and ask *them* what you should do, and they will tell you to do what's written on this sheet of paper." Then Paride made the same kind of remark as Anita's. "I shall take my gun," he said, "and the first German I see, I shall kill him, and then of course they'll kill me. But at least I won't go alone to the other world." Michele laughed and said: "That's fine, now you're beginning to talk sense."

We were all in a state of uncertainty, while Michele went on laughing and the others stared stupidly at the dying fire. At last Michele became serious and said: "Do you want to know what you ought to do?" Everyone looked at him hopefully. "You ought to do nothing at all," Michele went on. "That's all. Behave as if you had never seen this proclamation. Stay where you are, go on with your ordinary lives, ignore the Germans and their orders and their threats. If they really want to evacuate the area they'll have to do it, not by pieces of paper, which are worth nothing, but by force. The English have the force too; but, because of the bad weather, they can't use it and have come to a halt. It's the same with the Germans. If you don't move, they'll think twice before sending soldiers up here, over these mule tracks. And even if they came, they would have to take you away forcibly. Turn a deaf ear, in fact. Then we'll wait and see. Don't you know that the Germans and the Fascists have made proclamations all over the place, and always with the death penalty for anyone who disobeyed? I myself was in the army on July 25th, and I deserted, and then they made a proclamation ordering everyone, on pain of death, to rejoin his own unit. Instead of rejoining my unit, I came here. Do as I did, therefore, and don't move."

It was the simplest and most proper thing to think in that dilemma, but the thought had occurred to nobody because, as I have said, everyone looked upon the Germans as being in supreme authority and everyone was in need of some kind of authority, and besides, when something is printed on a sheet of paper, it seems to be a thing to which no possible objection can be made. Everybody, indeed, went to bed that night somewhat reassured, and with more confidence than they had had when they got up in the morning; and next day no one mentioned the Germans and their evacuation order. It was just as though the word had gone round that it should not be spoken of, that we should all behave as if nothing had happened. A few days went past and then it became clear that Michele had been right, for no one made any move either at Sant'Eufemia or, from what we heard, in other districts; and apparently the Germans changed their minds and gave up the idea of the evacuation.

For how many days did it rain? I should say it must have rained for at least forty days, as it did in the time of the Flood. And besides raining, it was also cold, for we were in the middle of winter, and the unpleasant wind blowing in from the sea in squalls full of dampness and mist was also very cold, and the water that the clouds discharged every day on to the mountains was mixed with snow and ice and pricked your face as though it were full of pins. Our only means of keeping warm was a brazier of embers which we put close against our knees; generally, however, we either stayed in bed, huddled up against each other, or sat in Paride's hut, in darkness, in front of the fire. It usually rained all the morning and then toward midday it would clear, but only partially, with a mass of ugly clouds, ragged and untidy, hanging suspended in the sky as though to recover breath, and the coast looking more dingy and foggy than ever. In the afternoon it would start raining again and go on raining through the evening and the night. We two were always with Michele, and he would talk and we would listen to him. And what did he talk about? About every sort of thing; he liked talking, and his tone was that of a professor or a preacher, and many a time I said to him: "What a pity you didn't become a priest, Michele! You would have preached splendid sermons on Sundays, you know. By this I don't mean to imply that he was a mere chatterer; he always said something that was interesting, whereas chatterers are boring and you stop listening to them. Michele always made you listen to him, and sometimes I put aside my knitting so as to attend more carefully to one of his arguments. While he was talking he was aware of nothing else—neither of the passage of time nor that the lamp was going out, nor that Rosetta and I wanted to be alone for some reason of our own. He went on and on, animated, monotonous, full of good faith, and when I interrupted him by saying: "Well, well, it's time to go to bed," or "Well, it's dinner time," he was always put out, disconcerted, and his face would take on a bitter expression, as much as to say: "That's what happens when you talk to silly, thoughtless women like these; it's a waste of breath."

During those forty days of rain nothing notable occurred except for one episode which concerned Filippo and his tenant Vincenzo. One morning when, as usual, it was drizzling and the sky was a seething mass of dark clouds rising ceaselessly out of the great boiling pot of the sea, Rosetta and I were present at the slaughtering of a goat which Filippo had bought from Paride and which he intended to re-sell piecemeal, after taking a share for himself. The goat, a black and white one, was tied to a stake, and the evacuees, for lack of anything better to do, were examining it and calculating how much it weighed and how much meat it would produce once it had been skinned and cleaned. While we were standing thus in the fine rain, our shoes deep in mud, Rosetta said to me in a low voice: "Mum, I'm sorry for that poor goat. It's alive now, and in a few minutes they're going to kill it. If I had any say in the matter, I shouldn't kill it." "What would you eat, then?" I said. "Bread and vegetables," she replied. "What need is there to eat meat? After all I'm made of flesh too and the flesh I'm made of isn't so very different from the flesh of that she-goat. What fault is it of hers that she's an animal and can't reason and defend herself?" I quote these words of Rosetta's to give an idea of how she still argued and thought at that time, in the midst of war and famine. Her words may perhaps sound oversimple and even foolish, but they bear witness to her own particular sort of perfection which made it impossible to attribute any kind of defect to her.

In the meantime the butcher, a man called Ignazio who looked like anything but a butcher—a melancholy, listless kind of person with a riotous mop of greying hair above his forehead, long side whiskers and deep-set blue eyes—had taken off his coat and stood there in his waistcoat. A couple of knives and a small basin had been placed on a little table near the stake to which the goat was tied, just as in a hospital before an operation. Ignazio took up one of the knives, tested its edge on the palm of his hand, then went up to the goat and seized it by the horns, throwing its head back. The goat rolled its eyes, which seemed to be starting out of its head with fright, and you could see it had understood; it gave a bleat that sounded just like a moan, as much as to say: "Don't kill me, have pity." But Ignazio caught his lower lip with his teeth and with one blow drove the knife up to the handle into the goat's throat, still keeping hold of it by the horns. Filippo, who was acting as his assistant, was quick to put the basin under the goat's throat; and the blood flowed out of the wound like a little fountain, black and thick and smoking hot in the cold air. The goat shuddered, then half-closed its eyes which were already grown dim, as though as the blood flowed into the basin so its life ebbed away, and with its life, the sight of its eyes. Finally it bent its knees and—still trustingly, you might say—let itself slowly fall into the hands of the man who had slaughtered it. Rosetta had walked away in the rain which was still falling and I should have liked to go and join her, but I had to stay where I was because there was not much meat and I did not wish to lose my share; besides, Filippo had promised me the entrails, which are so very good when roasted on a gridiron over a fire of wood and soft charcoal. Ignazio, meanwhile, had lifted the goat by its hind legs and dragged it off through the mud to hang it up on two posts, head downward and feet outspread. We watched him as he worked.

First of all he took hold of one of the forelegs and made a cut just above the hoof, as you might cut a hand at the wrist. Then he selected a thin but tough stick and inserted it between the wooly hide and the flesh of the foot: the skin of a goat is only lightly joined to its flesh, and is very easily detached, like a leaf that is ready to fall. Having inserted the stick, he twisted it in such a way as to make a hole and then, throwing it away, put the foot into his mouth like a whistle, and blew hard into it until the veins in his neck stood out and his face turned purple. He blew and blew, and the goat began to swell out more and more as Ignazio's breath penetrated steadily into it and circulated between the hide and the flesh. Ignazio still went on blowing and blowing, and finally the goat, blown up tight like a wine skin, was dangling between the two posts, almost twice as large as before. Then he dropped the foot, wiped his blood-soiled mouth, and with his knife made an incision in the hide throughout the whole length of the belly, from the groin right up to the neck. Then he started detaching the hide from the flesh with his hands. It was a truly strange thing to see how easily the hide came away—just like taking off a glove—as he pulled steadily at it and now and then used his knife to cut the filaments which still remained attached to it. Gradually he took off the whole skin and then threw it on the ground, hairy and bloodstained, like a cast-off garment; and now the goat was naked, and all red with a few white or bluish patches here and there. It was still drizzling but no one had moved. Ignazio took his knife again, opened up the belly of the goat lengthwise, thrust in his hands and immediately shouted to me: "Cesira, hold out your arm!" I ran forward and he pulled out the whole mass of the entrails, unwinding them one by one, in an orderly fashion, as though they had been a skein of wool. At intervals he cut them and put them over my arm, still warm and stinking unbelievably and dirtying me with dung. And meanwhile he kept saying, as if to himself: "This is a dish fit for kings, or rather, as it's for you women, I should say for queens. Clean them well and roast them over a slow fire." At that moment a voice was heard calling "Filippo! Filippo!"

We all turned around and there, coming up over the edge of the terrace, was first the head and then the shoulders and then the complete figure of Vincenzo, Filippo's tenant, at whose house we had lived before we came up to Sant'Eufemia. Looking more than ever like a great, ugly, plucked bird, with his hooked nose and his sunken eyes, breathless, soused with mud and rain, he began shouting from down below. "Filippo, Filippo, a terrible thing has happened. . . . a terrible thing has happened. . . ." Filippo who, like the rest of us, had been watching Ignazio, immediately ran towards him, his eyes starting out of his head. "What has happened—tell me—what has happened?" But the other man, who was cunning, pretended to be panting for breath from the steep climb and pressed his hand against his chest, repeating in a cavernous voice: "Something very terrible." By this time we had all abandoned Ignazio and his goat and had clustered around Filippo and his tenant; and the window of Filippo's cottage, which stood just up above, had opened and two women were looking out of it, Filippo's wife and daughter. Finally Vincenzo spoke. "What has happened," he said, "is that the Germans and the Fascists came and knocked on the walls and found the hiding-place, and then pulled the wall down." Filippo interrupted him with a yell: "They've stolen my stuff!" "Yes, indeed they have," replied the other man, "they've stolen the lot, they've left nothing, absolutely nothing." He said this in a loud voice, so that Filippo's wife and daughter, looking out of the window, heard it; and they started complaining bitterly and waving their arms as they hung over the window sill. Filippo wasted no time in further inquiries: "It's not true, it's not true," he began bawling. "It was you who stole the things, it's you who are a thief, and a German and a Fascist too . . . you and that bitch of a wife of yours and those two crooks of sons . . . Everybody knows about you. You're just a bunch of crooks, you haven't even any respect for San Giovanni." He was yelling like a lunatic; and then he snatched up one of Ignazio's knives from the little table, seized Vincenzo by the throat and was on the point of slashing him. Luckily the evacuees were quick to jump on him; and they held him by the arms, four of them, while he thrust forward his chest and his forehead, foaming at the mouth and shouting: "Let me go, let me kill him, leave me alone, I want to kill him." Meanwhile the two women at the window were in a state of wild agitation, screaming: "We're ruined. We're ruined!" and the rain was now falling heavily, soaking us all to the skin.

But Michele, who had stood watching the scene, almost with satisfaction, as though it gave him pleasure that his sister should have lost her trousseau and his mother her household goods–surdenly went up to Vincenzo, who was still protesting: "Me the thief, indeed! It was the Germans, it was the Fascists, we'd nothing to do with it." And Michele, just as if he had known about it, put his hand into Vincenzo's coat pocket and pulled out a little box, saying quietly: "This is the thief. It was you who stole the things. This ring belongs to my sister."

He had opened the box and now held up a small diamond ring which I learned later had been given by Filippo to his daughter as a birthday present. As soon as Filippo saw the ring he gave a great yell and, tearing himself away from the men who were holding him, rushed at Vincenzo with the knife held aloft. But his opponent was quicker than he; he broke away from the crowd of people surrounding him and rushed off down the path. Filippo would certainly have liked to pursued him, but he at once realized it would be useless: he himself was short and paunchy, whereas the other man was long and thin, with legs like an ostrich. So he stooped and picked up a stone and hurled it after Vincenzo, shouting: "Thief, thief!" But, if he himself made no movement, the other evacuees did, not so much because they minded about Filippo's possessions as because, once a quarrel starts, everyone gets excited and wants to come to blows. Two or three of the younger ones ran off down the terraces, flying after old Vincenzo who was running like a hare. They caught up with him, seized him by the arms and forced him to come up again. Filippo, who all this time had continued to throw down stones big enough to kill a man, was now waiting, panting and breathless, at the edge of the terrace, and in his hand he held Ignazio's knife, still red with the blood of the goat. Then Michele went up to his father and said to him: "I'd go back into the house, if I were you."

"But I'm going to kill him."

"You'd better go back into the house."

"But I want to kill him, I *must* kill him."

"Give me the knife and go back into the house."

To my astonishment Filippo, in face of the calmness of his son, also became calm. He put the knife on the table and went to his cottage, from where could be heard cries and groans as though from purgatory itself. In the middle of the terrace, in the steadily falling rain, nothing was left but the poor goat, split open, hanging on its two posts.

Soon Vincenzo and the young men who had pursued him arrived back on the terrace; and the peasants and evacuees immediately gathered round them, asking him how it had happened—more out of curiosity, I noticed, than reprobation. Vincenzo was quite ready to satisfy them. "I didn't want to," he said in that ogreish voice of his, "none of us wanted to . . . Gracious me, the San Giovanni . . . He held my son at his christening and I held his daughter . . . Blood's thicker than water, isn't it? I swear I would rather have cut off my hand than commit a robbery . . . May I be struck dead here on this spot if it isn't true!"

"Yes, yes, we believe you, Vincenzo, we believe you. But how did it come about then that you *did* commit a robbery?"

"It was a voice. For days and days I kept hearing a voice inside me repeating: 'Take a hammer and break down the wall. Take a hammer and break down the wall. . . .' A voice that wouldn't let me rest, night or day."

"And so, Vincenzo, in the end you took the hammer and broke down the wall . . . was that it?"

"Yes, that was it."

The whole group of evacuees and peasants burst into a great laugh, and then, after a few more questions, they left him and returned to Ignazio and his goat. Vincenzo, however, did not go away at once. He started wandering round the place, from one house to another, from one hut to another; and everywhere he asked for something to drink; and then he repeated the story of the voice and made everybody laugh; but he himself did not laugh, he stood there stupidly, like an ugly, sick bird, and seemed not to understand why people were laughing. At last, toward evening, he went off, very crestfallen, as though he himself and not Filippo were the one who had been robbed.

That same evening Michele came to the hut where I was roasting the goat's entrails in company with Paride and his family and said, purely as a comment: "My father isn't a bad man, but he was on the point of killing a man for a couple of pairs of sheets and a small quantity of gold. *None* of us, however, would be capable of killing even a hen for the sake of an idea."

Paride, looking into the fire, said very slowly: "Michele, don't you know that possessions mean more to men than ideas? Take a priest, for instance. If you tell him, in the confessional, that you have stolen something, he will tell you in a feeble sort of way to recite a few prayers to Saint Joseph as a penitence, and in the end he'll give you absolution. But if you go into the presbytery and steal something from *him*—some silver spoons and forks or anything you like—you'll see what a rumpus he'll make. Far from giving you absolution, he'll immediately send for the superintendent of police and have you arrested. That being so—I mean, if a priest, who is after all a priest, behaves like that, what d'you expect of people like us, who are not priests?"

This was the only notable event that occurred during the time of the rain. Otherwise there were just the usual things: endless talk about the war and the weather, and about what we should do when the English arrived and afterward; and—more than anything—long periods of sleep, of twelve or fourteen hours at a stretch, sleeping most of the time and occasionally waking up, and after listening for a short time to the rain battering on the tiles and gurgling in the gutter, falling asleep again more soundly than ever, lying in each other's arms on the mattress of dried maize leaves over that bed of loose planks which often opened up beneath us and threatened to drop us onto the ground. For Filippo's family, and in general for all the evacuees, the main occupation was one thing and one only—eating. For them, it was just one long banquet from morning till night, and they wallowed in an abundance of food. They must eat, they said, for it was the only way to chase away melancholy; they also said that it was better to use up their provisions, because when the English arrived there would be plenty of everything, prices would fall, and no one would have any further need of the provisions they now had. But I thought to myself: "To trust is good but not to trust is better." I too was convinced that the English would come, but when? All that was needed was for them to delay matters for a month or two, and we should die of hunger, the whole lot of us. While all the others were cramming themselves I started a rationing system in our own hut. We had only one proper meal a day, in the evening—a small potful of beans and a little meat, generally goat's flesh, a piece of bread, always the same quantity, and a few dried figs. Sometimes I made *polenta*, sometimes, instead of beans, there were chick peas or dwarf peas and, instead of goat, cow's meat. In the morning, on the other hand, I used to cut one slice of bread for myself and one for Rosetta, and with the bread we would eat a raw onion. Or again we ate no bread at all but nibbled carob beans. Rosetta used to complain of being hungry—after all, she was young—and then I used to encourage her to sleep because, as I knew, sleeping is like eating: you consume little and build up your strength. In short, I ordered my life carefully, like the peasants, who were prudent and downright miserly and doled out their provisions with the precision of a goldsmith. It is true that they were accustomed to scarcity of food and knew by instinct that, Germans or English, they would never have enough to satisfy their hunger, since they always lacked money and one harvest was never sufficient to carry them over to the next. I felt more like a peasant than an evacuee, and I could not help feeling a dislike for the evacuees, most of them shopkeepers who had made their money at the expense of other people and who were counting on going back to do the same thing again, as soon as the English arrived. Someone may object that I was a shopkeeper too, and that is true, but I was born a peasant and as a result of contact with peasants and with the soil I felt myself to be a peasant again, as at the time when I left my native village to go and get married in Rome.

At last, toward the end of December, we got up as usual one morning and saw that during the night the wind had changed. The sky was a hard, luminous, deep blue, becoming reddened by the dawn, and a number of small red and grey clouds, the last of the endless rain clouds, were moving away. Down below, in the direction of Ponza, the sea coast could be seen, brilliantly clear, dark blue, almost black in colour. The plain of Fondi, wintry now and more grey than green, was smoking in the morning mist, as often happens before a fine, dry day of dazzling sunshine. And down from the mountains came the *tramontana* wind, cold and crisp and cutting, making the bare branches of the tree beside our cottage knock together with a clanking sound. When I went out of doors I found the mud hard, encrusted, jagged underfoot, and it glistened here and there as though mixed with splinters of glass, for there had been frost during the night. This change in the weather revived hope in the hearts of the evacuees, who came out of their houses in the icy morning air and started embracing and congratulating one another. Surely now, with the fine weather, the English would make a great advance and all would be over.

The English indeed arrived, punctually, but not in the way the evacuees expected. About eleven o'clock on that first morning of fine weather we were out on the terrace basking in the sun like so many numbed lizards, when we heard a distant roar which, as it gradually drew nearer, became steadily fuller and more majestic and seemed to fill the whole sky with its sound. After a moment's uncertainty everyone realized what it was; and so did I, who had so often heard that same roar in Rome, both by night and by day: "The English! The airplanes! The English airplanes are coming!" And then from behind a mountain, in the shining, clear sky, appeared a leading group of four planes. White and beautiful they were and they glittered in the sun, looking like those little silver filigree brooches they make in Venice. Immediately afterward there appeared another four, and then four more, so that there were twelve in all. They flew straight, as though following an invisible thread; their roar filled the whole sky, and although that roar reminded me of so many unpleasant hours in Rome I felt somewhat elated at hearing it, for in that roar I seemed to be listening to a voice which, though terrible, was yet kindly to us Italians, a voice which was commanding the Fascists and the Germans to go. My heart filled with suspense and hope, I watched them as they made their way, straight and sure, toward the town of Fondi lying down there in the valley, with its assemblage of little white houses among the dark green orange groves. And then suddenly the sky around the airplanes was dotted with small white clouds, and a moment later came a resounding crack of sharp, hurried volleys from the German anti-aircraft guns. There seemed to be a great number of these guns; they were firing from all parts of the valley. You should have heard the evacuees: "They're firing at them, the poor fools . . . but they're firing to no purpose at all . . . They'll take all day to hit them. Go on, go on, fire away, you're not getting anywhere near him." And certainly their shots did not appear to touch the planes, which continued their steady advance across the sky. Then we heard a louder, deeper explosion and saw a small white cloud, not in the sky but on the ground, among the houses and gardens of Fondi. The planes were beginning to drop their bombs.

What happened after that first explosion, I shall remember for quite a long time, if only because I have never seen so many people pass so swiftly from joy to sorrow. The bombs were now falling thick and fast in the town, and the white clouds formed by the explosions were multiplying, one beside the other, as far as the eye could reach; and all the evacuees began wailing as they stood along the terrace, weeping and loudly lamenting in just the same way as Filippo's wife and daughter when Vincenzo announced that the Germans had stolen all their belongings. They shouted and ran up and down and waved their arms, as though they wanted to try and stop the airplanes: "My house, my house, the murderers! They're destroying our houses, oh dear oh dear oh dear, our houses, our houses!"—and all the time the bombs went on falling like ripe fruit from a tree when you shake it, the anti-aircraft guns fired continuously, furiously, with a deafening din that seemed to fill the heavens and make the earth tremble as well. The airplanes went to the far end of the valley, toward the coast, and then, far away where the sea sparkled in the sunshine, they turned around and came back again, and down went more bombs, while the evacuees, who for a short time had fallen silent, thinking that they were going away, started weeping and wailing again louder than ever. But just when the squadron, still inflexible and assured, appeared to be really moving away in the direction from which it had come, the second plane in the last group sent forth a great red burst of flame, like a scarf fluttering in the blue sky. The anti-aircraft guns had hit their mark and the plane hung behind the others and the scarf of flame fluttered around the little white machine, growing steadily in size and in redness. And now again you should have heard the evacuees: "Well done, Germans! Give it to them, give it to those murderers! Knock them down out of the sky!" Suddenly Rosetta cried: "Oh Mum, do look at the parachutists—how lovely!" And as the stricken plane glided off in flames toward the seacoast I saw the big white umbrellas of parachutes opening in the sky, and each one had a little black object dangling below it and swaying in the wind—an airman. Seven or eight of them opened in this way and floated very slowly down. The anti-aircraft guns were no longer firing and the burning plane, wobbling and losing height, disappeared behind a hill and shortly afterward we heard a tremendous explosion. Now there was silence, with nothing to be heard but a faint metallic echo in the distance from the direction in which the squadron had vanished, and the groans and laments of the evacuees on the terrace. The silvery parachutes went on floating slowly down, and the whole of the Fondi valley was enveloped in grey smoke, reddened here and there by the flames of fires. Such was the coming of the English.

On this occasion Michele's strange hardness of heart was proved in a way that I did not expect. That same evening, while we were talking in the hut about air raids, he suddenly said: "You know what these evacuees who are now whining about their houses used to say, when the papers announced that *our* air forces had laid flat —Coventrized, as they used to call it—some enemy town? They used to say: 'Well, if they get bombed, it means they deserve it.' " I asked him: "Don't you feel sorry for all these poor people who are now homeless and forced to make their escape across country, as destitute as beggars or gypsies?" "Yes," he said, "of course I feel sorry for them, but not more than for other people who lost their homes before. I tell you, Cesira, it's first one and then the other, everyone in his turn. These people applauded when the homes of the English and the French and the Russians were bombed, and now they're being bombed in their turn. Isn't that perfectly just? You, Rosetta, who believe in God, don't you see the finger of God in this?" Rosetta said nothing—as usual, when he spoke of religion— and that was the end of the conversation.

After that first air raid the evacuees went rushing down into the valley to see what had happened to their houses, and almost all came back with the good news that their homes for the most part were safe, and that all in all the destruction was not so terrible as it had seemed at first sight. A couple of people had been killed; an old beggar who was sleeping in an already ruined house on the outskirts of the town and, oddly, the Fascist known as Apeface who had threatened us with his gun when we were staying at Concetta's. Apeface died just as he had lived. That morning, taking advantage of the fine weather, he had gone to Fondi and had smashed the iron shutters of a notions shop. The bomb brought the house down on his head and they had found him in the midst of ribbons and buttons, his hand still clutching the goods he had stolen. "Well," I said to Rosetta, "as long as it's people like that who get killed, there's something to be said for war." But she surprised me by the sadness of her expression and her tear-filled eyes, and by saying: "You mustn't say that, Mum. . . . Even he was a man to be pitied." And that evening she insisted on saying a special prayer for him, for the repose of a soul blacker than the black shirt he was wearing when the bomb struck him.

I forgot to say that there was another man who met his death during that time; Tommasino. I know exactly how and why he died because I was with him when the event which caused his death occurred. In spite of the rain and the cold and the mud he had continued his business transactions. He bought from the peasants, from the Germans, from the Fascists, and re-sold to the evacuees. Things to eat were now very scarce, but he still found means of obtaining salt, tobacco, oranges, eggs. He had raised his prices, of course, and I am pretty sure he was making plenty of money. All day long he would go up and down the valley, regardless of the danger, not because he was brave but because money meant more to him than life. Always unshaved, with his trousers tucked up and torn, his shoes laden with mud, he was the very image of the Wandering Jew. He had found lodging for his family with some peasants who lived even higher up the mountainside than Paride, and if anybody asked him why he did not go and join them, he would say: "I have my business, I must attend to my business till the last possible moment." What he meant was the last moment of the war; he did not know that he would be carrying on his business till the last moment of his own life.

One day I put eight eggs in a basket and went down the mountain with Rosetta, intending to exchange them for an army loaf with the Germans who were encamped in the orange groves in the valley. It so happened that Tommasino was up at Sant'Eufemia on a business visit, and he offered to accompany us. It was the fifth fine day after that first air raid, when we started off. Tommasino, as usual, walked in front of us, going down over the rocks and the holes of the mule track without saying a word, absorbed in his calculations. The mule track zigzagged down the side of the mountain to the left, then at a point where a large rock that barred its passage, it ran across a piece of flat ground and on downward over the flank of the mountain on the right. The stretch of flat ground was a strange place: there were numbers of curious bare upright rock formations, smooth and rounded, grey like the skin of an elephant and perforated with holes and caves of different sizes; and among these rocks there were prickly pear trees, with green, fleshy leaves that looked like little swollen, thorny faces. The path wound among the prickly pear trees and rocks beside a small stream that was a joy to look at, with water clear as crystal on a bed of green moss.

Just as we reached the flat ground, with Tommasino about thirty yards in front of us, we heard the roar of planes. We paid no special attention; they had become a normal event and generally they passed straight over toward the front; one could be quite sure that they would not bomb the mountains, for it was not worth while wasting bombs, which cost money, on the rocks of the *macere*. All I did, therefore, was to say quietly to Rosetta: "Look at the planes!" In the shining sky we could see the squadron, silver-white, in three orderly rows, with a single plane, which appeared to be acting as guide, flying ahead of them. Then I saw a red banner stream out from this first plane, and I remembered that Michele had told me that such was the signal for dropping bombs. I scarcely had time for this thought before the bombs began raining down. We did not *see* the bombs, which fell far too fast, but almost immediately heard an immensely violent explosion very close to us, while the whole stretch of ground round us rocked as if there were an earthquake. In reality it was not so much the earth rocking; quantities of small stones, torn from the ground, were hurtling around us and, particularly—as I discovered afterward—sharp, twisted splinters of iron, each one of them at least as long as my little finger, a single one of which would have killed us instantly if it had entered our bodies. A thick, acrid dust had risen around us, making us cough, and, since I was able to see almost nothing through this opaque cloud and was, at the same time, struck by a terrible fear, I called to Rosetta. The dust was clearing a little now, and I saw on the ground a number of those iron splinters and a torn and mangled mass of prickly pear leaves; and then, all of a sudden I heard Rosetta's voice calling to me: "I'm here, Mum." I have never believed in miracles, but, to tell the truth, considering all those iron splinters that had hurtled around us at the moment of the explosion, I felt, as I happily embraced my Rosetta, that it had been truly a miracle that we had not been killed. I embraced and kissed her and ran my hands over her face and body, hardly able to believe that she was still whole; then I began looking for Tommasino.

I did not see him on the ground scattered with torn, crushed prickly pear leaves; but I could hear his voice somewhere, moaning: "Oh my God, *Dio mio*, *Madonna mia*, *Dio mio*, *Madonna mia*. . . ." I thought he must have been hit, and this filled me with remorse for the happiness with which I had found Rosetta safe and sound. I had no great liking for him, but after all he was a human being too, and had helped us even if it had been from self-interest. Expecting to find him lying on the ground in a pool of his own blood, I made my way toward the spot from which I heard his voice coming. This was a shallow cave, a sort of cavity in one of the big rocks, and there he was crouching, huddled like a snail in its shell, holding his head between his hands and moaning loudly. I realized at once that he hadn't a scratch and was suffering from sheer terror. "Tommasino," I said to him, "it's all over. What are you doing in that hole? Thank God, we're all safe." He did not answer me but went on whining: "Oh my God, oh *Madonna mia*. . ." I persevered: "Come on, Tommasino, get a move on. We must go down, or we'll be late." "I'm not moving from here," he said.

"Why," I asked, "do you want to stay here?" "I'm not coming down with you," he said. "I'm going right up to the top of the mountain, as high as I can get, and I'm going into some deep cave, and I'm never going to move again. I'm done for." "But, Tommasino, your business?" "To hell with my business." Hearing him speak like that of the business for whose sake he had hitherto defied so many dangers, I knew that he was in earnest and that it was useless to insist. I said: "At least come down with us today. You can be quite sure the planes won't come back again." But he answered: "You go on . . . I'm not going to move from here," and then he began trembling again and imploring the help of the Madonna. So I said good-bye and went on down the mule track in the direction of the valley.

We reached the bottom, and at the edge of the orange groves found a German tank covered with boughs of orange trees. There was a camouflaged tent painted blue and green and brown, and six or seven Germans were busy cooking while another was sitting under an orange tree playing an accordion. They were young men, with shaven heads and pale, puffy faces covered with gashes and scars; they had been in Russia before coming to Fondi, and there, as they told us, the war was a hundred times worse than in Italy. I knew them, as I had already done this eggs-and-bread bargaining with them once before. While I was still some way off, I held up the basket of eggs, and the man with the accordion immediately stopped playing, went into the tent and came out again with an army two-pound tinned loaf. We went up to him, and without looking us in the face, and holding the loaf to one side as though he were afraid I might snatch it, he removed the leaves covering the eggs and counted them in German. Not content with that, he took up one of the eggs and put it to his ear, shaking it to see if it was new-laid. I said to him: "It's quite all right, they're new-laid, you needn't worry; we've risk our lives to bring them down to you, and you ought to give us two loaves instead of only one." He did not understand and gave me a questioning look, so I pointed to the sky and made a gesture to illustrate the falling of the bombs and said "Boom, boom" to describe the explosion. At last he understood and made a remark in which occurred that word *kaputt* that they are always using, and which, as Michele explained to me once, means something like "dead and done for." I realized he was talking about the plane which had been brought down, and I answered: "For every one that you bring down, a hundred more will come. If I were you I should give up the war and go home to Germany. It would be better for everybody, both for you and for us." This time he said nothing, for again he had not understood, but he held out the loaf to me and took the eggs, with a gesture as much as to say: "Come back and we'll make this exchange again." So we said good-bye and went back up the mule track towards Sant'Eufemia.

That same day Tommasino climbed to the place high up above Sant'Eufemia where he had his family. Next morning he sent down a peasant with a couple of mules to fetch all his belongings, including mattresses and bedsteads, from his cottage in the valley, and had everything carried up to his mountain retreat. But the cottage in which his family was staying did not seem to him safe enough; a few days later he transported himself, his wife and children to a cave right underneath the very top of the mountain. It was a deep, spacious cave with an entrance that could not be seen from outside because it was entirely hidden by trees and brambles. Above this cave rose an enormous formation of rock, grey and lofty, shaped like a sugar loaf, and so huge that it could be seen easily from down in the valley; the ceiling of the cave must have been at least a hundred feet thick. He established himself with his family in this cave which in bygone days had been a refuge for brigands, and you would have thought that he now felt safe from bombs and that his terror would have left him. But so intense was his fear that it had entered into his blood like a fever and in spite of the cave and its protecting rock he never stopped trembling all day long, from head to foot, leaning against the wall with his head and shoulders wrapped in a blanket. He kept on repeating: "I feel sick, I feel sick," in a weak, complaining voice, and he could neither eat nor sleep; he was, in fact, pining away before one's eyes, melting away like a candle, a bit more each day. I visited him one time and found him pitifully thin and dejected, trembling as he leaned against the entrance of the cave, muffled up in his blanket, and I remember that, not realizing that he was seriously ill, I started teasing him a little, saying: "Why, Tommasino, what are you frightened of? This cave here is absolutely bomb proof. What are you frightened of? Do you think the bombs are going to crawl about in the wood like snakes and then creep through the entrance of the cave and find you in your bed?" He looked at me without any sign of understanding and kept on repeating: "I feel sick, I feel sick."

After a few days, we heard that he was dead. It was fear that he died of, for he had neither wounds nor sickness; simply the shock of the bombs. I did not go to his funeral because it would have made me too sad and there were quite enough sad things already. His own family went, and Filippo and *his* family. They did not put the dead man's body in a coffin because there were no planks and no carpenters; instead they tied it between two branches and the grave digger, a tall thin man with fair hair who was also an evacuee and now did a bit of black marketing, going round the mountain districts with his black horse, tied Tommasino on to the horse's saddle and carried him down the mule track to the cemetery. They told me afterward that they had been unable to find a priest because they had all run away, and so Tommasino, poor man, had to be contented with the prayers of his relations. The funeral had been interrupted three times by air raid warnings, and on the tomb, for lack of anything better, the family had placed a cross made of two small boards torn from a munition case. Later I heard that Tommasino had left his wife a good sum of money but nothing in the way of provisions; in all his various business negotiations he had sold everything, down to his last pound of flour and his last ounce of salt, and his widow found herself with money but with nothing to eat. She was forced to buy at double the price things which her husband had sold for half, and I believe that at the end of the war, of all the money that Tommasino had left her, practically nothing remained. This was partly due, also, to the devaluation of the lira. Would you like to know what Michele said about his uncle's death? "I am sorry," he said, "because he was a good man. But he died as plenty of people like him might die any day; running after money and deluding himself into thinking that it is the only thing, and then suddenly being frozen with terror at the sight of what there is *behind* money."

Chapter 6

THE FINE WEATHER brought with it not merely the bombs of the English but another scourge as well—round-ups by the Germans. Il Tonto had told us about them, but at heart no one had believed in them; now, however, some peasants who had fled up into the mountains brought the news that down in the valley the Germans had carried out a wholesale sweep and had netted all the able-bodied men, placing them in trucks and sending them off to forced labor at some unknown destination, some said to the fortifications at the front, others to Germany itself. Then came another unpleasant piece of news: one night the Germans had completely encircled a valley not far from ours, had gone up to the top of the mountain and then swooped down in open order, gathering the men like so many little fishes into their net and sending them away. There was great fear among the evacuees because among them there were at least four or five young men who had been in the army when the Fascist regime collapsed and had then deserted; and these young men were just the ones the Germans were looking for, because they regarded them as traitors and intended to make them pay for their betrayal by forcing them to work as slaves. The most frightened of all were the parents of the young men, and, more than any of them, Filippo, on account of his son Michele, who always contradicted him but of whom he was extremely proud. A meeting was held in Filippo's cottage and it was decided that as long as the danger of these round-ups lasted, all these young men should slip away during the next few days, each one on his own, far up the mountainside, and not come down again till dusk. Up there, even if the Germans should arrive, there were other paths leading to other valleys and over other mountains; and even the Germans would be discouraged if they saw that they had to travel several miles over high mountain paths just for the fun of catching a man or two. Michele, in truth, did not want to slip away like the others, not so much from arrogance as because he never wanted to do what other people did. But his mother implored him with tears to do it for her sake, even if he did not wish to do it for his own, and in the end he consented.

Rosetta and I decided to go up with him, not because we were afraid, for they were not carrying off women, but simply in order to have something to do, for we were dying of boredom where we were; and also in order to be with Michele, who was the only person up there whom we had grown to like. And thus began a strange life which I shall remember as long as I live. While it was still pitch dark Paride, who always got up first, would come and knock at our door, and we would dress in haste by the feeble light of the oil lamp. We would go out into the icy cold darkness, while shadows flitted up and down the terrace and lights appeared in the cottage windows one by one, and find Michele. He made a queer little figure, all bundled up in sweaters and scarves, stick in hand, looking like a dwarf in a fairy tale, one of the ones who live in caves and guard treasures. We would follow him without a word as he moved off up the mountainside.

It was dark when we started climbing up the frost-covered path through the thick, tall scrub that reached up to our chests. It was impossible to see anything, but Michele had a pocket flashlight and now and then shone the ray of the lamp on to the path, and so we made our way onward, without speaking. Meanwhile the sky would be starting to grow pale behind the mountains, turning gradually to a dirty grey, but with numbers of stars still shining for the last moment before day came. The mountains remained black against the background of this brightening, star-dotted sky, and then they too grew clear, revealing their green color with dark patches of wood and scrub. Now the stars were no longer there and the sky was turning from grey almost to white, and the whole expanse of scrub had become visible to us, dry and frozen and lifeless, silent and still asleep. But gradually the sky turned pink at the horizon and blue above our heads, and with the first ray of sunshine that shot out from behind one of the mountains sharp and sparkling as a golden arrow, all the colors leapt into life: the bright red of berries, the brilliant green of the moss, the creamy-white plumes of the reeds, the glossy black of withered branches. We had left the scrub now for an ilex wood which swathed the whole mountain almost to its top. These were very large ilexes, scattered over the slope at a considerable distance from each other, and they had grown without touching and stretched out their branches like arms hither and thither as though, what with the steepness of the slope and the wind, they wanted to take hands and support each other from falling. Twisted, widely scattered, they formed an open forest that allowed the eye to travel upward over the white stones of the mountainside to the topmost peak as it stood out against the blue sky. The path ran almost on the level through this forest; you could hear large numbers of birds, awakened by the sunshine, fluttering and twittering in the branches.

Michele looked happy as he walked briskly in front of us, twirling the branch which served him for a walking stick and whistling a little tune that sounded like a military march. After we had climbed still farther up the ilexes became gradually wider apart, smaller and more twisted, till finally there were no more of them, merely the path running obliquely across the slope, over blindingly white loose stones, and, a little higher up, the top of the mountain, or rather the pass between two peaks for which we were making. When we reached the end of the path, we found ourselves on a piece of level ground, surprising after all those stones since it was carpeted over with soft, brilliantly green grass, amongst which were scattered white rocks, rounded in form like the cruppers of a horse. In the middle of this emerald meadow was an old well with a parapet of unmortared stones. From this piece of flat ground there was a truly magnificent view, and even I, who am not particularly interested in the beauties of nature—perhaps because I was born in the mountains and know them too well—even I was left open mouthed with admiration the first time I went there. On one side the eye plunged down over the awe-inspiring mountainside, composed of terraces, like an immense staircase, right down to the valley and, beyond that, to the blue streak of sparkling sea, on the other side there was nothing to be seen but mountain after mountain, the mountains of Ciociaria, some of them sprinkled with snow or completely white, others bare and grey. It was cold up there, but not too much so, for there was pure, clear sunshine and no wind, at any rate during the whole period that we went there, which lasted about a fortnight.

We had to spend the whole day up there, so we spread out a blanket on the grass and threw ourselves down upon it. There we rested for a while, and then restlessness would come upon us and we would start wandering round and exploring. Michele and Rosetta would go off picking flowers or simply chattering, or rather he would be talking and she listening; more often than not I remained in the meadow. I liked being alone—a thing which in Rome was possible whenever I wished, but impossible at Sant'Eufemia because by night I slept with Rosetta and by day I could not avoid the evacuees. Solitude gave me the illusion that I had come to a stop in life and was able to look around; time was passing just the same, of course, but I was not conscious of it as I was when in company with others. There was a great silence; from some little valley down below there sometimes came the tinkling of sheepbells, but that was the only sound and it was not a disturbing noise but merely a sound that made the place quieter and the silence deeper. Sometimes it gave me pleasure to lean over the parapet of the well and look down for a long time. It seemed very deep, and it was made of dry stones all around down to the water, of which you could catch a glimpse. Maidenhair fern, so pretty with its stalks black as ebony and its fine, green, feathery leaves, sprouted thickly between the stones and was reflected in the dark water at the bottom. I used to lean over and look down and it reminded me of when I was a child, and to see myself reflected in a well inspired me with fear and at the same time attracted me. I imagined that wells communicated with a whole subterranean world inhabited by fairies and dwarfs, and was almost tempted to throw myself down into the water so as to enter that strange world and get away from my own. Or again I would look down until my eyes had become accustomed to the darkness and I could distinctly see my face reflected in the water, and then I would take a stone and drop it into the middle of the face and watch the face break in pieces in the rippling circles of water caused by the falling stone.

I also enjoyed wandering among the strange, round, white rocks that rose from the green grass in that flat meadow. During these explorations, too, I felt like a little girl again: I had hopes, almost, of finding something precious amongst the grass, partly because the grass itself, so emerald-like, seemed a rare thing, partly because this was one of those places in which, according to what I had been told as a child, a treasure might well be buried. But there was nothing except the grass, which is worthless and is given to animals; just once I found a four-leaved clover which I gave to Michele, and he, more to please me than because he believed in it, put it in his wallet. In this way, time passed, slowly; the sun rose high in the heavens and became burning hot —sometimes I undid my bodice and lay on the grass and had a sun bath, as if I were at the seaside. About lunchtime Michele and Rosetta would come back from their walk and we would sit on the grass and eat bread and cheese. I have eaten plenty of good things before and since, but that dark-colored, stale bread mixed with bran and maize flour, and that sheep's-milk cheese, so hard that you needed a hammer to break it, seem to me the most exquisite things I have ever tasted. Perhaps it was the appetite that came to us from our walk and from the mountain air which acted as a sauce; perhaps it was the idea of danger, which is also a rare seasoning; certainly I ate with a strange enthusiasm, as though I were realizing for the first time in my life what it means to eat and to take nourishment and to restore one's strength and feel that food is a good and necessary thing. There were many things of which I became aware for the first time, and strange to tell they were the simplest things, which usually one does without thinking about them, mechanically. Sleep, for instance, which I had never before thought of as an appetite, the satisfying of which brings pleasure and refreshment; bodily cleanliness, which just because it was difficult and almost impossible seemed an almost voluptuous pleasure; and everything connected with the physical side of one's being, to which, in a town, one devotes little time or attention. I believe that if there had been a man there who had attracted me and whom I could have loved, love itself would have had a new savor, more profound and more intense. It was as though I had become a beast, for I imagine that beasts, having nothing to think about but their own bodies, must experience the same feelings that I experienced at that time, compelled as I was by circumstances to be nothing more than a body which took nourishment, slept, kept itself tidy and tried to be as comfortable as possible. . . .

Gradually the sun moved around the sky and began sinking in the direction of the sea. When the coastline started to darken and redden with the lights of sunset, we set out on our return journey, not by the mule track but running straight down the slope where there was no path at all, slithering over grass and rocks, rushing over the loose stones and through the scrub. The journey which in the early morning had required two hours took us no more than half an hour on our return. We would arrive at supper-time dusty and covered with leaves and twigs, and would go at once to our supper in the hut. We went to bed early, and at dawn we were on the move again.

Not always was our green meadow so quiet and so remote from the war. I am not referring to the airplanes which frequently passed over our heads, nor to the explosions, the muffled sounds of which came up to us from the valley, showing that those miserable Germans were still in process of blowing up the dikes of the irrigation canals, thus letting loose both water and malaria over the whole of the valley region; what I mean is that the war made itself felt through people we encountered up there from time to time. This was because the pass, lonely as it was, lay in the path of all those who, keeping high up and avoiding the valleys, came down over the mountains from Rome and also from Northern Italy, both of which were occupied by the Germans, towards the south where the English were. For the most part these people were disbanded soldiers, or else poor people who wanted to get back to the villages from which they had been chased by the war, or prisoners who had escaped from some concentration camp. One of these encounters I remember extremely well. We were eating our usual bread and cheese when from behind one of the rocks there popped up two men armed with sticks who were so very odd to look at that I took them for savages. They were dressed in rags, and that did not frighten me because rags up there were a perfectly normal thing, but their shoulders, which were unbelievably broad, and their faces, which were entirely different from the faces of us Italians, made such an impression upon me that I was unable to move as they approached, and remained sitting there, paralysed with fear, my bread and cheese half way to my mouth. Michele, however, who was afraid of nothing and nobody—not so much from courage, perhaps, as because he trusted everybody—went up to these two men and started talking to them by means of gestures. Then we two plucked up courage and went up to them too. Their faces were yellow and flat and beardless, with long folds in the smooth skin following the lines of their cheeks; they had thick black hair, and small eyes slanting upward at the corners towards their temples; flat noses, and mouths like the mouths of skulls, full of broken, dark-colored teeth. Michele told us they were Russian prisoners but of some Mongol race such as the Chinese, and that he imagined they had escaped from some German concentration camp where they had been imprisoned. I couldn't take my eyes off those enormously wide shoulders, and I felt it had perhaps been imprudent not to hide or run away: those two men were so strong that if they jumped on us, on Rosetta and me, I mean, there would have been no escape. However the two Mongols behaved like decent people, and talking all the time by signs they stayed with us an hour or more, long enough to have a rest. Michele offered them bread and cheese and they ate it, but with discretion, and I am almost sure they thanked us. They laughed continuously, poor things, possibly because they could not manage to understand or make themselves understood; as though they meant to convey to us by their laughter that their intentions were good. Michele, talking all the time by signs, explained to them which way they ought to go, and after a time they started off among the rocks, looking for a distance like two big apes walking on their hind legs, and helping themselves along with sticks they had torn from trees.

Another time an Italian workman came past us who had been working on the fortifications at the front; he had run away because they were given nothing to eat and were treated like dogs and made to work like slaves. He could hardly stand on his feet. He was a handsome, distinguished-looking young man with a fine, dark face so thin that his cheekbones stuck out, and with deep-set, sad eyes and a body all skin and bone. He told us his family lived in Apulia and he hoped to be able to get to them by walking over the mountains. He had been walking for a week and was reduced to rags and tatters, his shoes worn right through and his clothes in pieces. He did not say much, partly because, owing to weakness, he could only speak very slowly and with an effort and only a few words at a time, as though he were trying to save his breath. But he did tell us that he had heard there had been a revolt in Rome and some Germans had been killed and the Germans had taken reprisals against the Italians, but he did not know when this had happened, nor how, nor where. Finally, still speaking of the Germans, he said: "They're hateful people. They know perfectly well now that they've lost the war, but as they like war and there's nothing to prevent them living on us, they'll go on doing so as long as they've a soldier left. And unless the war comes to an end first, they'll kill the whole lot of us with starvation and ill treatment. Either the war finishes or *we're* finished." He accepted some bread and cheese and also a little tobacco from Michele, and after staying with us in the meadow for barely half an hour he set off again, dragging his legs slowly along so that at each step he took it looked as if he would fall flat on the ground and never move again.

One morning we were basking in the sun when suddenly we heard a whistle. We immediately hid behind one of those big white rocks till we could see who it was. We never knew what might happen and were always on the alert, afraid that the Germans might come and round us up. After a while, Michele poked his head out, just in time to see another head retreating hastily behind a rock not far off. We went on thus, peeping at each other in turn, and then at last we saw that they were not Germans and they saw that we were Italians and so they came out. They were two soldiers belonging to Southern Italy, a lieutenant and a second lieutenant, they told us, but they were dressed in civilian clothes and, like so many others, were making their escape over the mountains in a southerly direction, with the intention of crossing the front and reaching the villages where their families lived. One of them was black-haired, tall, with a dark skin, a round face, eyes as black as coal, white teeth and lips that were almost purple; the other was fair, with a long face, blue eyes and a pointed nose. The dark one was called Carmelo, the fair one Luigi. Of all the encounters we had on that mountain-top this was perhaps the least pleasing, not so much because these two men were really disagreeable—in peacetime, I daresay, in their own homes, I should have had nothing against them—but because, as will be seen, war had had a bad effect on them, as it had on so many others, uncovering sides of their characters which otherwise would have remained hidden. And I wish to say at this point that war is a great test, and that men ought to be seen in war and not in peace; not at a time when there are laws and respect for others and the fear of God, but when all these things no longer exist and each man acts according to his own real nature, without restraint and without regard for others.

These two men had been with a regiment stationed in Rome, and at the time of the armistice, they had deserted and gone into hiding and then made their escape from Rome with the intention of finding their way back to their own villages. For about a month they had stayed with a peasant at the foot of the Monte delle Fate, and I at once had a bad impression of them on hearing them speak of this peasant—who, after all, had given them hospitality—in a contemptuous manner, as a poor ignorant rustic who could not even read and who had a house like an animal's den. One of them said, laughing: "Of course, we had to put up with it; in a time like this half a loaf is better than none." They went on to say that they had left the Monte delle Fate because the peasant had told them he couldn't keep them any longer because he had nothing left to eat, and the dark one remarked that this was not true and that if they had had any money the food would have been produced in no time; all peasants, he said, had an eye to the main chance. In the end they had started off southward and were hoping to get across the front.

By now it was lunchtime, and Michele, albeit rather unwillingly, suggested that they should share our usual bread and cheese. The dark one said they would accept the bread with pleasure, but as for the cheese, they already had a complete cheese, because they had stolen one from that miserly peasant without his noticing it. As he said this he pulled the cheese out of his knapsack and, laughing, flourished it in the air. This frank remark made me feel uncomfortable, not so much on account of the thing itself, quite ordinary in those times when everybody stole and theft had ceased to be theft, as because of its very frankness, which seemed to me unbecoming in a man like him, with the rank of lieutenant and obviously, from his manners, a gentleman. Besides, to my way of thinking, it was not nice to repay that poor man's hospitality by taking away the little he had. But I said nothing and we sat down on the grass and started eating, and while we ate we listened to the dark man, who talked all the time and always about himself, as of someone very important, both as a landowner in his own country and as an officer in the war. The fair man listened to him, half-closing his eyes in the sunshine, and every now and then contradicted him in an almost spiteful way, but the other man was not put out by this and went on with his boastful remarks. The dark man said, for example: "In my part of the country I have an estate. . . . " "Come on," said the fair man, "you mean two or three little fields the size of handkerchiefs." "No, an estate. You have to have a horse to go over it from one end to the other." "Get along with you, you can go on foot and do the whole thing in a few steps." Or again: "I took a patrol and went into the wood. There were at least a hundred enemy soldiers lying concealed in that wood." "Come on, I was there too, there were just about four or five in all." "I tell you there were at least a hundred. When they got up from behind the bushes where they were hidden, I didn't count them because at moments like that there are other things to do besides counting the enemy, but there must certainly have been a hundred of them if not more." "You're adding on a few, aren't you? There may have been five or six." And so on. The dark man talked very big, in a completely self-assured, swaggering tone; the fair man, in a lazy, weary sort of way, never let him get away with it. Finally the dark man told about what he had done on the day when the armistice had been declared and the Italian army had been disbanded. "I was with the Army Service Corps, near my own home, in charge of an army store full of everything you can think of. The very moment I heard the war was over, I had a truck loaded up with everything I could lay hands on, tinned food, preserves, cheeses, flour, all kinds of provisions, and off went the whole lot, straight to my home, where my mother was." He laughed with pleasure at the thought of this clever exploit, showing all his white, perfect teeth; and then Michele, who so far had listened to him without saying a word, remarked drily: "To put it briefly, you *stole* the things." "What d'you mean?" "I mean that one moment you were an officer in the Italian army and next moment you were a thief." "My dear sir,

I don't know who you are nor what your name is, but I could—" "Could what?" "Anyhow, who said I was a thief? I did what everyone was doing, and if I hadn't taken those provisions, someone else would have." "That may be so, but the fact remains that you stole them." "Be careful what you say, I'm quite capable of—" "Of what? Let's see what you're capable of." The fair man laughed and said to the dark man: "I'm sorry, Carmelo, but you've got to admit that this gentleman here has defeated you. *Touché*." The dark man shrugged his shoulders and said to Michele: "You're a miserable creature, and I don't intend to waste breath arguing with you." "That's just as well," said Michele with authority, "and I'll also tell you why you've behaved like a thief. Because, not content with having committed a theft, you now boast about it. You think you were very cunning. If you had done it and been ashamed of it, one might possibly think you had done it from real need . . . or carried away by seeing other people doing the same thing. . . . But you boast about it, thus proving that you aren't fully conscious of what you did and are ready to do the same thing again." The dark man, infuriated by this, rose to his feet, seized a branch and brandished it at Michele, saying: "Either you be quiet, or else—" But Michele had no time to react. The fair man took the wind out of his friend's sails by saying, with his spiteful little laugh: "*Touché* again, eh?" Then Carmelo turned his fury against *him*. "You be quiet! Didn't *you* take a share in it too? We were together, weren't we?" "I didn't give my consent, I merely obeyed. You were my superior. Ha, ha, *touché!*" Well, our lunch ended in silence, with the black-haired man looking really black and the fair man chuckling.

After lunch we sat in silence for a short time. But Carmelo could not swallow the matter of the thief and after a little he said to Michele, with an air of challenge: "You who are so ready to proclaim your opinions and to call people thieves who are worth far, far more than you are yourself—may one be allowed to know who you are? I am ready to say who *I* am—Carmelo Alí, officer, agriculturalist, with a degree in law and a decoration for valor, Cavaliere of the Crown of Italy. But you—who are you?" The fair man remarked with a chuckle: "You're forgetting to say that you're also the local Fascist Secretary, in our village. Why don't you tell him that?" Carmelo, annoyed, answered: "That's all over and done with, and that's the only reason why I didn't mention it. But you know quite well that, even when I was the local Fascist Secretary, no one ever found anything to say against me." Laughing, the fair man corrected him: "Except that you took advantage of your position to get hold of all the prettiest peasant girls who came to ask you a favor. Why, you're a great Don Juan, you know." Carmelo, flattered by this accusation, smiled slightly but did not reject it; then he turned toward Michele and demanded: "Well then, my dear sir, tell us of some title or degree, some honor or decoration, anything, in fact, that will help us to know who you are and by what right you criticize others." Michele looked at him fixedly through the thick lenses of his glasses; finally he asked: "What does it matter that I should tell you who I am?" "Well, for one thing, have you a university degree?" "Yes, I have. But even if I hadn't, it wouldn't make any difference." "What d'you mean?" "What I mean is that you and I are two human beings, and what we are, we are because of what we do and not because of any honors or degrees. And what you did and said shows you to be a man of shallow character, to say the least, and of a very elastic conscience. That's all." "*Touché*" said the fair man again, still laughing. This time the dark man took the line of not caring. He suddenly jumped to his feet and said: "It's stupid of me to lower myself by arguing with you. Come on, Luigi, or it will be getting late, and we still have a long way to go. Well, thanks for the bread, and you can be sure that, if you come to my home, I'll repay it with interest." Michele, punctiliously polite, answered calmly: "Yes, provided the bread isn't made with the flour you took from the Italian army." Carmelo had now gone on ahead; he merely shrugged his shoulders and said: "Go to hell, and the Italian army too." We heard the fair man, still laughing, say once more: "*Touché*."

Then they turned away behind a rock and disappeared out of sight.

On yet another occasion we saw a large number of people walking in single file, as though in procession, along a path skirting the mountainside. Then they crossed over through the pass. There were at least thirty of them, the men in their best clothes, black for the most part, the women in local costume with long skirts, bodices and shawls. The women were carrying bundles and baskets balanced on their heads, and the smallest of the children in their arms; the men were leading the bigger children by the hand. These people were inhabitants of a small village that lay on the line of the front. One dreadful morning the Germans had awakened them at dawn while they were still sleeping and had given them half an hour to get dressed and put together the most necessary of their belongings. Then they had loaded them into trucks and taken them off to a concentration camp in the neighborhood of Frosinone. But after some days they had escaped from the camp and now they were trying to get back over the mountains to their village, to find their own homes and start their ordinary life again. Michele questioned the leader of the group, a good-looking elderly man with a fine pair of grey mustaches, and the latter said simply: ". . . Even if it's only for the sake of our beasts. If we're not there, who's going to think of our beasts? The Germans?" Michele hadn't the heart to tell them that when they arrived at their village they would find neither houses nor beasts nor anything else. After they had rested for a few minutes, they started on their way again. I felt a great sympathy for these poor people, who were so calm and so sure of their own business, partly because there was a certain resemblance between them and Rosetta and me; they also had been chased out of their homes by the war, they also were fleeing over the mountains, destitute and bereft, like gypsies. A few days later, however, I heard that the Germans had caught them again and carried them back to the camp at Frosinone. After that I heard nothing more of them.

We lived this sort of life, going up to the pass at dawn and coming down again at sunset, for about two weeks; then it became clear that the Germans had ceased their round-ups, in that part of the mountains anyhow, so we came back and took up our usual occupations again. But I still felt a kind of nostalgia for those splendid days that I had spent high up on the mountain, face to face with solitude and nature. Up there there had been no evacuees or peasants to worry me with talk of the war, the English, the Germans, the lack of food; there had been none of the customary efforts to cook small quantities of poor material on green wood in a dark hut; there had in fact been nothing to remind us of the situation in which we were placed, except those two or three encounters that I have described. I might have thought I was on an expedition in company with Michele and Rosetta—that was all. And the green meadow where the winter sun grew so burning hot that it might have been the month of May, with the snow-capped mountains of Ciociaria on the horizon and, on the other side, the sparkling sea beyond the plain of Fondi, had seemed to me an enchanted spot in which a treasure might really have been buried, as in the stories I had been told as a child. The treasure beneath the ground did not exist, I knew; but I had found it, instead, inside myself, with as much surprise as if I had dug it up with my hands; and this treasure had been the profound calm, the complete lack of fear and anxiety, the confidence in myself and in outward things which, as I walked all alone, had grown up in my mind more and more as the days went past. Those were perhaps my happiest days for a great number of years, and, strange to say, they were precisely the days during which I found myself poorer and more destitute of everything than I had ever been, with bread and cheese for food and the meadow grass for my bed and not even a hut for shelter, more like a wild animal than a human being.

It was the end of December by now, and it was actually on Christmas Day that the English at last arrived. Not the English of the Garigliano army, you must understand, but two Englishmen who were escaping over the mountains and who descended upon us at Sant'Eufemia on the morning of the twenty-fifth. The weather was still brilliant—cold, dry and clear; and one morning, when I looked out of our cottage door, I noticed a little crowd collected on the terrace. I went over to them and saw both evacuees and peasants gathered round two young men who appeared to be foreigners: one of them was small and fair, with blue eyes, a straight, thin nose, red lips and a fair, pointed beard; the other tall and thin, with blue eyes and black hair. The fair one talked a halting Italian and told us that they were English, he himself a naval officer and the other an ordinary seaman, that they had been put ashore in the neighborhood of Ostia, near Rome, in order to dynamite something or other belonging to us unfortunate Italians, and that then, when the job was finished, they had gone back to the beach but the boat which had brought them had failed to come back and fetch them, so they had been forced to make their escape and go into hiding, like so many others. They had spent the rainy period in a peasant's house in the neighborhood of Sermoneta, but now that the weather was fine they intended to try and cross the front and reach Naples, where their headquarters was. These explanations were followed by a great many questions and answers; evacuees and peasants all wanted to know how the war was going and when it would end. But these two knew no more than we did: they had been living in the mountains these last months, seeing no one but illiterate peasants who scarcely knew that there *was* a war going on. So, when the evacuees discovered that they knew nothing and, furthermore, that they needed help, they all melted away, one after another, saying among themselves that these two were English and that it was dangerous to be in their company, that you never know, there were spies everywhere and, if the Germans got to know about it, it was quite likely there might be unpleasant results. So in the end the two men were left all alone in the middle of the terrace, in the clear, sparkling sunshine, ragged and unshaven and bewildered by the glances that encompassed them.

I must confess that I too was a little frightened to remain with them, not so much on my own account as for Rosetta; but it was Rosetta herself who made me ashamed of this fear by saying:

"Oh Mum, they look so lost, poor things. Besides, it's Christmas Day and they've nothing to eat, and I daresay they'd like to be with their families, and they can't. Why shouldn't we invite them to come and have dinner with us?" I admit I was ashamed and I felt that Rosetta was right and that I could hardly afford to despise the evacuees as I was doing if I then behaved like them. So we made the two men understand that we wanted them to come with us and we would all eat our Christmas dinner together, and they at once happily accepted.

I had made a special effort for that Christmas Day, chiefly for Rosetta's sake, for every year since she was born she had been accustomed to celebrating that day as well as any lady in the land. I had bought a fowl from Paride and roasted it with potatoes. I had made the *pasta* myself—not much of it, for I had very little flour—and I had made dumplings with stuffing. I had a couple of small *salame* sausages, and these I had cut into thin slices and had put them with some hard-boiled eggs. I had made a sweet too; for lack of anything better, I had grated some carob beans very finely, mixed this carob flour with some white flour, dried grapes, pine kernels and sugar, and had baked a *pizzetta* cake which was flat and hard but good. I had also managed to buy a bottle of Marsala from one of the evacuees; Paride had given me some wine. There was plenty of fruit: at Fondi the orange trees were full of oranges which cost very little, and some days before I had acquired several dozen of them and we were eating oranges all day long. I invited Michele too, asking him as he was hurrying off toward his father's cottage. He accepted at once, and I am pretty sure he accepted mainly out of dislike for his own family. But he said: "My dear Cesira, you did a good deed today. If you hadn't invited those two you would have lost the good opinion I have of you."

Be that as it may, he called to his father, and when the latter put his head out of the window he hold him we had invited him to dinner and that he had accepted. In a low voice—for he was afraid of being overheard by the two Englishmen—Filippo began entreating him not to go. "Don't go," he said. "They're a couple of runaways, and if the Germans get to know about it, we shall be in trouble." But Michele shrugged his shoulders and without waiting for his father to finish speaking came to our cottage.

I had laid the Christmas table with a heavy linen tablecloth which I had borrowed from the peasants. Rosetta had placed sprays of green leaves and red berries around the dishes, rather like the ones you see in Rome on similar occasions, which she had picked from bushes in the scrub. In one dish was the fowl, rather a small one for five people, in the others the *salame*, the eggs, the cheese, the oranges and the cake. I had made bread specially for that day, and it was still warm from the oven. I cut a slice for each person. We ate with the door open because there was no window in our room. Outside the door was the sunshine and the magnificent, sunlit panorama of the Fondi plain, stretching far, far away to the edge of the sea that glittered brightly in the sun. Michele, after the stuffed dumplings, started to attack the Englishmen on the subject of the war. He gave it to them hot and strong, speaking as one man to another; and they seemed rather astonished, perhaps because they had not expected speeches of this kind, in this place, from a ragamuffin such as Michele appeared to be. He told them they had made a mistake in not landing near Rome instead of in Sicily; that they could easily have taken Rome and the whole of Southern Italy without striking a blow. But by advancing step by step up the length of Italy, as they were doing, they were destroying Italy and, in addition, causing terrible suffering to the inhabitants, who found themselves caught between the devil and the deep sea. The two Englishmen replied that they knew nothing of all these things; they were in the Navy and they obeyed orders. Then Michele assailed them with another argument: why were they fighting the war, for what object? The Englishmen answered that they were fighting the war in order to defend themselves from the Germans, who were seeking to gain the mastery over everyone, including them. Michele replied that that was not enough: people were expecting them, after the war, to create a new world, with greater justice, greater freedom and greater happiness in it than in the former one. If they did not succeed in creating this world, they too would have lost the war, even if, in fact, they had won it. The fair-haired officer listened to Michele with some mistrust and answered him briefly and at long intervals; but it seemed to me that the sailor had the same ideas as Michele, although, out of respect to the officer, who was his superior, he did not dare to express them. In the end the officer cut short the discussion by saying that the essential thing, at present, was to win the war, and that in other respects he relied on his government which doubtless had a plan for creating this new world of which Michele spoke. We all of us realized that he did not wish to entangle himself in any embarrassing argument, and Michele, although he was a little upset, also realized this and now proposed that we should drink to the health of the new world that would be born out of the war. So we filled our glasses with Marsala and all drank to the health of the world of tomorrow. Michele was positively moved and had tears in his eyes, and, after this first toast, insisted on drinking to the health of all the Allies, including the Russians, who had, it seemed, won a great victory over the Germans only a few days before. And so we were all content, just as one should be on Christmas Day, and for a moment it seemed that there were no longer any differences of language or upbringing between us and that we were all really brothers. This day, which so many centuries before had seen the birth of Jesus in the stable, had again seen the birth of something that resembled Jesus, something new and good which would make men better. At the end of our dinner we gave a last toast to the health of the two Englishmen and then we all embraced each other, the whole lot of us; I embraced Michele, Rosetta and the two Englishmen, and they embraced all of us, and we all said to one another: "A happy Christmas and a happy New Year," and for the first time since I had come up to Sant'Eufemia I felt really content. After a little, however, Michele remarked that this was all very nice but that some limit must be put to self-sacrifice and altruism; and he explained to the two Englishmen that we two would be able to offer them hospitality for that one night at most, but that then it would be best for them to leave, for it would be really dangerous both for them and for us if they stayed: the Germans might get to know at any moment and then no one could save us from their vengeance. The Englishmen answered that they understood these difficulties and assured us that they would leave next day.

All that day they remained with us. They talked about all kinds of things with Michele, and I noticed that although Michele appeared to be extremely well-informed about *their* country—in fact almost better-informed than they were themselves—they knew little or nothing about Italy even though they were there at the moment and engaged in fighting a war there. The officer, for instance, told us that he had been at a university; he was, therefore, an educated man. But Michele, by slow degrees, made the discovery that he did not even know who Dante was. Now I am not an educated woman and what Dante wrote I have never read, but I did know the name, and Rosetta told me that the nuns at school had not only taught her who Dante was but had also made her read something of him. Michele whispered this fact about Dante to us; and, still in a low voice, at a moment when they were not listening to us, went on to say that it explained many things, as for instance the air raids which had destroyed so many Italian towns. The airmen who dropped the bombs knew nothing about us or about our monuments, ignorance made them calm and pitiless, and ignorance, added Michele, was perhaps the cause of all our woes and other people's too, for wickedness is only a form of ignorance and he who knows cannot really do evil.

That night the two men slept under a haystack, and early in the morning, without saying good-bye to us, they left. Rosetta and I were dead tired because we had stayed up late and were not accustomed to it, and that morning we slept till past midday. While we were still fast asleep there was a terrible bang at the door of our room, and a fearful voice saying something or other in a language I didn't know. "Good heavens, Mum," exclaimed Rosetta, clinging to me, "what ever is happening?" I lay still for a moment, scarcely believing my ears, and then again, suddenly, there was another bang at the door and another dreadful, incomprehensible cry. I told Rosetta I would go and see, and I jumped out of bed just as I was, in my petticoat, with bare feet and my hair all untidy, and opened the door and looked out. There stood two German soldiers, a sergeant and a private. The sergeant was the younger of the two; he was fair, with a shaven head, his face was white as paper, his eyes a washed-out blue, without eyelashes, and with no expression or light in them. His nose was a bit crooked and his mouth went the opposite way to his nose, and two long wounds across his cheek, healed up into pale, ridged scars, gave his face a curious look, as if his mouth went on toward his neck. The other was a middle-aged man, thickset and dark, with an enormous forehead, sad, deepset, dark blue eyes and the jaw of a mastiff. I was frightened, if only because of the sergeant's eyes, which were so cold and expressionless and of such an ugly blue that they looked like the eyes of a beast. However I did not show my fear, but shouted right in his face, as loud as I could: "What's the matter, you miserable wretch, do you want to knock the door down? Can't you see we're just a couple of women and that we're trying to sleep?" The sergeant with the pale eyes waved his hand, saying in bad Italian: "Good, good," and then, turning to the soldier, signaled to him to follow and went into the room. Rosetta, who was still in bed, looked on with eyes starting out of her head, the sheets pulled right up under her chin. The two of them ransacked the whole place, even under the bed; and the sergeant, in the fury of his search, even went so far as to raise the sheet from on top of Rosetta, as though she might have had whatever it was they were looking for under the bedclothes. Then they went out again. In the meantime a quantity of evacuees had assembled; and now, thinking it over, I am sure it was a miracle that those two Germans did not question the evacuees about the two Englishmen, for someone, more out of stupidity than anything else, would certainly have blurted out the whole story, and then—what would have happened to *us?* In any case, the fact that the Germans came up there the very day after the arrival of the two Englishmen has always made me suspect that there had been some sort of spying or gossip. But the Germans did not seem to want to make trouble, and confined themselves to a hurried visit without any interrogations.

The evacuees, not accustomed to seeing Germans up there, wanted to know how the war was going and whether it would be over soon. Somebody had gone meanwhile to call Michele, who knew a little German; and at the very moment when the two Germans were on the point of going they pushed him forward, much against his will, shouting: "Ask them when the war'll be over."

You could see from a mile off that Michele did not at all like speaking to the Germans. But he plucked up courage and said something. I shall now relate what the Germans and Michele said, for part of it Michele translated there and then for the convenience of the evacuees, and part of it he translated later for me, after the Germans had gone away. Well, Michele asked them when the war would be over, and the sergeant replied that it would be over soon, with victory for Hitler. They had some secret weapons, he added, and with these weapons they would throw the English back into the sea, in the spring at latest. He also said something that made a great impression upon the evacuees: "We shall take the offensive and throw the English back into the sea. And meanwhile the trains will be used for carrying munitions and we shall live on the Italians, and as for the Italians, who betrayed us, we shall leave them to die of hunger." He said this calmly and pitilessly, with an expression of conviction on his face, as though he had been speaking of flies or caterpillars instead of Italians, that is, of human beings. The evacuees fell silent at these words, because they had not expected them; for some unknown reason they thought the Germans were sympathetic toward them. Michele, who was now beginning to enjoy himself, asked the Germans who they were. The sergeant answered that he came from Berlin and in peacetime had a small cardboard-box factory there, but it had now been destroyed and so, he said, there was nothing left for him to do except fight in the war, as best he could. The private hesitated before replying, and then, turning away his sad, deepset eyes with a pained expression like a dog which has been beaten, said that he too came from Berlin and that for him too there was nothing left but to fight in the war, because his wife and his only daughter had been killed in air raids. They had both of them made more or less the same answer—that having lost everything in the air raids, the only thing they could think of now was carrying on the war; only it was clear as daylight that the sergeant, for his part, was carrying on the war with enthusiasm and passion, and with malevolence as well; whereas the private, so gloomy looking with that enormous forehead that seemed full of sadness, was now fighting more from despair than anything else, knowing that there was no one waiting for him at home. I felt that the private was perhaps not a bad man; but the fact of losing his wife and daughter might have made him bad; and if, let us suppose—God protect us!—they had arrested us both, he perhaps would not have hesitated to kill Rosetta, bearing in mind, precisely, that his own daughter had also been killed.

While I was thinking these things, the sergeant, who seemed to bear a real grudge against the Italians, suddenly asked why, when all Germans were at the front, there should be amongst the evacuees here so many young men standing about with their hands in their pockets. Then Michele, raising his voice till he was almost shouting, replied that he and all the others had fought for Hitler and for the Germans in Greece, in Africa and in Albania, and that they were ready to fight again, to the last drop of their blood; and that everyone up there could hardly wait for the moment when the great and glorious Hitler should win the war, as quickly as possible, and chase all those bastards of English and Americans back into the sea. The sergeant appeared rather surprised at this tirade; he looked up from under his eyelids at Michele in uncertainty, and you could see that he did not altogether believe him. However, they were words to which no exception could be taken and he could not say anything, even if he did not believe them. And so, after they had nosed about a little more among the cottages, and rummaged and searched here and there, but in a tired sort of way and without much interest, they went off again down to the valley, to the great relief of all of us.

But I had been shocked by Michele's attitude. I am not saying that he ought to have hurled abuse at the two Germans, but the fact remains that all those lies which he had shouted at them in such a brazen-faced way had astonished me. I said so to him, and he replied with a shrug of the shoulders: "With the Nazis, anything is permitted: you can lie to them, betray them, kill them, if possible. What would you do with a poisonous snake, a tiger, a mad wolf? You would try, obviously, to reduce it to impotence either by force or by cunning. You certainly wouldn't talk to it and try by some means or other to pacify it, since you would know perfectly well beforehand that this would be useless. And so it is with the Nazis. They have placed themselves outside human kind, like wild beasts, and therefore in dealing with them all means are legitimate. You, like that highly educated English officer, have never read Dante. But if you had read him, you would know that Dante says: *E cortesia fu in lui esser villano*."

I asked what this meant; and he explained to me that it meant that lies and treachery were too good for people like the Nazis. They didn't even deserve *that*. So I said—just for the sake of saying something—that among the Nazis there might perhaps be both good and bad, as always happens; and how was he to know that both of these two were bad? He started to laugh. "This isn't a question of good and bad," he said. "Of course they're good to their own wives and children, just as wolves and snakes are good to their young and their females. But to human kind—which after all is what counts—that is to you, to me, to Rosetta, to these evacuees and peasants, they are incapable of being anything but bad." "But why?" "Because," he said after a moment's reflection, "because they are convinced that what we call evil is good. And so it follows, they do evil, thinking that they are doing good. That is, they do their duty." I felt a little doubtful, thinking that I had not really understood. Michele, however, paid no further attention to me, but concluded, as if talking to himself: "That's it; the combination of evil and a sense of duty—that's what Nazism is."

Michele, in short, was an odd character, so very good and yet so very hard. I remember another time when we encountered the Germans. As usual, we had very little flour, and now, when I was making bread, I left in it not merely the finer part of the bran but the coarse bran as well. We decided to go down into the valley to see if we could find some flour in exchange for eggs. I had bought the eggs from Paride and I had sixteen of them, and I was hoping to be able to acquire a few pounds of white flour in exchange for these eggs, with the addition of some money. We hadn't been down to the valley since the day of the air raid which had so terrified poor Tommasino, and, to tell the truth, I went unwillingly, partly for this reason. I mentioned it in front of Michele and he offered to go with us, and I accepted with real pleasure because with him I felt safer, and he was the only person up there who inspired me with any courage or confidence. We put the eggs in a basket underneath some straw, and started off early in the morning. It was now the beginning of January and we were in the very heart of winter, and also, I felt—though I couldn't quite explain it to myself—in the very heart of the war, that is, at the darkest, coldest and most desperate moment of the despair that had now lasted for so many years. The last time I had gone down into the valley there were still leaves on the trees, yellow though they were; there was grass in the meadows; owing to the great amount of rain; and on the hillsides there were even a few flowers, the last of the autumn, such as cyclamen and wild violets. But now everything was dried-up and grey, scorched and barren in the cold, sunless air beneath an overcast, colorless sky. We had been quite cheerful when we set out but we quickly fell silent: the day was quiet as only days in the depth of winter can be quiet, and this quietness froze us and prevented us speaking. We went down across the side of the mountain on the right of the valley, then crossed the level stretch of ground where, among the prickly pears and the rocks, the bomb had fallen that day when we came down with Tommasino.

We walked steadily in silence for another half hour and at last came down to the point where the valley opened out on to the plain, to the little bridge, the fork in the road, and the cottage in which Tommasino had lived until the day of the fatal air raid. I recalled this spot as being smiling and pretty, and spacious too, and I confess I was surprised when I saw it now, looking so sad and grey and bare and mean. Have you ever seen a woman without any hair? I have; a girl from my village who had typhus fever and lost part of her hair and had the rest shaved off, down to nothing at all. She looked a different person, she even had a different expression, and she remained one of a big, ugly egg, with a smooth, bald head such as women never have and a face with no hair to shade it so that it looked crushed by a light that was too crude. In the same way, without the thick, green foliage of the three plane trees that shaded Tommasino's cottage, without the green vegetation that hid the rocks on the banks of the stream, without the plants at each side of the road and in the ditches, which I had not noticed at the time but which must have been there because I now felt the lack of them, without all these things the place seemed of no interest and had lost all its beauty. Just like a woman if you take away her hair. When I saw it looking so impoverished my heart ached, and it seemed to me that the place had a resemblance to our lives at that moment, they too being reduced to nakedness and disillusionment, with the war going on and on without end.

But enough of that. We turned into the main road, and a little farther on had our first encounter. A man was leading two brown, well-fed horses—very fine ones—along the road. These two horses were German but the man was wearing a uniform I had never seen, and, as soon as we caught up with him, he first looked at us, then gave us a greeting, and then, since we were going the same way, started a conversation in his odd, halting

Italian; and so we walked along, talking together. He was a man of about twenty-five, and of a beauty such as I have seldom seen in my life. He was tall, with broad shoulders and a slim waist almost like a woman's, graceful, and with long legs in yellow hide jack-boots. His hair was fair as gold, his eyes of a color between green and blue, almond-shaped, strange and rather dreamy, his nose straight, large and delicate, his lips red and well-cut; and when he smiled he showed very beautiful teeth, white and regular and a pleasure to look at. He told us he was not German but Russian, from some very distant country; he said the name but I cannot remember it. He said quietly that he had betrayed the Russians for the Germans because he did not care for the Russians; however he did not at all love the Germans either. He told us that he himself, together with other Russians who were also traitors, was attached to German headquarters for fatigue duties. He also said he was certain that the Germans would lose the war because they had disgusted the world with their cruelty and the whole world had turned against them. It was only a question of months, he said, before the Germans would be completely defeated, and then it would be all up with him, and at this point he made a gesture that froze my blood, putting his hand up to his neck, as much as to say that the Russians would cut his troat. He spoke calmly, as though his own fate were by now a matter of indifference, and he even smiled, not only with his mouth but with those strange, cerulean eyes which looked like two little pieces of the deepest part of the sea. It was clear that he hated the Germans and the Russians and even himself, and that death was of no consequence to him. He walked quietly along, holding the two horses by their bridles; and on that deserted road in the grey, frozen countryside there was nothing to be seen but him and his horses, and it seemed incredible that this very beautiful young man should be already condemned and should have to die soon, probably before the end of the year. At the fork in the road, where we parted, he said again: "These two horses are all that I have left in life and they're not even mine." Then he went off in the direction of the town. We watched him for a moment as he walked away, and I reflected that here was another effect of war. If there had not been a war, this handsome young man would have stayed in his own country and would probably have got married and had a job and become a good, honest man like many others. The war had made him leave his country and had made him turn traitor, and now the war was going to kill him and he was already resigned to death and this, among so many terrible things, was perhaps the worst of all, for it was the least natural and the least comprehensible.

We turned off to the left along a road which led toward the orange groves, hoping to exchange our eggs for some bread with the German tank crew whose tents were pitched at the edge of these groves, as we had done before. But we found no one. The tank men had gone and there was no sign of them but the trampled ground and a few torn trees with their leaves stripped from them: that was all. I said that we might as well continue along the same road, possibly the tank men or some other group of Germans might be encamped a little farther on. We walked on for another quarter of an hour without speaking, and finally met a fair-haired girl wandering along all alone, not like one who has a definite objective, but walking aimlessly. She was moving slowly, looking with a strange interest at the bare, grey fields and pulling off a morsel now and then from a piece of bread. I went up and asked her: "Can you tell me—do you know if there are any Germans anywhere along this road?" She stopped suddenly at my question and looked at me. She had a handkerchief tied round her head and was a good-looking girl, healthy and strong, with a broad, rather massive face and big, chestnut-brown eyes. She said at once, hurriedly: "Germans. . . of course there are Germans. . . and what if there are?" "But where are they?" I asked. She looked at me and now she seemed frightened, and then without answering she started to walk away. I caught her by the arm, repeating my question and she said in a low voice: "If I tell you, you won't go and tell anyone else where I keep my provisions, will you?" I was astonished on hearing these words, for they were at the same time in accordance with the circumstances and also completely absurd. "What do you mean?" I said. "What have provisions got to do with it?" She shook her head. "They come and they take," she said, "they come and they take. . . . They're Germans, of course. . . . But do you know what I said to them last time they came? I haven't anything, I said, I haven't any flour, I haven't any beans, I haven't any lard, I haven't anything at all. . . The only thing I have is milk for my baby. If you want that, take it—here you are." And, staring at me wide-eyed, she began unbuttoning her bodice. I was struck dumb, and so were Michele and Rosetta. She stared at us, moving her lips as if talking to herself, and meanwhile she had undone her bodice down to the waist; then, with one hand, the fingers held open, she drew forth her breast just as mothers do when about to suckle their babies. "This is all I have . . . take it," she kept repeating in a low voice. By now she had completely pulled out one of her breasts; and a fine, rounded, swelling breast it was, with the transparency of skin and the clear whiteness which generally go to show that the woman is a mother and is suckling her child. But after she had pulled it out she moved off again humming a tune in an absent-minded way, her bodice still open, one breast out and the other in. It moved me to see her go off like that, nibbling her piece of bread, with one breast exposed to the wintry air, the only living, white, warm, luminous thing to be seen at that moment, on that cold, bleak day without sunshine and without color. "She must be mad," said Rosetta at last. Michele agreed tartly: "Yes, indeed." We walked on in silence.

Since there were no Germans to be seen in any direction, Michele suggested going to see some acquaintances of his who, he thought had taken refuge in a hut amongst these orange groves. They were honest people, he said, and they might at any rate be able to suggest where we could find Germans who would exchange our eggs for some bread. We left the road and made our way along a small path through the trees. Michele told us that all these oranges belonged to the person we were going to visit, a bachelor lawyer who lived with his old mother. We went on for about ten minutes and finally came out into a small clearing, in front of a humble little hut with brick walls and a corrugated iron roof. The hut had two windows and a door. Michele went over to one of the windows, had a look and said the owners seemed to be there; he then gave two knocks. We waited and finally the door slowly opened and the lawyer appeared on the threshold. He was a man of about fifty, corpulent, bald, with a brow pale and glossy as ivory surrounded by a fuzz of ruffled black hair, watery, rather prominent eyes, a beaky nose, and a soft mouth curving back over a plump chin. He was wearing a town overcoat, of the type that men wear at night, of dark blue cloth with a black velvet collar, but underneath this smart coat he had on a pair of ragged old trousers and hobnailed, cow-hide army boots. I noticed immediately that he was upset at seeing us; however, he recovered himself quickly and threw his arms round Michele's neck with a cordiality that might even have been thought excessive. "My dear Michele! How splendid, how splendid! What good wind brings you here?" Michele introduced us and he greeted us distantly, with embarrassment and almost coldly. In the meantime we were standing around the door, and as he did not invite us to come in, Michele said: "We were passing this way so we thought we would pay you a visit." The lawyer gave a start, and replied: "That's fine. . . . Well, we were just sitting down to table. . . . Won't you come in and share our meal?" He hesitated and then went on: "Michele, I warn you. . . since I know your feelings, which are mine too. I've invited the German lieutenant who commands the anti-aircraft battery near here. I had to do this. Alas, you know what it is in these times." Sighing and making excuses, he led us into the hut. A round table was spread near the window, and was the only clean and tidy thing in the room; otherwise there was nothing to be seen but bits of rubbish, heaps of rags, piles of books, and a jumble of suitcases and boxes. Already seated at the table were the lawyer's mother, a little elderly lady dressed in black with a wrinkled, apprehensive face like that of a small, frightened monkey, and the Nazi lieutenant, a little fair man, flat as a sheet of paper in his tight-fitting uniform, with long legs in riding breeches and boots, which he stretched out under the table in an informal manner. He looked like a dog and had the face of a dog—all nose, eyes almost yellow and very close together, without eyelashes or eyebrows, an alert, hostile expression, a large, drawn-back mouth. Courteous and well-bred, he rose to his feet and greeted us with a click of the heels; but he did not shake hands with anyone and promptly sat down again, as much as to say: "I don't do this for you but because I am a well brought up person." The lawyer was explaining, in the meantime, that the lieutenant was attached to the anti-aircraft batteries—which we knew already; and that this luncheon was a matter of neighborliness. "And let us hope," the lawyer concluded, "that soon the war will be over and the lieutenant will be able to invite us to his home in Germany." The lieutenant said nothing, he did not even smile, and I thought that perhaps he did not know our language and had not understood. But then he suddenly said in good Italian: "Thank you, I never drink *apéritifs*," to the lawyer's mother, who, in a plaintive voice, was offering him a vermouth. I realized that he refused to smile because for some reason he was angry with the lawyer. Michele told the story of our encounter with the madwoman; and the lawyer remarked with indifference: "Oh yes, Lena. She's always been dotty. Last year, when there was all that confusion with troops coming and going, some soldier came upon her when she was wandering all alone as usual, about the countryside, and got her with child."

"And where's the child, now?" "Oh, it's kept by her family and brought up with every possible care. But she, poor crazy creature, has got it into her head that they want to take it away from her because she hasn't the milk to feed it. The odd thing is that it's she herself who suckles it regularly; I mean that at certain hours her mother puts it into her arms and she does what her mother tells her to do. All the same, she has this fixed idea that she can't give it enough to satisfy it." The lawyer spoke of this poor Lena as if she were something of no importance whatever. Upon me, on the other hand, she had left an impression so profound that it can never be effaced from my memory. To me, that bare breast that she offered to all and sundry, on the high road, seemed the clearest possible symbol of the situation in which we Italians found ourselves in that winter of 1944: bereft of everything, like the beasts that have nothing except the milk they give to their young.

All this time the lawyer's mother, frightened, trembling, apprehensive, was going back and forth to the kitchen carrying the dishes with both hands, like the Holy Sacrament. She placed some sliced sausage, *salame* and ham on the table, a German tinned loaf—just what we were looking for—and some good soup with vermicelli in it, and finally a big boiled fowl garnished with mixed pickles. She also brought in a bottle of good red wine. It was obvious that the lawyer and his mother had made a special effort to keep on the right side of this nasty young German who, with his battery, was now their neighbor. The lieutenant had a really unpleasant character, for the first thing he asked, when he saw the tinned loaf, was: "Might I inquire, *Signor avvocato*, how you managed to procure this loaf of bread?" The lawyer, who was sitting with his coat wrapped closely around him as though he had a high fever, answered in a hesitating, joking tone: "Well, it was a present; a soldier gave it to us as a present and we gave him a present too. . . . In war-time, you know—" "An exchange," said the other man, pitilessly, "that is forbidden. And who was this soldier?" "Ha, ha, Lieutenant, one can mention a sin but not a sinner. Do try some of this ham; *that* isn't German, it's produced locally." The lieutenant said nothing, and began eating the ham.

Then suddenly the lieutenant turned his attention from the lawyer to Michele. He asked him, point-blank, what his profession was; and Michele told him without hesitation that he was a professor and teacher. "A teacher of what?" "Of Italian literature." Then the lieutenant, to the lawyer's astonishment, remarked calmly: "I know your literature. I have even translated an Italian novel into German." "Which novel?" The lieutenant mentioned the name of the author and the title of the book, but I don't remember either of them now; and I could see that Michele, who so far had shown no interest in the lieutenant, seemed now to have become curious about him; and that the lawyer, seeing that the lieutenant spoke to Michele with almost consideration, as though they were on equal terms, had also changed his attitude: he now seemed pleased to have Michele at his table, and said to the lieutenant: "Oh yes, our friend Festa is a man of learning, a distinguished man of learning"—at the same time clapping his hand on Michele's shoulder. But it appeared to be a point of honor with the lieutenant to pay no attention to the lawyer though he was the master of the house and had invited him to lunch. Still turning toward Michele, he went on: "I lived for two years in Rome and studied your language, but my own special subject is philosophy." The lawyer tried to insinuate himself into the conversation by saying jokingly: "Then you'll understand why we Italians accept everything that has happened to us in recent times philosophically . . . ha, ha, yes indeed, philosophically." But once again the lieutenant did not even look at him. He was now talking quickly to Michele, bringing out quantities of names of writers and titles of books; evidently he knew a great deal about literature, and I noticed that Michele, grudgingly, and almost in spite of himself, was gradually giving way to a feeling, if not exactly of respect, at least of curiosity. They went on like this for a little and then, somehow or other, started talking of the war and of what the effect of war might be on a man of letters or a philosopher; and the lieutenant, after observing that it was an important experience, in fact even a necessary one, came out with this remark: "I experienced the most novel and at the same time most aesthetic sensation"—I repeat this word "aesthetic," although at the time I did not understand it, because the whole sentence made an impression on my mind as though branded there with fire—"during the Balkan campaign, and d'you know how, my dear Professor? When I cleared out a cave full of enemy soldiers with a flame thrower." The moment he uttered this remark all four of us—Rosetta, myself, the lawyer and his mother—were turned to stone. Afterward I thought that perhaps it was a mere boast and hoped he had never done it and that it was not true; he had drunk a few glasses of wine, his face had turned red and his eyes were rather bright; but at the moment I felt my heart sink and my whole body turn cold. I looked at the others. Rosetta had lowered her eyes; the lawyer's mother, nervously and with trembling hands, was smoothing out a fold in the tablecloth; as for the lawyer, he was behaving like a tortoise and had pulled his head back inside his overcoat. Only Michele was staring wide-eyed at the lieutenant; and he then said: "Interesting, no doubt about it, interesting. And an even more novel and aesthetic sensation, I suppose, would be that of an airman dropping his bombs on a village and leaving nothing, after he has passed, except a patch of dust where there were houses before." But the lieutenant was not so silly as to be unaware that Michele's remark was ironical. He said, after a moment: "War is an experience for which there is no substitute, and lacking which a man cannot call himself a man. . . . And by the way, Professor, how in the world does it happen that you're here and not at the front?" Michele asked in return, quite simply: "Which front?" and strange to relate, the lieutenant said nothing, he merely gave him an ugly look and returned to his plate.

But he was not pleased; you could see from a mile off that he was conscious of having around him people who, if they were not actually hostile, were anyhow not friendly. He left Michele alone—thinking, perhaps, that he was not sufficiently frightened—and attacked the lawyer again. "My dear sir," he demanded, indicating the table, "you appear to be rolling in abundance, whereas, everyone else around here is dying of hunger. Tell me, how have you managed to procure so many good things to eat?" The lawyer and his mother exchanged a significant glance, the mother's frightened and apprehensive, the lawyer's reassuring; and then the latter said: "I assure you we never eat like this on other days—far from it. We have done this in order to do honor to you." The lieutenant was silent for a moment, then he asked: "You are a landowner here in this valley, are you not?" "Yes, in a sort of way, yes." "In a sort of way? I'm told you own half the valley." "Oh no, my dear Lieutenant, whoever told you that was either a liar or an envious man or both. I own a few gardens—we call them gardens, these fine orange groves." "I'm told these so-called gardens are extremely profitable. You must be a rich man." "Oh well, Lieutenant, no; not exactly rich. I live off my own property." "And you know how your peasants live, all around here?" The lawyer, who by now had realized the turn the conversation had taken, answered with dignity: "They live well. Here in this valley they live as well as any." The lieutenant, who at that moment was cutting himself a piece of chicken, said without smiling, pointing his knife in the direction of the lawyer: "If these peasants here live well, I wonder what it's like with the ones who live badly. I have seen them myself, I have seen how your peasants live. They live like beasts, in houses that look like stables, eating like beasts and dressed in rags. No peasant in Germany lives like that. We in Germany would be ashamed to make our peasants live like that." The lawyer, partly in order to please his mother who was darting imploring glances at him, as much as to say: "Don't draw him out—keep quiet," shrugged his shoulders and said nothing. The lieutenant, however, persisted: "What have you to say, my dear sir, about all this; what answer are you going to give me?" This time the lawyer replied: "It's they themselves who wish to live like that. I assure you, Lieutenant, you don't know them." But the lieutenant said harshly: "No, it's you, the landowners, who wish the peasants to live like that. It all depends on *this*," and he touched his head, "on the head. You landowners are Italy's head and it's your fault if the peasants live like beasts." The lawyer was now looking really frightened and was eating with obvious effort, making a movement with his throat at every mouthful, like a hen when it swallows something in haste. His mother looked completely bewildered, and I saw her furtively put her hands together in her lap under the tablecloth: she was praying, placing herself in the hands of God. The lieutenant went on: "At one time I knew just a few of the towns of Italy—the most beautiful ones—and in those towns I knew only the monuments. But now, thanks to the war, I've come to know your country thoroughly; I've traveled over it from end to end and from one side to the other. And do you know what I say, my good sir? That you have differences between one class and another which are an absolute scandal." The lawyer remained silent; but he made a slight movement with his shoulders as much as to say: "And what can *I* do about it?" The lieutenant noticed it and jumped upon him: "No, my dear sir, this thing concerns you as it concerns all others of your kind—lawyers, engineers, doctors, professors, intellectuals. We Germans, for instance, have felt indignant at the enormous differences that exist between Italian officers and soldiers: the officers are covered with gold lace and wear special materials, they eat special kinds of food, they have special, privileged treatment in every possible way. The soldiers are dressed in rags, they feed like beasts, they are treated like beasts. What have you got to say about all this?" This time the lawyer spoke up. "I have to say that it is indeed true. And that I am the first to deplore it. But what can I do about it, all by myself?" "No, my dear sir," said the other man primly, "you shouldn't say that. This thing concerns you directly and if you and everyone else in your position really wanted the situation to change—well, there would be a change. Do you know why Italy has lost the war and why we Germans now have to waste precious soldiers on the Italian front? It is precisely because of that difference between soldiers and officers, between the people and you gentlemen of the ruling class. The Italian soldier doesn't fight, because he thinks that this is *your* war, not his. And he shows you his hostility precisely by not fighting. What have you got to say about all this?" The lawyer, perhaps because he was so irritated, managed, this time, to overcome his fear. "It's true," he said. "The people didn't want this war. But neither did I. This war was imposed upon us by the Fascist government. And the Fascist government is not *my* government, of that you may be sure." The other man raised his voice slightly. "No, sir, that is too easy. This government is your government." "My government? I suppose you're joking, Lieutenant." His mother intervened at this moment. "Francesco, please, please . . . for God's sake." The lieutenant insisted: "Yes, *your* government; do you want the proof of it?" "What d'you mean, proof?" "I know all about you, my dear sir; I know for instance that you're an anti-Fascist, a Liberal.

And yet, in this valley, you don't associate with peasants and workmen, but with the local Fascist Secretary. What do you say to that?" The lawyer shrugged his shoulders again. "At the present time I am neither anti-Fascist nor Liberal; I take no part in politics but look after my own affairs. Besides, what's that got to do with it? The Fascist Secretary and I went to school together, in fact we're more or less related because my sister married a cousin of his. There are some things that you Germans can't understand. You don't know Italy well enough." "No, sir, that is a perfect proof. You Fascists and anti-Fascists are all bound to one another because you're all of the same class . . . and this government is the government of the whole lot of you, both Fascists and anti-Fascists, because it's the government of your class. Facts speak for themselves and all the rest is mere nonsense."

There were beads of sweat now on the lawyer's brow, although it was cold inside the hut; his mother, not knowing what to do, rose to her feet, bewildered, and said in a trembling voice: "Now I'm going to go and make some nice coffee," and disappeared into the kitchen. The lieutenant meanwhile was saying: "I'm not like the majority of my fellow-countrymen who are so stupid about you Italians . . . They love Italy because it has so many fine monuments and because the landscapes of Italy are the most beautiful in the world. Or they find some Italian who talks German and are touched by hearing their own language. Or again someone gives them a good lunch such as you have given me to-day, and they make friends over a bottle of wine. I am not like these stupid Germans. I see things as they are and tell you about them to your face, my dear sir." Then, for some reason or other—perhaps because I felt sorry for the poor lawyer—I suddenly said, almost without thinking: "Do you know why this gentleman gave you this lunch?" "Why?" "Because you Germans frighten everybody and everybody's frightened of you, and so he tried to conciliate you, just as one might do with a fierce animal, by giving you something good to eat." Strange to say, the expression on his face, just for an instant, became sad, almost, and distressed: no one, even a German, likes to hear it said that he frightens people and that people are kind to him merely because they are frightened of him. The lawyer, terrified, tried to mend matters by intervening. "Please, Lieutenant, don't pay any attention to this woman. She's a simple sort of person, and there are things she doesn't understand." But the lieutenant signaled to him to be quiet, and asked: "Why is it that we Germans are so frightening? Aren't we men like other men?" Well into it now, I was on the point of answering him: "No, a man who is really a man, unless he's a heathen, doesn't take pleasure—as you were saying just now—in clearing out a cave full of living soldiers with a flame thrower," but luckily I hadn't time, for suddenly we heard sharp, intermittent firing, like that of anti-aircraft guns, alternating with the duller sound of exploding bombs. At the same time the air was filled with a distant rumbling which grew ever nearer and more distinct. The lieutenant leaped to his feet, exclaiming: "Aircraft! . . . I have to get back to my battery," and upsetting chairs and everything else in his way, he rushed out. The first to rouse himself after the flight of the lieutenant was the lawyer. "Quick, quick, come," he cried, "we must go to the shelter." He jumped up and led us out of the hut into the yard. There, in a corner, was a kind of opening, flush with the ground and protected by a little fortress of beams and sandbags. The lawyer went straight across to this opening and started going down into it by a wooden ladder, repeating: "Quick, hurry up, they'll be overhead in a moment." Indeed that rumbling sound had now become all-pervading, even above the bursts of firing from the anti-aircraft batteries, as though it were coming from just behind the trees that surrounded the clearing. Then it all died down and we found ourselves in the dark, in a small underground room which seemed to have been dug out right underneath the clearing. "Of course this wouldn't be any use against a direct hit," said the lawyer, "but at least it's a protection from the machine-gun bullets . . . There's more than three feet of earth above us, and there are the sandbags." So there we remained for I don't know how long, standing upright in the darkness, hardly daring to breathe; from time to time we could hear a few muffled bangs from the anti-aircraft guns, and that was all. Finally the lawyer opened the door slightly, made sure that all was quiet, and then we came out into the open. The lawyer pointed to some of the sandbags which had been holed or torn, and also picked up a brass shell-case, as long as our finger, saying: "If this caught you, it would kill you all right." Then raising his eyes toward heaven, he went on: "Blessed airplanes, may they come often! And let's hope they have delivered us from that lieutenant, who certainly *is* a fierce animal." His mother reproved him: "You must not say that, Francesco. After all, he's a Christian too, and one shouldn't desire the death of anybody." But the lawyer replied: "He—a Christian? Curses on him, curses on his battery, and cursed be the day when he arrived here. When he goes away, I intend to give a lunch a thousand times better than this. That's understood—you're all invited." Indeed he went on and on, cursing the German lieutenant with genuine hatred. We returned to the hut and drank some coffee and then the lawyer's mother took our eggs and gave us some flour and beans in exchange. Finally we bade them good-bye and left.

It was getting late by now and I was longing to be up at Sant' Eufemia again. Down in the valley we had had nothing but disagreeable meetings: first the Russian with the horses, then the poor madwoman, then that German lieutenant. As we were climbing up again, Michele said: "One thing made me particularly angry while he was talking." "What was that?" "That he was right, even in spite of being a Nazi." "Why?" I said; "even Nazis can sometimes be right." He bent his head. "No, never," he said. I should have liked to ask him how he accounted for the fact that this ferocious Nazi, who found a special kind of enjoyment in burning people alive with a flame-thrower, could nevertheless, at the same time, have studied the question of the injustice that existed in Italy. Michele had always told us that those who were conscious of injustice were fine people, the best of all, the only ones he did not despise. And now, if you please, this lieutenant, who was a philosopher into the bargain, was capable of perceiving injustice and yet at the same time found satisfaction in killing people. How could this be? It was not true, then, that justice was such a very good thing. But I had not the courage to communicate my reflections to him, partly because I saw that he was sad and discouraged. So we went up the valley and reached Sant'Eufemia long after dark.

Chapter 7

ONE JANUARY DAY, when the *tramontana* was still blowing in a sky as transparent and brilliant as crystal, Rosetta and I, on waking up, heard a distant, regular sound that seemed to come from far away and low down in the heavens, in the direction of the sea coast. There was a dull thud, just as though the sky had received a thump, and then a second thud shortly afterward, louder and clearer, which sounded like the echo of the first. Thump, thump, thump–so it went on, without ever stopping; and this dull, menacing sound made the day seem by contrast even more beautiful, the sunshine more brilliant, the sky bluer. Two days went by without this sound ever ceasing, night or day; and then one morning a shepherd boy came down from the scrub bringing a printed leaflet which he had found in a bush. This leaflet was a news sheet printed by the English but written in German for the benefit of the Germans, and since Michele was the only person up there who knew any German, it was brought to him. After reading it he explained to us that the English had carried out a landing in the neighborhood of Anzio, near Rome, and that there was now a big battle going on, with ships, artillery, tanks and infantry, and that the English were advancing toward Rome and, it appeared, were already in the neighborhood of Velletri. At this news all the evacuees fell into each other's arms, congratulating and kissing one another in their great joy. That evening nobody went to bed early, as usually happened, but strolled around among the cottages and huts, commenting on the landing and exulting in the fact that it had happened.

The following days, however, brought no news. The same dull sound of gunfire continued to reverberate far away and low down in the sky in the direction of Terracina, but the Germans were not falling back. After a few more days, the first accurate news arrived; the English had indeed made a landing but the Germans had promptly sent I don't know how many divisions of soldiers to stop them and, after much fighting, had succeeded in doing so. The English had dug themselves in on the beach, in a very small space, and the Germans were firing on this space with a large number of guns, as if at target practice, and would soon force the English to re-embark in the ships which were lying off the beach. At this news, there was nothing to be seen throughout Sant'Eufemia but long faces, and the evacuees said that the English were no good at fighting on land because they were sailors, and the Germans, on the other hand, had land fighting in their blood and the English would never get the better of the Germans. As for Michele, he didn't speak to the evacuees at all because, he told us, he did not want to make bad blood. But he assured us, quite calmly, that it was absolutely impossible for the Germans to win; and when I asked him one day why he thought so, he replied simply: "The Germans were beaten from the very beginning."

Here I wish to tell a little story to show how short of news we were up at Sant'Eufemia and how the peasants, most of whom were illiterate, distorted even the small amount that did come through to us. Since we were unable to discover anything precise about the Anzio landing, Filippo and another evacuee, also a shopkeeper, decided that they would pay Paride to go over the mountains to a village in Ciociaria, a very long way off, where they knew there was a parish doctor who owned a radio. It is true that Paride was illiterate and could neither read nor write, but he had ears and was able to listen to the radio like anybody else and if necessary, get the doctor to explain it to him. They also gave Paride some money so that if possible he might buy up something in the way of eatables—flour, beans, fats, anything that he could find. Paride saddled his ass and left one morning at dawn.

Paride was away for three days; he came back late one afternoon. As soon as they saw him appear on his way down the mountainside, pulling his ass by the bridle, the evacuees ran out to meet him and foremost among them Filippo and his shopkeeper friend. Paride said he had found nothing, or practically nothing, in the way of provisions; everywhere there was the same shortage of food and hunger as at Sant'Eufemia, or even worse. Then he went off to his hut followed by a procession of people. Inside the hut he sat down on a bench, and around him sat his family, Michele and Filippo and a whole lot of others. Many people remained outside the hut too, because there was no room inside but all the same they wanted to hear what Paride had heard on the radio.

Paride said he had listened to the radio and it did not say much about the landing, it only said that the English and the Germans were keeping to their positions and not moving. But he had talked to the doctor and to many others who had listened to the radio on other days and had thus learned why the landing had failed. Filippo asked him why the landing had failed, and Paride answered simply that it had been the fault of a woman. This piece of news left us all open-mouthed, and Paride went on to say that the admiral who was in command of the landing was an American, but in reality, though no one knew it, he was a German. This admiral had a daughter who was beautiful as a star, and she was engaged to the son of the general in command of all the American troops in Europe. But this young man, who was a cad, had given offense by breaking off the engagement, returning the presents and the ring and marrying someone else. So the admiral, the father of the bride, he who was really a German, had determined to avenge himself and had secretly informed the Germans of the landing, so that, when the English had appeared in front of Anzio, they had found the Germans all ready waiting with their guns. Now, however, the thing had been discovered; it had been ascertained that the admiral really was a German although he passed himself off as American, and he had been arrested and would soon be brought to trial, and, in short, it was quite certain that he would be shot. Paride's listeners were divided into two groups by this news. The more ignorant and simple ones shook their heads and repeated: "Of course, there's always a woman at the bottom of it. Scratch hard enough and you'll always find a skirt." But many others objected, saying it was impossible that the radio could have given out such rubbish. As for Michele, he merely asked Paride: "Are you sure the radio gave out this news?" Paride confirmed that the doctor and others too had assured him that this news had been communicated by the B.B.C. from London. "But tell me," said Michele, "are you quite certain you didn't hear it from some professional story-teller in the village square?" "What d'you mean-story-teller?" "Never mind, Anyhow, it's a new version of the exploits of Gano di Maganza; and very interesting too, it must be admitted." Paride, who did not understand irony, repeated that the whole story was guaranteed radio news. But a little later I asked Michele who this Gano di Maganza was, and he explained that he had been a general in the distant past, many centuries ago, and had betrayed his own emperor in a battle against the Turks. "Well then, you see," I said; "these are things that can happen. I'm not saying that Paride is right, but, after all, it's not absolutely impossible." He started to laugh, and said: "Would to God things still happened in that sort of way nowadays!"

And so there was nothing to be done but wait, seeing that the landing had failed for one reason or another. But as the saying goes, hope deferred maketh the heart sick, and up there at Sant'Eufemia, all through January and then through February too, we felt our hearts sickening a little more every day. The days were monotonous, too, for everything repeated itself now and the same things happened every day that had happened all through the last months. Each day we had to get up, cut wood, light the fire in the hut, cook something to eat, eat it, and then dawdle about on the terraces to while away the time until supper in the evening. Each day, moreover, the airplanes came and dropped bombs. Each day, from morning until evening and from evening until morning, we could hear the regular thud of those accursed guns at Anzio firing continuously, and it was evident that they never hit their mark, for, as we knew, neither the English nor the Germans had budged. Each day, in fact, was like the day before; but hope, now roused and impatient, made each day seem more than ever strained, exasperating, painful, wearisome, endless and unnerving. And the hours which, at the beginning of our sojourn at Sant'Eufemia, had passed so quickly now oozed slowly away, drop by drop, bringing an exhaustion and a despondency that I cannot describe.

But the thing that contributed most of all to make the monotony exasperating was the continual talk about things to eat. People talked about food more and more because there was less and less of it; and in conversation now it was no longer the nostalgia of people whose food is bad that was apparent, but the fear of people whose food is inadequate. Everyone ate but one meal a day and was very careful not to invite any friends. As Filippo said: "We're all friends for life, but at table, in these times, it's everyone for himself." The people who suffered least were those who had money, that is Rosetta and I, Filippo and another evacuee called Geremia; but even we, who were comparatively well off, felt that very soon money would no longer be of any use. The peasants, who at first had been so greedy for money because they never saw any in peacetime, were now beginning to find out that mony counted for less than property. They would say somberly, and in an almost vindictive tone: "The moment has now come for us peasants. It's we who have the upper hand now because it's we who have the provisions . . . You can eat provisions but you can't eat money." But I knew there was an element of boastfulness in this, because even they had not very much in the way of provisions: they were but poor mountain peasants who always had great difficulty in carrying over till the next year's harvest, and, when April or May came round, always had to raise some money and buy stuff to tide them over until July.

What did we eat, then? Once a day we ate a few boiled beans with a spoonful of lard and a little tomato paste and a small piece of goat's flesh and a few dried figs. In the morning we had carob beans or onions and one thin slice of bread. Our chief trouble was lack of salt, and this was terrible, for food without salt is almost impossible to swallow, and as soon as you put it in your mouth you begin to want to spit it out, so tasteless is it, with a kind of sweetness like that of something dead and decayed. There was not a drop of oil left; I had barely two finger-breadths of lard at the bottom of an earthenware pot. Once in a while we had a stroke of luck, as when I was able to buy five pounds of potatoes. On another occasion I managed to acquire from some shepherds a sheep's milk cheese weighing about two pounds, as hard as a rock but good and sharp-tasting. But these were strokes of luck, things that happened rarely, not to be counted upon.

The countryside, now that the first days of March had come, began to show signs of spring. One morning, looking down from the terrace, we saw through the mist the first quivering of white almond-blossom: it had all come out during the night and seemed to be trembling from cold, pale and spectral in the grey mist. To us evacuees this flowering seemed a joyful sign: spring was coming, the roads would dry up, the English would resume their advance. But the peasants shook their heads: spring meant hunger. They knew from experience that their provisions would not carry them over until the next harvest, and they tried to save them as much as they could, endeavoring by every means to find something to eat without cutting into their supplies. Paride, for example, set traps made of reeds in the bushes, to catch robins and larks, but these were so small that you needed four to make a mouthful. He also set other traps for the small, fiery-red foxes that exist in that locality; these he would skin, and then, after leaving them to soak in water for some days in order to soften them, would cook them with a sweet, strong-flavored sauce to disguise the gamey taste. But our greatest resource at this time was chicory; not the chicory that is eaten in Rome, which is always the same plant and never changes, but rather any kind of herb that can be eaten. I myself made more and more use of this so-called chicory; and sometimes I spent the morning picking it on the terraces with Rosetta and Michele. We would get up early, each of us armed with a small knife and a basket, and go off along the slope of the mountainside, sometimes below, sometimes above, gathering herbs. People have no idea of how many herbs there are which can be eaten—almost all of them, in fact. I already knew a little about them from having gathered them when I was a child, but I had almost entirely forgotten their names and species. Luisa, Paride's wife, went with me the first time in order to teach me, and quite soon I had become as good at it as the peasants and knew the various kinds of "chicory" both by name and by shape. I remember only a few of them now. We used to go, as I say, up and down over the terraces, and we were not the only ones, for everyone was picking chicory now and it was a strange sight to see the mountain slope dotted all over with people moving about with their heads down, one step at a time, like so many souls in purgatory. It looked as if everyone was searching for some lost object, instead of which it was hunger that caused them to search, not for something they had lost, but for something which they hoped to find. This chicory-gathering took a long time, two or three hours or even more, for in order to make a bare soup bowl of it you had to collect an apronful. It was not so plentiful that it sufficed for all the people who were looking for it, and, as time went on, you had to go farther and farther away and spend longer and longer hunting for it. All this hard work had little result; once boiled, two or three apronfuls of chicory became two or three green balls each of them the size of an orange. After boiling it I used to put it in a frying pan with just a taste of lard, and this, if it provided no nourishment, at least served to fill our bellies and to cheat our hunger. But the labor of collecting the chicory left us dead tired for the rest of the day. And at night, when I lay down beside Rosetta on our hard bed, with its sack of dried maize leaves, instead of seeing darkness when I closed my eyes I saw nothing but chicory, plants and plants of chicory dancing in front of me. In vain I would try to go to sleep, but for a long time I would see the chicory crossing and re-crossing and dissolving before my eyes, until at last, after long wakefulness, I would fall right into the chicory and go to sleep.

But, as I have said, the most wearisome thing of all was the fact that the food shortage encouraged the evacuees to talk of nothing but of things to eat. Filippo, especially, was always lapsing into conversations about food. Sometimes, as I passed along the terrace, I would see Filippo sitting on a rock surrounded by a group of evacuees, and I would go up to them and hear him saying: "D'you remember? One used to telephone to Naples and reserve a table at a restaurant. Then we would get into the car, four or five of us, all good trenchermen, and off we'd go. We'd sit down to table at one and get up at five. And what did we eat? Well, spaghetti with a fish sauce, with pieces of fish in it and cuttlefish and crayfish and oysters; dorado and grey mullet, roast or boiled, with mayonnaise sauce; dog fish with peas, slices of swordfish and bass and grilled tunnyfish; and octopus *alla luciana*, which is so delicious. Fish of all types, in fact, and in all kinds of sauce, for two or three hours. We sat down to table all in good order, irreproachable in every respect; we got up with our waistcoats unbuttoned, our belts let out, belching fit to rattle the window panes, and each of us weighing at least four or five pounds more than before. And on top of it we drank at least, *at least* a flask of wine a head. Ah, those feasts, when shall we ever see them again?" Then somebody said: "When the English arrive, there'll be plenty of everything again, Filippo." One day when, as usual, they were talking about food, I was present at a squabble between Filippo and Michele. Filippo was saying: ". . . Now listen, what I should like would be to have a fine pig and to kill it and cut steaks off it, lovely fat, thick ones, each weighing about a pound and a quarter. . . . You know, a pound and a quarter of pork is something that will bring you back to life." Michele who, it so happened, was listening to him, said all at once: "That would really be a case of cannibalism." "Why?" "Because it would be pig eating pig." Filippo was upset at hearing himself called a pig by his own son; he went very red and said sharply: "You've no respect for your parents." "Not only have I no respect for them," rejoined Michele, "but I'm ashamed of them." Filippo was again disconcerted at this harsh, uncompromising tone, but he merely remarked, more calmly than before: "If you hadn't had a father to pay for it, you would never have been educated as you were and you wouldn't be in a position to be ashamed of us now. It's my own fault." At these words, Michele remained silent for a moment. Then he said: "Yes, you're quite right. I did wrong to listen to you. In the future I'll keep away and you can talk as much as you like about things to eat." Then Filippo, moved I believe because it was the first time since we had been up there that his son had admitted he was right, said conciliatingly: "If you like, we'll talk about something else. You're right, what necessity is there to talk about things to eat? Let's talk of something else." But Michele suddenly flew into a rage and, twisting round like a viper, cried: "All right, what shall we talk about, then? About what we shall do when the English have arrived? About having plenty of everything? About the shop? About the things the tenant stole? What shall we talk about–eh?" This silenced Filippo, for these and a few other similar things were about the only things he could talk about, and Michele had mentioned almost all of them and there was nothing else that came into his mind. Michele, having uttered these words, walked away. Filippo, as soon as he was sure his son could not see him, made a gesture as much as to say: "He's an odd creature; one can't help being sorry for him." And all the evacuees tried to cheer him up by telling him the right was on his side. "Filippo, you have a son who knows a great deal. The money you spent on his education was well spent; that's the important thing, the rest doesn't count."

That same day Michele, feeling rather mortified, said to us: "My father is right, I am lacking in respect for him. But I simply can't help it; when he starts talking about food, I lose my head." I asked him why in the world it annoyed him so much to hear his father talk about food. He thought a moment and then answered: "If you knew you had to die tomorrow, would you talk about food?" "No." "Well, we're in that position. Tomorrow, or in a few years' time, it doesn't matter which, we shall die. Ought we then, while we are waiting for death, to talk about foolish things and be entirely taken up with them?" I did not quite understand, so I persisted: "But what ought we to talk about, then?" He considered again for a little and then said: "In the situation in which we find ourselves at present we ought, for instance, to talk about the reasons that have brought us up here." "And what *are* those reasons?" He started laughing and replied: "Each one of us has to find them for himself, on his own account." "Well and good," I said, "but your father talks about things to eat just because they're lacking and because we're, so to speak, forced to think about them." "That may be so," he concluded. "But the trouble is, my father always talks about things to eat, even when they exist and nobody's in want of them."

At the moment, however, things to eat were seriously lacking and everyone was now trying to save up what little he had. Whenever they talked about it to other people, they made great efforts to make them believe they had nothing at all. Filippo, for example, kept repeating almost every day to such of the evacuees as were poorer than himself: "I have no flour left now and only enough beans for a week. When that's week's over, may the Lord provide. . . ." Now this was not true, because everyone knew that he had another sack of flour, as well as a smaller sack of beans; but, for fear that someone might take them away from him, he no longer invited anybody to the house, and locked the door in the daytime and went off along the terraces with the key in his pocket. As for the peasants, they really were at the end of their provisions, for this was the time of year when they used to go down to Terracina and buy food to tide them over until the next harvest. But this year there was a shortage of food everywhere, and it was quite likely that you would find an even worse famine at Terracina than at Sant'Eufemia. Besides, there were the Germans who, whenever they could, carried everything off; and this was not because they were all of them thieves or bad men but because they were at war and waging war means not only killing but stealing as well. For instance, one day a German soldier turned up at Sant'Eufemia; he was alone, just as if he was going for a walk, and unarmed. Dark, with a round, kindly face and anxious, rather sad blue eyes, he wandered around for a long time among the huts talking to the peasants and evacuees. You could see that he had no evil intentions, in fact that he had a sort of sympathy for all these poor people. He said that in peacetime he was a blacksmith; and he also said he was a good accordion-player. So one of the evacuees went off to fetch his own accordion, and the German sat down on a stone and played to us, surrounded by children listening to him open-mouthed. He played well, and he played, among other things, a song which at that period, it seems, was sung by all the German soldiers—"Lili Marlene." It was a very sad song, almost a lament; and as I listened I reflected that, after all, these Germans that Michele hated so much and considered to be not even human were Christians like us, with wives and children at home; and that they too hated the war which kept them far away from their families. After "Lili Marlene" he played a lot of other tunes; and all these tunes were sad and moving; and some were really complicated, just as if they had been concert music. And he himself, with his head bent over the accordion, completely absorbed in the study of the keys as his fingers ran lightly over them, gave the impression of being a serious kind of man who knew the value of things and did not hate anybody, and who, if he had been able, would willingly have given up fighting. This likable German, after he had played for nearly an hour, went away again, but not without first patting the children on the head and saying a few kind words to us in his halting Italian: "Cheer up, the war'll be over soon." However, the path by which he started off down the hill passed close behind one of the huts; and the evacuee who lived there had put out a fine shirt with big red checks to dry on the fence. The German stopped, felt the material of the shirt as if to see whether it was of good quality, then shook his head and went on down the path. But half an hour later there he was again, all out of breath from having run up the hill. He went straight to the hut, took the shirt off the fence, put it under his arm and ran off again down to the valley. You see what I mean? He had gone off after playing the accordion to us and patting the children on the head, and he was an honest man, but that shirt had taken his fancy, and all the time he was going down the hill he had not been able to stop thinking about it, and in the end temptation had been stronger than conscience and he had come up again and taken the shirt. As long as he had been playing the accordion, he had been the man who in time of peace had been a blacksmith; when he took the shirt he had been the soldier who does not know the law of *meum et tuum* and who has no respect for anyone or anything. In short, as I have already said, war means not only killing but stealing as well; and a man who, in peacetime, would not kill or steal for all the gold in the world, in wartime rediscovers, at the bottom of his heart, the instinct to steal and kill which exists in all men; and he rediscovers it just because he is encouraged to rediscover it; in fact he is told all the time that this instinct is the right instinct and that he must trust to it, otherwise he is not a real soldier. So he says to himself: "I'm at war now. I shall go back to being what I really am, when peace comes. For the moment I can let myself go." Unfortunately, however, no one who has stolen or killed, even in war, can ever hope to go back, afterward, to what he was before—in my opinion, anyhow. It would be—if I may make a comparison—as though a woman who was still a virgin allowed her virginity to be broken under the illusion that she could go back to being a virgin again later, by some extraordinary kind of miracle that has never been known to happen. Once a thief and a murderer, even in uniform and with a chest covered with medals, always a thief and a murderer.

The peasants knew that the Germans had this little weakness for picking and stealing, and had organized a kind of alarm service—a number of little boys stationed at intervals all up the valley, right to Sant'Eufemia. No sooner did a German appear on the mule track than the first of these little boys would immediately shout, with all the breath in his body: "Malaria!" And the next one, higher up, would repeat the cry: "Malaria!" And then another and another and another: "Malaria!" And then, at this repeated cry, there would be a general helter-skelter flight at Sant'Eufemia, someone carrying a bag of beans, someone else a bag of flour or a pot of lard or some sausages and all going to hide their burdens amongst the bushes or in the caves. Sometimes a German really did arrive, some soldier who had ventured up there for no particular reason and who wandered around among the houses with everyone following behind in a procession and somebody carrying the joke to the point of making gestures at him, hands to mouth, as much as to say they were hungry. But often it was a false alarm and, after an hour or so, seeing no German face appear, the evacuees would take their belongings back again from their hiding places.

Since food was becoming scarcer and scarcer and my own provisions were almost exhausted, I determined to make a serious effort to procure some more; I had the money, and it might be that in some less exposed place there might still be something to buy. Early one fine morning we started off, Rosetta, Michele and I, aiming for a place in the mountains called Sassonero, about four hours' walk from Sant'Eufemia. We aimed at reaching this place about midday, when we would make our purchases, if such a thing was possible, have something to eat and then make our way back to Sant'Eufemia before nightfall.

We started when the sun was still hidden behind the mountains, though it had already been light for a time. A slight wind was blowing off the snow, numbing our noses and ears, and when we reached the pass we found a few white patches of it melting on the emerald-green grass. The sun had come out at last, and it was less cold, and the great panorama of the mountains of Ciociaria, all besprinkled with snow beneath the shining sky, was so beautiful that we paused for a moment to gaze at it. I remember Michele saying with a sigh, almost in spite of himself, as he looked at the mountains: "How beautiful Italy is!" I said, laughing: "Michele, you say it as if it displeased you." "That's true;" he replied, "it does rather displease me because beauty is a temptation."

From the pass we took a path among the rocks which was at first ill-defined, no more than a track through the grass, but which soon became clearer. It followed the ridge of the mountain, with precipitous slopes on each side, one of which went straight down without interruption to Fondi, while the other, less deep, fell away to a deserted valley, thick with scrub. The path, keeping all the time along the ridge, went twisting on for some distance like a snake, then began to descend slantwise toward this same wild little valley, among scrub and oak-trees. We went down to the bottom of this deserted valley, more like a ravine, and walked along a small stream half hidden among the bushes. In that profound silence the stream made a light and cheerful sound as its waters ran over the stones. Then the path started to rise up the other side of the ravine, reached another pass and, after going down a way, led us, climbing again, up another hill, till finally we reached the bare, stony summit, where a black wooden cross, extremely ancient, stood planted among the rocks. Beyond this summit, still continuing our way along the mountain ridge, we came to one end of a strange place we had seen from above before we went down into it. This was a level plain, as flat as the palm of your hand, lying below an immense red crag, and with rocks and a few oak trees scattered about it. The oaks were large and ancient, with bare, grey branches stretching forth into the air like the grey locks of witches: the rocks were both large and small but all shaped like sugar loaves, black and smooth as if they had been turned on a lathe. Among these rocks and oak trees were huts with blackened thatched roofs from which smoke was issuing, and in front of these huts were women cooking in the open, or hanging out clothes on ropes to dry, and numbers of children playing on the rough ground. Men were not to be seen, for this was a village of shepherds and the men, at this hour of the day, were with the flocks up on the mountains. As we came down to the huts we saw the blackened mouth of a cave; underneath the great crag I have already mentioned. One of the women told us that there were evacuees living inside it. I asked this woman whether she had any provisions to sell, but she shook her head gloomily. She added, in a reserved tone, that possibly the evacuees might be able to sell me something. And this seemed strange to me, for evacuees do not sell, they buy.

We went on toward the cave, if only to obtain information of some kind, seeing that it was impossible to get a word out of these wild and mistrustful shepherds' wives. As we approached the cave the ground seemed to be all covered with quantities of bones, big and small, mixed with the loose stones—no doubt the remains of the goats and sheep eaten by the evacuees, but besides the bones there was also a great deal of rubbish, such as rusty tins, rags, old boots, bits of paper. It looked like one of those building sites in Rome where people throw out all the refuse from the surrounding houses. Here and there you could see burnt patches on the ground, with dead embers surrounded by little heaps of grey ash. The entrance to the cave was very large, blackened all around, and dirty and smoky. There were nails fixed in the stone and from them hung pots, ladles, rags, and even a quarter of a newly butchered goat from which blood was still dripping. When we looked into the cave I was astonished: lofty and deep, its ceiling blackened by smoke and its inner part so dark that you could not see the end of it, it looked like an enormous bedroom, its whole extent being lined with beds and pallets side by side, like a hospital or the dormitory of a barracks. There was a strong smell, like that of a work-house or a doss-house, and at the first glance I could see that the beds were untidy, with the covers in disorder and dirty beyond words. The evacuees were all over the place, some were sitting on the edge of their beds, scratching their heads, or doing nothing; some were lying on their beds, wrapped in their blankets; some were walking up and down in the small space available. One group, sitting on two beds around a small table, were playing cards, like the men at Sant'Eufemia, their overcoats on and their hats on their heads. In one of the beds I noticed a half-dressed woman giving her baby the breast; in another there were three or four children tucked up close together, motionless, as though dead, presumably asleep. The inner part of the cave was, as I have said, in darkness: but you could catch a glimpse of piled-up household implements and a great heap of odds and ends, such belongings, no doubt, as these poor refugees had managed to carry away with them when they made their escape.

Close to the entrance to the cave I noticed an unusual thing: an altar made out of packing-cases and covered with a fine embroidered tablecloth. On the tablecloth stood a crucifix and two silver vases in which there had been arranged, for lack of flowers, some leafy ilex boughs. Underneath the crucifix, instead of little figures of saints or other objects of worship, I saw a number of watches—there must have been a dozen of them—arranged tidily in a row. They were old-fashioned watches such as are carried in waistcoat pockets, most of them being of white metal, but a couple of them of gold. Beside the altar, sitting on a stool, I saw the priest. I say the priest because I recognized him by his tonsure, but in all other respects it would have been difficult to imagine that he was a priest. He was a man of about fifty, with a dark, thin, serious face. He was not wearing the usual black cassock but was dressed all in white, with a white undervest, a white band around his waist, white trousers or rather, long, loose drawers like a zouave's, and black stockings and shoes. He had removed his cassock and was sitting there merely in what he was wearing underneath it. He sat quite still, his head lowered and his hands clasped in his lap, moving his lips hurriedly as though he were praying. Then he raised his eyes toward me—

I had approached, in the meantime, in order to examine the altar—and I saw that they were the eyes of a man possessed yet at the same time unseeing.

I said to Rosetta in a low voice: "This man is mad," yet I spoke without surprise, for by now I had ceased for some time to be surprised at anything. He, meanwhile, was staring fixedly at me, with a look which became gradually permeated with a curious expression, as of one who recognizes somebody by slow degrees. All at once he rose to his feet and took hold of me by the arm. "That's fine," he said, "you have come at last. Now, wind up these watches for me."

I turned back toward the cave, feeling rather alarmed, all the more so because his hand was gripping my arm with terrifying force, clutching it like the talons of a hawk or a kite. One of the evacuees who was playing cards, who had evidently been following the scene out of the tail of his eye, called out, without turning round: "Wind up the watches, just to please him. His church and his house were destroyed and he escaped with only his watches, and now he's lost his reason. But he does nobody any harm . . . you needn't worry."

Partly reassured, Rosetta and I each took one of the watches and wound them up—or rather, we pretended to do so, for they were already wound and all of them going perfectly well. He stood watching us in the way priests do, legs wide apart, hands clasped behind his back, a frown on his face, his head bent. When we had finished, he said in a deep voice: "Now you have wound them up, I can at last celebrate Mass. Well done, well done; at last you've arrived." Fortunately, at that moment, another inhabitant of the cave came up to us, a young nun, the sight of whom reassured me at once. She had a pale face, a perfect oval in shape, with black eyebrows joined together in the middle and forming a black bar above her black, shining, quiet eyes which looked like two stars on a summer night. What made the greatest impression upon me, however, and really astonished me, was her wimple and all the white portions of her nun's dress: these were white as snow and, incredible as it seemed in that place, starched to perfection. I cannot imagine how she managed to keep herself so immaculately clean in that filthy cave. With great politeness she turned to the priest and said in a sweet voice: "Come along, Don Matteo, come and have something to eat. But first you must put something on. You can't very well sit down to eat in your drawers." Don Matteo, his legs wide apart, a true zouave from top to toe, listened to her open-mouthed, bewilderment in his eyes. Finally he muttered: "What about my watches? Who's going to take care of my watches?" The nun replied in her quiet voice: "They've wound them up for you; they're all going perfectly. Look, Don Matteo, they all tell the same time, which is just dinner time." In the meantime she had taken down the priest's black cassock from a nail in the wall and was helping him to put it on, very politely, just like a nurse with a madman in an asylum. Don Matteo allowed himself to be dressed in his dusty, grease-spotted cassock; then, passing his hand over his uncombed head, he went off with the nun supporting him by the arm to the back part of the cave, where a big, black, smoking pot could be seen on a tripod. Then, turning to us, she said: "Come along, you three, there's enough for you too."

We went over toward the pot, around which a number of other evacuees had gathered. Among these I noticed one who seemed very plaintive and petulant—a short, fat little man, very ill dressed in ragged clothes, ill-kempt and unshaven. He had a tear in his trousers, right in the seat, and a piece of white shirt was hanging out. He whimpered as he held out his plate: "You always give me less than the others, Sister Teresa; why should I have less than the others?" Sister Teresa did not answer him; she was busy filling the bowls, giving each one a piece of meat and two ladlefuls of broth; but another evacuee, a middle-aged man with black mustaches and a red face, said sarcastically: "Ticò, why don't you make the Sister pay a fine? After all, you're a municipal inspector, you ought to make her pay a fine for giving you less soup than the others." Then, laughing, he said to Michele: "We're a fine collection of people here. The priest is mad, the policemen have been deported to Germany, the inspector goes about with his shirt hanging out of his trousers, and the mayor—that's me—is hungrier than anyone else. There's no authority left, and it's a miracle that we don't cut each other's throats." The nun, without raising her eyes from the pot, replied: "No, it's not a miracle, it's God's will that men should help each other." Ticò, in the meantime, was grumbling: "Don Luigi, you always want to make jokes . . . Don't you know that an inspector without a uniform is just a poor wretch like anybody else? Give me back my uniform and I'll be able to keep order again." And I reflected that fundamentally he was right. In certain cases anyhow, the uniform is everything. Even that good nun, with all her sweet character and her religion, would not have had so much authority if, instead of her nun's habit, she had been dressed in rags like myself and Rosetta.

We ate the soup, a thin, greasy broth in which the flesh of an old he-goat had been boiled until the soup smelled and tasted of goat to such an extent that, in spite of my hunger, I could hardly manage to swallow it down. While we were eating we listened to the usual subjects of conversation that we knew so well—the food shortage, the arrival of the English, the air raids, the round-ups, the war. Finally, when I felt that the right moment had come, I hazarded the question as to whether any of them could sell us any provisions. They were dumbfounded, as indeed I had imagined they would be. They had nothing; like us, they bought what they could here and there or were just coming to the end of what they had brought with them. They advised us to try the shepherds who lived in the huts, out in front of the cave. "We buy from them," they said. "They always have some cheeses, a goat or two. Go and see if they're willing to sell you something." So I said that a woman had sent us to *them*, stating that shepherds had nothing at all to sell. The mayor shrugged his shoulders: "They say that because they don't trust people and want to keep prices high. But they have their flocks and they are the only ones who have anything to sell, hereabouts."

We thanked the nun and the evacuees for the soup and, passing in front of the altar covered with the mad priest's watches, came out of the cave again. Just at that moment a small flock of sheep and goats was making its way between the rocks and the huts, led by a coarse-looking man with white sandals, black trousers, a band round his middle, a black jacket and a black hat. One of the evacuee women, who was standing near the entrance to the cave nibbling a piece of bread, pointed to him and said: "There, that's one of the *Evangelisti.* He'll sell you some cheese if you pay him well for it." So I ran after the man and shouted to him: "Have you any cheese you can sell me?" He did not answer me; he did not even turn around but went straight on, apparently deaf. I shouted again: "Signor Evangelisti, will you sell me some cheese?" Then he spoke: "My name's not Evangelisti," he said, "it's De Santis." "I was told," I said, "that you were called Evangelisti." "No," he replied, "we belong to the Evangelist church, that's all."

To be brief, he did finally hint that he might possibly be able to sell us some cheese, so we followed him into his hut. First of all he put the sheep into a hut next door to his own, calling them by name, one by one: "Bianchina, Paciocca, Matta, Celeste. . . ." and so on, then he closed the door behind them and led us into his own hut. This was a hut just like the one in which Paride lived, only larger and—I don't know why—drearier, emptier, colder; but perhaps this was just an impression, due to his not very friendly welcome. A number of women and children were sitting around the usual fire on the usual benches and the usual blocks of wood. We sat down too, and he clasped his hands together and started praying, and they all imitated him, even the children. I was flabbergasted at seeing them pray, for the peasants, in our part of the country at any rate, rarely pray and then only in church; but I recalled the answer he had given on the subject of the Evangelist religion and realized that they were quite different from us, they believed in a different way. Michele, who seemed interested, asked them, as soon as the prayer was finished, how in the world they came to be Evangelists; he appeared to know what this word meant. The ugly man replied that he and two of his brothers had been over to work in America and there they had met a Protestant pastor who had convinced them and so they had been converted to the Evangelist religion. Michele asked him what impression America had made upon him and he answered: "We embarked at Naples and disembarked at a small town on the Pacific coast and then we went by train to some forests, because we had been engaged as wood cutters. Well, from what I saw of it, it seemed to me to be a country full of forests." "But didn't you see any towns?" "No, only the one where we disembarked, a small town. We stayed two years in the forests and then came back to Italy the same way as we went." Michele looked surprised, and amused too, because, as he told me afterward, there were immense cities in America and they had seen nothing but trees and so they thought that America was just one big forest. They went on talking like this about America for a little; then, as it was getting late, I mentioned the cheese. The man fumbled about in the dark in the thatching of the roof and pulled out two very small yellowish sheep's-milk cheeses, saying quite simply that, if we wanted them, they would cost so much. We all jumped, for it was an unheard-of price, even in those times of shortage; and I said to him: "My goodness, is your cheese made of gold?" "No," he answered gravely, "it's better than gold, it's cheese. You can't eat gold, but cheese you can." Michele said sarcastically: "Does the Gospel teach you to ask prices like that?" He did not reply, so I pressed him: "Just now Sister Teresa, in the cave over there, said that God wishes men to help one another. *You* have a fine way of helping people." Quietly, but quite brazenly, he replied: "Sister Teresa belongs to a different religion. We are not Catholics." "What d'you think it means, then, to be an Evangelist?" interposed Michele again. "Selling at double the price of other people who are Catholics?" He answered with his usual gravity: "To be an Evangelist, brother, means observing the precepts of the Gospel. We do observe them." He always had a ready reply, in fact, and there was nothing to be done; he was as hard as a rock. Finally he said: "If you like, I could sell you a lamb . . . a nice fat one, for Easter. I have some up to about twelve pounds in weight. I would let you have one at a fair price." I reflected that Easter was indeed drawing near and that we needed a lamb, so I asked him the price and gave another jump: at that price we ought to have been able, very nearly, to buy the sheep that had produced the lamb as well. All of a sudden Michele said: "You know what you Evangelists are? You're downright starvation-mongers, that's what you are." "Peace, brother," said the man, "the Gospel lays it down that men should love one another." Finally, in desperation, I told him that I would buy a sheep's-milk cheese, but that he must let me have it at a lower price. What do you think his answer was? "A lower price? That is the lowest price I can manage. But you'd better leave it alone, sister, because, if you buy it at *my* price, you'll be angry with me afterwards, and if I sell it to you at *your* price, *I* shall be angry with *you*. Whereas the Gospel lays it down that men should love one another. Leave it alone, and then we can go on loving each other." I took no notice of this piece of advice and went on arguing for a long time, but he was inflexible and there was no way of convincing him, and whenever I got him with his back to the wall, proving conclusively to him that he was a robber, he wriggled out of it with some maxim or other from the Gospel, such as: "Do not be carried away by anger, sister. Anger is a grave sin." In the end I paid his exorbitant price, and all I could get out of him was that he should add a slice of butter-milk curd, which we ate there and then with a little bread. Then we went away, and although we parted very coldly, he said good-bye to us from the doorway in this manner: "God be with you, my brethren." Almost in spite of myself, I thought secretly: "As for you, may the devil carry you off and drag you down to hell."

This expedition brought us nothing but that one cheese—and to think we had walked all those miles over the mountains and that each of us had more or less finished off a pair of sandals! However, as often happens in such situations, our reward came a few days later without any effort on our part, as if by the intervention of Providence: the grave digger who went around the mountain districts with his black horse in search of food sold to us a good quantity of haricot beans at a fair price. He had acquired them from some Yugoslavs who had been banished to the island of Ponza and who, at the moment of the armistice, had escaped from there to a valley not far from ours; now, from fear of the Germans, they were on the move again and were unable to take all their provisions with them. The grave digger, a fairish young man, tall and thin and lively, also brought us some news of the war, which he had had from these people. He said that at a town called Stalingrad, which was in Russia, the Germans had taken a terrible beating, that the Russians had taken prisoner an entire army with all its generals, and that Hitler, discouraged, had ordered a retreat. He also said it was only a question of days, now, or at most of weeks, and the war would be over. This news filled the evacuees with joy, but not the peasants. The greater part of the men from Sant'Eufemia who had gone to the war were, it so happened, at Stalingrad, and had written from there. Many of the women now feared for their husbands' and brothers' lives, and they were right, for it became known later that not one of them had escaped.

During the whole month of March, as the days grew longer and the mountainside began slowly to turn green again and the air became softer, the bombardment of Anzio, on one side, and of Cassino, on the other, continued. We were about halfway between Anzio and Cassino, and all day and night we heard the guns firing in both these places, ceaselessly, as if in rivalry. Toom, toom, said the Anzio gun, first with the parting, then with the arriving, explosion; toom, toom, replied the Cassino one, from the other side. The sky seemed like a drumhead with the guns resounding dully and somberly upon it. It was very moving to hear so gloomy and menacing a sound on those days of brilliant weather; it suggested the thought that the war now formed part of nature, that the sound was in some way connected with the sunlight and confused with it, and that the spring, too, was sick from the war, just as men were sick from it. The rumble of gunfire, in fact, had entered into our life, just as rags and famine and danger had entered it, and, since it never ceased, it became—like rags and famine and danger—a normal thing to which we had become so accustomed that, if it had ceased—and indeed one fine day it did cease—we should have felt almost surprised. What I mean is that you can get accustomed to anything and that war too is a matter of habit, and what changes us is not the extraordinary things that happen for a time but this very fact of becoming accustomed to a thing, which shows, in fact, that we accept what happens to us and cease to rebel against it.

By now, at the beginning of April, the mountainside was lovely to look at, all green and full of flowers, and the air was mild and you could stay out of doors all day long. But behind all these flowers that were a pleasure to the eye there was, for us evacuees, an ever present thought of hunger, for flowers come out when plants have attained their greatest development and have become hard and fibrous and can no longer be eaten. These flowers, so lovely to look at, meant that our last resource, chicory, was finished; and that this time, really and truly, we could only be saved by the prompt arrival of the English. The trees, too, were in blossom, the peach trees and the almonds, the apples and the pears, scattered over the mountainside, looking like white and pink clouds hanging in the soft, windless air; but in the case of the trees, again, we could not look at them without reflecting that their blossom would have to turn into fruit and that the fruit, which would have provided us with nourishment, would not appear for months to come. And the corn, which was still in blade—short, green, tender, velvety looking—had also an unnerving effect upon me: a long time would have to pass before it was tall and yellow and could be reaped and threshed and the grain taken to the mill and the flour kneaded and put into the oven in so many lovely two-pound loaves. Ah, beauty can be appreciated on a full stomach; but when your stomach is empty, all your thoughts turn in the same direction and beauty seems a deception or, even worse, a mockery.

Talking of corn in the blade, I remember something that happened during that time which gave me an exact notion of what famine can mean. One afternoon I went down, as often, to Fondi, in the hope of buying some bread, and, as we came down into the valley, we were flabbergasted to see three horses belonging to the German army quietly grazing in a field of corn. A soldier without any sign of rank, possibly a Russian renegade like the one we had met on that other occasion, was in charge of the horses, and was sitting idly on the fence with a blade of grass between his teeth. To tell the truth, never had I realized, as I did at that moment, what war means, and how, in time of war, the feeling heart no longer feels, and a man's neighbor no longer exists, and everything is possible. It was one of those brilliant days, full of sunshine and flowers, and we three—Michele, Rosetta and I—stood near the fence and gazed open-mouthed at those three well-fed horses which, poor things, unaware of what their masters were causing them to do, innocently cropped the tender corn with which, when it ripens, bread is made for human beings. When I was a child my parents used to tell me that bread is sacred and that it is a sacrilege to throw it away or waste it and that you are committing a sin even if you place the loaf upside down; and now I saw that this bread was being given to beasts, when so many people in the valley and up in the mountains were suffering from hunger. Michele at last expressed all our feelings by saying: "If I were religious, I should say that the Apocalypse had come, when horses shall be seen grazing upon corn. Since I am not religious, I say merely that the Nazis have come, which, perhaps, is the same thing."

A little later that same day we had confirmation of the German character, so strange and so different from ours; they are full, no doubt, of all sorts of good qualities, but always with something missing, as if they were not complete human beings. We paid another visit to the lawyer at whose house we had met that unpleasant German officer who told us he took such pleasure in clearing out caves with a flame-thrower; and there we again found a German, a captain. The lawyer told us: "This one isn't like the others, this one is a really well-bred person, he talks French, he has lived in Paris and he thinks as we do about the war." We went into the hut and the captain, as all Germans do, rose at our entrance and shook hands with us, clicking his heels. He was certainly a man of refinement, a gentleman—slightly bald, grey-eyed, with a thin, aristocratic nose, a haughty expression on his lips, handsome, in a way, and almost Italian-looking—if there had not been something stiff and uneasy about him which you never see in an Italian. He spoke Italian well and paid us a lot of compliments about Italy, saying that it was his second country and that he went every year to the sea, to Capri, and that the war, if it had served no other purpose, had at least allowed him to visit a great many beautiful places in Italy which he did not know. He offered us cigarettes, asked about Rosetta and myself, finally spoke of his own family and even showed us a photograph of his wife, a pretty woman with magnificent fair hair, and their three children, also very pretty, little angels, in fact, all three of them golden-haired. As he took back the photograph, he said: "Those children, at this moment, are happy." We asked why and he answered that they had always longed to possess a little donkey and that just recently he had acquired one at Fondi and had sent it as a present to them in Germany. In his enthusiasm, he started going into details: he had found just the little donkey he was looking for, of Sardinian breed, and, since it was still being fed by its mother, he had sent it to Germany in a military convoy, with a soldier specially appointed to give it milk continually: there was also a cow with the convoy. He laughed, well satisfied, and then went on to say that his children were certainly at that very moment riding the little Sardinian donkey, and that was why he had said that they were happy. The rest of us, including the lawyer and his mother, were astounded: it was a time of famine, there was nothing to eat, and yet this man found means of sending a donkey to Germany and had the milk given to it which might have been allotted to Italian babies who were in need of it. Where was his love for Italy and the Italians, if he was unaware of so simple a fact? And yet I reflected that he had not done it out of malice; he was certainly the best German I had so far encountered; he had done it because he was a German, and the Germans, as I have already said, are made in a special way, with all sorts of good qualities, no doubt, but all in one direction, whereas in the other direction they haven't a single one—like trees growing against a wall which have all their branches on one side, away from the walls.

Michele, now that there was so little to eat, was trying to help us in every possible way, either openly, by bringing us a part of his own breakfast or supper, under the disapproving eyes of his family, or in secret, by actually stealing things from his father on our behalf. When he came to see us one day I showed him all the bread we had left, one small loaf which was two thirds maize flour into the bargain. He said that from now on he would provide us with bread, taking it a little at a time from the box in which his mother kept it. And so he did. Each day he brought us a few slices of bread, and it was still white bread, without any maize-flour or bran in it, the only white bread that was now made up there, although Filippo never stopped wailing and lamenting and told anybody who was willing to listen to him that he and his family were reduced to starvation. One day, however, instead of bringing us the usual three or four slices, Michele, for some reason, brought us a couple of complete loaves; they had been making bread that same morning and he deceived himself into thinking they would not notice. But they did notice and Filippo made the devil's own row, shouting out that someone had stolen his provisions. He did not say it was loaves that had been stolen, otherwise he would have been contradicting himself, since he was forever saying that he had no flour left. Filippo instituted an inquiry in the manner of a detective, measuring the height and width of the window; examining the ground underneath it to see if the grass had been trampled; scrutinizing the window-frame in case any small pieces of plaster had become detached; and in the end he became convinced that, given the small size of the window and its height from the ground, it must have been a child who got into the house and committed the theft, but that the said child could not have reached the window without the help of an adult. In short, at the conclusion of his inquiry, he decided that the child was without doubt a boy called Mariolino, son of one of the evacuees, and that the adult who had helped him was obviously his father. And all would have ended there, if Filippo had not communicated these suppositions to his wife and daughter. What for him had been only suppositions immediately became, for the two women, certainties. First they started ignoring the evacuee and his wife, passing them by with silent haughtiness; then they went further and started dropping hints: "Was the bread good today?" or: "Keep an eye on Mariolino . . . he might break his neck climbing through windows"; and finally they spoke out quite plainly: "You're a family of thieves, that's what you are." A violent quarrel started, a scene beyond description, with shrieks and cries mounting to heaven. The evacuee's wife, a sickly little woman, ragged and bedraggled, kept screaming at the top of her voice: "Go on! Go on!"—but I don't know what she meant; and Filippo's wife, on her side, was shouting into the other woman's face that they were thieves. And so, with one of them repeating those two little word: "Go on!" and the other screaming that they were thieves, they moved forward, facing one another, with a circle of evacuees round them, but without touching each other, like two infuriated hens. In the meantime we two—though not without remorse—were eating Filippo's bread at that very moment, in the dark so as not to attract attention, one mouthful to each scream from the two women; and I cannot deny that that stolen bread seemed to me almost more tasty than our own, simply because it was stolen and because we were eating it in secret. Anyhow, from that day on Michele took care to cut the bread very thin, in such a way that his family should not notice, a slice here and a slice there; and they did not notice and there were no more scenes.

April went by, with flowers and weak stomachs, and May came bringing heat; and now, besides hunger and despair, there was the torment of flies and wasps. In our room there were so many flies that the whole day was spent in driving them away; and at night, when we went to bed, the flies went to sleep on the cords on which we hung up our clothes, and there were so many of them that the cords were black. The wasps, too, had nests under the roof and went in and out in clouds, and woe betide anyone who touched them, for their stings were fierce. We sweated all day long, partly, perhaps, from weakness, and with the coming of the heat—perhaps because we could not wash or change our clothes—we realized that we were nothing but a pair of old rag-bags, like the ageless and sexless hags who stand begging at convent doors. The few clothes we had were now ragged and smelly; our sandals (it was a long time since we had had any shoes) were pitiful too, botched up as they were by Paride with pieces of old tires; and as for our room, after being a refuge for the winter it was now made uninhabitable by the flies, the wasps and the heat and had become worse than a prison. Rosetta, for all her sweetness and patience, perhaps suffered from this state of things more than I did, for I was born a peasant whereas she was born in a town. So much so, that she said to me one day: "You're always talking about things to eat, Mum. But I would willingly agree to go hungry for another year if I could only have some clean clothes and live in a clean house." There was even a water shortage now, for there had been no rain for a couple of months, and she could no longer pour a bucket of water from the well over her head, although now she had most need of it.

During May I came to hear of something which may give an idea of the despair to which the evacuees were now reduced. It appeared that there had been a meeting in Filippo's house in which only the men had taken part, and it had been decided that if the English failed to arrive before the end of May, the evacuees—who all possessed arms, either revolvers, or shotguns, or knives—would compel the peasants to pool their provisions for the common good, either voluntarily or forcibly. Michele had been present at the meeting and had immediately protested, as he told us afterwards, declaring that he would take the part of the peasants. "All right then," one of the evacuees had answered him, "we'll treat you like the peasants, in that case, and consider you as one of them." I daresay this meeting did not mean very much because, after all, the evacuees were decent people and I doubt if they would have been capable of making use of their arms; but it does give an indication of the degree of despair which by now everyone had reached. Others, I knew, were getting ready, now that the weather was good and the ground had dried up, to leave Sant'Eufemia and to try either to go south through the lines or north, where it was said there was no lack of food. Others, again, talked of going to Rome, on foot, because, they said, in the country they leave you to die of hunger but in a town they can't *not* help you, because they're afraid of a revolution. And so, under the burning May sun there seemed to be a general spirit of restlessness and disintegration. Each person was now thinking again only of himself, and many were now disposed to risk their lives simply to escape from a state of stagnation and endless waiting.

And then on a day like any other day, the great news arrived: the English had launched an offensive in earnest and were advancing. I will not stop to describe the joy of the evacuees who, for lack of any better way—being unable to drink as there was no more wine, or to eat because there was no more food—gave expression to their feelings by embracing each other and throwing their hats into the air, Poor things, they did not know that this English advance would in itself bring us fresh troubles. Our difficulties were only beginning.

Chapter 8

WHEN I WAS A CHILD, a shopkeeper in my village had a collection of numbers of the *Domenica Illustrata* dealing with the first war, and with the shopkeeper's children I used to look at this collection, which contained many fine colored plates illustrating the battles of the war of 1915. I imagined a battle to be as I had seen it in these pictures: guns firing, clouds of dust, smoke and flame; soldiers advancing to the attack, bayonets fixed and colors flying; hand-to-hand fighting, men falling dead, others still rushing onward. To tell the truth, I liked these pictures, and it seemed to me that war was not as ugly a thing as people said. Or rather, it *was* ugly, but I felt that if a man likes to kill and to display his own courage or show his initiative and his contempt for danger, war provided the opportunity he needed. And I also felt that people ought not to think that everyone loves peace. There are plenty of people who feel very much at their ease during a war, if only because it enables them to give vent to their own violent and bloodthirsty instincts. That was how I argued, until I saw real war.

One day Michele told me that the battle for the break-through at the front was almost over, but I still felt uneasy, because no matter how far I looked in any direction, I could not see the slightest sign of fighting. It was a brilliant, serene day, with just a few pink clouds moving slowly on the horizon, seeming almost to touch the tops of the mountains behind which lay Itri, the Garigliano; the front. To the right the mountains rose green and majestic in the golden sunlight, to the left, beyond the plain, the sea sparkled with a smiling, bright, springlike blue. But where was the battle? Michele replied that the battle had been going on for at least two days and was being fought out behind the Itri mountains. I was unwilling to believe this because, as I have said, my notion of a battle was quite different; and so I told him. Michele started laughing and explained to me that the battles I had so much admired on the covers of the *Domenica Illustrata* no longer occurred. Nowadays guns and planes were able to make short work of soldiers at a great distance from what was strictly called the front; nowadays a battle resembled the operation carried out by a housewife with a spray gun, who kills all the flies without dirtying her hands and without even touching them. Modern war, said Michele, had nothing whatever to do with charges and assaults and hand-to-hand fighting; valor had become useless; the winner was the one who had the most numerous and the longest-range guns, and the planes with the widest radius of action and the greatest speed. "War has become an affair of machines," he concluded, "and soldiers are little more than clever mechanics."

Well, this invisible battle went on for a day or two longer. And then one morning the guns came so close that they made the walls of our room tremble. Boom, boom, boom—they seemed to be firing from just behind the corner of the mountain. I got out of bed in great haste and rushed out of doors, almost expecting to see the hand-to-hand fighting I have spoken of. But there was nothing. It was the usual beautiful day, calm and full of sunshine, and the only difference was that at the horizon, down at the far side of the plain, there were numbers of very thin, red streaks rising from behind the enclosing hills; they rose in a flash, like red wounds in the sky, and then melted away as though penetrating behind the blue. It was explained to me that these were shells whose trajectories, owing to a momentary condition of the atmosphere, could be seen with the naked eye. These red streaks looked just like razor cuts in the sky, with blood flowing from the wound for a moment and then ceasing immediately. First we would see the razor cuts, then we would hear the roar of the gun, and immediately afterward a furious mewing sound passed in a blast of air right over our heads. At almost the same time, from behind the mountain, would come the deafening burst of the shell as it reached its mark, making the whole sky resound like an empty room. The guns were firing over our heads at somebody behind our backs, and this, as Michele explained to me, meant that the battle was now moving northward and that the Fondi valley was already liberated. I asked where the Germans had gone to and he replied that they had almost certainly fled towards Rome. The battle for the break-through was over, and the guns were hammering at the Germans in retreat. In short, no hand-to-hand fighting, no bayonet charges, no visible dead and wounded.

That night we saw that the sky in the direction of Itri was brighter, and occasionally red, as if with a sudden burst of flame, and the razor cuts of the shell trajectories still continued, reminding one of a firework display against that black, starry sky, except that there was a continuous gush of fine streaks of fire in place of the slow flowering of display pieces. The explosions were different; duller, deeper, menacing, not cheerful like the noise of fireworks. We watched the sky for some time and then went to bed and slept as best we could, for it was hot and Rosetta would not stop talking. Early in the morning we were awakened by a deafening explosion, very close to us. We jumped out of bed and discovered that they were firing straight at us. For the first time I realized that the guns are far worse than airplanes; the latter can at least be seen, and as soon as you see them you can run to shelter, or at any rate you have the comfort of seeing what direction they are taking; but guns you never see, they are beyond the horizon. And although you can't see them they are looking for you, and you don't know where to hide yourself, because the gun follows you everywhere like a pointing finger. People came and told us that a shell had burst a short distance from Filippo's house. Michele came running along and said, with great satisfaction, that it was now only a matter of hours; but I answered him that being killed might be only a matter of seconds; at which he shrugged his shoulders and replied that we must now consider ourselves immortal. As if in answer, there was a terrifying explosion right on top of us. The walls and floor shook; plaster and dust rained down upon us from the ceiling; and for a moment the air was darkened to such an extent that we thought the shell must have landed on the house. We rushed out and saw then that it had exploded on the terrace, collapsing part of it and making a great hole full of freshly upturned earth and uprooted plants. As for Michele, I am not saying that he was frightened, but he did now realize I was not wrong when I said it might only be a few seconds before we were killed; so he told us we must come with him: he knew where to go; what we must do, he said, was to put ourselves in dead ground. We ran along the terrace, to the other extremity of the ravine, and went to a hut made of boughs which was used as a shelter for animals and which stood on a spur of rock. "This is dead ground here," said Michele, pleased at being able to show off his military knowledge. "We can sit down here on the grass . . . the gunfire won't reach us here." Dead ground, indeed! No sooner had he finished speaking than there was a violent explosion and we were enveloped in smoke and dust, and through the smoke and dust we saw the hut bend over to one side and then remain like that, looking like one of those crooked card-houses made by children. Michele no longer talked about his "dead ground." He had made us throw ourselves down on the grass and now, without raising himself, he shouted to us: "Follow me to the cave. We'll go into the cave. But don't get up, crawl along like me." The cave he was speaking of was just behind the hut, a very small cave with a low entrance in which the peasants had rigged up a hen-house. We crawled along the ground behind him and into the cave, among the hens which were clucking in terror at the far end. The cave was too low for us to stand upright, and we lay there side by side, dirtying our clothes with the excrement that covered the floor, while the hens, with courage renewed, walked over us and pecked among our hair. Explosions followed each other thick and fast around the cave, and I said to Michele: "What a good thing this was dead ground!" Finally the explosions became less frequent, and then there was nothing more, except for the sound of shells passing over us to hammer some place at the back of Sant'Eufemia. Michele said the shells which had hit the hut had probably been fired by the Germans, with high-angle mountain mortars; and now we could come out safely because the Germans had stopped firing and the English were not firing on us. We crawled out of the cave and went back home again.

It was one o'clock now, time to have some bread and cheese. Just as we were eating it, Paride's son came running up, out of breath, and told us that the Germans had arrived. We did not understand, because we thought that after all that bombardment it was the English who ought to be arriving; and I argued with him, thinking that he was only a child who misunderstood. "You mean the English?" "No, the Germans." "But the Germans have run away." "No, I'm telling you that they've just arrived." And then Paride himself came and cleared up the mystery: a group of fleeing Germans had indeed arrived and they were sitting in the shade of a straw stack, and nobody could make out what they wanted. "Well," I said to Michele, "what do the Germans matter to us? We're waiting for the English, not the Germans. Let's leave the Germans to stew in their own juice." But Michele paid no attention to me; his eyes had lit up when he heard Paride's story. He hated the Germans and at the same time was attracted by them, and he was excited and pleased by the idea of seeing them defeated and in flight, after having so often encountered them arrogant and victorious. He said to Paride: "Let's go and see these Germans." Rosetta and I followed them.

There were five Germans, and in all my life I have never seen people more hard-driven and exhausted than they were. They had thrown themselves down on the straw, one here and one there, and lay with arms and legs flung wide, as though dead. Three of them were asleep or anyhow were lying with their eyes shut, another lay flat on his back, with eyes open, staring at the sky, and the fifth was also lying on his back but had made himself a pillow of straw and was looking straight in front of him. I noticed this last one particularly: he was almost an albino, with pink, transparent skin, blue eyes with almost white eyebrows and eyelashes, and very pale fair hair, fine and smooth. His cheeks were grey with dust and streaked as though tears had flowed down them over the dust and had then dried, his nostrils were black with earth or some sort of filth, his lips were cracked, and his eyes circled with red, with two black streaks under them which looked like scratches. Germans, as we all know, always have tidy uniforms, as clean and freshly ironed as though they had just come out of moth balls. But the uniforms of these five were crumpled and unbuttoned; they even seemed to have changed colour, as though they had come into contact with a blast of gunpowder or lamp black. Evacuees and peasants were standing in a circle around them, gazing silently at the Germans as though at some incredible sight; the Germans neither spoke nor moved. Michele then went up and asked them where they had come from. He spoke in German, but the albino, without moving—just as if the back of his neck had been nailed on to his straw pillow—replied, speaking slowly: "I can talk Italian . . . I know Italian." So Michele repeated his question in Italian, and the other answered that they had come from the front. Michele asked what had happened. The albino, still lying there as though paralyzed, said in a somber, threatening, exhausted voice, uttering each word slowly and separately, that they were gunners. They had been subjected for two days and two nights to a terrible bombing from the air, and that their guns and the ground they stood on had been blown up. In the end, after seeing the greater part of their comrades killed, they had had to retire and make their escape. "The front," he concluded slowly, "is no longer on the Garigliano but further north and we must reach it. . . . Further north there are other mountains and we shall still resist." Although they were reduced to such a state that they seemed to be dead, they still talked of fighting and resisting.

Michele then asked who had broken through the front, the English or the Americans; and this was an imprudent question, for the albino gave a sort of mocking laugh and said: "What does it matter to you who it was? You know that your friends will soon be here, and that's enough." Michele pretended not to notice his sarcastic, threatening tone and asked what he could do for them. "Give us something to eat," said the albino.

We had really come to an end of everything by this time and with the exception possibly of Filippo, I don't believe the whole lot of us, evacuees and peasants combined, could have put together one single loaf. We looked at one another in consternation, and I, interpreting the general feeling, exclaimed: "Something to eat? Who, here, has anything to eat? If the English don't bring us something as quick as possible, we shall all die of starvation. You'd better wait for the English too, then you'll get something to eat."

I saw Michele make a gesture of disapproval, as much as to say: "You idiot!" and realized I had said something wrong. The German was staring hard at me, as if he wanted my face to become thoroughly impressed on his memory. He said slowly: "Very good advice; wait for the English." He lay still for a moment longer, then raised his arm with an effort and started fumbling in his breast under his jacket. "I said we wanted something to eat," he said. In his hand was a huge black pistol and he pointed it at us, still without moving or changing his attitude in any way.

A terrible fear came over me, perhaps not so much on account of the pistol as of the look in the albino's eyes, which was just like that of a wild animal caught in a trap yet still snarling and showing its teeth. Michele, on the other hand, remained unmoved and merely said to Rosetta: "Will you please run and tell my father to give you some bread for a group of Germans who are in need of it?" He said these words in a special kind of way, as though to suggest to Rosetta that she must explain that the Germans were demanding this bread at the point of the pistol. Rosetta ran to Filippo's house.

While we were waiting for the bread, we all stood quite still, forming a circle around the straw stack. After a moment the albino began again. "It's not only bread we need. We also need someone to come with us and show us the way, so that we can go on north." "There's the path," said Michele, pointing to the mule track that went up the mountainside. "I can see that too," said the albino.

"But we don't know these mountains. We need someone. That girl, for instance." "Which girl?" "The girl who's gone to get the bread." My blood froze at these words: if they carried Rosetta off there was no knowing what might happen, there was no knowing when I should see her again. But Michele, without losing his composure, said at once: "That girl doesn't belong to these parts. She knows them even less than you do." "Well then," said the albino, "*you* come with us. You belong to these parts, don't you?" I wanted to shout to Michele: "Tell him you're a stranger," but I hadn't the time. Too honest to lie, he had already answered: "Yes, I belong to these parts, but I don't know the mountains. I've always lived in the valley." The albino almost laughed. "To listen to you," he said, "one would think nobody knows these mountains. You will come. You will see that you'll find you know them very well." Michele made no reply to this; he merely frowned over the top of his glasses. In the meantime Rosetta had returned, out of breath, with two small loaves which she now placed on the ground, on top of the straw, stretching out her hand and leaning forward just as you might with a fierce animal that you don't trust. The German noticed her gesture and said, with a note of exasperation in his voice: "Put the bread in my hand. We're not mad dogs that bite." So Rosetta picked up the bread again and held it out to him. The German put the pistol back in its holster, took the loaves and sat up.

The others, too, had now sat up; it was clear that they had not been asleep but had followed the whole conversation, though with their eyes shut. The albino took a knife out of his pocket, cut up the two loaves into five equal parts and distributed them to his companions. They ate very slowly, with us standing around all the time in a circle and not uttering a word. When they had finished—and it was a long business, for they ate, so to speak, crumb by crumb—a peasant woman silently handed them a big copper basin of water and they drank, some of them two ladlefuls and some as many as four; they were just about dead with hunger and thirst. Then the albino pulled out his pistol again.

"We must go," he said, "or it'll be too late." He addressed these words to his companions, who immediately began pulling themselves slowly to their feet. Then he turned to Michele: "And you're coming with us to show us the way."

We were dismayed, for we all thought that the albino had not meant what he said; now it was clear that he had meant it seriously. Filippo had been present during the Germans' meal. When he saw the albino point the pistol at Michele he gave a kind of groan, and with a courage no one knew he possessed, thrust himself between the pistol and his son. "This is my son, do you understand? He's my son."

The albino said nothing. He made a gesture with his pistol as though he were chasing away a fly. Filippo, refusing to stand aside, shouted: "My son doesn't know the mountains, and that's Gospel truth. He reads and writes and studies—how could he know the mountains?"

"He's coming; that's enough," said the albino. He had risen to his feet now, and without lowering the pistol was adjusting his belt with his other hand.

Filippo looked at him as though he had not properly understood. I saw him swallow and pass his tongue over his lips: evidently he felt that he was choking, and at that same moment, for some reason, I recalled the phrase that he used to repeat with such pleasure: "No fools here." Poor man, he was neither foolish nor clever now, he was a father, and that was all. He stood for a moment as though thunderstruck, and then cried out again: "Take me! Take me instead of my son! *I* know the mountains. Before I was a shopkeeper I was a pedlar. I've been all over these mountains. I'll guide you carefully, all across the mountains, right to your headquarters. I know the easiest paths, and the most secret ones. I'll show you the way, I promise you." He turned to his wife and said: "I'm going. Don't worry, I'll be back by tomorrow evening." Suiting action to the word, he pulled up the band of his trousers and, composing his face into a smile—which seemed acutely painful—he went up to the German and put his hand on his arm, saying with an effort at off-handed ease: "Well, let's get started, we've a long way to go."

But this was not at all the German's intention. He said calmly: "You're too old. Your son will come, it's his duty," and brushing Filippo unceremoniously aside with the barrel of his pistol, he went over to Michele and signed to him, again with the pistol, to precede him. "Come along," he said. Someone shouted: "Michele, make a bolt for it!" You should have seen that German! Exhausted as he was, he turned like lightning in the directon from which the shout had come and fired. The bullet was lost among the stones of the terrace, but the German had succeeded in intimidating the peasants and evacuees and preventing them from doing anything to help Michele. They scattered in terror and came together again in a circle a little farther off, and in silence they watched the German as he walked away, pushing Michele in front of him with the barrel of the pistol in his back. Thus they went away, and the scene of their going is still as clear before my eyes as if it were happening now: the German with arm bent pointing the pistol, Michele walking in front of him with one trouser-leg longer than the other, the longer one ending almost under his heel, the shorter one showing his ankle. Michele was walking slowly, hoping, perhaps, that we would turn on the Germans and give him a chance to escape; the way in which he dragged his legs gave me the feeling that he was pulling a heavy chain along behind him. The procession of Michele and the Germans filed past us and slowly disappeared into the scrub. Filippo gave a kind of roar and made as if to rush after them. Peasants and evacuees immediately jumped on him and held him back, still roaring and repeating the name of his son and weeping big tears which made streaks down his face. Michele's mother and sister had now come running up and had difficulty in understanding what had happened; they kept asking for explanations and as soon as they understood, they started weeping and crying out Michele's name. His sister was sobbing loudly, and between her sobs she kept saying: "Just at this moment, when it was all going to be over so soon, just at this moment. . . ." We did not know what to say, because when there is a real sorrow with real causes words cannot lessen it and the only thing to do is to put an end to the cause of the sorrow, and this we could not do. Finally Filippo recovered himself and, taking his wife around the shoulders and helping her along said to her: "He'll come back all right.... There's no doubt he'll come back.... He'll show them the way and then he'll come back." The daughter, though she was weeping too, supported her father: "You'll see, Mum, he'll be back by this evening." But her mother said what mothers often say in such cases, and alas, their guesses are generally right, because a mother's instinct is stronger than any reasoning. "No, no," she said, "I know he won't come back. I shall never see him again."

Here I must confess that in the confusion caused by the bombardments, the defeat of the Germans, the break-through at the front and the end of our sojourn in the mountains, this matter of Michele did not make the impression upon us that it ought to have made. We too believed—or rather, we tried to deceive ourselves into believing—that he would come back without fail. This was partly because we felt that if we did *not* believe in his return we would have found ourselves incapable of sharing in the grief of the Festa family, for our thoughts and our hearts were elsewhere. We were both of us brimming with the news of the liberation, so longed-for and so long waited for, and we did not realize that the disappearance of Michele, who had been to us like a father and a brother, was a more important thing than the liberation and at least should have had the effect of embittering and saddening it for us. But so it was: selfishness, which had lain silent as long as there was danger, made its presence felt again now that the danger was over. And I myself, as I went back to the cottage after Michele had vanished, could not help saying to myself that it was a piece of truly good fortune that the Germans had taken Michele instead of Rosetta and that, after all, Michele's disappearance was mainly the concern of his own family, since we were on the point of parting from them and should never see them again. We would be going back to Rome and taking up our old life again, and would recall this long sojourn in the mountains only rarely and in a vague sort of way, saying perhaps to one another: "Do you remember Michele? I wonder what happened to him? And do you remember Filippo and his wife and daughter? I wonder what they're doing now?"

That night we slept close in each other's arms in spite of the heat, because the guns continued firing and from time to time shells landed close by and we felt that, if we were hit, at any rate we should die together. To say we slept is only a manner of speaking; we dozed for five or ten minutes, and then an unusually loud explosion would make us jump and sit up in bed; or else we would wake up for no particular reason, probably through agitation and nervousness. Rosetta was worried about Michele; and I understand now that she, unlike me, felt that his disappearance was not a thing to be taken so lightly as I wanted to make her believe. I heard her asking me in the darkness: "Mum, what will they do with Michele now?" Or: "Mum, do you really think Michele will come back?" Or again: "Mum, what will happen to poor Michele?" I felt that she was fundamentally right to be worried, but it almost made me angry because it appeared to me that our stay at Sant'Eufemia was now over, and we no longer ought to think of anything but ourselves. I answered first one thing and then another, trying to reassure her; and in the end, losing patience, I said: "Now do go to sleep; even if you don't sleep, you can't do anything for him. In any case I'm sure they haven't done him any harm. By this time he's already started back across the mountain to get to us here." "Poor Michele," she said, and that was all, for after these words she really did fall asleep.

When I awoke next morning I found that Rosetta was no longer lying beside me. I rushed out of the house; it was already late and the sun was high, and I realized that the gunfire had ceased and that there was a great stir all over the village. Evacuees could be seen coming and going hither and thither, some of them saying good-bye to the peasants, some carrying out their possessions, some of them actually going off in single file down the path leading to Fondi. All at once I had a terrible fear that Rosetta had vanished like Michele; and I began running about calling her. Nobody paid any attention to me, and I suddenly realized that what I had been thinking with regard to Michele was now being turned against me:

Rosetta had gone, everyone was attending to his own affairs, no one was willing to stop and hear what had happened to me. Luckily, just when I was becoming desperate, Luisa, Paride's wife, put her head out of the hut and said: "Rosetta's here, eating *polenta* with us." Feeling rather mortified, I went into the hut and sat down with the others around the table on which stood the bowl of *polenta.* As usual, no one was saying a word; the peasants, as always, appeared completely absorbed in the operation of eating, even on that day on which so many new things had happened and were about to happen. Only Paride, as if to give expression to a general thought, suddenly said—without a trace of sadness, just as though he were saying it was a fine day, or something of that sort: "So now you'll be going back to town to be ladies again . . . and we go on toiling here." He wiped his mouth, took a ladleful of water to drink, and then went out, as he always did, without any sort of farewell. I told Paride's family that we would pack up our belongings and would then come back and say good-bye to them. Then I left the hut with Rosetta.

I had now one sole desire, one great, impatient, joyful longing—to get away as quickly as possible. Nevertheless I said: "We must go and find the Festas and hear what's happened to Michele." I said it reluctantly, for it might be that Michele had not come back, and in that case I feared that the sorrow of the Festa family would be bound to disturb my own joy. But Rosetta answered quietly: "The Festa's aren't here. They went down this morning, at dawn. And Michele hasn't come back. They hope they may find him in the town." I felt greatly relieved at these words, with a relief no less selfish than my reluctance of a moment before, and I said: "Then we've only to pack up and leave as quickly as we can." Rosetta went on: "I got up at dawn, while you were still asleep, and went to see the Festas. Poor things, they were really in despair. For them this wonderful day is a terrible one, because Michele has not come back." I was silent for a moment because I felt ashamed, and I reflected that Rosetta was a much better person than I was. She had got up at dawn to go and see the Festas, and she had not been afraid, as I had been, that their sorrow would spoil her joy. I embraced her and said: "My precious daughter, you're a much better person than I am, and you did what I didn't have the courage to do. I am so glad this torment is over because I was almost frightened of going to see the Festas." "Oh," she replied, "it wasn't any effort to me to do it; I did it because I was fond of Michele. It would have been an effort to me *not* to go. All night long I never closed an eye because I could not help thinking about that poor boy. And his mother was right: he didn't come back."

The time had come for us to leave. We pulled out the two fibre suitcases we had brought from Rome and put into them the few rags we possessed, together with one or two petticoats, a couple of sweaters which we had made for ourselves up there, using the peasants' knitting-needles and greasy wool, and a few stockings and handkerchiefs. I also packed what was left of our provisions—the sheep's-milk cheese I had bought from the Evangelists, two or three pounds of haricot beans and a small dark loaf of bran and maize flour. I hesitated as to whether I should take the two or three plates and glasses I had acquired from the peasants; then I decided to leave them behind and arranged them tidily on the window-sill. That was all; and, having shut the suitcases, I sat down for a moment on the bed beside Rosetta and looked around me at the room, which already had the sad, empty look of a house that one is about to leave forever. No longer now did I feel so impatient or so joyful, in fact I had a feeling which was painful. I reflected that these dirty walls and this muddy floor held the memory of the bitterest and most terrible days of my life, and I suffered at leaving them even though I longed to do so. The nine months I had spent in that room I had lived through day by day, hour by hour and minute by minute with all the intensity of hope and of despair, of fear and of courage, of the will to live and of the desire to die. I had been waiting, however, for one thing above all others—the liberation; which had about it the quality of justice as well as of beauty and which concerned others as well as myself. And then I understood that anyone who waits for a thing like that lives with a greater power and truth than those who wait for nothing. And, passing from my own humble case to something far greater, it seemed to me that the same could be said of all those who wait for much more important things, such as the return of Jesus to earth or the establishment of justice for poor and lowly people. And to tell the truth, when I left that room for good and all, I felt I was leaving, not exactly a church, but a place that was almost sacred because in it I had suffered so much and had waited and hoped not only for myself but for others as well.

We had balanced our suitcases on our heads and were just going to the peasants' hut to say good-bye to them, when the people around us on the terrace suddenly fled in every direction. This time it was not the sound of heavy gunfire but a regular crackling sound, precise and angry, which seemed to be coming from the thorny scrub-patches high up toward the top of the mountain. One of the evacuees stopped for a moment and shouted to us: "Machine guns! It's the Germans firing on the Americans with machine guns." Then he ran away. By this time everybody had rushed off to hide in caves or holes in the ground, and we two were alone in the middle of the terrace, and the crackling noise did not stop but became more persistent. For a moment I too thought of running off to take shelter, but then a violent reluctance came over me at the idea of taking up all over again the life of fear that I had been leading for nine months. Enraged at the thought, I said to Rosetta: "Machine guns indeed! I don't care a damn about them and I'm going down just the same!" Rosetta made no objection; from very boredom and weariness she had become courageous. We gave up our intention of saying good-bye to the peasants who had been our hosts for such a long time—we had no idea where they were hiding now—and started off, regardless of the machine guns, walking slowly. We began going down, terrace after terrace, and the further we went the more we realized how right we had been not to run and hide, for the crackling sound could no longer be heard and everything appeared normal —merely a beautiful May day like many others, with a scorching sun and hedges smelling of wild roses and dust, and bees humming, just as if there had never been a war at all.

But a war there was, and very soon we saw signs of it. First of all we met two soldiers whom I judged to be Americans more from what they said to us than from their uniforms, which I did not know. They were dark, small, slight young men, both of them, and they came out of the scrub almost on top of us. One of them said: "Hello," or something like that; and the other said some more words in English that I did not understand. They crossed in front of us and then, leaving the path, started climbing up again through the scrub, bending down, rifles in their hands, looking up from under their steel helmets in the direction of the mountain top. These were the first Americans we saw, and we saw them by pure chance; and all war, now that I come to think of it, is a matter of pure chance; everything happens without reason, and you move a step to the left and are killed or you go to the right and are safe. I said to Rosetta: "You saw those two, they're Americans." "I thought Americans were tall and fair," said Rosetta, "but they were dark and small." At the moment I did not know what to answer, but later on I found out that there are kinds of races and colors in the American army, Negroes and whites, far and dark, tall and short. These two, as I discovered later, were Italian-Americans, and there were a good number of these, at any rate in the units which occupied our own area.

As we went on down the hill we came upon a Red Cross post in the shade of a carob tree. There was a camp bed, and a medicine cupboard, and a few soldiers, and at that moment two more soldiers brought in a wounded companion on a stretcher. We stopped to watch the two soldiers as they left the path and proceeded with some difficulty toward the post, carrying the stretcher. The wounded man kept his eyes closed and looked as if he was dead. But he was not dead, for the two who were carrying him were talkng to him, as much as to say that he would be all right, that they would be there in a moment, and he was nodding his head slightly as though answering that he understood and they mustn't worry about him. However, as one watched this scene on the mountain slope in the sunshine, with the flowering scrub hiding the two stretcher bearers up to their waists, one was almost inclined to believe not only that the wounded man was not dead but that the soldiers were not soldiers and the Red Cross post was not a Red Cross post and that in short the whole occurrence was not really true but was just a strange and absurd thing that had no explanation and no significance. I said to Rosetta: "That man has been hit by the machine guns. It might have happened to us," and I believe I said this in order to convince myself that the machine guns really existed and that the danger was to be taken seriously. All the same, I didn't feel entirely convinced.

We at last reached the bottom, at the fork in the road by the river near which was the cottage in which poor Tommasino had lived. Last time we had seen this place it had been deserted, like all places occupied by the Germans, who seemed to make a desert around themselves; wherever they went people hid themselves and disappeared. Now it was swarming with people, peasants and evacuees, some of them on foot, some with donkeys and mules, all of them laden with their belongings, all coming down like us from the mountains to go back to their homes. We walked along with this crowd, and they were cheerful and talked as if they had known each other for a long time. "The war's over," they said, "everything's past and done with; the English have arrived, and we shall have abundance of everything"; they seemed to have forgotten their year of sufferings. In company with this crowd we reached a crossroads where a road led in the direction of the mountains, and here we met the first column of Americans. They were moving in single file; and this time I saw that they were really Americans—that is, different both from the Germans and the Italians. They had their own characteristic way of walking, slouching along with a listless, discontented sort of air, and each of them wore his steel helmet in a different way, some on one side, some over their eyes, some on the back of their necks. Many of them were in shirt sleeves, and all of them were chewing gum. They looked as if they were taking part in the war unwillingly but without fear, like people who were not born for fighting—as are the Germans, for instance—but who do it because they were dragged forcibly into it. They did not look at us; you could tell that since landing in

Italy they had seen many mountain roads, so many poor people laden with bundles like us, so many brilliant mornings like this, that by now they were hardened to such sights. They filed along in the direction of the mountains, moving slowly and always with the same even pace. Finally, after the last three or four—the weariest and most indifferent of all—had gone past, we started off along the main road again.

This road led to Monte San Biagio, which is a village perched up on the hills that enclose the Fondi valley to the north; a little farther on it joined the national highway, the Via Appia. When we arrived at the Via Appia we stood open-mouthed at the spectacle of the entire American army advancing. To say that the road was crowded would be an understatement, nor would it be accurate, for there was no crowd and the road was filled from side to side with machines of every kind, all painted green, with the five-pointed white star on them, the star of America which is so very different from the big star of Italy that brings luck, so they say, but only luck, whereas the American star seems arrogant in its power and gives strength to all who follow it. I said machines, not motorcars. For there were on that road, so closely jammed together that they were hardly moving, machines of every sort and kind. There were small, open cars all made of iron, brimming over with soldiers holding their rifles between their legs; gigantic tanks, heavily armored and with caterpillar wheels, whose guns brushed against the boughs of the plane trees shading the road; trucks small and large, open and closed; smaller tanks, toylike almost, but also equipped with upturned guns; and even vehicles like complete railway carriages, enormous, armor-protected, with cabins in which you could catch glimpses of dial-plates full of switches and levers and electric wires. To tell the truth, anyone who has not seen the American army advancing along a road has no idea of what an army is. This great river of machines big and small, all carrying the white star which seemed to be a positive obsession, advanced very slowly, slower than walking pace, stopping at every moment and then starting again, just like the cars in the Corso in Rome at the time of day when there is most traffic. And everywhere there were soldiers, clinging to the tanks, the cars, the lorries or piled up on top of them, some sitting and some standing, always with the same look of patience, indifference, or even boredom, always chewing gum, some of them actually reading little newspapers full of pictures. Slipping in and out between the machines were motorcycles with one or two men on them dressed in leather. They were the only ones who were able to move quickly, and they looked like so many sheepdogs scurrying around an enormous, slow, lazy flock of sheep. When I looked at this procession of machines, so close together that if you threw a penny into the middle of them it would never reach the ground, I wondered to myself that the Germans did not take advantage of it to send their planes over and carry out a great slaughter. And this, more than anything else, made me realize that the Germans had now lost the war and could do no more harm because their nails had been cut and their teeth drawn—which, in the case of an army, means their guns and their planes. Once again I understood what modern war is. Not the hand-to-hand fighting which I had so much admired in the magazine illustrations of 1915, but a thing entirely remote and indirect: first the planes and the guns have a good preliminary clean-up; and after that the main body of the troops advances, rarely coming into contact with the enemy but going forward sitting comfortably in motor vehicles with their rifles between their legs, chewing gum and reading picture papers. Someone told me afterward that in some places these troops had had heavy losses. But never against other troops; as a result, rather, of the enemy's guns firing on them in an attempt to halt them.

There could be no question of crossing or going back up this road; it would have been like crossing a river in flood at its deepest point. We turned back, and, reaching a minor road, started off in the direction of the town. We arrived there in ten minutes, but here again we saw it was no use stopping. All the houses were lying in great heaps of ruins; where there were no ruins, there were huge pools of stagnant water; and in the small amount of space left vacant there was a swarming, seething mass of American soldiers, evacuees and peasants. It was like a fair, except that there was nothing to buy or sell apart from the hope of better days to come, and those who could have sold this hope—that is, the Americans—seemed indifferent and distant, while those who would have liked to buy it, the peasants and the evacuees, did not appear to know how to make the purchase. They wandered around among the Americans, asking them questions in Italian, and the Americans did not understand and answered in English, and then the peasants and evacuees went away disappointed, only to start again, after a short time, with the same result.

In front of one small house which for some unexplained reason had remained standing, I saw a commotion going on and went over to see what was happening. There were some Americans on the balcony and they were throwing down sweets and cigarettes to the evacuees and the peasants, and the latter were all hurling themselves on these things, scrambling and scuffling in the dust; it was really an indecent spectacle. You could see perfectly well that these sweets and cigarettes were of no great importance to them, but that they were nevertheless fighting for them with all this ferocity because they felt that the Americans were expecting them to behave like that. In those few hours, in fact, the atmosphere had already been created which I had occasion to observe, later, in Rome during the whole period that the Allied occupation lasted: the Italians would ask for things in order to please the Americans and the Americans would give the things in order to please the Italians, and neither of the two was aware that they were giving the other no pleasure whatsoever. And I do not believe that anyone desires these things but that they happen of themselves, as if by mutual agreement. The Americans were the conquerors and the Italians the conquered, and that was that.

I went up to a small military car which was standing still in the middle of all this crowd; two soldiers were sitting in it, one of them red-haired and freckled and blue-eyed, the other dark, yellow-faced, with a pointed nose and thin lips; and I said to them: "Please tell me what is the best way for me to get to Rome?" The red-haired man never even looked at us, he just went on chewing gum, absorbed in his little newspaper; but the dark man fumbled in his pockets and pulled out a packet of cigarettes. "No," I said, "I'm not asking for cigarettes, anyhow, we don't smoke; just tell us if there's any way we can get to Rome." "Rome?" he finally repeated. "Rome–nothing." "But why?" "Rome–Germans." Meanwhile he was fumbling in his pockets again, and this time he pulled out the usual sweets. But I refused these too. "If you want to give us anything," I said, "give us a loaf of bread; what use are sweets to us? Are you trying to sweeten my mouth? You won't do that, it'll stay bitter for quite a long time." He did not understand, and then, from under the seat, he pulled out a camera and gave us to understand, by a gesture, that he wanted to take a photograph of us. This time I lost patience and cried: "Ah, so you want to photograph us like this, do you, all ragged and grimy and looking like a couple of savages? Thank you very much, you can put away your camera again." Since he persisted, however, I took the camera out of his hands and put it down on the seat, as much as to say: "Stop it!" This time he understood; he turned to his companion and said something in English, and the other man answered grudgingly, without lifting his eyes from his paper. Then the dark man signaled to us to get into the car; we obeyed, and the red-haired man, coming to life, seized the wheel and started off. The car shot away like a rocket through the scattering crowd and took us into the town, climbing over the mountains of ruins and driving through the pools of water; evidently it was able to go anywhere. The dark man, in the meantime, was examining Rosetta's feet; she, like me, was wearing sandals. Finally he asked: "Shoes?" and leant down to touch her sandals; then, following the strings of the sandals, his hands traveled upward over her calf. I gave his hand a sharp smack and said: "Hands off. Yes, they're sandals, that's what they are; is there anything so special about that? But you shouldn't take advantage of it to put your hands on my daughter." Again he pretended not to understand and, pointing to Rosetta's sandal, took up his camera and said: "Photograph?" So I replied: "We may be wearing sandals but that doesn't mean we want you to photograph them. Why, the next thing would be that you'd go home and say that we Italians all wear sandals and don't know what shoes are. In your country you have the Redskins, and what would *you* say if *we* took photographs of them and then went about saying that you Americans all look like that, with feathers on your heads, like so many turkey-cocks? I come from the Ciociaria and I'm proud of it; but for you I'm just an Italian, a Roman or whatever you like, so don't go on being a nuisance with your silly photographs." In the end he understood it was no use insisting, so he put down his camera again. Meanwhile, leaping and bouncing over mounds of rubble and through pools of dirty water, we had gone half across the town and arrived in the main square.

Here there was an enormous crowd—again it looked as if there was a fair going on—and the crowd was thickest around a house which must have been the town hall and which by some miracle was not in ruins; there were merely a few holes and some bits of peeling plaster on its façade. The red-haired man, who so far had never said a word and had not even looked at us, made a sign to us to get out. The dark man also got out, told us to wait, and disappeared in the midst of the throng. He came back a moment later with another American in uniform, a young officer who looked like a real Italian, dark, with sparkling eyes and white, regular teeth. The latter immediately said: "I can speak Italian," and went on discoursing to us in what he believed to be Italian but which was, more or less, a Neapolitan dialect of the lowest kind, such as is spoken by the dockers in the port at Naples. Anyhow, he understood us and made himself understood, and I said to him: "We two come from Rome and we want to get back to Rome. You must give us instructions about what we should do to get there." He started to laugh with all his brilliant white teeth and then answered: "The only way is for you to dress up as a soldier and get into a tank and join in the battle that's going on for the capture of Rome." This made me uneasy, and I said: "But haven't you occupied Rome?" "No," he said, "the Germans are still there. And even if we had occupied it, you couldn't go there until special orders came through. Without those orders, nobody will be able to go to Rome." I felt much upset at this, and cried out: "Is *this* your liberation, then? To die of hunger and be left homeless just as before, and worse than before?" He shrugged his shoulders, and said that there were military reasons. He added that provision had been made that in the territories occupied by them no one should die of hunger; in proof of this he would give me some food, now, at this very moment. And indeed, smiling all the time with those dazzling teeth, he told us to follow him and led the way into the town hall, where we found a pandemonium not to be described, with a crush of people pressing forward and shouting and protesting at the far end of a big white, empty room in which there was a very long counter. Behind the counter were some Fondi people wearing white arm bands, and on the counter a number of piles of American tinned food.

The Italian-American officer led us up to the counter and used his authority to make them give us several of these tins. I remember he gave us six or seven tins of meat and vegetables, two of fish, and a big round tin, weighing a couple of pounds or more, of plum jam. We placed the tins in our suitcases and then pushed and shoved our way out. The two soldiers in the car had already vanished. The officer gave us a fine military salute and a smile, and then went off.

We started wandering among the crowd, aimlessly, like everyone else. I felt less worried now, with those tins in our suitcases, for eating is the first consideration; and so I amused myself by watching the spectacle of Fondi liberated. I was able in this way to take note of certain things which made me realize that the situation was not at all as we, up at Sant'Eufemia, had pictured it while we were awaiting the arrival of the Allies. The famous abundance of which everyone talked did not, in the meantime, exist. It was true that the Americans were giving away cigarettes and sweets, of which they seemed to have a truly enormous reserve; but otherwise, as could already be seen, they were being very careful. And to tell the truth I did not much care for the demeanor of these Americans. They were kind, it must be admitted, and therefore to be preferred to the Germans, who certainly made no excessive use of kindness; but their kindness was indifferent, remote, and they treated us, in fact, like a lot of little boys who are causing annoyance to the grownups and must therefore be kept quiet with—of course—sweets. And sometimes they were not even kind. In order to get into the center of the town of Fondi it was necessary to have a pass, or at least to be taking part in the work which the Italians and the Americans together had organized to repair the wreckage of the air raids. Rosetta and I found ourselves at a point in the main road where a barrier had been set up, with two soldiers and a sergeant. Two Italians approached—educated men, both of them, as you could see from their manners, although they were both in rags. One of them, a white-haired old gentleman, said to the sergeant: "We are engineers, and we were told at Allied headquarters to report today for the works in progress here." The sergeant, a tough man with a face like a closed fist, all bare and bumpy, said: "Where's your pass?" They looked from one to another, and the old man said: "We have no pass. They just told us to report." Then the sergeant, in a most offensive way, began shouting: "And you report at this time of day? You ought to have reported at seven o'clock this morning with all the other workmen." "They only told us a short time ago," said the younger of the two, a man of about forty, thin, distinguished-looking, extremely nervous, with a sort of tic which caused him to twist his head to one side every now and then, as though he had a stiff neck. "That's a lie—you're just a couple of liars." "Be careful what you say," said the younger man resentfully. "This gentleman and I are engineers, and—" He was on the point of continuing, but the sergeant interrupted him: "Shut your mouth, you shit, or else I'll swipe you a couple that'll keep it shut for you." The younger of the two engineers must have been, as I have said, a nervous wreck, and these words had the same effect on him as the two blows would have had. He went white as a sheet and I thought for a moment that he was going to kill the sergeant. Luckily the older man interposed, in a conciliating manner, and in the end, what with one thing and another, they did in fact get past the barrier and go on their way. I saw several such incidents that day. They were always provoked by American soldiers who were, in reality, Italian-Americans. The real English-Americans—by which I mean those who for the most part were tall, fair and thin—behaved in a different way, distant, but polite and respectful. But these Italian-Americans were a miserable lot and you never knew how to deal with them. Perhaps they felt they were too much like Italians and wished to convince themselves that they were different and superior. Perhaps they had a grudge against Italy, from which their families had fled, destitute and homeless, to America; or perhaps in America they were looked down upon and therefore tried to get themselves respected, for once in their lives, here in Italy. Anyhow the fact remains that they were the most ill-mannered of all—or, if you prefer it, the least polite. And every time I had to make a request of the Americans I always prayed to God that I should have to do with an American—yes, even of Negro descent, rather than an Italian-American. Furthermore, they insisted on telling us that they spoke Italian, instead of which they talked strange Southern Italian dialects such as Calabrian, Sicilian or Neapolitan, and you had to be very clever to understand them. It is true that when you came to know these men better you found that, after all, they were good, honest people. But the first encounter was always disagreeable.

We wandered around for a little longer among the ruins, in the midst of the crowd of Italians and soldiers, and then started off along the main road where there were still several houses left intact, for the bombings had been concentrated mainly on the town itself. At a point where the mountain thrust itself out, at a sharp angle, into the plain, and the road wound round it in a curve, we suddenly espied a cottage. The door was open, and I said to Rosetta: "Let's see if we can fix ourselves up here for the night." We went up three steps and found a single, completely empty, room. The walls had once been whitewashed; but now they were dirtier than those of a stable. Amongst patches of what looked like soot, amongst peeling plaster and gaping holes, were numbers of drawings, done in charcoal, of naked women, of women's faces, and of other things which I will not mention—the usual sort of filth that soldiers scrawl upon walls. On the floor in one corner a heap of ashes and black, dead embers showed they had lit a fire there. The two windows had no glass in them and there was only one shutter—I suspect that the embers were the remains of the other. I told Rosetta that it would be a good plan for us to install ourselves here for two or three nights; I had seen a straw stack in a field not far off, and we would bring in a heap of straw and make a kind of bed for ourselves. We had no blankets or sheets but it was warm now and we would sleep in our clothes.

We cleaned up the room as far as possible, taking away the worst of the dirt, and brought in enough straw to make a bed. "It's odd, though," I said to Rosetta, "that no one except us has thought of using this cottage." The explanation of this odd fact became plain a few moments later when we went out and walked along the road under the mountainside. At a very short distance from the house there was a wide clear space and also a group of trees. In this space the Americans had planted three huge guns, so big that during the rest of the war I never saw their equals. They were pointed to the sky and had enormous barrels, thick as tree trunks at the bottom and tapering gradually up to their mouths; these were painted bottle green and were so long that they disappeared beyond the foliage of the great plane trees beneath which they lay. Mounted on caterpillar wheels, they had, at the base of each gun, dials and wheels and switches and handles, which suggested that they must be extremely complicated to work; and around them were trucks and armored vehicles in which—so we were told by some peasants—were the shells; these, judging by the guns, must also have been immense. The soldiers in charge of these guns, some of whom were lying flat on their backs in the grass while others perched on the guns themselves, were in shirt sleeves, all of them young and carefree, looking as if they were there for a picnic rather than a military action; some were smoking, some chewing gum, some reading newspapers. One of the peasants explained to us that the soldiers had given notice that all those who stayed in cottages in the neighborhood of the guns did so at their own risk, for the Germans might start a counter-bombardment and a direct hit on the ammunition would blow up and kill everyone within range of at least a hundred yards. I understood now why our little cottage had remained empty and I said: "I see we've fallen out of the frying pan into the fire. There's a chance that we may be blown up in company with all these young men." But what with the sunshine, and all those soldiers lying about in their shirt sleeves on the grass, and the greenness of everything, and the soft air of that beautiful day, it seemed really impossible that we should be killed. "Well," I said, "never mind, we're not dead yet and I daresay we shan't die this time either. We'll stay in the cottage." Rosetta, who always did what I wanted, said that it didn't matter to her: the Madonna had protected us so far, and would continue to protect us.

Truly it was just as though it had been a Sunday with a fair going on and everybody out and enjoying the lovely holiday afternoon in peace and quiet. The road was filled with peasants and soldiers smoking American cigarettes and eating American sweets and rejoicing in the sunshine and freedom as though they were one and the same thing, and as though sunshine without freedom would have had neither light nor warmth and freedom had not existed as long as winter lasted and the sun had remained hidden behind the clouds. Everything, in fact, was now natural, as if all that had occurred up till then had been against nature; and now at last, after a very long time, nature had taken the upper hand again. We spoke to various people and they all said that the Americans had distributed supplies of food and that there was already talk of rebuilding Fondi and making a much finer town of it than before, and that now the bad times were over and there was nothing more to fear. But Rosetta was tormenting me to find out about Michele, for even in the midst of joy she had this thorn in her heart; and I asked several people about him but no one knew anything. The Germans had gone and no one wanted to think about sad things—just as I had been afraid to go and say good-bye to Filippo, who had been unable to join in the general exultation of leaving Sant'Eufemia. "Filippo?" people said. "Oh, no doubt he's probably organizing the black market." Of his son nobody could say anything; they all called him "the student" and, as far as I could make out, considered him to be an idler and an eccentric.

We ate one of the American tins of meat and vegetables and some bread a peasant gave us, and then, since the heat was intense and we had nothing to do and were dead tired, we went into the cottage, shut the door and threw ourselves down on the straw to sleep. We were awakened late in the afternoon by an immensely violent explosion: the walls trembled as if they had been made but of paper. At first I was in doubt as to the origin of this explosion, but then there was another one and I understood: the American guns, no more than fifty paces away from us, had gone into action. Although we had slept for some hours we were still very tired, so we remained lying in the corner of the room, our arms round each other in the straw, stunned and unable even to speak. The gun went on firing all the rest of the afternoon. After the first surprise I had fallen into a doze again, and in spite of the terrible violence of the explosions I heard the gun in a state between waking and sleeping, and the reports mingled strangely with my reflections, which in turn seemed to follow the rhythm of the reports. The gunfire was regular, and my thoughts soon adapted themselves to this regularity and were no longer disturbed by the din. First there would be a tremendous explosion, deep-sounding, hoarse, harrowing, as though the very earth had vomited up the sound; all the walls would tremble and pieces of plaster would fall from the ceiling. Then there would be silence, and then a fresh explosion, again making the walls tremble and the plaster fall from the ceiling. Rosetta pressed up against me, saying nothing, but I was thinking. Each one of these explosions filled me with joy; and this joy increased with each explosion. These guns were firing on the Germans and the Fascists, and I became aware that I hated both Germans and Fascists, and these explosions seemed to me to be coming, not from guns but from some force of nature such as thunder or an avalanche. These reports, so regular, so monotonous, so determined, were driving away winter and sorrows and dangers and the war and the food shortage and hunger and all the other unpleasant things that the Germans and the Fascists had brought down on our heads for so many years. "Dear guns," I thought, "blessed guns, guns of pure gold." I welcomed each explosion with a feeling of joy that sent a thrill through my whole body; and each silence almost with fear, because I was afraid the guns might stop firing. As I lay with closed eyes I seemed to see a vast room, such as I had seen so often in the newspapers, a room with a lot of fine pillars and a lot of paintings, and this room was all full of Fascists with black shirts and Nazis with brown shirts, standing stiffly, as the papers said, to attention. And behind a vast table stood Mussolini, with his great broad face, his threatening eyes, his thick lips, his chest sticking out and covered with medals, and a white plume on his head; and beside him was that other miserable wretch, that bastard, his friend Hitler, with his ill-omened, cuckold face, his little black mustache that looked like a toothbrush, his eyes like a wet fish, his pointed nose and on his forehead that insolent lock of hair. I could see every detail of this great room just as if I had been there myself; those two men standing behind the table and at both sides of the table Fascists and Nazis, the Fascists on the right, all black, always black, with the white death's head on their black caps; the Nazis on the left, with their brown shirts and red arm-bands with black crosses on them that looked like nasty insects running along on four feet, their fat faces shaded by the peaks of their caps, their stomachs packed tightly into the tops of their riding-breeches. I looked and looked and looked, and I enjoyed the sight of all those faces of scoundrels and bastards and cuckolds who had gone unpunished, and then my thoughts traveled to one of the big guns close beside the cottage under the plane trees. I saw an American soldier who was by no means standing stiffly to attention and who had no swastikas, no black or brown shirt, no death's heads on his cap, no dagger stuck into his belt, no glossy jack-boots nor any of the other trimmings with which the Germans and the Fascists adorned themselves, but was dressed simply and since it was hot had his shirt sleeves rolled up over his arms. And this young American, perfectly calm, chewing gum all the time, took up an enormous shell in his arms and slipped it into the breech of the gun and then turned the levers on the dial. The gun went off, shuddering as it did so and making a jump backward; and then into my dream came the din of the real gun really firing, and my dream was no longer a dream but reality. And in my mind I followed the shell as, whistling and whining, it cleft the air, and I saw it plunge into the great room, blowing them all sky-high—Fascists and Nazis, Hitler and Mussolini, with all their death's heads and their plumes, their swastikas and daggers and jack-boots. This gave me great joy, and I realized that such joy was not good because it was the joy of hatred, but there was nothing I could do about it; it was clear that I had been hating the Fascists and the Nazis all the time, without knowing it, and now that the big gun was firing on them, I was pleased.

Since that time I have heard a great deal of talk about liberation, and have realized that liberation was a thing that really happened, for that afternoon I felt it as you feel a physical fact, as you feel comfort and relief after you have been tied up; as you have a sense of freedom after you have been shut up in a room under lock and key and then the door is suddenly thrown open. And that gun firing on the Nazis, in spite of its being a similar gun to those which the Nazis were using to fire on the Americans, spelled liberation for me; something which had a blessed force stronger than their hateful force, something which made them afraid after they had made everybody else so deeply afraid, something which was destroying them after they themselves had destroyed so many people and so many towns. This gun was firing on the Nazis and the Fascists and each shot it fired was a blow against the prison of lies and fear which they had built up over so many years, and this prison was big as the sky and now it was crumbling in every direction beneath the onslaught of the gun and everyone could breathe again, even they, the Fascists and the Nazis, for soon they would no longer be compelled to be Fascists and Nazis but would go back to being human beings like everyone else. Yes, that evening I was aware of liberation in this way, and although later this liberation came to signify a great many other things which were very unpleasant, I shall always remember, as long as I live, that afternoon and that gun. I felt liberation as a happiness which made me rejoice even in the death that the gun dispensed, and made me hate for the first and only time in my life, and made me enjoy the destruction of other people with the same feeling with which one enjoys the coming of spring and flowers and fine weather.

And so I passed that afternoon, sleeping or rather dozing, with the gun's tremendous lullaby sounding in my ears. The house trembled at each report, plaster fell on my head and body, the straw was prickly and the floor underneath the straw was hard; yet those were among the best hours of my life, and I can say this now, today, in full consciousness of what I am saying. From time to time I opened my eyes and looked out of the window and saw the green boughs of a plane tree in the lovely May light; later, this light became lower and the boughs darker and less luminous, and still the gun went on firing and I hugged Rosetta tightly and felt happy. I slept for at least an hour, with a black, heavy sleep, and then I woke up and again heard the gun booming away outside and realized that the gun had never stopped firing and again I felt happy. Finally, at twilight, when it was already almost dark inside the room, the gunfire unexpectedly ceased. The silence that succeeded it seemed numbed and paralysed after so many repeated explosions—a silence which, as I noticed, was made up of the normal sounds of life: a church bell ringing somewhere or other, voices of people passing along the road, a dog barking, an ox lowing. We lay with our arms round each other for another half hour, in a state of drowsiness, then we got up and went out. It was dark and the sky was full of stars, and there was a strong smell of cut grass in the soft, windless air. But from the Via Appia, not far away, there still came the clank of iron and the rumble of engines: the advance continued.

We ate up the contents of another tin with a little bread, and flung ourselves down on the straw again and went to sleep at once, clasped closely together and this time without the sound of the guns. I do not know how long we slept; perhaps four or five hours, perhaps more. I only know that I suddenly sat up, terrified; the room was filled with a dazzling, quivering green light; everything was green, the walls, the ceiling, the straw, Rosetta's face, the door, the floor. This light seemed to become more intense, like a certain kind of physical pain which grows more acute every moment and it seems impossible that it should increase any more, so violent and intolerable is it already. Then suddenly the light went out and in the darkness I heard the hateful howl of the warning siren, which I had not heard since we left Rome, and I realized there was an air raid. I shouted to Rosetta: "Come on, hurry, let's get out of the house!" and at the same time I heard the deafening burst of bombs falling quite close and, between the explosions, the furious roar of planes and the sharp reports of anti-aircraft guns.

I seized Rosetta by the hand and rushed out of the house. Then there was a terrific crash: a bomb had fallen behind the house and I felt the blast from it on my skirt, as though an enormous draft had blown upon it, glueing it to my legs. It made me think I had been hit and was perhaps already dead. However I ran on, across a cornfield; dragging Rosetta by the hand, and then I stumbled and found myself in water. It was a brook, full to the brim, and the coldness of the water calmed me a little, and I stood still in water up to my waist, hugging Rosetta to my breast, while all around us a red light danced and in this light could be seen the ruined houses of Fondi, with their varying colors and outlines, just as in daylight, and all over the countryside the explosions continued. The sky above us was all a-flower with little white clouds, puffs of smoke from the anti-aircraft fire; and through all the confusion came the continuous harsh roar of airplanes flying low and dropping bombs. Finally there was one last explosion, louder than all the rest—it was as if the sky had been a room and someone had banged the door violently before going away;—and the red glow vanished almost entirely, except in one corner of the horizon where there seemed to be a fire. The din of the airplanes died down and the anti-aircraft guns fired a few more shots, and after that there was nothing.

As soon as the night's blackness and silence had returned and the stars had reappeared in the sky over our heads, I said to Rosetta: "We'd better not go back to the cottage. Those bastards may start dropping their bombs again, and this time they might really kill us. Let's stay here; at least there isn't a house to fall on our heads." So we crawled out of the water and threw ourselves down flat on the ground beside the brook. We did not sleep, though we dozed again, but not so happily as in the house while the gun was firing. The night was full of noises; we could hear distant shouts and screams, the clanking of engines and the stamp of feet and countless other strange sounds. The darkness was unquiet, and I felt it to be full of dead and wounded from the German bombs, and now the Americans were hurrying about to collect these dead and wounded. We dozed off finally, and then woke up in the grey light of dawn and saw that we were lying in a cornfield. Beside my face rose the tall yellow stalks, and among the stalks were a few poppies of a glorious red, and the sky above my head was white and cold, with a few bright golden stars still shining. I looked at Rosetta as she lay beside me, still asleep; and I saw that her face was smeared with dry, black mud, and her legs and her skirt, up to her waist, were black with mud too, and so also were my own legs and skirt. I felt rested, however, for I had been sleeping most of the time since early afternoon of the day before. "Shall we move?" I said to Rosetta; but she murmured something I did not understand and twisted herself around and put her face in my lap, throwing her two arms round my hips. And so I lay down too, although I was no longer sleepy; and there I remained, with the corn around us, my eyes closed, waiting for her to finish her sleep.

She awoke, at last, when full daylight had come. When we had risen from our bed of corn and turned to look across the field in the direction of the cottage, we discovered that the cottage was no longer there. In the end, after looking carefully for some time, I saw a pile of rubble at the edge of the field, at the point where I remembered that the house had stood. "Do you see?" I said to Rosetta; "if we'd stayed in the house we'd be dead." She answered in a calm voice, without moving: "Perhaps it would have been better, Mum." I looked at her and saw a distraught, despairing expression on her face, and with sudden decision I said: "By hook or by crook we're getting away from here today." "How?" she asked. "We've got to go," I said, "and go we shall."

In the meantime, however, we went to look at the cottage and saw that the bomb had exploded right beside it, pushing the whole thing into the road—which was almost blocked by rubble. The bomb had made a big, shallow, ragged hole of fresh brown earth mingled with torn-up grass, and there was a pool of yellowish water in the bottom of it. Now we had no roof over our heads and, what was worse, our suitcases, with the little we possessed, were buried in the ruins. All at once I felt truly desperate and, not knowing what to do, I sat down on a heap of rubble and stared straight in front of me. As on the previous day, the road was swarming with soldiers and evacuees, but they walked straight on without looking either at us or at the ruins—a perfectly normal sight, nowadays, and nothing to make a fuss about. Then a peasant stopped and greeted us; he was a man from Fondi whom I had known when I used to come down from Sant'Eufemia in search of provisions. He said it was the Germans who had done the bombing during the night, and he told us that about fifty people had been killed, thirty soldiers and twenty Italian civilians. He spoke of the case of a family of evacuees who, like us, had spent almost a year in the mountains and had then come down at the moment when the Allies had arrived and had established themselves in a cottage on the road, only a short distance from ours. There had been a direct hit on the cottage and they had all been killed; wife, husband and four children. I listened to these things without saying anything, and so also did Rosetta. In former times I would have exclaimed: "Why, how terrible! Poor things! What a dreadful disaster!" But now I didn't feel in the mood to say anything. Our misfortunes actually made us indifferent to the misfortunes of others. And I reflected afterward that this, undoubtedly, is one of the worst effects of war: that it makes people unfeeling, that it hardens their hearts, that it kills pity.

So we spent the morning sitting on the ruins of the house, feeling dazed and incapable of thinking about anything. We were so numbed, and in so shocked and painful a state, that we had not even the strength to reply to the occasional soldiers and peasants who bothered to address us as they went by. I remember that an American soldier, seeing Rosetta sitting motionless and dazed on the stones, stopped to speak to her. She did not answer but sat there looking at him. He spoke to her first in English, then in Italian, and finally he took a cigarette out of his pocket, slipped it into her mouth and walked away. Rosetta stayed just as she was, her face smeared with dry, black mud and the cigarette in her mouth, drooping from her lips; and it would have been a funny sight if it hadn't been so overwhelmingly sad. Midday came and I decided, with a great effort, that we must do something, if only in order to find something to eat, for eat we must; and I said to Rosetta that we would go back to Fondi and look for that American officer who spoke Neapolitan and seemed to have a kindly interest in us. We walked back slowly and unwillingly into the town. Here the usual fair was going on, among the piles of rubbish and the pools of water, the trucks and the armoured cars, with the American police heavily overworked in an attempt to give some sort of a direction to this inert, aimless crowd. We reached the main square and went to the town hall building, where there was the same tumultuous throng as the day before and the same food distribution was taking place. This time, however, it was more orderly: the police had formed the crowd into three rows, each leading toward an American standing behind the counter on which the tins of food were stacked; beside each American stood an Italian with a white arm-band; these were town councillors, who had been given the job of helping in the distribution. Amongst the others behind the counter I saw the American officer I was looking for, and I told Rosetta we would take our place in the row that led up to him: in this way we would have an opportunity of speaking to him. We waited for a long time in line with all those other poor people, until our turn finally came. The officer recognized us and smiled at us with all his dazzling teeth. "What's happened, haven't you left for Rome yet?" he said.

I pointed to my clothes and Rosetta's. "You see what a state we're in," I said.

He looked at us and immediately understood. "Last night's air raid?"

"Yes, and we've nothing left. The bombs destroyed the cottage where we were sheltering, and our suitcases were buried in the ruins together with the tins of food you gave us."

He had stopped smiling now. Rosetta, particularly, with her gentle face all smeared with dried mud, banished all desire to smile. "I can give you some food, as I did yesterday," he said, "and also a few things to wear. But that's all I can do."

"Send us back to Rome," I said; "we've got our home there and our belongings and everything we need."

But he gave the same answer he had given the day before. "*Our* men haven't reached Rome yet; how can *you* go there?"

This silenced me, and I said nothing. He took some tins of food from the pile, handed them to us, and then told one of the Italians with the armbands to take us to some place where they were distributing clothing. As we were on the point of leaving him I said: "My parents live in a village near Vallecorsa—or rather, they did live there; I don't know where they've gone to now. Do at least help us to get to my village. I know everyone there, and even if my parents are not there I shall find some way of getting settled."

He looked at me and answered, kindly but firmly: "I'm afraid you can't make use of army vehicles to get from one place to another. It's forbidden. Only Italians who are working for the

American army can make use of our vehicles, and then only in connection with their work. I'm sorry, but I can't do anything for you." Having said this, he turned to two other women who were standing behind us, and I, seeing that he had nothing more to say to us, followed the Italian with the armband.

Once we were in the street, this man, who had heard our conversation, said to us: "There was a case only yesterday of two evacuees, a husband and wife, who were sent back to their village in an army car. But they were able to prove that they had given hospitality during the winter to an English prisoner. As a reward, the authorities made an exception to the rule and sent them back to their village. If you two had done the same thing, I don't believe there would be any difficulty in your getting to Vallecorsa."

Rosetta, who had so far said nothing, suddenly exclaimed: "D'you remember, Mum—those two Englishmen? We could say we gave them hospitality."

Now it so happened that those two Englishmen, before they left us, had given me a note written in their own language and signed by both of them, and I had put it in the bag together with the money. Of money there was not much left now, but the note should still be there. I had forgotten about it; but at Rosetta's words I hastened to feel in my pocket, and indeed I found it. The two Englishmen had begged me to hand over this note to an officer, as soon as their own troops arrived. "We're safe, then," I said joyfully; and I related the story of the two Englishmen to the Italian, and how we two had been the only ones to give them hospitality on Christmas Day because all the other evacuees had been afraid to help them, and how they had gone away again next day and that very morning the Germans had come to look for them. "Come with me to get these clothes," said the Italian. "Then we'll go to headquarters and I'm sure you'll get everything you want."

We went to another house where the distribution of clothes was going on, and there they gave us each a pair of men's shoes with rubber soles and no heels, and some green stockings that came half way up the leg, and a skirt and a blouse of the same color. These were the clothes worn by the women in their army, and we were delighted to put them on because our own clothes were by now reduced to rags and were dirty with dried mud. We received a piece of soap and washed our faces and hands, and we combed our hair and thus we were almost presentable. The Italian said to us: "That's fine, you look like civilized people now, instead of a couple of savages. Now come with me to headquarters."

Headquarters was in yet another house. We went upstairs, and everywhere army police were asking where people were going and were receiving information and giving directions. We went up from one landing to another, with soldiers and Italians coming and going all the time, till we reached the top floor. Here our Italian friend went and spoke to a soldier who was standing on guard in front of a door, and soon he came back and told us: "Not only are they interested but they want to see you in a minute or two. Sit down on this sofa and wait."

It was scarcely five minutes before the soldier came and ushered us in. It was an entirely empty room except for a desk behind which was sitting a fair, middle-aged man with a red toothbrush moustache, blue eyes and a freckled face. He was stout and cheerful. He was in uniform, and I don't understand their ranks, but I heard later that he was a major. There were two chairs in front of the desk; and he rose politely when we came in, invited us to sit down and then, when we had done so, sat down himself. "Would you like to smoke?" he asked us in good Italian, holding out a packet of cigarettes. I refused, and he immediately began: "I was told you had a note for me."

"Here it is," I said, and handed it to him. He took it and read it through two or three times with close attention, and then, looking at me fixedly, with a serious expression on his face, said: "This note is very important, and you are giving us valuable information. We have been without news of these two men for a long time, and we are very grateful to you for what you did for them. Now, could you give me some idea of what they were like, these two?"

I described them as well as I could. "One was fair and small, with a pointed beard. The other was tall and thin and dark, with blue eyes."

"What sort of clothes were they wearing?"

"Black oilskin wind jackets, I think, and long trousers."

"Had they any caps?"

"Yes, they had kind of uniform caps."

"Were they armed?"

"Yes, they had pistols. They showed them to me."

"And what were they intending to do when they left you?"

"They were intending to get to the front, keeping to the mountains all the way, pass through the lines and reach Naples. They had spent the winter in a peasant's house at the bottom of the Monte delle Fate, and now they were hoping to reach the front and get through the lines. But I doubt if they succeeded because everybody said it was impossible to cross the front on account of the German patrols and the machine gun and artillery fire."

"In fact," he said, "they did not cross it, for they never arrived in Naples. What date was it when they were with you?"

I told him the date, and after a moment he went on: "And how long did you keep them?"

"Only one day and one night, because they were in a hurry and also because they were afraid someone might give them away. And indeed, no sooner had they gone than the Germans arrived. They spent Christmas Day with us and we had a fowl and a bottle of wine together."

He smiled and said: "The wine and the fowl that you shared with them represent only a small part of the debt we owe you. Now tell me—what can we do for you?"

Then I told him the whole story: that we had nothing to eat; that we did not feel like staying at Fondi, partly because we had no house to go to, the one in which we were sheltering having been destroyed in last night's bombing; that we wanted to go to my own village near Vallecorsa, where I supposed my parents to be and where, at any rate, we could live in my own home. He listened to me with a serious look, and then said: "What you are asking me is, strictly speaking, forbidden. But then, giving hospitality to English prisoners, under the Germans, was forbidden too, wasn't it?" He smiled and I smiled. After a moment he resumed: "This is what we'll do. I shall say that you're leaving by car with one of our officers to collect information in the mountains about these two missing men. We should in any case have carried out this inquiry, though not at your village as it's impossible that they could have passed that way. This means that the officer will first take you to Vallecorsa and then make his inquiries afterward."

I said I thanked him very much, and he replied: "It's *we* who thank *you.* And now, will you give me your names?"

I told him, and he wrote everything down carefully and then rose to say good-bye to us, and carried his politeness so far as to accompany us to the door and hand us over to the soldier on guard, to whom he said something in English. The soldier, also, at once became very polite and invited us to follow him.

We went with the soldier to the far end of a bare, white passage and he showed us into an empty but clean room in which there were two army beds; he told us that we could sleep there that night and that next day, in accordance with the major's orders, we would be going somewhere else. There he left us, closing the door behind him, and we sat down on the two beds with a sigh of satisfaction. We felt quite different now from what we had felt hitherto. We had clean clothes, we had washed, we had food to eat, army beds to sleep on, a roof over our heads and—most important of all—we had the hope of better days to come. We were, in fact, completely changed, and we owed this change to the major and his kindly words. How often have I thought that a human being has the right to be treated as a human being and not as a beast, and that treating a human being as such means giving him the opportunity to keep clean, in a clean house, showing sympathy and consideration for him and, above all, giving him hope for the future! If this is not done, man, who is capable of anything, becomes a beast in no time at all, and if you want him to be a beast and not a human being, it's no use asking him to behave like a human being.

Well, we hugged each other and I kissed Rosetta and said to her: "Now I'm sure everything will come right, really and truly, this time. We'll spend a few days in the village and we'll have plenty to eat and a good rest, and then we'll go back to Rome, and everything will be just as it was before." Poor Rosetta, she said, "Yes, Mum," just like a lamb being led to the slaughter, not knowing what is happening and licking the hand that guides it toward the knife. That hand, alas, was mine, and I did not know that it was I who, of my own free will, was conducting her to the slaughter, as will be seen later.

That day, after eating one of our tins of food, we lay dozing all the afternoon on our army beds. We had no desire to go wandering around the streets of Fondi; it was too melancholy, with that fair-ground throng of ragamuffins and soldiers and all those ruins reminding us of the war at every step. And we were still terribly fatigued. We had spent the night in the open, after a great many terrors and other emotions, and we felt as if all our bones were broken. So we slept, and from time to time woke up and then went to sleep again. My bed was in front of the window which, having no shutters, was filled with blue sky, and each time I woke up I noticed that the light had changed both direction and intensity as the sun went from high noon to the western horizon. I felt happy again that day, just as I had the day before when listening to the gun, but this time it was on Rosetta's account that I was happy, when I saw her sleeping in the bed beside mine, safe and sound after so many vicissitudes and dangers. It seemed to me that I had done well and had succeeded in bringing myself and my daughter safely home through the storm and tempest of war: Rosetta was well, I myself was well, nothing really serious had happened to us, and soon we should be going back to Rome, back into our own flat, and I should be opening the shop and everything would begin again, just as before. Better than before, in fact: for Rosetta's young man, who certainly would be spared too, would come back from Yugoslavia and he and Rosetta would be married. As I lay there half asleep, I saw her coming out of a sun-filled church, dressed in white, with orange blossoms around her head. She was on the arm of her husband, and behind her came myself and all the other relations and friends, smiling and happy. Then, not satisfied with seeing her in the porch, I made a jump backward, inside the church itself, as I wanted to see the pair of them kneeling in front of the altar while the priest who had married them was pronouncing his little discourse on the duties and obligations of holy matrimony. But even this did not satisfy me, and I made another jump, forward this time, and saw Rosetta with her first baby: we were sitting at table, she and her husband and I. The baby started crying in the next room, and Rosetta fetched him and sat down again and unbuttoned her bodice and gave the baby her breast, and the baby took hold of it with his mouth and his two hands. She bent over the baby to take a spoonful of soup; and now there were no longer three but four of us round the table, Rosetta's husband, Rosetta, the baby and I. As I looked at this picture, half-asleep, I reflected that I was now a grandmother, and I did not mind that, since I had no further desire for love-making and wanted to become an old woman and live for many years as a grandmother alongside Rosetta and her children. During this time, while I was having these dreams, I peeped now and again at Rosetta as she lay on the bed beside mine, and I was pleased that she should be there to prove that these dreams could quickly become realities.

Evening came, and I pulled myself up and looked around. Rosetta was still asleep; she had taken off her skirt and bodice and in the twilight I could just see her bare shoulders and arms, white and plump, the shoulders and arms of a young, healthy girl; her petticoat had risen up over her leg, which was bent so that the knee was almost on a level with her mouth; and her thigh, too, was white and plump, like her shoulders and arms. I asked her if she wanted anything to eat; and after a moment, without turning, she shook her head slightly and murmured a word of refusal. Then I asked if she wanted to get up and go downstairs into the streets of Fondi: again there was the same movement, again the faint refusal. So I threw myself down on the bed again, and this time I fell sound asleep; the truth was that we were both exhausted by so many emotions, and this stubborn need for sleep was rather like winding up a watch that has stopped for a long time, and you wind and wind and it seems endless, because the watch has run down completely and lost the power to start going again.

Chapter 9

WE WERE AWAKENED at dawn by someone knocking so loudly that you might have thought he wanted to break the door down. It was the soldier who had helped us the day before, and he told us that the car which was to take us to Vallecorsa was ready and that we must hurry up. We dressed quickly, and as I dressed I realized that I felt strong as never before; those hours of sleep had brought me back to life again. I saw also, from the energy with which she washed and dressed, that Rosetta too felt strong and lively. Only a mother can understand these things; I remembered Rosetta the day before, dazed from lack of sleep and emotion, her face smeared with dried mud, her eyes sad and bewildered. It gave me pleasure to look at her now as she sat on the bed with her legs dangling. She stretched herself, raising her arms in the air and thrusting out her lovely plump white bosom that looked as if it must burst out of her chemise; then she went to the basin in the corner and poured cold water from the jug and vigorously washed herself, throwing the water over her face and over her neck and arms and shoulders. With her eyes shut she felt for the towel and rubbed herself until her skin was red, then she took her skirt and slipped it on over her head as she stood in the middle of the room. All these were normal gestures and I must have seen her go through them countless times. But they made me conscious of her youth and her restored strength, just as one feels the youth and strength of a fine tree standing firm in the sunshine yet with all its leaves moving gently at every slight puff of a spring breeze.

Well, we dressed and ran down the still deserted stairs of the empty house. In front of the door stood a small open car of the kind used by the Allied armies, hard and with seats made of iron. At the wheel was an English officer, fair and ruddy, with an expression of embarrassment or annoyance on his face. He indicated the seats behind him and told us, in bad Italian, that he had orders to take us to Vallecorsa. He did not seem very agreeable, but I think it was more from shyness and embarrassment than because he felt any dislike for us. In the car were two big cardboard boxes filled with tins of provisions, and he told us in the same embarrassed tone of voice that the major had sent them to us with his compliments and best wishes for a good journey, excusing himself for not coming to say good-bye to us because he was extremely busy. While these preliminaries were going on, a number of evacuees, who had probably spent the night in the open, gathered around the car watching us in silence, with envy on their faces. They envied us because we had found a way of getting away from Fondi, and also because we had all those tins of food, and I could not help a feeling of vanity, though not entirely unaccompanied by remorse. I did not yet know how little, in reality, we were to be envied.

The officer started the engine and the car darted off through the puddles and the ruins in the direction of the mountains. We turned off by a secondary road and soon began speedily climbing between two mountains, through a narrow, deep valley, along the side of a stream. We remained silent and the officer remained silent—we because we were tired of talking by signs and grunts like deaf mutes, and he out of shyness or because he was bored at having to act as our chauffeur. Anyhow, what could we have said to this officer? That we were pleased to be leaving Fondi? That it was a lovely May day, with a blue, cloudless sky and a sun that made the whole green, exuberant countryside glow with light? That we were going to the village where I was born? That there we should find ourselves in our own home? None of these things would interest him and he would have been right to tell us so, and that he was merely doing his duty, which was to take us to a certain place, and that it was better for us to remain silent, and furthermore, he had to drive and must not be distracted. And yet, although I was thinking these things, I felt an acute desire to speak to this officer and to find out who he was, where his family lived; what he did in peacetime and whether he was engaged to be married, and so on. I realized that now that danger was past I was returning to the normal feelings of normal times. I was again taking interest in people and things outside myself and my own and Rosetta's safety. I was beginning to live again, and that means doing all sorts of things for no reason at all, either out of sympathy or caprice or impulse or, indeed, simply for fun. This officer aroused my curiosity, just as when you have had a long illness and begin to be convalescent, everything arouses your curiosity, everything that you set your eyes on, even the most insignificant things. I looked at him and observed that he had really magnificent fair hair, the color of gold, with numbers of smooth, shining locks crossing and interweaving like the strands of a fine basket and then escaping in so many capricious points at the back of his neck. This golden hair tempted me to put out my hand and stroke it, not because the young man pleased or attracted me in any way; merely because life had become a pleasure again and his hair was truly alive. I had the same feeling for the trees with their young foliage, and for the foundation of clean, well-cut stones which supported the embankment on the other side of the stream, and for the blue sky and the bright May sunshine. Everything gave me pleasure and I had an appetite for everything.

After running for some time beside the stream in the narrow, deep valley we came out into the main road, and the stream joined a small river, wide and clear, which flowed along a more spacious valley. The mountains did not now rise so steeply above the road, they sloped gently away from it; and they were no longer so green but bare and stony. The whole landscape became steadily more naked, more deserted, more severe. This was the landscape in which

I had grown up as a child and I recognized it more and more clearly, so that the depressing, almost frightening feeling of its wildness and solitude was partly softened for me by the sense of coming back to a place which was familiar. It was a brigands' landscape, and even the May sunshine failed to make it any more kindly or welcoming; there was nothing but slopes sprinkled with stones and rocks and amongst the stones and rocks very little vegetation; and the black, clean, glossy road winding through this great stony expanse looked like a snake that has been woken by the first warmth of spring. There was neither a house nor a cow shed nor a hovel nor a hut to be seen, nor yet a human being nor an animal. I knew that the valley went on like this, bare and silent and deserted, for miles and miles, and that the only village to be found in it was my own village, which was nothing more than a group of houses situated along the road and around the square in which stood the church.

We continued in this way for some distance, and then the village came in sight at a bend in the road. Everything was just as I remembered it: the beginning of the village marked by two houses which I knew well, one on each side of the road. They were old houses in the country style, built of stones from the mountainside, without any whitewashing, dark and modest, with roofs of green, mossy tiles. Impulsively I tapped the English officer on the shoulder, saying that we would get out here; we had arrived. He drew up immediately, and I, vaguely regretting that I had made him stop, told Rosetta we had arrived and must get out. The officer helped us unload the two boxes of provisions, which we placed on our heads. Suddenly, in an almost affectionate manner and with a smile, he said, in Italian: "Good luck to you!" and then, wheeling around very rapidly in a semicircle, was off like a rocket. A few seconds later he had disappeared around the bend in the road and we were alone.

It was only then that I became aware of the complete silence and the deserted look of the place. There was no one to be seen, nor any sound except the soft, faint rustle of the spring breeze blowing along the valley. Then, as I looked at the two houses at the entrance to the village, I noticed that the windows were shut up, with the shutters closed, and the doors at ground level were barred with two planks nailed crosswise over them. I saw that the village must have been evacuated and, for the first time, I realized that I had done wrong to leave Fondi: there was the danger of air raids there, it was true, but there were also plenty of people and one was not alone. I felt my heart sink, and in order to cheer myself up I said to Rosetta: "It may be that there's no one in the village; they may all have been evacuated. In that case we won't stay here but we'll walk on to Vallecorsa, only a few miles further. Or we'll get a lift in a truck. This is a well-traveled road and there's always somebody passing."

As if to confirm my words a long column of trucks and army cars came into sight round the bend. Their appearance encouraged us; they were allies, therefore they were friends and in any difficulty we could always appeal to them, as we had done at Fondi. I stood back to one side of the road together with Rosetta, and watched the column as it filed past us. At its head was a small open car like the one that had brought us there, with three officers in it and a little flag stuck on the bonnet. It was a blue, white and red flag, the French flag, as I learned later, and the officers were French officers, with képis on their heads like little round pots with hard peaks coming down over their eyes. Behind this car came number of trucks, cram-full of troops, but these were not soldiers like the ones we had seen so far, they were men with dark skins and faces like Turks—as far as the red scarves in which their faces were enveloped would allow us to see; and they were dressed in garments like white sheets with dark-colored capes over them. Later, I learned the origin of these soldiers. They came from Morocco, and Morocco, it appears, is a country a very long way off, somewhere in Africa, and, if it had not been for the war these Moroccans would never, never have come to Italy. The column was not so very long; the whole of it filed past in a few minutes and went on into the village; and it finished with another small car like the one at the head. Then the road became deserted and silent again. "They're allies, certainly," I said to Rosetta, "but I don't know what race they belong to; who has ever seen people like that?" Then we too started off in the direction of the village.

There is a rock jutting out from the mountainside on to the road just before you come into the village, and beneath this rock there is a kind of grotto with a spring in it. I said to Rosetta, as we walked along with the boxes balanced on our heads: "Let's go in, I'm thirsty and I want a drink." That was what I said, but what I really wanted was to have a look at the grotto, because when I was a child, and then a little girl, and then a bigger girl, I used to go to this grotto several times a day with a big copper pot on my head, to fetch water. I would stay there and chatter for ten minutes or even more with others who went there for the same purpose, and sometimes also I would meet people from neighboring villages there, with little barrels tied on the backs of their donkeys, for the water of this spring was famous and it was the only spring in the locality that did not dry up but continued always to produce an abundance of ice-cold water. I remember that as a child this grotto had seemed to me a strange and mysterious place which had partly frightened and partly attracted me, and often I used to lean across the rim of the stone basin that was fitted into the grotto, with the whole upper part of my body hanging over it, and look at my reflection in the black water and gaze for a long time at the thick maidenhair ferns that concealed the spring itself. I enjoyed contemplating the image of myself upside down, so clear and full of color; I enjoyed looking at the exquisite ferns with their tiny green leaves and their little stalks as black as ebony; I enjoyed examining the velvety moss, all scattered over with bright drops like pearls and with constellations of minute red flowers, which covered the rocks. But the grotto attracted me chiefly because someone in the village had told me that if I dived down into the water and swam down deeper and deeper, I should arrive all of a sudden in a subterranean world, far more beautiful than the world up above, with caves full of treasure and many dwarfs and beautiful fairies. This fairy story had made a great impression upon me, and even when I was almost grown and no longer believed in it I never went into the grotto without recalling it and without feeling a kind of uncertainty and doubt, just as though it were not a fairy story but a real fact and as though I could still make that deep dive, if I wished to, and go underground and visit the fairy caverns.

So Rosetta and I now went to the grotto, and I put down my big box on the ground and went up the two or three steps and looked into the grotto with my chest pressed against the rim of the stone basin, beneath the dangling stalactites which, as in the old days, were dripping and clothed in green, brilliant moss. Rosetta looked in too, and for a moment I gazed at our two faces reflected in the black, still water, and I sighed at the thought of all the things that had happened since the time when, as a little girl, I used to bend over this same water and look at my reflection in this same way. Underneath the thick maidenhair fern, at the bottom of the basin, I could see, as then, the faint ripple produced by the spring and I could not help thinking that this spring would go on bubbling up, sweetly and quietly, for ever and ever, long after Rosetta and I and everyone else had left this world and when hardly even a memory of this terrible war would remain. Everything came to an end, I thought to myself, and I was no longer a child and had a grown-up daughter, but the spring never came to an end and went on bubbling up as it always had. I stooped down and drank, and I believe a tear fell from my eye into the water; Rosetta, beside me, also drank, but did not notice it. Then we wiped our mouths, put the boxes back on our heads and went off to the village.

As I had imagined, it was completely deserted. It had been neither bombed nor devastated in any way, but merely abandoned. All the houses, humble as they were, built of rough stone without any plastering and standing back to back along the road, were intact, but the windows were shut and the doors barred. We walked for some distance between the two rows of dead houses and I had a feeling almost of fear, as when you walk in a cemetery and think of all the people lying under the gravestones. We passed in front of my parents' house, which was also closed and barred, and I gave up the idea of even knocking at the door and hastened my step without saying anything to Rosetta; finally we reached a wide sloping space with steps leading up to the church, a real country church of old blackened stone, rustic and ancient and devoid of finery or ornament. The space in front of the church was just as I remembered it, with its wide steps of dark cobbles edged with white stone; four or five trees planted irregularly and now laden with bright foliage; and, a little to one side, an old well with a parapet of the same blackened stone as the church and a rusty iron windlass. I noticed that the church door, underneath the little porch with its two pillars, was half open, and I said to Rosetta: "The church is open, so let's go in and sit down for a bit and have a rest, and then we'll walk on toward Vallecorsa." Rosetta followed me without saying anything.

We went in and I became aware that the church had been, if not exactly devastated deliberately, at any rate lived in by soldiers and reduced to the state of a stable. It consisted simply of a long, narrow, whitewashed room, with a roof of great black beams and an altar at the far end, the latter surmounted by a picture representing the Madonna and Child. The altar was now bare, without ornaments or anything else; the picture was still there, but it was crooked, as though there had been an earthquake. The benches, which had once stood in rows up each side of the church right to the altar, had all gone except two, which were placed lengthways, opposite each other, the wrong way round. Between these two benches was a quantity of grey ash and black cinders, showing that a fire had been lit there. The church was lighted by a great window above the entrance door which had once had stained glass in it. Nothing remained now but a few sharp fragments; there was bright daylight inside the building. I went up to the two remaining benches, moved one of them round so that it faced the altar, put down my box on it and said to Rosetta: "That's what war is, you see: they don't even have any respect for churches." Then I sat down and Rosetta sat down beside me.

I experienced a strange feeling, for I found myself in a holy place with no desire to pray. I turned my eyes toward the ancient picture hanging crooked above the altar, with the Madonna, all greasy from the black smoke of candles, no longer looking down towards the benches, but slantwise toward the ceiling, and it seemed to me that if I wanted to pray I ought first of all to straighten the picture. But even so, perhaps I should not have been able to pray; I felt numbed and apathetic and bewildered. I had hoped to rediscover the village where I was born and the people among whom I had grown up and, of course my parents as well, instead of which I had found nothing but an empty shell: they had all gone away, perhaps even the Madonna too, disgusted at her picture being handled in this way and left so crooked. Then I looked at Rosetta beside me and saw that she, unlike me, was praying, her hands clasped together, her head bent, her lips moving slightly. "You're quite right to pray," I said in a low voice. "Pray for me too . . . I haven't the heart for it."

At that moment I heard a faint sound of footsteps and voices from the direction of the door. I turned round and caught a glimpse like a flash of lightning of something white which appeared in the doorway and immediately disappeared again. I thought that I recognized one of those strange soldiers I had seen shortly before when the convoy passed us on the road, and seized with a sudden uneasiness I got up and said to Rosetta: "Let's go away . . . we'd better go." She rose at once, crossing herself. I helped her to put the box on her head, put the other one on my own head, and then we walked to the door.

I started to push open the door, which was now closed, and found myself face to face with one of those same soldiers, who looked like a Turk, dark and pock-marked, with a red hood pulled down over his black, brilliant eyes and his body wrapped in a dark cape over his white robe. He placed a hand on my chest and pushed me back inside, saying something that I did not understand, and I saw that behind him there were others, but I could not see how many because he seized me by the arm and was pulling me into the church, while the others came rushing in after us. "Stop! What are you doing?" I cried. "We're evacuees," and I let go of the big box that I was holding on my head and it fell to the ground and I heard all the tins rolling about, and then I began struggling with the man, who had now taken hold of me around the waist and was leaning heavily on me, with his dark, ruthless face pressed forward against mine. I heard a shrill scream from Rosetta, and I tried with all my strength to free myself and rush to her help, but the man held me tightly and I struggled in vain, for he was strong and even as I thrust my hand against his chin and pushed his face away from me I could feel him dragging me back toward a dark corner of the church. Then I screamed too, with a scream even shriller than Rosetta's, and I believe I put into it the whole of my despair, not only at what was happening to me at that moment but also for everything that had happened to me since the day I left Rome. The man seized me by the hair with such terrible force that he seemed to be trying to pull my head right off my neck, and still he was pushing me back and finally I felt myself falling with him onto the floor. He was on top of me and I was struggling with my hands and legs, and all the time he held my head down on the floor by pulling my hair with one hand, and meanwhile I felt him fumbling with the other hand at my clothes, pulling them up to my stomach and then putting his hand between my legs. I screamed again, but with pain this time, for he had seized hold of me by the hair on my body with the same force with which he was pulling the hair of my head to keep my head still. I felt my strength failing me and I could scarcely breathe, and meanwhile he was tugging at the hair on my body and hurting me, and then in a flash I remembered that men are very sensitive in that particular place. I put my hand down to my belly and encountered his hand, and he, at the contact of my hand, thinking perhaps that I was yielding to him and wanted to help him take his pleasure with me, immediately relaxed his grip in both places and smiled at me with a horrible smile that showed his black, broken teeth. I pushed my hand underneath him and seized hold of his testicles and squeezed them with all the strength I had. Then he let out a roar, seized me again by the hair or my head and beat the back of my head against the floor with such violence that, though I scarcely felt any pain at all, I fainted.

I don't know how long it was before I came to. I found that I was lying in a dark corner of the church; the soldiers had gone and there was silence. My head was hurting me, but only at the back where it joined my neck. Otherwise I had no pain, and I realized that that terrible man had failed to do what he wanted because I had gripped him in that way, and he had beaten my head on the floor and I had fainted and, as everyone knows, it is difficult to handle a woman who has fainted. But, reconstructing the scene afterward, I concluded that another reason why he had done nothing to me was that his companions had called him over to hold Rosetta still, and he had left me and gone over to her and had then, like all the others, vented his lust on her. But Rosetta, alas, had not fainted, and everything that had happened she had seen with her own eyes and felt with her own senses.

I remained lying there for some time, almost incapable of moving, then I tried to rise and at once felt a sharp stabbing pain in the back of my neck. I forced myself to get to my feet and looked round. At first I saw nothing except the floor of the church littered with the tins of food which had tumbled out of the two boxes at the moment when we were assaulted; then I raised my eyes and saw Rosetta. Either they had dragged her or she had fled to just below the altar, and there she was lying, flat on her back, her clothes pulled up over her head, naked from the waist down to the feet. Her legs had remained open, just as they had left them, and you could see her belly, white as marble, and the fair, curly hair like the head of a little goat, and on the inside part of her thighs and on the hair there was blood. I thought she was dead, partly on account of this blood which, although I knew it was the blood of her slaughtered virginity, was blood nevertheless and suggested ideas of death. I went over to her and called "Rosetta" in a low voice, almost despairing of having any answer from her; and indeed she neither answered nor moved. I was convinced that she was really dead, and I stooped down and pulled away the clothes from her face. She was staring at me with wide-open eyes, without saying a word or moving, with a look in her eyes that I had never seen there, like that of an animal caught in a trap and unable to stir and waiting for the hunter to give it the final blow.

I sat down close beside her, below the altar, and I put my arm around her waist and lifted her up a little, and I held her close to me and said: "My precious daughter," and I could not say any more because I was weeping and the tears flowed thick and fast down my cheeks and I drank them and tasted their full bitterness, all the concentrated bitterness that I had gathered during the whole of my life. Meanwhile I was exerting myself to make her clean and tidy again, and took my handkerchief and wiped away the still fresh blood from her thighs and her belly. Then I pulled down her petticoat and skirt and then, still in floods of tears, I put back inside the brassière her breasts which those barbarians had pulled out and I buttoned up her bodice again. Finally I took out a small comb the English had given me and combed her disheveled hair slowly and gently, a little at a time. She submitted quietly to all this, lying still and saying nothing. By this time I had stopped crying, and I was upset that I could not cry any more or scream or give way to despair. I said to her: "Do you feel able to leave here now?" and she answered "Yes" in a very low voice. I helped her to get up and she staggered and was very pale, but in the end she walked away, with me supporting her, toward the door. But halfway down the church, when we were near the two benches, I said: "We must pick up all these things and put them back in the boxes. We can't leave them here. Do you feel like doing this?" Again she said "Yes," so I filled the two boxes again with the tins which were scattered about the floor, and one I placed on her head and one I took on my own, and at last we left the church.

The back of my head was hurting me more than I can say, and as I came out through the porch there was a mist in front of my eyes, but I summoned up all my courage when I thought of what Rosetta was suffering at that same moment. We went very slowly down the wide, slippery steps of the little square outside, beneath a sun which was already high and which shed its lovely clear light upon the blackened cobbles. Of the Moroccans there was not a sign; after doing what they had done they had, thank God, departed—perhaps to go and do the same thing again in some other place in the district. We went thus through the whole village, between the two rows of shuttered, silent houses, and then started off along the sunlit, clean, bright road, with the spring breeze blowing softly in our ears and seeming to tell me that I must not be upset, for everything would go on as before, as always. We walked on for nearly a mile without speaking, very slowly; but finally, feeling the pain in the back of my neck steadily increasing and knowing that Rosetta was utterly exhausted, I said: "We'll stop at the first barn we come to and rest until tomorrow morning." She said nothing; and thus began the silence that had descended upon her at the moment when the Moroccans had raped her and that was to last for such a long time. We went on for about a hundred yards and then I saw a small open car coming toward us with two officers in it, two French officers, as I knew from their pot-shaped képis. I was seized by an indescribable impulse and took a stand in the middle of the road, signaling to them with my free arm, and they stopped. I cried furiously at them: "Do you know what they've done, those Turks that you're in command of? Do you know what they dared to do in a consecrated place, in a church, under the eyes of the Madonna? Well?—do you know what they've done?" They did not understand, but looked at us in astonishment; one of them was dark, with a black mustache and a red face bursting with health; the other was a fair-haired, pale, sharp-faced little man with blue eyes and a squint. "This daughter of mine here," I shouted again, "they've ruined her, d'you see?—they've ruined her for good and all, a daughter who was an angel and now it's worse than if she was dead. Do you understand, do you see what they've done?" The dark man raised his hand and waved it, as much as to say "That's enough," and then said in Italian, but with a strong French accent: "Peace, peace!" "Yes, peace indeed," I yelled at him, "a fine sort of peace! This is your so-called peace, you bastards!" The fair man said something or other to the dark man, as if to signify that I was mad; in fact he touched his forehead with his finger and smiled. Then I lost my temper, and I shouted again: "No, I'm not mad—look at this!" and throwing down the box of tins on the ground I ran over to Rosetta, who had stayed a way behind, in the middle of the road, motionless, with her box on her head. Rosetta did not move, she did not even look at me, and I snatched at her dress and tugged it up over her belly, uncovering her beautiful, straight, white legs close together; I knew I had wiped away the blood and that perhaps there would be hardly a trace of it left; instead of which, as I uncovered her, I saw at once that the blood had started flowing again, and her thighs were all bloodstained, and there was a trickle of blood right down to her knee, of red, living blood that shone in the sunlight. "There, look at that and tell me if I'm mad!" I cried, disconcerted and also rather frightened by the quantity of blood. At the same moment I was aware of the car rushing swiftly past, close beside me, and, when I raised my head, I saw it already disappearing around a bend in the road.

Rosetta continued to stand quite still, like a statue, with the box on her head and her arm raised to hold it, and her legs pressed together. Suddenly I was afraid that she had gone mad from fright, and as I pulled down her dress I said to her: "My darling, why don't you speak? What's the matter? Please say a word to your Mum." She said in a quiet voice: "It's nothing, Mum. It's a natural thing and it's stopping already." At that I breathed again, for I had feared that she might have gone stupid from shock; and, feeling somewhat cheered, I asked her: "Do you feel like walking on a little, now?" "Yes, Mum," she answered; and I put the box back again on my head and started off again with her along the main road.

We walked on for nearly a mile and the pain in the back of my head was getting worse and worse and every now and then I was almost fainting, with the whole landscape going black in front of me, as though the sun had suddenly gone out. Finally, at a bend in the road, we saw a small hill, rounded in shape and covered with scrub, backing on the high mountains behind. On the top of this hill, in the scrub, we could see a hut of the same kind that the peasants at Sant'Eufemia used for their animals. I said to Rosetta: "I can't manage any more and I know you're exhausted too. Let's go to that hut. If anybody's there they'll be Christian folk and allow us to spend the night. If there's no one, so much the better; we'll stay there today and tomorrow, and as soon as we feel better we'll move on again." She said nothing, but I was less uneasy now because I knew she was not mad but only badly shaken. I felt, however, that she was no longer the same as before and that something had changed not merely in her body but in her soul. And even though I was her mother I had no right to ask her what she was thinking about, and decided I could demonstrate my full affection for her only by leaving her in peace.

After a long climb, we reached the hut. As I had expected, it was a shepherds' hut, with a low wall of unmortared stones, a thatched roof which came down almost to the ground and a wooden door. We put down our boxes and tried to open the door, but it was bolted and padlocked and the door itself was made of thick planks; not even a man could have forced it. While we were shaking the door we heard faint bleating sounds, like the bleatings of goats, but not loud or resentful as when goats are in the dark and want to come out; these were feeble and plaintive. "They've shut up their animals in here and gone away," I said. "We must find some way of letting them out." Having said this, I went to the side of the hut and began tearing away the thatch of the roof. This was difficult, because the thatch was compressed and clogged together by rain and smoke and the long passage of time since it had been applied, and each bundle of thatch was tied by strong tendrils to the boughs which supported it. By tearing away pieces and slackening and undoing the tendrils, I succeeded in pulling out a few bundles of the thatch and making a hole level with the top of the low wall. When I enlarged this hole a black and white goat poked its head out, placing its feet on the wall, looking at me with its golden eyes and bleating faintly. "Come on, my beauty," I said. "Jump, jump!" The poor thing did not have the strength to pull itself up, for it was weakened by hunger. I widened the hole a little more, while the goat remained with its feet on top of the wall, looking at me and bleating softly; and then I took hold of it by its head and neck and pulled, and it made an effort and jumped down. Another goat appeared in the hole, and again I pulled it out, and then a third and a fourth. Finally no more goats appeared, but I could still hear a sound of bleating inside the hut. I made the hole larger and jumped in. There I found a pair of kids too small to jump up to the opening. In one corner was a white goat lying motionless on its side, with a kid crouching close beside it, its feet folded underneath its body and its neck stretched out to suck at its mother's teats. At first I thought the goat was lying still in order to allow the kid to suck, but the mother-goat was dead. Her head was lying back limply, with the mouth just open, and there were flies at the corners of her mouth and around her eyes. The goat had died of starvation, and the three kids were still alive because they had been able to suck their mother's milk until her last breath. Leaning out through the hole, I put the kids down on the ground at the foot of the low wall. The four goats I had already set free were biting at the leaves on the bushes and devouring them with furious eagerness, as if blinded by hunger; the kids joined them, and very soon both goats and kids could no longer be seen, as they had disappeared browsing into the scrub. Their bleatings could still be heard, getting clearer and stronger, as though their voices were being restored at each mouthful and the poor creatures wanted to let me know that they felt better and that they thanked me for saving them from starvation.

With an effort I pulled the corpse of the dead goat out of the hut and dragged it as far as I could into the scrub. Then I took all the straw that I had torn off the roof and some more from the hole, and spread it out in one corner of the hut, making a sort of pallet. "I'm going to lie down," I said to Rosetta. "I want to sleep. Why don't you come too?" "I'm going to sit outside in the sun," she replied. I said nothing and lay down. I could see the blue sky through the hole in the roof, and the sun cast a ray of light onto the floor, which was sprinkled with little black balls of goats' dung, as bright and neat as laurel berries; and there was a good smell of stable. I felt as if my bones were broken and I realized that my exhaustion made me incapable of feeling real sorrow over what had happened to Rosetta: what had happened was incomprehensible and absurd; every now and then I saw again her beautiful white legs, the thighs pressed close together and the muscles in relief, tensed with the effort, and her standing there motionless in the middle of the road and the blood on her thighs with a trickle of it reaching down to her knee and the glitter of the living blood in the sunshine. The more I contemplated this picture, the less I understood it. Finally I fell asleep.

I slept for perhaps half an hour, then woke up with a jump and at once called loudly and anxiously to Rosetta. There was no answer. I called again and uneasily got up and climbed out through the hole. I walked around the hut; there were our two big boxes full of tins standing against the wall, but there was no sign of Rosetta.

I was seized with a violent fear and thought she might have run away in shame and despair, or that she might actually have gone down to the road and thrown herself under a truck or car in a moment of hopeless depression. I could hardly breathe and my heart started thumping in my chest and I began calling Rosetta, turning in one direction after another as I stood in front of the hut door. No one answered. I left the hut and started off aimlessly through the scrub.

I followed the path, which in some places was wide and clear and dusty and then again merely a vague track amongst the tall bushes. Suddenly I came out beside a rock which jutted out vertically above the road. There was a tree there, and the rock was shaped like a chair from which you could look down and see a good stretch of the road as it wound through the narrow valley, and down below the road was the bed of the stream, littered with white stones, with channels of clear water that ran sparkling among the stones and vegetation. Down below and a long way off was Rosetta. I understood why she had not heard me: she was below the level of the road, in the middle of the stony bed of the stream, and was moving in a leisurely, careful fashion, stepping from one stone to another and taking care not to wet her feet, and from the way in which she moved I could tell that she had not gone down to the stream from despair. She stopped at a point where the stream became narrower and deeper, and knelt down and put her face to the surface of the water to drink. When she had done this she rose to her feet again, looked about her, lifted up her clothes as far as her groin, uncovering her legs. I thought I could see the dark streak of dried blood reaching down to her knee. She crouched down with her legs apart and started to wash herself, scooping up water in the palm of her hand and applying it to her belly and between her legs. She held her head to one side and washed in a leisurely, methodical manner, indifferent to the fact that she was exposing her shame to the sunshine and open air. All my frightened conjectures were dispelled: Rosetta had left the hut and gone down to the stream merely to have a wash. I must confess I was conscious of a feeling of painful disappointment. Certainly I had not hoped that she would kill herself; I had in fact been terrified of it; but to see her doing something so entirely different gave me a feeling of disappointment, and a fear for the future. It seemed to me that she was bowing to the new destiny that had begun for her in the church when those barbarians had taken her virginity from her, and that her stubborn silence was more the result of resignation than of rage. And I reflected later, when this impression of mine was confirmed, that during those few moments of agony my poor Rosetta had grown abruptly into a woman, both in body and mind; into a hardened, experienced, bitter woman bereft of all illusion and all hope.

Sitting on the rock, I watched her for a long time. After drying herself as best she could, still with almost the immodesty of an animal, she came back up the bed of the stream and then climbed up and crossed the road. I got up from the rock and went back to the hut: I did not want her to think that I had been spying upon her. She reached the hut a few minutes later, with a face that was not so much composed and calm as devoid of all expression. Feigning an appetite, I said to her: "I'm quite hungry, shall we have something to eat?" In a colorless, indifferent voice she answered: "If you like"; and we sat down in front of the hut on some stones and I opened a couple of our tins of food. I was surprised and somewhat pained to see her eat with a good appetite—quite greedily, in fact. Again, I certainly hadn't hoped that she would *not* eat—but to see her eat with such avidity surprised me, for I had thought that after what had happened food wouldn't interest her. I didn't know what to say, and watched her in a dazed sort of way as she took pieces of meat out of the open tins with her fingers, crammed them into her mouth and chewed them furiously. Finally I said: "My precious daughter, you mustn't think about what happened in the church, you must never think about it again, and then, you'll see–" But she interrupted me, saying sharply: "If you don't want me to think about it, you'd better start by not talking about it." I was upset, because her tone of voice was new to me: a tone with a touch of irritation, and at the same time arid and unfeeling.

We stayed there for four days and four night, sleeping at night inside the hut, rising with the sun, eating the tins of food the English major had given us, quenching our thirst at the water of the stream and speaking only when it was necessary. During the day we wandered about aimlessly in the scrub; sometimes we slept in the afternoon too, on the ground under a tree. The goats, after feeding all day long, came back of their own accord to the hut, and we helped them to jump inside and then they slept with us, lying close against each other in a corner, together with the kids which were now being suckled first by one and then by another of them and which had by now entirely forgotten their dead mother. Rosetta remained in the same apathetic, indifferent, remote state of mind; as she had requested, I spoke no more of what had happened in the church. Never since then have I mentioned it to her, not even once, and the pain it gave me has remained in me like a thorn and will never cease because never again will it find any expression. It was during those four days, I am convinced, that the real change came about in Rosetta's character, either because she thought over what had happened on her own account and in a way entirely her own, or was transformed into a different person in spite of herself and without being aware of it by the very force of the outrage she had undergone. I was at first surprised at so complete and so radical a change in her, as if from white to black, but afterward it seemed to me that things could not have gone differently. I have already mentioned that she was inclined by nature to a strange perfection; whatever qualities she had, she had thoroughly and completely, with no uncertainties or contradictions, so much so that I had almost convinced myself that my daughter was a kind of saint. Now this saintly perfection, made up, as I have already said, chiefly of inexperience and ignorance of life, had been mortally wounded by what had happened in the church; and it had then changed into an opposite kind of perfection, without any of the half measures, without the moderation and the prudence that belong to normal, imperfect, experienced people. Hitherto I had seen her all piety and goodness, purity and sweetness; now I had to be prepared for the probability that from now on she would turn to the opposite extreme, with the same absence of doubts and hesitations, the same inexperience and the same completeness. And very often, in concluding my reflections on this painful subject, I said to myself that purity is not a thing that you can receive at birth, as a gift of nature, so to speak; it is a thing that is acquired through the trials of life; anyone who has received it at birth loses it sooner or later, and loses it all the more disastrously for having been confident of possessing it; and, in short, it is almost better to be born imperfect and gradually to become, if not perfect, at any rate better, than to be born perfect and to be then forced to abandon that first transient perfection for the imperfection that life and experience bring with them.

Chapter 10

In the meantime the tins of food given us by the English major were growing perceptibly fewer, more especially as Rosetta appeared to be as hungry as a wolf; and I decided that we must leave our little hill as soon as possible. I had not the courage to go to Vallecorsa or any other place in the district, fearing that we would run into the Moroccans again, for as far as I could make out they were distributed all over the Ciociaria. I said to Rosetta: "I think our best plan is to go back to Fondi. There we shall find some means of getting to Rome, if the Allies have reached it by now. In any case, air raids are better than Moroccans." Rosetta listened to me and was silent for a moment, then she came out with a remark which was instantly painful to me: "No, better the Moroccans than the air raids, for me, anyhow. What can the Moroccans do to me that is worse than what they've already done? But I don't want to be killed." We argued for a time and I finally convinced her that the wisest plan was to return to Fondi: now that the Allied army was advancing northward the air raids ought to have stopped. And so, one morning, we left the hut and went down on to the road.

After several army trucks had gone past—I knew they didn't pick up civilian passengers—there suddenly appeared an ordinary truck, empty and coming almost gaily—at breakneck speed, anyhow, and zigzagging a bit—down the deserted main road. I stood in the road and waved my arms and the truck stopped at once. At the wheel was a fair-haired, blue-eyed young man wearing a fine red sweater. He stopped and looked at me, and I cried: "We're a couple of evacuees; can you take us to Fondi?" He gave a whistle, and replied: "You're lucky, I'm on my way to Fondi. A couple of evacuees, are you?—where's the other one?" "She's coming now," I said, and gave the signal we had previously agreed upon to Rosetta, whom I had told to stay back on the path behind a bush, for fear of another unpleasant encounter. She came out and walked down the middle of the sunlit road with our only remaining box balanced on her head. I could get a better view of the young man now, and I realized that he was made unattractive by reason of the dissolute, vulgar, violent look in his blue eyes and his over-red mouth. My unfavorable impression was confirmed when Rosetta came up beside the truck. He did not look her in the face but to her breast which, because her arms was raised to hold the box in place, was pulled upward and bulged out prominently under the thin stuff of her bodice. He gave an ill-mannered laugh and cried to Rosetta: "Your mother told me you were an evacuee but she didn't tell me what a pretty girl you were." Then he got out and helped her up on to the seat beside him, putting me on her other side. I was aware that I had made no protest at his disrespectful remark, whereas only a few days earlier I should have answered him sharply and quite likely would have refused to let him give us a lift; and suddenly I realized that I too had changed, in relation to Rosetta, anyhow. Meanwhile the young man had started up the engine again and we moved off.

For some little time we said nothing, and then, as always happens on such occasions, the exchange of information began. About ourselves I said little; but he appeared to be a great chatterbox and told us everything about himself. He said he belonged to this district and had been in the army at the time of the armistice and had deserted in the nick of time. After hiding out in the mountains he had been caught by the Germans;

a German captain had taken a fancy to him and, instead of sending him to work on the fortifications, had put him in a mess hall. Never in his life, he said, had he eaten more or better, and with the general shortage of food, the provisions he had at his disposal had enabled him to obtain everything he wanted from women: "Such a lot of pretty girls used to come and ask me for something to eat. And I gave it to them—but on one condition, of course. You wouldn't believe it, but I never found *one* who refused. Ah, hunger's a fine thing, it makes even the proudest women see reason." In order to change the subject I asked him what he was doing now, and he said that he had gone into partnership with some friends and they were using the truck to transport evacuees who wanted to get back to their villages, getting paid very well for it, of course. "I won't charge you two anything," he said at this point, casting an oblique glance at Rosetta. He had a deep, hoarse voice; and the fair curls on his great, thick neck made his head look like the head of a he-goat, and there was something of the he-goat in the way he looked at Rosetta, especially when he glanced at her breast, as he did whenever he could. He told us his name was Clorindo, and he asked Rosetta what *her* name was. She told him, and he remarked: "It's a pity, it's really a great pity the food shortage is over. But I'm sure we can come to some arrangement in spite of that. Do you like nylon stockings? Would you like a nice length of woolen stuff for a dress? Or a nice pair of kid shoes?" After a moment's pause Rosetta said: "Who wouldn't?"—and he laughed and repeated: "We'll come to some arrangement, we'll certainly come to some arrangement." I was horrified, and couldn't help exclaiming: "Be careful what you say . . . Who do you think you're talking to?" He looked at me askance, and finally said: "Ugh, don't be so nasty about it! Who do I think I'm talking to? Why, to a couple of poor evacuees who need help."

As you can see, he was a cheerful sort of fellow, though fundamentally vulgar, brutal and immoral. During this idle conversation we reached the top of the pass, after which the road goes down toward the sea, and he began to drive like a lunatic, letting the truck go at breakneck speed, with the engine turned off, taking the bends on two wheels and singing a rude song at the top of his voice. And truly there was something to sing about, for it was a marvellously beautiful day and at the same time there was the feeling of newly acquired freedom in the air, after all those months of slavery. And I cannot deny that in his way he made us feel, by the lack of restraint with which he behaved, that this freedom now really existed. Only *his* freedom was the freedom of the rogue who never intends to respect anything or anybody again; whereas ours was simply the freedom to go back to Rome and start leading our old life once more. When the truck gave a jolt at a bend in the road I was thrown forward and noticed that he was driving with one hand, while the other lay on the seat with Rosetta's hand clasped in it. I was astonished when I saw that she allowed her hand to be clasped in this way, and I was also astonished that I made no protest. This was *her* freedom, I thought to myself, and it flashed across my mind that I had ceased to be able to do anything. The Madonna had not performed the miracle of preventing the Moroccans from doing their butchery in front of the altar, and I, infinitely weaker than the Madonna, was unable to prevent this young man from taking Rosetta's hand.

We reached the bottom of the hill and came out on to the main road I knew so well, with the mountains on one side and the orange groves on the other. The last time we were here the place was swarming with soldiers, evacuees, tanks and all sorts of vehicles, and now I was struck by the silence and solitude that had taken the place of what had looked like a milling crowd at a fair. Had it not been for the sunshine and the green trees jutting out over the road above the flowering hedges I might well have thought it was still winter, at the worst moment of the German occupation, when terror sent everyone into hiding like rabbits into their holes. There was no one on the road except an occasional peasant driving his donkey in front of him; there was not a sound to be heard. We drove along this main road at a great speed and came into Fondi. Here too there was solitude and silence, made worse still by the ruined houses, the piles of rubble and pools of stagnant water. The few people who were wandering around these streets full of holes and rubbish and patches of quagmire looked every bit as hungry and miserable as they had looked a month before, under the Germans. I said so to Clorindo, and he answered cheerfully: "Oh yes, people said the English would bring abundance with them. They do bring it, but only during the two or three days when they halt in their advance. During those few days they distribute sweets and cigarettes, flour and clothes. Then they go away and the abundance comes to an end and people are just as they were before, worse, in fact, because now they have nothing to look forward to."

I realized he was right. The Allied armies would stop for a moment in the places they were gradually taking back from the Germans, and for a day or two these armies would bring back some life to the slaughtered countryside. Then they moved forward again and everything went back to the same point as before. "And what are we to do now?" I asked Clorindo. "We can't stay in this hopeless place. We have nothing. We've got to get back to Rome." As he steered the truck through the ruins, he replied: "Rome hasn't been liberated yet. The best plan is for you to stay here for the time being." "And what are we to do here?" He answered, in a reserved tone of voice: "I'll look after you." His tone seemed strange to me but I said nothing. He was driving out of Fondi again, and turned onto a small road among the orange groves. "There's a family I know living in these orange gardens," he said lightly, "and you'd better stay here until Rome is liberated. As soon as it's possible, I'll take you to Rome myself."

Again I said nothing; he pulled the truck over to the side and stopped, explaining that we would have to walk through the grove to his friends' house. The place did not seem strange to me now; it is true that there were endless orange groves and this was just another path, but I could tell from certain signs that it was not the first time I had walked along this path, among these orange trees. We walked on for another ten minutes or so and came into a clearing, and then I understood: before me stood the pink house belonging to Concetta, the woman with whom we had stayed during the first days we had spent at Fondi. "No," I said resolutely, "I don't want to stay here." "Why?" "Because we stayed here before, months ago, and we had to run away because they're a family of crooks and this woman Concetta wanted Rosetta to go and act as a strumpet for the Fascists." He burst into a hearty laugh: "That's all a thing of the past, that's all over and done with. The Fascists aren't here now and Concetta's sons aren't crooks, they're my partners in business, and you needn't worry, they'll treat you with the greatest respect. Oh, that's all a thing of the past." I started to insist and to repeat that I had no wish to stay in the house at any price, but I didn't have the time. Concetta herself came out of the house and ran across the clearing, as gay and enthusiastic and excited as ever. "Welcome, welcome to you!" she cried. "How small the world is! Well, well, you ran away, you two, you ran away without saying a word, without paying what you owed us. But you did the right thing, you know, running away to the mountains, because not long afterward my sons had to go into hiding because of the round-ups those beastly Germans were carrying out. You did the right thing, you had more sense than we did; we stayed here and had all sorts of troubles. Welcome, welcome, I'm very pleased to see you in good health; after all, as long as a person has health he has everything. Come in, come in, Vincenzo and my sons will be delighted to see you. Besides, you arrive with Clorindo, and that's just like arriving with a son of mine. Clorindo's part of the family now. Come into the house, you're very welcome." It was the usual Concetta, and my heart sank when I reflected that we were at the same point as before, worse than before, in fact, and that we two had run away from her house to avoid the very same danger into which we had afterward so irreparably fallen, at my own village. But I said nothing and allowed myself to be kissed and embraced by this hateful woman, and so did

Rosetta, who had now become so apathetic and indifferent that she seemed like a puppet. Vincenzo came out of the house, looking more like a bird of ill omen than ever, shockingly thin, his nose even more beaklike, his eyebrows sticking out even farther, his eyes even more glittering than the last time I had seen him. And while Vincenzo was muttering something incomprehensible and clasping my hand in both of his, Concetta had the gall to say: "Vincenzo told us that you were with the Festa family, he told us he had seen you up at Sant'Eufemia. Well, well, it's been a bad winter for the Festas too. First it was we here, who couldn't resist the temptation of all those lovely things hidden in our wall, and then it was their son Michele. Poor things, we gave them back every bit of the stuff we pinched—except, of course, what had already been sold—because we're honest people, we are, and for us other people's property is sacred. But their son—who can give them back their son?—poor things, poor things!" I felt my heart sink at these words, so carelessly spoken and so cruel, and I went cold all over and knew I had turned as pale as a corpse. I asked in a feeble voice: "Why, has something happened to Michele?" She answered enthusiastically, as though she were giving us a splendid piece of news: "What, didn't you know? He was killed by the Germans." We were standing in the middle of the threshing floor and suddenly I felt faint, as I became aware that I had loved Michele as if he had been my own son. I sat down on a chair near the door and put my hands over my face. Concetta continued, excitedly: "Yes, they killed him while they were running away, the Germans did. Apparently they had carried him off to show them the road. As they were going over the mountains they came upon an isolated place where there was a peasant family; and since Michele no longer knew which was the best way to go, the Germans asked these peasants where the enemy had gone. They meant the English, of course, who, for them, are the enemy. But these peasants, poor creatures, who like all of us were convinced that the enemy meant the Germans, answered that they had fled toward Frosinone. The Germans, hearing themselves called enemies, were furious of course, because no one likes being considered an enemy, and they pointed their guns at the peasants. Michele flung himself in between, shouting: 'Don't shoot, they're innocent,' and he was killed with all the rest of them. An entire family destroyed—oh well, you know, war is war—an entire family massacred, a real slaughter indeed, men, women and children, and Michele on top of the heap, with a whole lot of bullets in his chest which they'd fired at him when he threw himself into the middle. We knew about it because a little girl hid behind a haystack and escaped and then came down and told the whole story. But surely, didn't you know? All Fondi is talking about it. Ah well, war is war, you know."

So Michele was dead. I sat still, my face between my hands, and realized I was crying because my fingers were wet. I heaved a deep sigh and began sobbing quietly to myself. It seemed to me that I was weeping for all of us, for Michele, whom I had loved like a son; for Rosetta, who perhaps would have been better dead, as Michele was; and also for myself, for I had no hope left after having hoped so much for a whole year. Meanwhile I could hear Concetta saying: "Weep, weep, it'll do you good. I wept too, when my sons ran off into the mountains, I wept ever so much and then I felt better. Oh yes, go on weeping, it means you have a good heart and you're quite right to weep, because Michele, poor boy, was a real saint, and besides, he was so learned that, if he wasn't dead, he would certainly have become a government minister. War is war, as we know, and in this war everybody's lost something. But the Festas more than anyone; for people who have lost their belongings can replace them again, but a son you can't replace, oh no, you can't replace a son. Go on weeping, then, it'll do you good."

I went on weeping for some time, conscious of the others around me talking of their own affairs. At last I raised my head and saw Concetta, Vincenzo and Clorindo arguing about a deal in flour or something of the kind in a corner of the threshing room, and Rosetta standing apart from them, waiting for me to stop crying. It frightened me to see that her expression was completely apathetic and indifferent, her eyes dry, just as though she had not heard anything, or as if Michele's name meant nothing to her. It seemed to me that she had ceased to feel anything, like a person who has had a burn and then hard skin forms over it and he can put his hand on burning coals without feeling anything. When I saw her so dried-up and apathetic my grief at Michele's death swept over me again, for I reflected that he had been truly fond of her and that he was the only one who might perhaps have been able to bring her back to normal, and now he was dead and there was nothing to be done. At that moment I was almost more upset by the manner in which Rosetta had received the news of Michele's death than by the death itself. Concetta was right, war is war and now even we had a share in the war and were behaving as though war and not peace were the normal condition of man.

At last I got up, and Clorindo said: "Now let's go and see where you can sleep," and we followed Concetta to the well-known shed where they kept the hay. There was no hay there now, instead there were three beds with mattresses and blankets, and Concetta said: "These beds belong to the poor man who kept the inn at Fondi. Poor people, they had everything taken away, the inn is empty, there's nothing left in the inn, even the chamber pots were taken away. We've made a little money with these beds during the winter. There were evacuees coming and going, people who had lost everything, poor things, and we charged them so much a night and made a little money. They're not there now, the landlord and his family, they ran away, poor creatures; some say they're in Rome, some in Naples. When they come back we'll give them back their beds, of course, because we're honest folks; but in the meantime we're making a little money, yes indeed we are. Oh well, war is war, as we all know." At this point Clorindo put in: "You're not going to charge these two ladies anything." To which she answered with enthusiasm: "But of course not, I wouldn't think of it. We're just one big family." Clorindo went on: "And you'll give them their meals too, and we'll settle up afterward." "Their meals—of course I will," she said. "Just simple things, you know, just country fare. They'll have to get used to it, of course, just country fare." They went away and I shut the door of the shed and sat down in semi-darkness on one of the beds, beside Rosetta.

We were silent for a little, and then I burst out violently: "What's the matter with you, I should like to know; what's the matter? Aren't you sorry Michele's dead—tell me, aren't you sorry? I thought you were fond of him." I couldn't see her face in the half-darkness because she kept her head down, but I heard her answer: "Yes, I'm sorry." "Is that the way you say it?" "How ought I to say it?" "Now come on—what's the matter? Speak, tell me! You haven't shed even one single tear for that poor boy, and yet he died to defend poor people like ourselves, he died like a saint." She said nothing; and then I, seized by a kind of frenzy, shook her by the arm, saying again: "What's the matter! What's the matter with you?" She freed herself in an unhurried way and said slowly and precisely: "Leave me alone, Mum." I said nothing more; I sat there motionless for a moment or two with my eyes wide open, staring in front of me. She got up and lay down on one of the other beds, turning her back on me. In the end I lay down too and soon fell asleep.

When I awoke night had fallen and Rosetta was no longer on the bed beside mine. I lay quite still for some time, feeling incapable of rising or indeed of doing anything at all, not so much from fatigue as from lack of will-power. Through the walls I heard the voice of Concetta talking to someone. I pulled myself together and got up and went out. Concetta had laid the table on the threshing floor, near the door of the house, and her husband was there but Rosetta and Clorindo were not. "Where is Rosetta," I asked, "have you seen her?" "I thought you knew," answered Concetta, "she's gone with Clorindo." "What do you mean?" "Yes," she said, "Clorindo has gone off with the lorry to take some evacuees to Lenola. So he took Rosetta with him because he didn't want to drive back all alone. I expect they'll be back here tomorrow afternoon." I was flabbergasted. In former times Rosetta would never have done such a thing—go away like that without telling me, and with a man like Clorindo into the bargain. I could scarcely believe it, and I insisted: "But didn't she leave any message?" "No, nothing. She merely asked me to tell you. She didn't want to wake you up because she's a good daughter. Besides, you know, youth is youth; she likes Clorindo and wants to be alone with him. We mothers, you know, become an embarrassment to our children after a certain age. My sons run away, too, to be alone with girls. And Clorindo is a very good-looking young man; he and Rosetta really make a handsome couple." Then, in an unguarded moment, I said: "If certain things hadn't happened, she wouldn't even have looked at this fellow Clorindo." The moment I had uttered these words I was sorry I had done so, but it was too late now, for that evil woman was all over me, asking: "What happened? It's true, it *did* seem a bit strange that Rosetta should go off with him like that, without thinking twice about it, but I didn't attach much importance to it,—youth is youth, you know. But tell me, what was it that happened?"

For some reason or other, partly because of the rage that this conduct on Rosetta's part aroused in me, partly in order to give vent to my displeasure by telling someone, if only Concetta, I succumbed and told the whole story—about the church and the Moroccans and what they had done to Rosetta and me. Concetta was ladling out the soup, and as she did so she kept on saying: "Poor thing, poor girl, poor Rosetta, I am so terribly sorry, I am so terribly sorry." Then she sat down, and when I had finished my story, she said: "Well, you know, war is war. And those Moroccans, after all, they're young men too, and when they saw your daughter, who's so young and pretty, well, they couldn't resist and they yielded to temptation. War, you know—" But she was unable to finish, because all at once I jumped up like a fury, my knife in my hand, and shouted: "You don't know what all this has meant for Rosetta. You're a tart and the daughter of a tart and you want all women to be tarts like yourself. But if you start talking like that again about Rosetta I'll kill you! God's truth I will." She jumped back, and joining her hands together, cried: "Christ, why do you get so angry? What did I say, after all? That war is war and that youth is youth and that the Moroccans were young men too! Don't get angry, Clorindo will take care of Rosetta now, and you'll see, as long as *he* takes care of her, she won't want for anything. He deals in the black market and has all kinds of food and he has clothes and stockings and shoes—don't you worry; Rosetta has nothing to fear with him." I saw that it was a waste of breath talking to this woman, and I put down my knife and swallowed my soup without saying a word. The food turned into so much poison inside of me; I could not stop thinking about Rosetta, about how she used to be and how she was now. She had gone off with Clorindo, like any tart that gives herself to the first man who puts his hands on her, and she hadn't told me she was going away, and it was quite likely that she didn't even want to live with me any longer. Supper came to an end in silence, and I went to the shed and threw myself down on the bed, but this time I did not go to sleep; I lay there with my eyes wide open and my ears straining and my whole body rigid with a kind of fury.

Next day Rosetta failed to return. I spent the whole day in a state of agitation, wandering around among the orange groves and going out on to the main road every now and then to see if she was coming. I had my meals with Vincenzo and his wife, the latter still trying to comfort me in the same stupid, excitable way, repeating that with Clorindo Rosetta was in good hands and would not want for anything. I said nothing, knowing well that it served no purpose, and I couldn't even become angry.

After supper I shut myself up in the shed again and finally went to sleep. About midnight the door opened very softly and in the moonlight, I saw Rosetta come in on tiptoe. She walked over to the small table that stood between our two beds and, after a short pause, lit the candle. I half-closed my eyes, pretending to be asleep. She was standing in front of me, and I could see by the candlelight that she was dressed in new clothes. She was wearing a two-piece suit of some thin red material, a white blouse, stockings and shiny black shoes with high heels. First she took off her jacket, and after giving it a long look placed it on the chair at the foot of the bed. Then she took off her skirt and laid it beside the jacket. She was now in a black, open-work undergarment of the kind that gives glimpses of white skin here and there. She sat down and took off her shoes, and after she had held them up to the light of the candle to gaze at them, she placed them side by side under the bed. After her shoes, she took off her undergarment, slipping it down over her arms. And then, while she was slipping it off, standing up again now, and finding it difficult and twisting her sides and legs this way and that, I saw she was wearing a black garter belt which fitted tightly round her hips and came down over her thighs. Rosetta had never had a garter belt, black or any other color; usually she wore garters just above the knee. This garter belt changed her completely, her body no longer looked the same. Before, it had been a healthy young body, strong and clean, the body of the innocent girl that she was; now, with this garter belt, so very tight and so very black, it had something provocative and vicious about it: the thighs looked too white, the hair too blond, the buttocks too exuberant, the belly thrust too far forward. It was not the body of Rosetta who had been my daughter, it was the body of Rosetta who made love with Clorindo. I looked up at her face, and this had changed too. The greedy, absorbed, wary expression I saw there made me think of Rosetta as a woman of evil life coming home late at night, after spending many hours on the streets and in disreputable hotels, and counting up her profits for the day.

I was no longer able to control myself and cried "Rosetta!" She raised her eyes quickly in my direction, and said slowly and unwillingly: "Yes, Mum?" "Where have you been?" I asked her. "You've kept me in anxiety for three days. Why didn't you let me know? Where have you been?" She looked at me and said: "I went with Clorindo and then I came back." I was sitting up in bed now, and I went on: "But, Rosetta, what's happened to you? You're not yourself any more, Rosetta." She answered in a low voice: "Yes, I am—why shouldn't I be?"

Deeply grieved, I said: "But, my dear girl, this man Clorindo—what do we know about him? What is there between you and Clorindo?" This time she did not answer, she just sat there with downcast eyes, but her body answered for her, her body which was now naked except for her garter belt and her brassière. Then I lost patience. I got up from the bed, seized her by the shoulders and shook her, crying: "You'll drive me to despair with this silence of yours. *I* know why you won't answer; do you think I don't know? You won't answer because you've behaved like a common slut and now you're Clorindo's whore and you don't want to say anything because you don't care a damn for your mother and you want to go on acting like a tart as much as you please." She said nothing, and I went on shaking her, then I lost my temper and shouted: "At least you can take this off!" and I started trying to tear off her garter belt. She neither moved nor made any protest, but sat there with her head bowed, crouching close against me, and I pulled at the belt but it would not give away. I threw her down on the bed and she fell with her face on the blanket and I gave her two good slaps on her buttocks. Then I threw myself down, panting, on my own bed and shouted at her: "You don't seem to understand what you've turned into; how is it you don't understand?" I expected that she would make some sort of protest this time. Not at all; she had now pulled herself up and appeared to be preoccupied entirely with her stockings, which I had partly unfastened when I was trying to pull off her garter belt. One of her stockings had a run from the thigh to below the knee, and she wet a finger with saliva and dabbed the spot to prevent it going any farther. Then she said: "Why don't you go to sleep, Mum? Don't you know it's very late?" She spoke in a sensible sort of tone, and I realized there was absolutely nothing to be done. I lay with my back to her as she moved about, and I could see her shadow, thrown by the light of the candle on the wall in front of me, but I did not turn around. At last she blew out the candle and I heard her bed creak as she lay down and turned about until she found the best position for sleeping.

There were any number of things I would have liked to say to her now, things which, while there was still light and I could see her, I had been incapable of uttering, such was the rage inspired in me by the sight of the great change in her. I wanted to tell her that I understood her; that I understood that, after what had happened with the Moroccans, she was no longer the same person and now wanted to go with a man in order to feel herself a woman and so obliterate the memory of what they had done to her; that I also understood that, having endured what she had endured, under the very eyes of the Madonna, without the Madonna doing anything to prevent it, she now felt that nothing in the world mattered, not even religion. I would have liked to say all these things to her and—oh, yes—to have taken her in my arms and kissed her and caressed her and wept with her. At the same time I felt I was no longer capable of talking to her nor of being sincere with her, because she had changed and, in changing, had changed me too, and so everything was changed between us. Again and again I thought of getting up, lying down on her bed beside her and embracing her; but in the end I gave up the idea and finally fell asleep.

Next day and the days following, the same state of affairs continued. Rosetta scarcely spoke to me—but not as though she was offended, rather as though she had nothing to say; and Clorindo was with her all the time and made no bones about putting his hands on her right under my eyes, taking her around the waist and stroking her face and so on; and Rosetta allowed him to do all this with an air of gratified, almost grateful submission; and Concetta was continually clasping her hands together and exclaiming that they really and truly made a very handsome couple; and I secretly railed at them and felt an inward despair, but I could neither do nor say anything; I was incapable of it. One day I tried reminding her of her fiancé who was in Yugoslavia, and what do you think she answered me? "Oh, I expect he's found some Slav woman or other. In any case I can't wait for him all my life."

She did not stay around the pink cottage. Clorindo took her

off all the time in his truck, which had become in a manner of speaking their home. And you ought to have seen how she obeyed him and ran after him! All Clorindo had to do was to appear in the clearing and call her, and she would drop everything and hurry away. And he didn't call her by using his voice, but simply by whistling, as you do with a dog; and she, it appeared, liked being treated like a dog. You could see from a mile off that he held her to him by that thing which she had never tasted before, and which was new to her and which now she couldn't do without, just as a drinker cannot do without wine or a smoker without cigarettes. Yes, she had now acquired a taste for what the Moroccans had imposed upon her by force, and this was perhaps the saddest aspect of the change in her, the one which I found it hardest to accept: that her revolt against the force that had destroyed her should express itself by consenting to, and seeking out, that very same force.

She and Clorindo used to go off in the truck to Fondi and the villages around Fondi, and sometimes they would go further afield, to Frosinone or Terracina or even to Naples, and then they would stay away all night. Each time she came back she seemed more and more attached to Clorindo and—to my eyes, which noted even the slightest change—more and more of a whore. There was no more talk of going back to Rome, and in any case the Allies had not yet reached it. Clorindo let it be understood that even when the Allies had taken Rome it did not mean that we would be able to leave Fondi. People would not be allowed to go to Rome for a long time, it would be declared a military zone, it would be necessary to get all kinds of passes to go there, and there was no knowing when it would be possible to obtain such passes. The future that had seemed so clear and bright to me at the moment of the liberation had now become dark and obscure, partly because of Rosetta's conduct and partly because of the presence of Clorindo. I myself no longer knew whether I really wanted to go back to Rome and take up my old life again; it would never be the same, for we were no longer the same.

Those days that I spent at the pink cottage in the orange groves were among the worst of the whole of that period, for I knew that Rosetta was going to bed with Clorindo—not merely because I guessed it but because I saw it and they did it right under my eyes. Sometimes, for instance, we would be in bed when the customary whistle would come from the clearing, Rosetta would quickly get up, and when I asked angrily: "Where are you going to at this time of night?" she would not even answer me, but would dress in a hurry and rush out; and on her face would be that tense, greedy, absorbed expression which I had seen there the first time when she came back from Lenola. I am almost sure that one night Clorindo was in the shed, for I was woken up by a noise from Rosetta's bed and by a sort of whispering, and I sat up and strained my ears to listen. In the dark, I asked Rosetta if she was asleep, and she answered in a tone of annoyance: "Yes, of course I was asleep—what else would I be doing? I was asleep and now you've woken me up." I lay down again, unconvinced, and I suppose they must have lain still and silent until they were persuaded that I had gone to sleep again; and that Clorindo must have gone away, stealthily, at dawn. But I did not wish to light the candle on that occasion because in my heart of hearts I preferred not to see them together in bed. Although I was not asleep when he left I pretended to be, and kept my eyes shut so that I knew nothing about it except what I deduced from a faint creaking of the door as it opened and then closed again. More often than not, however, they went off to conduct their love-making elsewhere, leaving in the truck after supper and not coming home till late at night. This happened almost every day; it was an entirely physical love which could never be satisfied, and Clorindo had two permanent black circles under his eyes and seemed actually to have grown thinner; while Rosetta was growing visibly into more of a woman, with that languid, satisfied look that women always have when they do this thing frequently and willingly, with a man whom they like and who likes them.

After a month of this life I began trying to comfort myself

with the idea that after all Clorindo was a good-looking young man who made plenty of money with his truck and his activities in the black market, and that in the end he would marry Rosetta and everything would come right. I did not feel comfortable about this because I didn't care for Clorindo, but I felt I must put a good face on it, as they say; and, after all, it was Rosetta who had to marry him. If she liked him there was nothing I could do about it. I supposed that they would get married and live at Frosinone, where his family was, and that they would have children and that perhaps Rosetta would be happy. This prospect comforted me a bit but I continued to be uneasy because Clorindo never mentioned marriage and neither did Rosetta. One evening after supper I plucked up courage and said to her: "Well, I don't want to know what you do or what you don't do when you're together, but I would at least like to know whether he has serious intentions and, if he has—as indeed I hope he has—when you're thinking of getting married."

She was sitting on the bed, in front of me, intent on taking off her shoes. She straightened herself, looked at me, and then said simply: "But Clorindo's married already, Mum; he has a wife and two children at Frosinone."

The blood rushed to my head; after all, I come from the Ciociaria, and we *ciociari* are a hot-blooded race and we'd put a knife into you as soon as look at you. Without even realizing what I was doing I jumped off the bed, hurled myself on top of her, seized her by the neck, banged her down on the mattress and started showering blows upon her. She tried to protect herself with her arm, and I went on hitting her and shouting: "I'm going to kill you. . . . You want to be a tart but I'll kill you first." She defended herself from my blows as best she could and made no protest, nor did she react in any way. In the end I was completely out of breath and I left her, and still she did not move but remained just as she was, flat on the bed, her face buried in the pillow, so that you couldn't tell whether she was crying or thinking or what she was doing. I stared at her as I sat panting on my bed, and a terrible despair came over me; I saw that I might actually have killed her, and it would not have served any purpose at all. I was now powerless and no longer had any authority over her, and she had broken away from me for good and all. I said angrily: "What I'm going to do now is to talk to that scoundrel Clorindo. I want to see what sort of an answer he has the impudence to give me." At these words she raised herself up, and I saw that her eyes were dry and that her face wore its usual apathetic, indifferent expression. She said quietly: "You won't be seeing Clorindo again because he's gone back to his family. He had nothing more to do at Fondi. He's gone back to Frosinone, and this evening we said good-bye, and I shan't see him again either, because his father-in-law threatened to take back his daughter, and since it's the wife who's got the money Clorindo had to obey." Once again I was left breathless. I had not expected her to announce with such complete indifference that she had parted with Clorindo, just as if the matter had nothing to do with her. After all, he had been the first man in her life, and I had almost hoped, secretly, that they really loved one another; but there was no truth in that at all, they had gone together just as a man goes with a prostitute and the pair of them, after the love-making is over and the love-money has been paid and received, have nothing more to say to one another and part without regret.

My poor daughter was indeed utterly changed, as I repeated to myself yet again; but I, accustomed to looking upon her as my own Rosetta, would never be able to understand to what degree she had changed. I felt bewildered, and I said: "You just acted as his mistress and now he's sent you packing and gone away himself; and you say it like that!" "How ought I to say it, then?" she replied. I made an angry movement, and she shrank back in fear as though she were afraid that I intended to hit her again, and this went to my heart, for a mother does not want to be feared but loved. "Don't worry," I said, "I'm not going to touch you. . . . It's just that my heart bleeds to see you reduced to this." She said nothing and went on undressing. Suddenly, in a loud, exasperated voice, I cried: "And who's going to take us to Rome, now? Clorindo said he would take us as soon as Rome was liberated by the Allies. Rome has been liberated, but Clorindo has gone, so who's going to take us? Tomorrow I intend to go back to Rome, even if I've got to walk." "We can't go to Rome for some days yet," she replied calmly, "however, one or other of Concetta's sons will take us there one of these days. They will be here tomorrow evening; they went with Clorindo to Frosinone, and now the partnership is dissolved and they've taken Clorindo's truck. Don't worry, we'll get to Rome all right." This piece of news, again, did not please me. So far Concetta's sons had never put in an appearance, being engaged, so it seemed, in black market traffic in Naples; but I remembered them as being even more repugnant than Clorindo, and I did not at all care for the idea of making the journey to Rome in their company. "Nothing in the world matters to you now—isn't that so?" I said to her. She looked at me and replied: "Why do you torment me so, Mum?"—and in her voice there was almost an echo of the old affection, and this moved me. "My precious daughter," I said, "it's because I have an impression that you're changed and that you don't feel anything for anybody now, not even for me." "Yes, I may be changed," she said, "I don't deny it; but for you I'm still just the same as before." So she recognized that she had changed; but at the same time she reassured me by giving me to understand that she still loved me as before. Not knowing whether I ought to feel grieved or comforted, I remained silent and the discussion came to an end.

Next day, as Rosetta had told me, the truck arrived from Frosinone, but with only one of Concetta's sons in it, Rosario, the other having gone on to Naples. Of the two—both of them repugnant, as I have already said—Rosario was the one I disliked most. Not very tall, massive, sturdy, with a dark, square, brutal face, a low forehead with the hair growing half-way down it, a short nose and a prominent jaw, he was a real boor, a country lout, and, to make matters worse, neither honest nor intelligent. At table he said to Rosetta: "Clorindo sends you his greetings, and says he'll come and see you in Rome after you get there."

Rosetta answered sharply without raising her eyes: "Tell him not to come, I don't wish to see him again." I understood then that Rosetta's indifference was a pretence, and that she had been attached and was perhaps still attached to Clorindo; and the fact that she might be suffering on account of that completely despicable man made me feel even more disgusted at the idea that, to him, she was of no importance. "Why?" asked Rosario; "are you angry with him now? Don't you still like him?" It made my blood boil to see Rosario speaking to Rosetta without respect or politeness, as if she were a tart who had no right to protest or show indignation; and it made my blood boil even more when Rosetta replied: "Clorindo did something to me that he ought not to have done. He never told me he was married. He told me only yesterday, when we decided to part. As long as it suited his convenience, he kept it from me; and as soon as it suited his convenience to tell me, he told me." It seemed to be my fate no longer to understand Rosetta or what was happening to her. I was painfully astonished to learn that she had not known until the last moment that he had a wife and children. And she spoke of it in this offhand tone, as of some slight, unimportant piece of spite, just like a tart without pride or dignity who knows quite well that she cannot gain the respect of the man she loves! It took my breath away. Rosario was saying, with a snigger: "But after all, why did he have to tell you? There was no question of you two getting married, was there?" Rosetta bent her head over her soup plate and said nothing. But that odious Concetta butted in. "That's very old-fashioned," she said. "Everything's changed with the war, as we know; young men pay court to girls without telling them that they're married, and girls go to bed with young men without asking them to marry them. Very old-fashioned—everything's different now—what does it matter if a man's married or not married, if he has a wife and children or not? Very old-fashioned. The important thing is that they should be fond of each other, and certainly Clorindo was very fond of Rosetta; if you want a proof of that, you've only to see how he dressed her up. Before she met him she looked like a gipsy girl and now she looks like a perfect lady." Concetta, who was always ready to defend crooks since she was a crook herself, was, however, telling a fundamental truth when she spoke these words: the war really had changed everything, and I had proof of it under my own eyes, in my own daughter, who had changed from an angel of purity and goodness to an apathetic, mindless whore.

All these things I knew, but what I saw and what I heard made my heart bleed, and I suddenly burst out against Concetta. "Everything's changed?—rubbish!" I cried. "It's you who were simply waiting for a war—you and your sons and that crook Clorindo and those Moroccan murderers and the whole lot of you—so that you could let yourselves go and do all the things you would never have dared to do in normal times. Rubbish! And I tell you, all this won't last so very long, and one of these days everything will come right again and then you and your sons and Clorindo will find yourselves in trouble, in bad trouble, and you'll discover that morals and religion and law still exist and that honest people count for more than crooks." At these words Vincenzo, half dotty as he was—he who had stolen all his landlord's belongings—shook his head and said: "Golden words, golden words indeed!" But Concetta merely shrugged her shoulders and said: "What are you getting so excited about? Live and let live, that's what I say." Rosario laughed outright and said: "You, Cesira, you're a pre-war woman, and all of *us*—my brother and I, Rosetta, my mother and Clorindo—*we* all belong to *after* the war. Now look at me, for instance, I went to Naples with a load of American food and army sweaters, sold it at once, made up a load of stuff to sell in Ciociaria—and here's the result," and he took out a bundle of bank notes and waved them under my nose. "I made more in one day than my father has in the last five years. Everything's changed, the old days are gone, and you've got to get used to the idea. And why do you get so worked up about Rosetta? She's realized, too, that there was one way of thinking before the war and a different way now, and she's cottoned on to it and learned how to live. Perhaps you never liked making love, and I'll bet they taught you that unless the priest gives his blessing love isn't love—that love can't exist at all. But Rosetta knows that priest or no priest love is always love. It's true, isn't it, Rosetta? Tell your mother you know it." I was dumbfounded; but Rosetta, quite calm and serene, appeared almost to take pleasure in the way in which Rosario spoke, and he went on: "For instance, not long ago we were all together in Naples, Rosetta, Clorindo, my brother and I, all friends together, without any jealousy or complications. And although we had Rosetta with us, and we all of us liked Rosetta, yet Clorindo, my brother and I remained just as good friends as before. And we had a good time, all four of us, we had a good time, didn't we, Rosetta?" I was trembling all over like a leaf; Rosetta had not only been Clorindo's mistress, which was bad enough, but the plaything of the whole gang. It was quite likely that she had gone to bed not only with Clorindo, but also with Rosario and his brother and, I daresay, with a few Neapolitan crooks as well—the type that live on women and pass them around as if they were so much merchandise. She was a poor abandoned creature to whom men could do whatever they liked, for her will-power had been smashed at the moment when she was raped by the Moroccans, and at the same time something previously unknown to her had entered into her flesh like a fire. It was burning within her and making her long to be treated by all the men she came across in the same way as the Moroccans had treated her.

Rosario got up and loosened his belt and said: "I'm going out in the truck—do you want to come with me, Rosetta?" Rosetta nodded, put her napkin on the table and started to get up, wearing that same greedy, lustful, absorbed expression that I had seen on her face the first time she had gone off with Clorindo. "No," I said, "don't you move, you stay here!" There was a moment of silence, and Rosario looked at me with astonishment, as much as to say: "Why, what's going on? Is the world upside down?" Then he turned to Rosetta and ordered: "Come along, get a move on!" Again I said, not now in a tone of command but rather of entreaty: "Rosetta, don't move!" But she had risen by now, and she said "See you later, Mum" and without turning around, she went and joined Rosario, who had already walked away as though quite sure of himself. She slipped her hand under his arm and disappeared with him into the orange grove. So, at a touch of the rod, she had obeyed Rosario, as before she had obeyed Clorindo, and now he was taking her off to some meadow to make love and there was nothing I could do about it. "Of course," cried Concetta, "a mother has the right to forbid her daughter anything she wants to, of course she has. But a daughter also has the right to go with the man she likes—why not indeed? And mothers never see eye to eye with the men their daughters like, but all the same youth has its rights and we mothers have to understand and forgive, we have to understand and forgive." I said nothing, I sat with my head bowed, like a withered flower, under the light of the acetylene lamp around which cockchafers went buzzing through the air, falling dead from time to time when burnt by the flame. And I reflected that my poor Rosetta was just like one of these cockchafers: the flame of war had scorched her and she was dead, for me at least.

Rosetta came back very late that night and I did not hear her when she came in. Before I went to sleep I thought for a long time about her, and about what had happened to her and what she had become; and then my thoughts had turned to Michele and for the rest of the time I was awake I thought only of him. I hadn't had the courage to go and visit the Festas and tell them how grieved I had been at the death of their son and that, for me, it had been just as if a son of my own, born of my own womb, had died. Nevertheless the memory of his death, so cruel and so bitter, had remained all this time like a thorn in my heart. I reflected that war was war, as Concetta was always saying, and that in war it is always the best who are lost because they are the most courageous, the most unselfish, the most honest, and some of them get killed like poor Michele and some of them are maimed for life like my Rosetta. The worst people, on the other hand, those who have no courage, no faith, no religion, no pride, who kill and steal and think of themselves and follow their own selfish interests—these come through safely and prosper, and become even more brazen and depraved than they were before. It also occured to me that if Michele had not died he might perhaps have given me some good advice and I wouldn't have left Fondi for my own village, and we wouldn't have encountered the Moroccans and Rosetta would still have been the angel of goodness and purity that she had been before. I said to myself that it was a sad pity that he was dead, for to us he had been father, husband, brother and son, and, although he was good as a saint he could also be harsh and without pity for crooks of the type of Rosario and Clorindo. He had had a kind of strength which was lacking in me, for he was not only good but also learned and judged the affairs of life from above, not in an earthy sort of fashion like myself.

There came over me a despair and a frenzy that I cannot describe; I did not wish to live any longer in a world like this, in which good men and honest women had ceased to count for anything and criminals behaved as if they were the masters. With Rosetta in her present state of degradation, life now had no more meaning for me, and even in Rome, with my flat and my shop, I should never be the same as before and should have no further pleasure in living. Suddenly I felt that I wanted to die. I jumped out of bed and, my hands twitching with impatience, lit the candle and went to the far end of the room to fetch a rope that Concetta used for hanging out the clothes to dry after she had done the washing. In the same corner of the shed there was a straw-seated chair; and I climbed on to the chair, rope in hand, having made up my mind to fix it to a nail or one of the joists of the roof and then fasten it around my neck, kick the chair away and drop down, thus putting an end to everything, once and for all. But just at the moment when, holding the rope in my hand, I was looking up to the ceiling in search of something to which I could tie it, I heard the door of the shed being quietly opened. I turned around and saw Michele—positively Michele himself—standing on the threshold. He was exactly as

I had seen him that last time, when the Nazis had taken him away, and I noticed that as on that occasion one of his trouser legs was longer than the other and came right down on to his shoe, while the shorter one barely reached his ankle. He was wearing his glasses, as usual, and in order to see me better he lowered his forehead and looked at me over the top of the lenses, as he used to do when he was alive. He made a quick gesture, as if to say: "No, don't do that, not that, you mustn't do that." I asked: "Why shouldn't I?" He opened his mouth and said something that I did not understand; he continued to speak and I tried to hear him and I did not hear anything; it was like trying to hear someone who is behind a window pane—and you can see his lips moving but you can't hear anything. "Please speak louder," I cried, "I can't understand you," and at the same moment I woke up, soaked with sweat. The whole thing had been a dream; the attempted suicide, Michele's intervention and his words that I could not hear. But a violent, bitter, consuming regret at not having heard what he said to me persisted; and for some time I went on tossing in my bed, wondering what it could have been. I was sure that he had been telling me why I ought not to kill myself, why it was worth while to go on living and why life, in any case, was better than death. Yes I am sure he had been explaining to me the meaning of life, which escapes us while we are alive but which must be quite clear and vivid to the dead; and it was my misfortune that I had not been able to catch what he was saying. The dream had been a kind of miracle, and miracles, we know, are miracles because anything can happen in them, even the most incredible and unusual things. There had been a miracle, or rather half a miracle: Michele had appeared to me and had prevented me from killing myself, but through some fault of my own—no doubt because I was not worthy of it—I had failed to understand why I ought not to do it. And so I had to go on living, but I should never know why life was to be preferred to death.

Chapter 11

Now, at last, came the great day of our return to Rome; but how different it was from what I had imagined in my dreams about the liberation during the nine months I had spent at Sant'Eufemia! I had dreamed, then, of a gay, cheerful homeward journey in some kind of an army truck, with some of those big, fair young men, English or American, who would also be happy and agreeable and cheerful; and at my side would be Rosetta, gentle and quiet as an angel; and perhaps Michele might even be with us, and he too, for once, would be happy. My mind would be filled with expectation for the sight of the dome of St. Peter's on the horizon—the first thing you see of Rome—and my heart brimming with hope and my head buzzing with plans for Rosetta and her marriage and the shop and the flat. During those nine months I had studied every detail of this return journey, and every detail of every detail. I had pictured our arrival at home, with Giovanni welcoming us, calm and smiling, the dead cigar in the corner of his mouth, and the neighbors crowding around us with all the embracing and smiling and saying: "Well, well, we've managed it . . . we'll tell you later how it all happened." I had thought of all these things and an endless number of others; I remember that in thinking of them I had often caught myself smiling with anticipated delight; and in any case it had never crossed my mind that these things could fail to come true. In short, I had not foreseen that—as Concetta was always saying—war is war; by which I mean that war, even after it is over, still goes on, like a savage beast at the point of death which still seeks to do harm and can still strike out. And now the war, just as it was leaving us, had dealt us this stroke: the Moroccans had ruined Rosetta, and the Nazis had killed Michele, and my daughter and I had to go back to Rome in the truck of that crook Rosario. Instead of my mind being occupied with all the cheerful things I had expected to be thinking and feeling, it was filled with sadness and disappointment and despair.

It was a morning in June, but already the heat and light of full summer was in the burning sky and on the dry, dusty earth. Inside the shed Rosetta and I were finishing dressing, for Rosario's truck was waiting for us on the road. Rosetta had spent part of the night away from the shed, and I, who had seen her coming in stealthily, still had that feeling of impotence of which I have already spoken; my mind was overflowing with things I wanted to say but my mouth was no longer able to express them. Finally, however, while she was washing herself at the basin in the corner, I managed to say: "I should like to know where you were last night." I expected silence again, or some brief reply, but this time it was not like that. She finished drying herself, then turned around and said to me in a clear, firm voice: "I was with Rosario and we made love together. And don't go asking me what I do and where I go and who I'm with, because you know now: I make love with anyone I can, wherever I can. And I want to tell you this too: I like making love, and I can't do without it and I don't wish to do without it." "But with Rosario, my dear child!" I exclaimed. "Don't you realize what sort of a person Rosario is?" "He or another," she said, "it's all the same to me. I've already told you: I want to make love because it's the only thing I like and the only thing I feel like doing. And from now on it's always going to be like that, so don't ask me any more questions because I shall always have to give you the same answer." She had never spoken so clearly before, in fact it was the first time she had spoken to me on the subject; and I realized that until she had been cured of this frenzy I should have to do as she told me: hold my tongue and ask no questions. I finished dressing in silence and she did the same.

When we came out of the shed we found Rosario sitting at a table with his mother, eating onion salad and bread. Concetta came over to us and at once started off on one of her rambling, excited speeches which had irritated me so much when I had first got to know her and which now, as you can imagine, were ten times worse. "So you're going away, you're going back to Rome, you lucky people, how fortunate you are, you're going away and leaving us, we poor country folk, you're leaving us here, in this desert where there's nothing left at all and everyone's starving and all the houses are ruined and everyone's penniless and in rags like a lot of gipsies. You lucky people, you're going back to live like ladies in Rome, where there's plenty of everything and where the English will be giving all the year around what they gave here for only three days. But of course I'm glad because I'm very fond of you and it's always nice when people we're fond of are lucky and get on well." To cut short these effusions, I said: "Yes indeed, we're lucky. We really are fortunate, there's no denying it. Above all, to have met a family like yours." But she did not see the irony. "You may well say we're a good, honest family," she replied. "You've been very well off here, we've treated you as our own kith and kin, you've eaten and drunk, you've slept and done just as you like. Ah well, there aren't very many families like ours." "Fortunately not," I wanted to reply, but I restrained myself. I was longing to get away, even in the company of the hateful Rosario, and not to stay one moment longer in that clearing shut in on all sides by thick, thick orange groves, which was like a prison to me. We said good-bye to Vincenzo, who said in his half-witted manner: "Are you going away already? Why, you've just arrived! Why don't you stay on till the August holiday, at least?"—and to Concetta, who insisted on embracing us and kissing us on both cheeks with loud, smacking kisses which, like her words, appeared to be delivered almost in mockery. Finally we started off down the path, turning our backs forever on that accursed pink house. On the road stood the truck. We got in, Rosetta beside Rosario and I beside Rosetta.

Rosario started the engine and said, as he let in the clutch: "Off we go to Rome!" and the truck moved off quickly down the road in the direction of the highway. It was well on in the morning by this time, and the sunshine was blazing hot and dry, and full of the cheerful strength of youth; the road was white with dust, the hedges also were white with dust, and whenever the truck slowed down you could hear the chirping of thousands of young cicadas hidden amongst the foliage. When I heard the chirping of the cicadas, when I saw the bright white dust on the road and the hedges, and larks diving down to peck amongst the mules' excrement and then whirring up again into the luminous sky, tears came into my eyes. This was indeed the real country, my own beloved countryside in which I had been born and brought up, and to which I had turned, in the perplexities of famine and war, as one turns to a very ancient mother who has experienced everything and has yet remained kind and good and who knows everything and forgives everything. But the country had betrayed me and everything had ended badly, and now I myself had changed although the country had remained the same as ever. The sunshine warmed everything except my frozen heart, and the cicadas which are so lovely to hear when you are young and love life were now almost annoying because I had no hope left, and the smell of the dry, hot dust which is intoxicating to the senses when they are still virginal and unsatisfied, now seemed to suffocate me, as though a stifling hand were placed over my nose and mouth. The country had betrayed me, and I was going back to Rome in despair, without any hope. I wept quietly and drank the bitter tears that flowed from my eyes, trying to keep my head turned away so that Rosario and Rosetta should not see me. But Rosetta noticed, and suddenly asked me: "Why are you crying, Mum?"—in a voice so soft and gentle that it almost made me hope that by some miracle of Heaven she had become my old Rosetta again. I was going to make some sort of an answer when I saw that she had her hand on Rosario's thigh, high up, close to his groin; and I realized that for some minutes they had been sitting silent, without moving. I knew that this silence, this immobility were due to the pursuit of their own pleasure which they were carrying on under my very eyes, and that the sweetness in Rosetta's voice was not the sweetness of innocence but of the amorous pleasure in which they were indulging, without modesty and without shame, even at that hour of the morning, like beasts that do it at all times and in all places. Then I said: "I'm crying for shame, that's why I'm crying." Rosetta made a movement as if to withdraw her hand, but the hateful Rosario caught hold of it and pulled it back. She resisted for a moment, or so it seemed to me, then he let go of her hand and she did not withdraw it again, and once more I realized that what she was doing was a stronger thing than my shame, or than hers either–supposing her to be still capable of feeling any such thing.

We were driving now along the Via Appia, between the rows of great plane trees whose thick, new foliage joined above our heads. It was like driving through a green tunnel; here and there the sunshine, piercing through the leaves, cast its rays across the surface of the road, making the dull asphalt seem like some luminous, throbbing substance, like the back of an animal warmed with living blood. I turned my head so as not to see what Rosario and Rosetta were doing; and to distract my mind from sad thoughts I watched the landscape. Here were the floods caused by the Germans when they blew up the dikes, their blue waters, ruffled by the breeze and broken by tufts of trees and ruins, spreading far and wide where once there had been cultivated fields and farms. After we had passed San Biagio, the road ran along the seashore. The sea was calm, but a slight, fresh breeze was blowing over it and causing the innumerable blue waves to go all crisscross; and each wave had a bright, sparkling eye of light in it, so that the whole sea seemed to be smiling in the sun. Soon came Terracina, and it made an even deeper impression upon me than Fondi–an utter desolation, with all the houses flayed by machine-gun fire and pitted with holes, and their windows black like the eyes of blind people or, worse still, blue, when there was nothing left but the façade of the house; and mountains of dusty debris and ditches full of yellow water everywhere. There was no one at Terracina, either in the main square, where the basin of the fountain was full to the brim with rubble, or in the long, straight streets, bordered with ruins, that ran down toward the sea. I felt that the same thing must have happened at Terracina as at Fondi: the first day, a kind of fair ground, a huge crowd, soldiers, peasants and evacuees, distributions of food and clothes, joy and hubbub—life, in fact. Then the army had moved on toward Rome, and life had vanished and nothing had been left but a desert of ruin and silence. Beyond Terracina we drove along the road that runs straight to Cisterna, with the thick, green water of the irrigation canal on one side and a vast plain on the other, flooded in places and extending to the foot of the pale blue mountains that bounded the horizon. In the ditches at the side of the road you could see the carcass of some military vehicle, its wheels in the air, already rusty and unrecognizable, as though war had passed that way many years before; and again, in a cornfield, you could distinguish the long, thin gun of a tank, motionless, pointing at the sky, and, as you came nearer, there was the whole tank submerged beneath the tall ears of corn, still and gaunt like some great animal stricken and left to die. Rosario was now driving very fast, with one hand on the wheel, and his other hand was clasping Rosetta's, in her lap. I could not bear this sight, one more indication of the change in her, and for some reason I remembered that Rosetta sang very well and had a beautiful voice, sweet and musical. When she was at home and going about her household occupations she had a habit of singing to keep herself company, and I was often charmed when I listened to her, for in her voice, as it rose calmly and cheerfully and seemed never to tire or lose the thread of the song, was the whole of her character, as she was then and had now ceased to be. As we traveled along the road between Terracina and Cisterna I felt an impulse to revive the illusion of

Rosetta as she had once been, even if it was only for a single moment. "Rosetta," I said, "why don't you sing something? You used to sing so well, why don't you sing us a nice song? Otherwise, what with the hot sun and the long straight road, we shall end up by falling asleep." "What would you like me to sing?" she asked, and I mentioned, at random, the name of a song which had been popular a couple of years before. She started singing in a clear voice, sitting quite still and holding Rosario's hand in her lap. But I soon became aware that it was no longer the same voice; it seemed less decided and less melodious and sometimes went out of tune, and she too must have noticed it, for suddenly she stopped singing and said: "I'm afraid I can't go on, Mum, I don't feel inclined for it." I wanted to answer: "The reason why you don't feel inclined and why you can't sing is because you're holding that hand in your lap and you're not yourself and you've lost the feeling you once had which used to make you fill your chest and sing like a bird. That's the reason." But I hadn't the courage to speak. "Well," said Rosario, "if you like, *I'll* sing;" and he started off, with his harsh voice, on a coarse, rude song. I now suffered more than ever, both because of Rosetta's inability to sing and because *he* was singing. In the meantime the truck rushed on at breakneck speed, and soon we arrived at Cisterna.

Here too, as at Terracina, there was nothing but desolation. I remember particularly the fountain in the square, in a semicircle of tottering houses full of gaping holes, its basin full of rubble, and in the middle of the basin a pedestal with a statue on it. The statue had no head, only a black iron hook, and only one arm, and that lacked a hand. It looked like a living person, just because it had no hand or head. There was not even a dog to be seen, the people were either up in the mountains or hiding among the ruins. After passing Cisterna the road runs through scanty groves of cork trees and there was neither a house nor a human being to be seen—nothing, as far as the eye could reach, but the green earth and the twisted, red tree-trunks which looked as though they had been flayed. The day was not so fine now: a small fan-shaped formation of grey clouds had come up from the direction of the sea, and this fan had then opened wider and wider and had now become immense, its handle being over the sea and its ribs of thick grey clouds spread out across the vastness of the sky.

The sun had vanished, and the whole landscape, with these twisted red cork trees that looked as if they were in pain from being so red and twisted, had turned to a single color, wan and dull and toneless. The solitude was complete, and although the noise of our engine never ceased for an instant one could guess that there was a great silence, with no more song of birds or cicadas. Rosetta was dozing now, Rosario was smoking as he drove, and I let my eyes follow the succession of white milestones or plunge deep into the cork woods, without seeing anything or anybody. As I sat looking at the cork woods I was suddenly flung forward against the windshield. As I fell back again I saw that a curve of the road was barred across its whole width by a fallen telegraph pole, and at the same moment three men came out from behind the cork trees and walked forward, waving their arms, signaling for the truck to stop. Rosetta woke up and said: "What is it"—but no one answered her because I did not understand what was going on, and Rosario had already jumped out of the truck and was walking purposefully toward the three men. I remember the men very well and would recognize them, even today. They were dressed in rags, as everyone was in those days, and one was small and fair and broad-shouldered, in a brown velveteen suit; the second was tall, middle-aged, thin as a rake, with a lean, lined face, deep-sunk eyes and untidy greying hair; the third was a very ordinary looking young man, dark with a broad face and black hair, not unlike Rosario. The latter, as he got down from the truck, had quickly taken a small parcel out of his pocket and pushed it in under the dashboard. I was sure that this packet contained money, and I suddenly realized that these three men were robbers. Then everything happened in a single moment while Rosetta and I watched, motionless and paralyzed with astonishment, through the glass of the windshield, dirty with squashed insects and dust and streaks of rain. Through this dirty glass we watched Rosario go up to the three men with determination—he was undoubtedly courageous—and we saw the three men stand and face him with a threatening sort of attitude. I could see the face of the fair man who was talking to him: he had a red, crooked mouth with a kind of eruption or festering sore at the corner of it. The fair man spoke and Rosario answered; the fair man spoke again and, at Rosario's second answer, seized Rosario by the collar of his coat, up under his chin. Rosario moved his shoulders to free himself, first to the right and then to the left, and at the same moment I saw him, quite clearly, put his hand to his hip pocket. I heard a shot and then two more, and I thought it was Rosario who had fired. On the contrary; for Rosario now turned as if to walk back to the truck, with his head down moving very uncertainly. Then he fell on his knees, supporting himself with his hands on the ground, stayed a moment in that position with his head lowered, as though pondering, and finally fell over sideways. The three men, paying no attention to him, came across to the truck.

The short, fair man, still grasping the revolver in his hand, pulled himself up by the door and looked in the cab. "Come on, you two," he said, panting, "get out. Quick!" He flourished the revolver, not so much to threaten us as to make us understand that we had got to get out. The other two men were moving the telegraph pole off the road. I realized we had to do what we were told and said to Rosetta: "Come on, we must get out"; and started to open the door. But the fair man, who was already halfway in the truck, suddenly leant out again, looking at the road, and I saw that the other two were making signs as if to warn him of some new development. He let out an oath, jumped down from the truck and ran back to his companions. All three of them rushed away through the cork wood as fast as they could go, and very soon, zigzagging from one tree trunk to another, they disappeared. For a moment there was no sign of anything except for the telegraph pole pulled to one side and the body of Rosario lying motionless in the middle of the road. "What are we to do now?" I said to Rosetta, and at that moment there appeared beside us a small open car with two English officers in it and a soldier driving. The car slowed down because the body of Rosario was blocking the road, not so much, however, that it was not possible to get past by keeping close to the ditch. The two officers turned to look at the body and then at us two, then I saw one of them make a sign to the driver, as much as to say: "Let the dead bury their dead; drive on!" and the car started again, creeping close round Rosario's body, then quickening its speed and disappearing around the bend in the road. I remembered the money that Rosario had hidden under the dashboard; I reached under, took the packet and thrust it into the bosom of my dress. Rosetta saw me make this movement and threw me a glance which seemed to me one of reprobation. Then suddenly there was a violent screech of brakes and a truck stopped abruptly beside ours.

It was an Italian this time, a small man with a big, bald head, a pale, sweaty face, round, prominent eyes and long side-whiskers which came halfway down his cheeks. His expression was frightened and disgruntled but not unkindly, as of one who is led by duty to perform an act of courage and secretly curses his fate which has forced him to be courageous in spite of himself. He asked hurriedly: "What's happened?" without moving from his seat, his hand on the gear shift. "They stopped us," I said, "and they killed this young man and then ran off. They meant to rob us. And now we two, who are evacuees—" "Which way did they go?" he interrupted. I pointed in the direction of the cork wood; he rolled his frightened eyes to that side, and then said: "For the love of God, jump into my truck if you want to go to Rome, but quick, be quick, for the love of God." I saw that if I hesitated another moment he would be gone, so I made haste to get out, pulling Rosetta after me by the hand. Then he cried to us again in a voice of distress: "Move that body, get it out of the way, otherwise how can I go past?" I saw that his truck, which was considerably wider than the English officers' little car, would not be able to pass between the ditch and Rosario's body. "Be quick, for the love of God," he repeated in his plaintive voice, so I pulled myself together and said to Rosetta: "Help me," and went over to the body, which was lying on one side with one arm raised above the head as though to cling on to something that there had not been time to grasp. I stooped down and took hold of one of the feet, and Rosetta stooped down and took hold of the other; and so, with an effort, for he was very heavy, we dragged him to one side, toward the ditch, with his head and shoulders on the ground and his arms stretched out at full length trailing lifelessly behind over the asphalt. Rosetta let go of his foot and I did the same, but I bent down hastily over the dead man, with an instinctive movement, fearing, almost, that I was going to discover he was still alive: the truth of the matter was that I had his packet of money in my bosom and I was anxious to keep it, knowing that in our present situation it would come in very useful, and I wanted to make sure that he was really dead. And dead he was; I knew it by his eyes, which had remained open and which were glossy and fixed and staring at nothing. In that difficult moment I behaved like a vile and selfish person—just as Concetta would have behaved, with her conviction that "war is war." I had taken the dead man's money; I had feared, on account of the money, that he was not dead after all; but, having once ascertained that he really was dead I wanted to make up for that ugly fear by an act of faith which would cost me nothing. Quickly, while the man in the truck was shouting impatiently at me: "He's dead, there's nothing to be done," I stooped down and made the sign of the Cross with my index and middle fingers on Rosario's chest, at the point where his black jacket was marked with a large dark stain. My fingers lightly touched the jacket and I felt that it was wet; then, as I was running with Rosetta toward the truck, I took a furtive look at the fingers with which I had made the sign of the Cross and saw that their tips were red with living, newly shed blood. At the sight of this blood, I felt a kind of horror at myself for having made that hypocritical sign of the Cross on the body of the man I had just robbed, and I hoped that Rosetta had not noticed it. But as I wiped my fingers on my skirt I saw her looking at me and realized that she had seen me. Then we both got in beside the driver and the truck moved off.

The man crouched over the steering wheel as he drove, gripping it with both hands, his eyes starting out of his head, his face pale and full of fear. I was still preoccupied with the packet of bank notes in my bosom, and Rosetta sat looking straight in front of her, with a motionless, apathetic face in which it was impossible to find the reflection of any feeling whatsoever. It occurred to me that for reasons of our own, the three of us had shown no pity at all for Rosario, who had been killed like a dog and abandoned on the highway. The driver, in his terror, had not even got out of his truck to see whether Rosario was dead or alive; my own chief anxiety had been to make sure that he really was dead, because I had taken his money; and all Rosetta had done had been to drag his body by one foot toward the ditch, as though it had been the stinking, obstructive carcass of some animal. There had been neither pity, nor feeling, nor human sympathy; a human being died and other human beings remained indifferent, each for his own reasons. In short, it was the war, as Concetta had said, and I had now come to fear that this war would continue to survive in our souls long after the real war was over. But Rosetta was the worst case of the three; not more than half an hour before she had been love-making with Rosario. She had aroused his desire and had satisfied it; she had given him pleasure and received pleasure from him; and now she sat dry-eyed, motionless, indifferent, apathetic, without a shadow of feeling in her face. I thought over these things and said to myself that everything went in the opposite way to which it ought to go, and the whole of life had become absurd, without head or tail, and important things were no longer important and things that had no importance had become important. Then an odd and unexpected thing happened: Rosetta began to sing. At first in a hesitating, strangled sort of voice, then in a voice that became clearer and firmer and more sure of itself, she started singing the same song that I had asked her to sing not long before. As I have said, it was a song that had been popular a couple of years before, and Rosetta had been in the habit of singing it while she was attending to her domestic tasks. In itself it was nothing much, in fact it was rather sentimental and silly, and at first I thought it strange that she should sing it at this moment, just after Rosario's death: it seemed a further proof of her insensibility and indifference. Then I remembered that when I had asked her to sing she hadn't been able to and said she didn't feel inclined to; and I had reflected that the reason why she could not sing was that she was no longer the same person as before. Now I said to myself that by starting to sing again she perhaps meant me to understand that it was not true she had changed and that she was still the Rosetta of former times, good and sweet and innocent as an angel. I looked at her and I saw that her eyes were full of tears. The tears were brimming over from her wide-open eyes and sliding down her cheeks, and all at once I felt completely sure: she was not changed, as I had feared; these tears she was shedding were partly for Rosario, who had been killed without pity, like a dog, and partly for herself and for me and for all those who had been stricken and maimed and destroyed by the war. This meant that not only had she not changed, fundamentally, but that I had not either, although I had stolen Rosario's money, nor had all those whom the war had made like herself, throughout the whole time it lasted. Suddenly I felt comforted, and spontaneously, from the comfort I felt, sprang the thought: "As soon as I get to Rome, I shall return this money to Rosario's mother." Without saying anything I slipped my arm under Rosetta's and clasped her hand in mine.

She sang that same song over and over again as the truck drove on toward Velletri; and then, when the tears ceased to flow from her eyes, she ceased to sing. The driver, who was not unkindly, possibly understood something of what was going on, for he suddenly asked: "What was he to you, that young man who was killed?" I hastened to reply: "He was nothing at all, just an acquaintance, a black market man who had offered to take us to Rome." The driver was seized with fear again, and went on hurriedly: "No, don't tell me anything, I don't want to know anything, I know nothing and I've seen nothing; when we get to Rome we part and I shall act as if I'd never seen you or known you." "It was you who asked me," I pointed out. "You're right," he said, "but consider it unsaid, please forget about it."

At the farthest end of the wide green plain there appeared a long streak of uncertain color, whitish and yellowish—the suburbs of Rome. And beyond this streak, hanging above it, grey against a background of grey sky, very far away and yet clear, rose the dome of St. Peter's. God knows how earnestly I had hoped throughout the whole of the past year to see that beloved dome again on the distant horizon, so small yet so vast that it could almost be mistaken for a feature of the landscape; so solid, although no more than a shadow; so reassuring because it was familiar and I had seen and studied it a thousand times. That dome, for me, was not merely Rome, it was my life in Rome, the serenity of days lived at peace with oneself and with others. Far away on the horizon, that dome was saying to me that I could now return home confidently and that, even after so many changes and tragedies, the old life would take up its course again. It also told me that I owed this new-born confidence to Rosetta, and to her singing and her tears. And that, had it not been for this sorrow on Rosetta's part, there would have arrived in Rome, not the two unoffending women who had left it a year before, but the thief and the prostitute which they had become, during the war and because of the war.

Sorrow. I thought of Michele, who was not with us in this eagerly longed-for moment of return and would never be with us again. I remembered the evening in the hut at Sant'Eufemia when he had read aloud to us the passage from the Gospel about Lazarus, and had been so angry with the peasants who had failed to understand anything, and had cried out that we were all dead and waiting for resurrection, like Lazarus. At the time Michele's words had left me in doubt, but now I saw that Michele had been right, and that for some time now Rosetta and I had indeed been dead, dead to the pity that we owe to others and to ourselves. But sorrow had saved us at the last moment, and so in a way the passage about Lazarus held good for us too, since at last, thanks to sorrow, we had emerged from the war which had enclosed us in its tomb of indifference and wickedness, and had started to walk again along the path of our own life, which was, maybe, a poor thing full of obscurities and errors but nevertheless the only life that we ought to live, as no doubt Michele would have told us if he had been with us.